The National Ass

(NA

By: Dagny Jackson

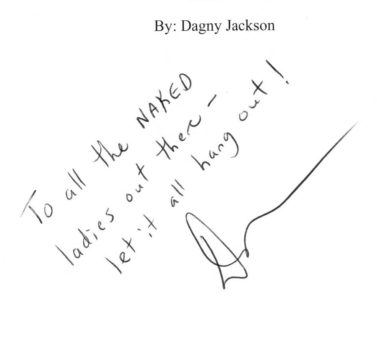

To all the NAKED ladies out there — let it all hang out!

To my kids, Jackson, Oliver and Erin. To my best guy, Matt, and to my parents, John and Tina, who were the inspiration for this story.

Dear Readers:

If you would like to get in touch with the author, please do so at kindred.dames@gmail.com

Part 1

Who Needs a Support Garment When You Have a Support Group?

Carol-Barbara Hoofnagle sat at the kitchen table, sipping her morning coffee. She watched her dog, Bubba, who in turn, watched her husband, Carl.

Carl was busy peering out the kitchen window. He thought he was being stealth, but Carol-Barbara knew better. He was snooping on the new neighbors moving in next door, and he couldn't have been more blatant about that fact if he'd had a pair of binoculars pressed to his eyes.

Carol-Barbara knew that Carl was especially concerned about the newcomers because the car they drove sported a license plate from New Jersey. In Dogwood County, Virginia no one ever showed up to put down roots sporting a New Jersey license plate. It was just plain unheard of.

As for the dog, he sat cross-legged, waiting patiently for his walk, but there was desperation in his eyes.

"Carl, why don't you take Bubba out? He's about to bust." Carol-Barbara was trying to get Carl out of the window before someone noticed the gray-haired peeping Tom with his face pressed to the glass. Her husband was unresponsive to her cues.

"Carl!" Carol-Barbara raised her voice in that shrill tone that Carl always likened to the sound of a cat that hadn't quite made it through the storm door before its tail got caught.

That worked. Carl snapped out of his trance and whirled around to face Carol-Barbara, nearly tripping over Bubba as he did so.

"Dang it, Carol-Barbara! What is it?" He snapped.

"The dog needs to go out," she said calmly. She would forgive him his tone of voice, this time, knowing he was stressed by the fact that people, about which he knew nothing, were going to be their closest neighbors. In a small town, this was grounds for anxiety.

Carl took a deep breath and sighed. The dog followed suit. "Fine. Come on, Bubba."

"You'll be able to get a better look at them from outside, anyway." Carol-Barbara teased.

"Better look at who?" Carl was defensive.

"A better look at the new neighbors; the ones you were stalking through the window."

"I beg to differ. I was checking the weather." Carl replied, unconvincingly.

"And how is it?" Carol-Barbara played along with him.

"Bleak." Carl responded, though Carol-Barbara knew the forecast was for a near-perfect day.

She glanced out the window just in time to see the car from New Jersey speed off from the driveway, bright sun glinting off its windshield. A bumper sticker on the back of the car read, "Yeah, I'm from New Jersey. What makes you so special?"

Though there was no chance of rain, Carol-Barbara understood what Carl meant about bleakness.

"I'd say there's definitely a chance of storms," she said pointedly, not liking the idea of new people moving in next door any more than he did.

"One of these days, Carol-Barbara, I swear on my life, we are moving to some tropical paradise in where no one can bother us."

Carl hooked Bubba to his leash, muttered something under his breath about Dogwood County living up to its name and "going to the dogs," and slammed the front door behind him.

Solitude.

Carol-Barbara loved Carl, but since he'd retired from the phone company two years ago, he'd been under foot. Staying home with him had been every bit as demanding as the years she'd stayed home with the kids before they finally started grade school.

At least the kids grew up. Carl had done all the growing he was going to do. A man without something to do was like a bicycle without a rider; both would just hang around rusting until somebody got on them, and that's exactly what Carol-Barbara had done a few weeks ago- gotten on Carl about finding something to do outside of the house. So, he'd finally gone out and applied for a job as a greeter at the local All-Mart, though he wouldn't be allowed to start until the doctor got his sugar and blood pressure under control, and that, according to Doc Bowman, could take several more weeks.

Carol-Barbara slugged the last of her coffee and took a quick glance at the clock on the microwave. It was nearly nine. She could count on Carl being gone for a good long stretch. Of course, he wouldn't be walking the dog the whole time. Since it was Saturday, he was bound to run into Butch Martin doing yard work. They would end up talking, probably about the new neighbors, and by then it would be time for Butch to take a break. The two men would head to the Moondollar Café for coffee and Anita's famous cream cheese biscuits. Carl had put on 15 pounds since he'd retired, in no small part due to those biscuits. Carol-Barbara wasn't happy about that, but it was almost worth it, as it got him out of the house, and out from under her feet every so often.

The way she figured it, she had at least an hour and a half of not having to worry what Carl was getting himself into, and she had work to do.

Carol-Barbara readied herself with a notebook and pencil. She still preferred this method to the laptop she'd received for Christmas from her son, Adam. It was a very nice laptop, according to Adam, as if she would know the difference between a good one and a bad one. It was loaded and ready, he'd told her, for anything she set her mind to.

Oh sure, she enjoyed checking email, getting pictures of her granddaughter, that sort of thing. For brainstorming, though, there was nothing like a pencil and paper. It made her feel powerful, ripping the paper off the new yellow notepad, excitedly putting the words down, then slicing through the ones she decided against with her red pen, until finally she'd made a proper list:

Naomi Martin- diabetes

Charlene Updike- widowed

Anne Townsend- stroke

Martha Fitzgerald- divorced

Susie Perkins- son recently killed in Iraq

Diane Suffolk- not entirely sure, but seems to be carrying a heavy emotional load

Last, she wrote her own name.

Carol-Barbara Hoofnagle. **B**eside it she wrote- *breast cancer survivor.*

She touched her chest, that place where two size C's used to exist, and where now there was nothing.

The other women on this list had felt loss, too- maybe not exactly like hers, but it was there. Theirs was the kind of loss that made some people curl up and die, but not these ladies. They were strong, salt of the Earth women, and they would make one hell of a support group.

Part 2

Cat Scratch Fever

Carol-Barbara tucked an invitation into a matching envelope and sealed it with one of the fancy stickers that had come with the stationery set her daughter, Lauren, had given her for Mother's Day two years prior. She repeated this process six more times. Each sticker bore a silver calligraphy "H" for Hoofnagle on a mauve background outlined in silver. She'd been using them sparingly, for special correspondence only. These invites, she considered, were very special. She didn't mind that she was using up six of the last seven stickers and envelopes in the package. Placing the last sticker on the last matching mauve-colored envelope, she then began addressing them to the women she had decided would most benefit from being part of a support group.

She hadn't thought much past who she would invite, but now that the invitations were almost ready to be mailed, she allowed herself to daydream about what they would do at meetings. Carol-Barbara had visions of them sipping tea and baring their souls to one another in a way that would make each of them feel that the heartaches they had gone through in life had been worth it. She believed that which hadn't killed her made her stronger, but there would have to be more going on at these meetings than just digging up old wounds and rehashing them. That would get real old, real fast.

Perhaps, she thought, they could go on field trips. The thought excited her. They would take day trips to museums, have lunch at restaurants their husbands would never agree to go to, and eat things like Indian Palak Paneer and Pad Thai. If they were feeling really exotic, they would go for sushi-- and not the kind with the fake cooked crab meat that was often passed off as fish, but the real kind. She would throw all caution to the wind for raw tuna wrapped in seaweed.

Just as Carol-Barbara was addressing the last envelope, she heard Carl come through the back door. He was cursing under his breath, though not so much so that Carol-Barbara couldn't still hear it from the next room. What was he doing back so soon? She rose, peeked through the doorway, and saw Carl picking briars out of Bubba's fur.

"Carl, what happened?"

"Yankee cat next door, that's what happened!" He pulled a briar out from behind Bubba's ear. Bubba yelped in protest.

"Careful!" She moved towards them. "Here, let me do that."

Carl stood and began pacing. "Bubba and I were just minding our own business, strolling up the street to Butch's place, when out of the clear blue came this cat, all hyped up on catnip or something. It just attacked Bubba for no reason at all!"

"And the briars?" Carol-Barbara pulled the last visible briar from the scruff around Bubba's neck. "Where did they come from?"

"You know Bubba. He's a lover, not a fighter. He was scared to death. I guess I didn't have a tight enough grip on him and he took off into the woods. I spent the last 30 minutes trying to get him out. I finally found him up under a bramble bush. "

"What makes you think the cat is from next door?" Carol-Barbara gave Bubba a final once-over before standing to face Carl.

"You ever see a pink cat with a rhinestone collar around here before today?"

"A *pink* cat? No. I can't say that I have." Carol-Barbara tried to envision such a thing. Surely it wasn't the poor creature's natural color.

"Besides, I saw the woman come out and retrieve the thing from their doorstep. And guess what? She had a tattoo! Right on her bicep! I'm telling you C.B. we got trouble next door. This is just the beginning!" Carl only called her CB when he was really serious about something.

Taking a deep breath through her nose and breathing out through pursed lips, Carol-Barbara considered the possibility that Carl was right. Perhaps the people next door were trouble. But what had Pastor Bening told their church congregation only two Sundays ago about how a good Christian should handle troubled people? Why, with open arms and a genuine offer of friendship, that's how.

She thought for a moment about the best way to handle this situation, and then it came to her. There was one mauve envelope and one matching sticker left in her fancy package of stationery. Carol-

Barbara decided right then and there who was going to get it.

Part 3

What Goes Up Must Come Down- or Does It?

Carol-Barbara climbed the front steps of the house next door and rang the doorbell. She could hear it chiming, sounding just as it had when Betty Horton was still living there, before her kids moved her to a nursing home in North Carolina.

She waited. No one came, so she rang it again, finishing off with a knock for good measure. This time she heard footsteps. They were quick, high-pitched footsteps. When the door opened, Carol-Barbara saw why. The woman that answered the door wore the pointiest stiletto heels that Carol-Barbara had ever seen. They reminded her of a poster advertising female escorts she'd seen in a phone booth once when she and Carl attended George W. Bush's 1988 Presidential Inauguration in Washington.

She pulled her attention away from the stilettos, and tried to look the woman in the eye, but something else grabbed her attention before she could bring her gaze that high; cleavage; more cleavage than anyone should be showing before noon on a Tuesday. Carol-Barbara couldn't help wondering if it was the result of implants or the best push-up bra ever made.

Carol-Barbara shifted her eyes and noticed the woman bore a tattoo on her right bicep, just as Carl had said. She couldn't tell what it was for sure, but it seemed to involve a lizard-type creature surrounded by little hearts.

With great difficulty, Carol-Barbara shifted her gaze again, and this time was met with a stare from the creature that had started all this; because in her arms, the tattooed woman held a pink cat with a rhinestone collar.

"Oh, Hi!" You must be from ova next door. " The woman spoke with an accent that seemed to exclude r's from the words she used. "I'm ya new neighba, Honey Van Honk." She put her hand out to shake Carol-Barbara's.

Carol-Barbara forced herself to bring her gaze to the woman's eyes. When she did, she was met with a face that was, despite its body's gravity-defying cleavage, not much younger than her own. This caused Carol-Barbara to snap out of her trance. How long had she been staring anyway? There was so much to take in- the stilettos, the pink cat, the tattoo, the cleavage. Finally, she found her voice.

"I'm Carol-Barbara. Carol-Barbara Hoofnagle. I live there." She pointed to her house, afraid to take her eyes off Honey's for fear she would get sidetracked again. The pink cat hissed at Carol-Barbara as she put out her hand to shake Honey's.

"Oh!" Carol-Barbara retracted her hand for fear of being bitten.

"Poopsie! That's bad mannas!" Honey scolded the cat and gently dropped her to the ground. The cat ran back into the house.

Honey turned back to Carol-Barbara. "Sorry about that. She's such a little brat. Especially with the move and all. Now, how can I help you?"

Carol-Barbara had almost forgotten why she had made the trek from her house, when the feel of the invitation in her hand reminded her. For just a second she thought she might have made a mistake deciding to invite the woman. She thought about making something up, some other reason for why she now stood on the steps of her house, but she quickly decided that wouldn't be in keeping with the "love thy neighbor, love thyself" sermon Pastor Bening had given.

She held the invitation out towards Honey. "I thought you might like to come to a gathering I'm having. It's not so much a gathering as a support group. Not that you need a support group." She was rambling now. "I just thought you might want to meet some of the local ladies. Seeing as how you're new and all." She thought she sounded like an idiot, but the woman seemed pleasantly surprised.

"Oh, well, that's nice." Honey took the invite from her, but accidentally dropped it on the porch between them. As she leaned over to pick it up, Carol-Barbara could practically see down her shirt, and her previous question was answered. Even the greatest push-up bra couldn't defy Newton's most famous law. They most certainly had to be implants.

Honey stood back up quickly, and Carol-Barbara barely had time to wipe the look of shock off her face.

Then, from inside the house, Carol-Barbara heard a man's voice.

"I'm hungry! Make lunch already would ya, Honey?" The voice bellowed.

Honey turned towards the house to yell back. "Don't get ya tighty whities in a twist! I'm comin' already!" She turned back around to face Carol-Barbara. "That's my husband, Roland." Then Honey leaned in close to Carol-Barbara, "See, ya neva know. I just might need a support group." she chuckled.

Carol-Barbara was sure she smelled alcohol on Honey's breath.

Carol-Barbara gave a half-laugh. "Okay, well, sounds like you're being summoned, so I won't keep you. Hope to see you at the meeting." Carol-Barbara forced a smile and a wave before she raced down the porch steps.

Lord help her, she thought, what had she just done?

Part 4

What Does a Man Have to Do to Get Some? (Respect, That Is)

Carl slammed down the phone. Once again, Doc Bowman's nurse had just informed him, he had failed his physical, and wouldn't be allowed to start work at the All-Mart. His blood pressure was through the roof.

Poor Carl. At least, that's what he interpreted Bubba big brown dog eyes saying as he looked up at him from the foot of Carl's recliner.

Of course, it was hard to tell what a dog was really thinking. Bubba could have just as well been reflecting on the smells coming from Carol-Barbara's meatloaf as it baked in the oven. Or, he might have been wondering when he would get to go outside for a pee-break. Maybe, Carl considered, Bubba was even contemplating how to set the U.S. economy straight. Still, Carl preferred to believe his loyal dog was feeling sorry for him. God knows, nobody else was lately.

Carol-Barbara had been spending most of her time planning her get-together for tomorrow night. Carl couldn't understand why Carol-Barbara needed a support group anyway. Hadn't he given her all the support she needed for the last 40 years? What were these ladies going to do, sit around and rehash every crisis they'd ever faced? Was that even healthy? They should learn to keep it inside like he did, and not bother the whole world with their drama. That's what women were, he decided, the longest running drama in the universe. Tomorrow night the house

14

would be full of cackling, screeching, crying women, airing their feelings out right in his living room. His blood pressure rose a few points just thinking about it.

He had really hoped to be out of the house for the big event, but instead he'd be parked in his recliner watching reruns of Matlock and trying to relax; doctor's orders. Doc Bowman had put him on a heavy duty medication, and he wanted Carl to stick around the house for a couple of days in case he had a bad reaction to it. Plus, the medication made him have to pee every 15 minutes, so being near a bathroom at all times was key.

The phone rang on the table beside him, jolting him from his thoughts. Then, it rang a second time.

"Carol-Barbara! Answer the phone!" Carl hated answering the phone. It was never for him anyway, unless it was bad news.

When it rang a third time, and it was clear Carol-Barbara was not going to get it, Carl reluctantly picked up the receiver.

"Hello." He sounded bothered.

"Hello, Carl!" The voice on the other end shouted.

Speaking of cackling and screeching women, Carl could tell that the voice belonged to one of the most annoying people in all of Dogwood County; Carol-Barbara's friend, Martha Fitzgerald. He had often thought that she sounded like the witch from The Wizard of Oz when she finally got what she deserved. No matter what Martha was saying, all

Carl could ever hear was "I'm melting! I'm melting!"

"Where's Carol-Barbara?" The voice on the other end shrieked.

"Martha, it's you. I almost didn't recognize your voice," Carl lied. "Let me get her for you."

Carl covered the receiver with his hand. "Carol-Barbara! Phone for you!" He put the receiver back up to his ear and waited to hear Carol-Barbara pick up the extension.

When she didn't, he hollered again, "CB! Phone!" Still no answer.

Carl put the phone back to his ear. "Just a minute, Martha. I'll have to go find her."

"Make it quick, Carl. I don't have all day to wait around." Martha snapped.

I do, Carl thought. In fact, unfortunately, that's all I have to do today. He placed the receiver back on the table and heaved himself out of the recliner. Bubba sat up and yawned.

"I feel the same way old buddy," Carl stepped over Bubba just as Carol-Barbara came through the kitchen door.

"I didn't know you went out." Carl was surprised to see her with two big grocery bags in her hands.

"I told you I was running to the store for a few things. Didn't you hear me?" She set the paper grocery bags down on the floor.

"No. I didn't hear you say that," he admitted.

"You were supposed to check on the meatloaf while I was gone." Carol-Barbara stepped quickly to the wall oven and lowered the door to check on the meatloaf.

"I was?" He genuinely hadn't heard her ask him to do that.

"Oh, Carl." She poked at the meatloaf. "Well, it's a little more done than usual, but I guess it will be alright." She slipped a hot pad over her hand and slid the pan out of the oven.

"By the way, the wicked witch of the west is on the phone." Carl joked.

"Who?" Carol-Barbara asked.

"Martha," he laughed.

Carol-Barbara walked over to the kitchen phone and picked up the extension.

While Carol-Barbara went over the plans for tomorrow's get-together with Martha, Carl sauntered back into the den. He could hear Martha's high-pitched voice transmitting over the receiver that was still off the hook. Bubba perked his ears at the noise. Carl quietly placed the receiver back into position.

"Hear that, old man?" He said to Bubba. There'll be a whole house full of that tomorrow. Carl sighed. So did Bubba.

Part 5

Party Time

Friday evening arrived and Carol-Barbara was excited.

The door to Carl's den was shut; an attempt by him to pretend the entire evening wasn't happening. He'd earlier expressed his displeasure at the fact that he would be eating the plain baked fish and steamed broccoli that Carol-Barbara made for him, while the ladies would be enjoying her home-made appetizers.

"I'm a second-class citizen tonight," he'd told her earlier. "Like Rodney Dangerfield – no respect."

Carol-Barbara briefly wondered why he had to act that way, but then, realizing it was in no small part due to his news from the doctor the day before, she took a deep breath and made a concerted effort to let it go. Instead, she prepared for her friends to arrive.

She'd taken care with the menu planning and would be offering them a variety of appetizers, as well as a special punch that was made with fresh fruit, lime Kool-Aid and champagne. She'd also made a non-alcoholic version for the ladies who wouldn't, or shouldn't, imbibe.

She wondered which drink Honey Van Honk would choose, if she showed up at all. Carol-Barbara had heard nothing from the house next door since she'd hand-delivered Honey's invitation three days prior.

Everything was ready, and now all that was left to do was wait. At seven o'clock the doorbell rang. Carol-Barbara stood, smoothing her skirt as she opened the front door.

All two hundred and twenty pounds of Naomi Martin stood on the front porch. She carried a lovely cake in her hands.

"It's sugar-free," Naomi pronounced as Carol-Barbara thanked her and welcomed her into her home.

"Thanks, Naomi," Carol-Barbara took the cake from her hands and welcomed her inside.

Right behind Naomi was Anne Townsend, who insisted on walking up the stairs by herself, though she had lost use in most of her left side since the stroke. Widowed Charlene Updike, who had driven Anne there, tried to help her up the steps, but Anne wouldn't hear of it. After many painstaking moments, Anne made it to the door, and was welcomed by Carol-Barbara with a big hug.

Martha Fitzgerald followed closely behind them, complaining about how she'd been stuck behind an Amish wagon on the way.

"Get a car!" She claimed she had yelled out the window at them, though they all knew she had probably only thought it, and not actually said it.

Diane Suffolk and Susie Perkins were the last to show. Susie's son had been killed in Iraq and Susie couldn't drive past her son's burial place without stopping to talk to him. Diane was driving them to Carol-Barbara's, and had happily agreed to stop at the cemetery. This made them slightly late, but it was worth it. Susie said the autumn leaves looked so pretty scattered around Michael's grave in the last moments of the day's sunlight. She wouldn't have missed it for the world.

The ladies chatted, snacked on the goodies Carol-Barbara had prepared, and drank the punch. Carol-Barbara noticed the punch with the champagne in it had been nearly drained. Apparently her friends enjoyed their bubbly.

This brought to mind her new neighbor. She guessed that Honey had decided not to show. She wondered if she should feel insulted or breathe a sigh of relief. Carol-Barbara decided it was time to get down to business, Honey or no Honey.

Carol-Barbara read aloud the pledge she had written for them to recite at the beginning of every meeting. The ladies repeated after her, line by line.

I am a woman, smart and strong,

To the union of womanhood, I belong,

Though I may know some times of strife,

I'll keep on trying all my life,

Controlling what I know I can,

Leaving the rest in a higher hand.

Carol-Barbara relaxed a little and began enjoying herself. She was proud. Her friends seemed to be enjoying themselves, and she was feeling powerful and strong; two things she hadn't felt in quite a while.

That was just about the time Honey came busting through the front door, and all eyes were on her-certain parts of her more than others.

Part 6

What's in a Name?

Honey Van Honk arrived at Carol-Barbara Hoofnagle's house wearing, in part, a black shirt studded with rhinestones. To Carol-Barbara, it looked like something she had made herself with one of those Bedazzlers that was advertised on TV in the wee hours of the morning when people were most susceptible to the idea of needing a machine that could make anything sparkle. That wasn't so bad, except the shirt featured a V-neck that scooped almost down to her belly button, showing ample cleavage. This topped a short denim skirt that was, as Martha Fitzgerald would describe two days later in her Bible study class "cut up to her crack."

The shoes Honey wore added another dimension to her outfit. They were red and shiny, of the platform variety. The outfit as a whole shouted a streetwalker past her prime.

The ladies were curious about this stranger, and their curiosity was amplified by the fact that Carol-Barbara had conveniently forgotten to tell her friends that she had invited her new neighbor to join their group. After all, she didn't have to tell them everything, did she? It was her house, her club. She could invite who she wanted, and, for what reason she couldn't yet understand, she'd chosen to invite former New Jersey resident Honey Van Honk.

Truth be told, she hadn't thought the woman would actually show up, and Carol-Barbara had suffered what her husband would have crudely referred to as a "brain-fart" when she saw Honey walk through her front door. In fact, she'd forgotten to properly introduce her to the rest of the ladies. Honey, never one to be shy, started the introductions herself.

"How are youz all doin? I'm Honey, Honey Van Honk. I'm Carol-Barbara's new neighba, down from Jersey!" There was a moment of silence until Naomi Martin, a one-woman Dogwood County welcome wagon, broke through it.

"Hello, Honey! Welcome to Dogwood County!" Naomi boasted as she stuffed her seventh bite-sized ham and cheese sweet potato biscuit of the evening into her mouth.

The other ladies weren't quite as welcoming as Naomi had been. Being a group of modest, church-going women, they couldn't understand why someone would leave the house in a get-up like the one Honey was wearing. Most of them wouldn't have worn an outfit like that in the privacy of their own bedrooms. There was an awkward moment of silence, tinged with a bit of jealously that none would ever admit to, as each woman wondered silently to herself what she might look like in that outfit. Not that it would ever happen.

Thankfully, Honey broke the silence with the presentation of a bag of gifts she'd brought with her. From her bag she produced the first of three items. It was a liquor bottle with a picture of a pig wearing a bonnet on the front. What in the world a pig wearing a bonnet had to do with alcohol, Carol-Barbara didn't have the faintest idea. Honey set the liquor bottle down next to the punch Carol-Barbara had so carefully prepared in the glass bowl she and Carl had received as a wedding gift.

"Fine Swine. Not half-bad, and a real bargain at $7.98 a fifth," Honey pointed out. "Plus, it's cherry flavored."

"Oh, I love cherries," Naomi inserted.

"You're diabetic, Naomi. That stuff'll kill you," Martha reminded her. "Hell, it would probably kill any of us," Martha mumbled under her breath.

Next, Honey pulled out a crumpled half-eaten bag of Doritos, which she also placed on the table. The big red bag looked like trash next to the centerpiece Carol-Barbara had lovingly crafted from fat pine cones and vibrant autumn leaves she'd gathered from the woods earlier that morning. What else could Honey have in her bag of tricks?

Last, Honey placed a set of six shot glasses on the table next to the liquor. Each one was unique to the other in that it had a picture of a different half-naked man flexing his muscles. Susie Perkins stepped from her place behind Diane Suffolk and walked towards the table. She picked up one of the glasses and read aloud.

"Tenth Annual Jersey Shore Brains and Brawn Contest 1996." Looking like he'd been on steroids since puberty, the man on the glass definitely sported more brawn than brains. Susie picked up another glass. This one had a man wearing glasses and nothing but a tie on his upper half as he flexed his less-than- stellar muscles. Obviously, he was the brains.

Carol-Barbara considered her table was beginning to look more like a sorority house gathering.

"I won these in a dart competition years ago, and forgot all about them until we moved. Aren't they cute?" Honey chimed.

"Yes, cute," piped Diane, who preferred cats to men whether they had brains, brawn or both.

Sometime after the presentation of the shot glasses, Carol-Barbara started to regain her senses and spoke up, "Ladies, if you've all had enough in the way of refreshments, I'd like to ask you to have a seat so we can discuss plans for our group."

Naomi reached for one more biscuit and Martha smacked her hand away. "You're going to put yourself into a diabetic coma."

Naomi retracted her hand and the two ladies made their way to the circle of chairs Carol-Barbara had set up in the middle of the living room.

"Mind if I pour myself a drink first?" Honey was twisting the cap off the liquor bottle and pouring herself a shot before Carol-Barbara could even answer her.

"Uh, no, of course not." Carol-Barbara took a seat next to Charlene Updike and waited while Honey threw back the shot, then filled a paper cup with ice and poured some more of the reddish-colored liquor into it. Carol-Barbara assumed she would mix it with some of the punch, maybe to dilute it a bit, but Honey turned the cup up and sipped it straight. She then grabbed the bag of

Doritos and plopped herself down in the empty seat on the other side of Carol-Barbara.

"Now, the first order of business for the group is," Carol-Barbara was rudely interrupted.

"You keep saying 'the group.' What do youz call yourself?" Honey asked.

"What do weez—I mean *we* call ourselves?" Carol-Barbara raised her eyebrows at Honey, who was shoving a Dorito into her mouth.

"Yeah, you know, don't youz guys have a name?" She said through bites.

"Ooh, a name! That sounds like fun!" Naomi offered.

"Yeah, and maybe we could have t-shirts made up," Martha said sarcastically.

Carol-Barbara hadn't thought about having a name for the group, but she admitted it did seem like a good idea.

"I guess you're right," she offered. "Any ideas?"

"It needs to be catchy," suggested Charlene. "Maybe something that forms an acronym."

"A what?" asked Susie.

"An acronym. You know, like SCUBA," Martha offered.

"Doesn't Scuba just mean Scuba?" Susie questioned.

"It stands for Self-Contained Underwater Breathing Apparatus," Martha bit back.

"Oh," responded Susie, feeling a little stupid. "I didn't know that."

"Well, it needs to be something that brings us together, a common thread," replied Diane.

"We're all old," Martha tactlessly pointed out. "How about Association of Old Ladies?"

"No," Diane replied. "That would make our acronym AOL, and that's already taken."

Carol-Barbara spoke up. "Forget about the acronym for a minute. I invited everyone here because I feel like we have something in common, like we're kindred spirits." She glanced at Honey. "For the most part," she added.

"And we are all old, you have to admit." Charlene put in.

"Speak for yourself," Honey protested as she uncrossed and re-crossed her slender legs, repositioning herself in her chair and slurping what was left of her drink.

"None of us are spring chickens is what I mean." Charlene added.

"Maybe there's a nicer way to say old." Carol-Barbara suggested.

"How about elderly?" Diane pointed out. "We could use that in our name."

"So I guess we're back on the acronym thing again?" Carol-Barbara asked.

"Guess so," Martha replied.

"So the Association of Kindred Elderly Women?" Carol-Barbara poised. "Only that doesn't form an acronym.

"Let's be dames. Doesn't that sound more regal?" suggested Naomi.

Carol-Barbara thought it sounded like something out of a gangster movie, but everyone else seemed to like it.

At this point, Anne Townsend, who had been relatively quiet, as it had become harder for her to speak since the stroke, spoke up. "I told my sister-in-law about the group, and she says she'd like to join, if there's a spot available."

"Doesn't Betty live in North Carolina now?" Diane questioned.

"Yes, but she has a computer in the nursing home and she says she can get updates through email. Her granddaughter even set her up with a Facebook account. "

"Betty Horton is on Facebook?" Carol-Barbara thought for a minute about her 90 year-old former neighbor who had lived in what was now Honey's house. Why, oh why had Betty's family gone and moved her to that home in North Carolina? Carol-Barbara grieved inwardly.

"Oh, yes, she's very computer savvy, "Anne offered.

"Okay, she's in then I guess. No skin off my back." Carol-Barbara easily gave in, as she wanted to get this over with.

"That means we could technically be a national association." Susie offered. "Since we have a member who is outside our state." She felt better having contributed this, especially after she'd felt so stupid not knowing about the SCUBA thing.

"So, then, we're the National Association of Kindred Elderly Dames." Carol-Barbara surmised. "Is everybody in agreement with that?" The ladies all excitedly agreed they were.

"Ha! That spells NAKED!" Honey pointed out.

"We'll, I'll be darned if it doesn't." Carol-Barbara stated. And leave it to you to figure that out.

Part 7

The Best Laid Plans

"Is it safe to come out?" Carl peeked his head out from behind the door and had a cautious look around. He'd barricaded himself in his den and watched reruns of Matlock all evening while his wife, Carol-Barbara, held court in the living room with her lady friends.

"It's over." Carol-Barbara sat in a chair with her feet resting on the ottoman. She looked spent.

Carl emerged from his man-cave. Bubba followed closely on his heels; yawning and stretching in the manner that had given the yoga pose the name 'downward facing dog.'

"So, how did it go?" Carl was curious.

"It wasn't how I envisioned it." Carol-Barbara seemed disheartened.

Carl knew her well enough to know that she planned things in such detail that rarely could something live up to her visions. He would ask her for more info, but first he sauntered over to the buffet table to assess the leftover situation.

He'd been waiting for some of her homemade sweet-potato biscuits with shaved Virginia ham ever since he saw her assembling them earlier that day. He was in luck. The last two fluffy biscuits called his name from a gold-encrusted serving platter. He reached for them. They were almost in his grasp when, with a single look, Carol-Barbara reminded him how much sodium the Virginia ham contained and how that would raise his blood pressure by a good ten points which would raise his chances for having a stroke, thereby leaving her widowed in her golden years. Of course, she didn't say it in so many words, but he'd heard it all before and could read between the lines.

All she really said was, "You still want that job at the All-Mart?"

Her words amped his blood pressure nearly as much as the salt would have. Of course he wanted the job as greeter at the All-Mart. It was a job coveted by most of the retired men in Dogwood County, and Dr. Bowman said he couldn't in good conscience sign Carl's employment form until he had lowered his blood pressure. Carl reluctantly put the biscuit down.

"Didn't you enjoy the fish I made for you?" Carol-Barbara glared at him over her glasses.

"Sure," Carl lied.

The only way Carl liked fish was fighting at the end of a hook. The truth was he'd given most of the dinner she'd made for him to the dog. Bubba didn't care about the lack of sodium in his food, just so long as he got to eat from a real plate instead of his dog bowl.

"You can have something from the veggie platter," she advised him.

"Great," Carl mumbled under his breath. He reached for a carrot stick and aimed for the dressing in the middle of the platter.

"And no ranch dip," Carol-Barbara ordered.

Carl shoved the plain orange stick into his mouth and crunched unhappily, then changed the subject back to her party. "So, what didn't go the way you planned it tonight?"

"For one, we scarcely did anything productive except agree on a name for the group," she complained.

"What are you calling yourselves?" Carl questioned.

"Would you believe The National Association of Kindred Elderly Dames?" Carol-Barbara retorted.

"That's not so bad," Carl encouraged.

"Have you thought about what the first letters of those words spell when strung together?" She watched Carl's face as he pieced it together.

"NAKED," he paused. "Exactly what kind of group have you started here, CB?" Carl joked.

"I know. It makes us sound like some kind of old strippers' union or something," she lamented.

"It'll turn out. Just give it some time." Carl felt for her. It didn't sound as though the name had been her idea. He wanted to make her feel better. "You know, it doesn't have to mean naked like that. You can be naked with your emotions; since that's what a support group is all about, baring your emotions and all."

Carol-Barbara reflected on his suggestion. "I suppose," she paused. "Do me a favor. Pour me a little bit of the stuff in that bottle into one of those glasses." Carol-Barbara pointed to the table next to where Carl was standing.

"This stuff?" He pointed to the bottle of reddish liquid sitting next to a set of shot glasses that he was sure hadn't been a part of their barware collection prior to tonight. If Carol-Barbara was asking him to pour her a drink, things really must have been stressful for her this evening. He'd only ever known her to initiate a drink a handful of times in their 40 year marriage. Oh, sure, if everyone was drinking champagne at a wedding or eggnog on Christmas Eve, she'd have a little, but for her to ask him to pour her a drink when there was no real celebration going on was rare.

Actually, now that he thought about it, the last time she had asked him to pour her a drink was when she was extremely stressed out. That was two years ago when her breast-cancer biopsy came back positive.

For a moment he wondered if she had received some bad news from Dr. Bowman. Could that explain why she seemed extra stressed tonight? She hadn't had a check-up for three months, and that one had been a glowing report. Doc had given her the all-clear. Besides, Carl considered, she would have told him if something was wrong. It wasn't like Carol-Barbara to keep things inside. Whatever was bothering her definitely stemmed from tonight's goings-on.

He turned his attention back to the bottle. "Where did this come from?"

"From a certain someone next door who decided to make her presence known." Carol-Barbara referred to their new neighbor, Honey Van Honk, who was recently transplanted from New Jersey

"So our new friend showed up after all," Carl stated. "And apparently bearing gifts, as well." He reached for one of the shot glasses next to the bottle and read aloud, "Tenth Annual Jersey Shore Brains and Brawn Contest 1996. "Nice." He placed the glass back on the table.

"Yes, nice," she retorted.

"You sure you want to drink this stuff?" Carl inspected the bottle with the picture of the pig in the bonnet on the front of it. Then, he twisted off the cap and had a sniff of the liquid inside. "Phew. *Fine Swine*, huh? Smells more like pig's butt."

"Just give me a little taste." Carol-Barbara insisted. "I want to see for myself what the big deal is."

"Okay, but if you're going to do this, you're not going down alone." Carl picked up one of the shot glasses and poured it about half full. He handed it to Carol-Barbara and poured a full one for himself. He waited for a sermon from her about the effects of alcohol on blood pressure, but it never came.

"You really think everything will be okay with my group?" Carol-Barbara questioned her husband.

Carl placed a reassuring hand on Carol-Barbara's shoulder. "I really do. After all, it was only the first meeting." He paused. "And if not, you always have stripping," Carl chided.

"Ha," she rolled her eyes at him. He bent down and kissed her on the cheek.

"And now, let's have a toast." He held his glass forward towards hers. "To the National Association of Kindred Elderly Dames!"

She reluctantly clinked her glass against his.

"Bottoms up." Carl turned up the shot glass and drained it, pursing his lips afterwards. "Tastes a little better than it smells. What is that, strawberry?"

"Cherry." She took a tiny taste of the sweet liquid, then another.

"What do you think?" Carl was curious.

"It's not something I'd want to keep around the house all the time, but, surprisingly, it's not bad."

"Kind of like Honey Van Honk, maybe?" Carl answered.

The look on Carol-Barbara's face told him she was taken aback.

"Think about it. She was brave enough to show up here without knowing a soul. She even brought gifts. And she was an invited guest, after all." Carl pointed out.

Surely the drink had already gone to his brain. These words were coming from a man who only a few days ago had been complaining about Honey and her crazy pink cat chasing down his poor defenseless dog. Yet, as she thought about what he said, she knew he was right.

Suddenly, Carol-Barbara felt very guilty. She had gone and invited Honey to her house, and then treated her in the most unwelcome way. It wasn't as though Honey had crashed the party. And she'd brought gifts, inappropriate as they may have seemed. The worst part about Carol-Barbara's realization was that Honey didn't seem to notice how terribly she had been treated by her hostess. This made her think that Honey must be used to being treated badly. The thought made her sad.

As she finished off her tiny glass of cherry-flavored *Fine Swine* liqueur, Carol-Barbara thought about a quote she'd once heard by a writer named B.C. Forbes. *"You have no idea how big the other fellow's troubles are."* She vowed to try not to judge Honey so harshly.

Sweet Potato Biscuits

1 cup mashed sweet potato

1/3 cup or more milk

1 and ½ cups flour

1 Tbs baking powder

1 tsp salt

6 Tbs cold butter, unsalted, cut into pieces

Preheat the oven to 425 degrees. Mix the wet ingredients (minus the butter) and the dry ingredients separately.

Cut the butter into the dry ingredients and then mix everything together (wet and dry). Mixture will be coarse.

Using flour on your hands to keep the dough from sticking, pat the dough out until it's about ½ inch thick. Cut out biscuits with a biscuit cutter. Once you have used all dough, place biscuits on a baking tray and bake for about 12 minutes, checking often to make sure they don't burn.

Part 8

Miss Popularity

The phone rang one week to the day after Carol-Barbara held her first meeting of the NAKED Ladies, as they had come to be called. She was surprised to hear Debbie St. James' voice on the other end.

Debbie and Carol-Barbara had been in the same water aerobics class for about three years, but recently Debbie rarely spoke to anyone else in the class. Carol-Barbara got the feeling Debbie felt superior because her husband, Dixon, had been appointed to the Dogwood County planning commission back in the spring.

"I hear someone had a swinging party last week!" Debbie's emphasis on the word "swinging" made it sound like Carol-Barbara's support group meeting had actually been some kind of illicit 1970's style key-swap party.

"Something like that," was all Carol-Barbara could think to say.

"And I also hear you have a fascinating new addition to the neighborhood." Debbie referred to Honey Van Honk as though she were a newly built gazebo or in-ground pool for the members of the community to take advantage of in their down time. Of course, if Honey had been either one of those things, Debbie would surely have already known more about her by now, since her husband Dixon was so connected in the county. He surely saw every building permit that came into the county planning office.

Unlike new construction, though, Carol-Barbara imagined that Dixon had not been able to provide Debbie with much information about the new people who had moved into the old house that sat on the hill next to her. She also imagined that not knowing much about Honey or where she came from was getting to Debbie. The woman prided herself on knowing everything there was to know about everyone, and storing the info away for future use.

"Yes, we have a new neighbor. She's quite a personality." Carol-Barbara practiced referring to Honey in the nicest way possible. Remember, she told herself, no judging Honey when you don't know the whole story. This was her new mantra to herself.

"And this will be a regular thing with you?" Debbie prodded. "These little gatherings, I mean."

"That's the idea," Carol-Barbara retorted.

It was more than the idea, actually. The plan was that the members of her group would gather at least once a month, and not necessarily at Carol-Barbara's house. She had plans for them to get out of their surroundings every once in a while and expand their horizons. She was already making preparations for the group to make a trip into Richmond to visit the new Fine Arts Museum. She didn't necessarily want to tell this to Debbie, though. Knowing her, she'd probably tell Carol-

Barbara she needed to file a permit to transport old ladies across county lines.

"And will your next meeting be anytime soon, say, within the next couple of weeks?" Debbie pushed.

Now Carol-Barbara was really worried. Exactly what was Debbie getting at? Had Carol-Barbara broken some Dogwood County law? Perhaps she'd had too many people crowded into her living room at once and broken a fire code? Maybe there was a rule about how many times a group could gather in a month's time without getting authorization from the county? Was she in trouble for serving the cherry liqueur Honey brought to the party, or the champagne punch? Did she require a liquor license to serve alcohol in her own home?

"Just exactly what are you getting at, Debbie?" Carol-Barbara finally came right out and asked.

"My sister and I want to join you next time." She said it as casually as if the two got together for weekly coffee dates and exchanged cards at Christmas; rather than the less friendly relationship they truly shared. This included Debbie rushing past her without so much as a greeting on her way into exercise class and going out of her way to avoid her when they both happened to be shopping at the All-Mart.

Carol-Barbara's heart stopped beating, or at least that's what it felt like. "You----what?"

"Elsa and I want to join you. Do you think you'll have another meeting before the holidays?" Debbie sounded excited.

Debbie and her sister, Elsa? Carol-Barbara hadn't planned on that, and couldn't think what to say in response, so she said nothing.

Debbie sensed the uncomfortable pause. "That is, unless it's an exclusive club. I mean, we're not trying to insert ourselves where we don't belong," Debbie sounded a bit haughty.

Carol-Barbara had to think quickly. As far as she was concerned, she had asked who she asked and that was that. She'd honestly never even considered the fact that other people might hear about it and want to join. How did she feel about that? Was it an exclusive club? How would she feel if she were excluded? Besides, if she did exclude Debbie there would likely be hell to pay, and she did, in fact, like her sister, Elsa, who had once been a babysitter to her children when they were young.

"Carol-Barbara, are you there?" The voice on the other end was jolting. Carol-Barbara got her wits back about her.

"What? Oh, yes, that's---- fine-- I guess."

"Are you sure? I don't want to intrude." Debbie sensed the hesitancy in Carol-Barbara's voice.

"Don't be silly. We'd love to have you. The more the merrier." How could she really say no, after all?

"I'm so glad to hear you say that, Carol-Barbara. We could all use some support, you know!"

The rest of the conversation went more smoothly, and she hung up the phone after promises of sending Debbie an email with details of the next meeting.

The excitement Carol-Barbara felt at knowing that her first meeting had been a success was palpable. Still, Carol-Barbara didn't trust Debbie completely. She was smart enough to know that Debbie never did anything that wasn't advantageous to Debbie.

Even so, she had to do a little dance in the kitchen to celebrate. Carl walked in just as she completed her second grapevine across the kitchen floor.

"What's gotten in to you?" Carl opened the refrigerator, searching for something legal to eat. He'd already had his allotment of carbs for the day, and the only thing he was supposed to have after 8:00 in the evening was water or decaf coffee with fake sweetener, but he thought he might be able to get away with sugar free yoghurt this evening, considering Carol-Barbara seemed to be in such a good mood.

He casually reached for one of the small containers on the door of the fridge without even looking at the writing on the container. He didn't really care which flavor he held in his hand. He'd tried many of them, and they had all been good; pumpkin pie, boysenberry cheesecake, and his favorite, chocolate cherry mousse. Of course, not a single bite of real cheesecake or chocolate mousse existed in the six ounce containers. He thought about how years of eating too much of the real stuff had contributed to his high blood pressure and borderline diabetes, but thanks to the miracle of chemical science, he could still taste the flavors.

To get away with eating one at this hour, the idea was to look so casual about opening and eating it, that Carol-Barbara wouldn't think a thing about it. He closed the refrigerator door and turned to face her.

"So, who was on the phone?" He held tight to the container and peeled back the foil lid.

"Debbie St. James," she stopped dancing to enunciate the name.

"Ooh la la. What did you do to deserve a call from her majesty?" Carl was keenly aware of Debbie's reputation as a diva.

"Would you believe she heard about my meeting last week and wants to join us?" Carol-Barbara got a glass from the cabinet and filled it with water. All that dancing had made her thirsty.

"You're kidding. She would lower herself to come to our humble abode?" Carl opened the utensil drawer and reached carefully for a spoon, wondering if Carol-Barbara would take this opportunity to stop him from eating the yoghurt.

"I think, actually, they're going to join us for a museum trip into Richmond. And she's bringing her sister, Elsa, with her, as well."

"Oh, good. You're taking it on the road. At least then Bubba and I won't have to hide in the den all night while you ladies take over the living room."

He glanced towards the corner of the kitchen at Bubba, who was snoring peacefully in his dog bed.

"Debbie does worry me a bit. I'm never sure what her true motives are," Carol-Barbara confessed.

"Look at it this way, you were afraid things hadn't gone well last week, but people are talking it up. Like they say in Holly wood, 'Any publicity is good publicity.' You're famous."

"I wouldn't go that far," Carol-Barbara corrected him. True, people were apparently talking about her get-together, but wasn't there also another saying, 'Here today, gone tomorrow?'

Carl took a bite of his ill-gotten yoghurt and gagged. "What the?" He glanced down at the container, no longer trying to be stealth.

"Fat free sour cream," Carol-Barbara smugly informed him. "Serves you right."

Part 9

Launder, Rinse, Repeat

"Hallelujah!" Carl dropped the phone back on the receiver.

"Good news?" Carol-Barbara asked without looking up from the vegetable stir-fry she was preparing for dinner.

"You could say that," Carl teased. "That was Dr. Bowman."

"Well, don't keep me in suspense." Carol-Barbara pressed him.

"The blood test from yesterday shows my blood pressure is down." Carl grinned.

"That is good news." Carol-Barbara praised.

"Oh, it gets better," Carl added. "Doc Bowman is willing to sign the paper so that I can start working."

"Well, thank the Lord!" Carol-Barbara had been waiting months for Carl's health to improve enough to allow him to work part-time as a greeter at the local All-Mart. She knew he'd needed an outlet since he retired, and, selfishly, she hoped this opportunity would get him out from under her feet for a few hours a week, if he could stay healthy. The news prompted her to toss some more garlic into the stir-fry. She'd read somewhere that it did a body good.

Carl sipped the last of the four ounces of heart-healthy red wine Carol-Barbara allowed him per night, and plopped himself down in a kitchen chair. A clap of thunder startled them both.

"Seems a little late in the season for a thunderstorm." It was November, and around Dogwood County thunderstorms were rare past the end of summer. A bolt of lightning lit up the dusky sky just before a huge clap of thunder exploded.

"That was close," Carol-Barbara pointed out.

"Yeah. I watched the Weather Channel this morning. It wasn't supposed to rain today at all," Carl stated.

"I guess Mother Nature doesn't get cable," Carol-Barbara smartly replied.

It thundered again. This time it sounded even closer.

"Is Bubba inside?" Carl had let the dog out in the back yard to get some fresh air. The invisible fence they'd had installed was one of the best things they'd ever done for the dog.

"I'll get him." Carl stood up from the kitchen table and walked toward the back door. He reached for the doorknob just as a bolt of lightning struck so close that Carl could feel the hairs on the back of his hand stand up. The lights in the house flickered.

He turned the doorknob and pulled the door open. Bubba had been sitting so close to the door that he practically fell in. He looked relieved. Just as Carl was pulling the door shut, lightning struck again. There was the sound of an explosion somewhere nearby and the electricity went out in the house.

"Oh, great," Carol-Barbara muttered. "The biscuits are only half-way done in the oven. Think it will come back on soon?"

Carl was serious. "I think that last bolt struck a transformer. Nothing short of climbing up there and replacing it will fix that. And I can't imagine Dogwood County Electric sending anyone out until morning."

The rain had started coming down in sheets.

"Darn, darn darn!" Carol-Barbara hated storms. When she was a little girl, the big, old tree that held her tree house had been blown apart by lighting. The incident had left an indelible imprint on her psyche.

"I'll get some candles." She walked over to the drawer where she kept a supply of candles and matches just for this very occasion. She rummaged through the drawer finding three long tapered candles and a book of matches. Just enough light shone through the kitchen window to allow her to place the candles in the holder on the table. She lit each one, and then, looking up, was startled to see a man's face staring back at her in the kitchen window. She gasped and covered her eyes. When she removed her hands from her eyes the face had disappeared.

"Carl! A man!" Carol-Barbara pointed to where the face had been.

Carl raced to the window. He looked out, but saw nothing in the near-dark. "Are you sure? I don't see anything."

This time a motion near the window on the other side of the kitchen caught her attention.

"There!" She pointed in the direction of the movement.

Carl raced to the other side of the kitchen in time to see a man crouching down in the rain under the kitchen window. "I see him!" Carl headed towards the back door.

"You're not going out there, are you?" Carol-Barbara was worried.

"There's a peeping Tom staring at my wife through the kitchen window. Of course I'm going out there!" Carl insisted, grabbing the baseball bat he kept behind the door on his way out.

Thunder crashed and lightning flashed for what seemed like an eternity before Carl reappeared at the door. He was soaked to the bone, and so was the man standing next to him.

Carol-Barbara didn't recognize the man. "Well?" She waited for an explanation. The man reached his hand out to greet her. "I'm Roland Van Honk. I believe you are acquainted with my wife."

Carol-Barbara hesitantly reached out her hand to shake his. So this was Honey's husband! But what was he doing spying on them through the window in a thunderstorm!

She noticed that he was holding something protectively under his coat.

"Roland here lost something and thought he might find it in our yard," Carl informed her.

"And did you?" Carol-Barbara was still suspicious of the man.

Roland carefully pulled what he had been protecting from under his coat. Though right now it looked more like a drowned rat, Carol-Barbara recognized it as her new neighbor Honey's pink cat. Only it wasn't so pink anymore, and Carol-Barbara realized that a pool of pink-tinged water was forming on her kitchen floor. So, this was actually a white cat. She'd known the pink color of the cat hadn't been natural, but she hadn't anticipated the color would come off so easily.

"I'm sorry to startle you, ma'am. The cat got spooked when the storm started and bolted out the front door. Honey made me come find her."

Carol-Barbara realized it all made sense now. This man hadn't been spying on her. He'd been sent out in the storm to retrieve Honey's precious cat.

"Let me get you a towel." She disappeared from the room for a moment to retrieve a towel from the hall bathroom. It was white, as were all their towels, but it wouldn't be for long, judging from the amount of pink that was coming off the cat. She handed the towel to Roland.

Roland rubbed the cat vigorously, and the animal looked none too pleased about being man-handled.

"It's just food coloring, so it comes right off. Honey thought using anything more permanent to color her might be bad for Poopsie's health," Roland explained.

Carol-Barbara wondered why Honey felt she had to color Poopsie at all. Why not just leave the poor cat in its natural state? "I see," she replied.

Roland finished using the towel and, as expected, it was stained pink. He walked a few steps to place it in the sink. Carol-Barbara noticed he was walking with a bad limp.

"Gosh, I'm sorry about your towel," Roland apologized.

"Nothing a little bleach won't get out," she assured him.

"The rain has slowed. I should be going." Roland hobbled back towards the door, with Poopsie in his arms.

"Are you sure? You're more than welcome to have a seat and relax until it stops completely," Carl offered. "Especially since I almost clubbed you," he held up the baseball bat he was still holding.

"Yes, won't you?" Carol-Barbara supported her husband's suggestion.

"No, thank you. Honey will be worried about the cat." Roland said it as though he was all too aware that he took second place to a feline.

In response to Roland's insistence that he leave, Carl opened the kitchen door to let him out. When he did, Bubba, who had been taking cover from the storm under the kitchen table, now suddenly decided to creep out from his hiding place. When he emerged, Poopsie leaped from Roland's arms and took off out the back door. Bubba took off after her.

"Oh, no!" Carol-Barbara shouted in response to the current state of affairs.

"Don't worry! The invisible fence will stop him!" Carl pointed out, just as Bubba defied Carl's statement by sailing directly past the point where the invisible fence was buried, with nary a shock to his system.

"Wrong. That thing runs on electricity, and the electricity is out," Carol-Barbara reminded him.

"Damn! Double damn!" And those were the last words Carol-Barbara heard out of Carl's mouth as he and Roland took off after their wayward pets, yet again.

About twenty minutes went by. When Carl returned, he was covered in mud. So was Bubba. Instead of ruining yet another towel, Carol-Barbara rubbed Bubba down with the same white towel Roland had used to dry Poopsie. Now the towel was pink and brown. "Nothing a little bleach won't get out," she said for the second time that night.

Next, she put a tired, cold Carl into the tub to warm up. Thank goodness their hot water tank ran on natural gas, so they had hot water even when they didn't have electricity.

Later they ate their cold dinner by candlelight. As Bubba munched on half-cooked biscuits under the table, Carl sneezed.

"I hope you're not getting sick." Carol-Barbara stated. "So what happened out there anyway?"

"Those animals ran all the way down to the river. I thought for a minute they would keep going, but you know how cats hate swimming."

"And Roland? Is he okay?" She had developed a concern for the man with the limp.

"With his bad leg he just couldn't run as fast as me. I had to hold that cat until he caught up, and you know I'm allergic," Carl reminded her.

That explained the sneezing, Carol-Barbara thought.

"You know he mentioned the limp is from an old Honey incident?" Carl added.

Carol-Barbara wasn't sure she'd heard him correctly. Had he said 'hunting' incident or 'Honey' incident? She asked him as much.

"I said Honey incident," Carl corrected her. "Whatever that means."

It was getting harder and harder to give Honey Van Honk the benefit of the doubt. What in the world had she done to give her husband a permanent limp?

"By the way," Carl added. "I have a little pink on my shirt from holding that cat."

"Nothing a little bleach won't get out," she said a third time. Now if only bleach would clean up all the messes in her life.

Part 10

In Her Shoes

One fine day, Carol-Barbara decided to ride into town with Carl.

'Town' was Waynesville, so named for its founder, Orion Wayne, who had been a hero during the Revolutionary War. The town was the Dogwood County seat, so any business that needed to be done, was done in Waynesville. Carol-Barbara asked Carl to drop her at the post office before he headed to the All-Mart to turn in his application. He didn't want to waste a minute, now that Doc Bowman had given him the okay to start working.

There was a long line at the post office, but Carol-Barbara didn't mind. Sure, she could have used her email for this task, and saved herself time and money, but her friends deserved to get proper invitations to the next meeting of The National Association of Kindred Elderly Dames. She'd even sprung for some new stationery for the occasion.

Instead of meeting at her house, this time they would be carpooling into Richmond for a field trip to the Fine Arts Museum. Carol-Barbara planned this trip because she thought it would be good for them to get out of Dogwood County for the day and broaden their horizons. There was a special showing of Picasso work at the museum, and the artist, in all his strange asymmetry, was one of her favorites.

As she took her place at the end of the post office line, Carol-Barbara noticed her new neighbor, Honey, struggling to put a huge package up on the counter for the postal worker to weigh. This was no easy task since Honey was wearing a skin-tight leopard print dress and her trademark four inch stilettos. After she got the box onto the scale, Carol-Barbara watched Honey fill out a slip of paper and then show her I.D. to the postal worker. She then handed him a wad of cash as payment.

What was in that box? Carol-Barbara wondered. As she so often did, Carol-Barbara let her mind wander. What else did she have to do but daydream and shuffle forward in line with the rest of the post office sheep?

Honey's box had the word SONY printed on the side and it was big, about as big as a new TV box, and not the new flat-panel kind—she hated those flimsy, cheap-made things. They never lasted. No, this box belonged to something bigger, like the kind of TV set she and Carl still had in their den, with the giant back-side containing the picture tube. Why would Honey be shipping an old TV?

She considered that Honey might simply be reusing the box, and that it didn't contain a SONY electronic product at all. Maybe it contained something entirely different, something that was only masked by the fact that it was in that box, possibly even something immoral, illicit, or illegal!

Perhaps the box was full of liquor and cigarettes. Was Honey illegally shipping Fine Swine and Marlboro Reds to her friends back up North? Carol-Barbara had heard about people making trips to the South, where taxes on that sort of thing were cheaper, and then hauling it all back up North to sell, making a tidy profit on the black market. It seemed like something Honey might do.

Or possibly, Carol-Barbara thought in a dark moment, it was Roland. That's it, she tried to convince herself. Honey had some time in the past given Roland a permanent limp, probably in a vicious attack, and now she'd done him in all together and was mailing what was left of him to some bogus address out of the country, never to be seen again!

Yet, she deliberated, hadn't Honey showed her I.D. to the guy behind the counter? She didn't seem to be hiding anything. So it probably wasn't Roland in the box. Chances were it probably wasn't even anything illegal.

Carol-Barbara was jolted out of her thoughts by someone squealing her name. She had been staring into the distance, thinking outlandish thoughts of heavily-taxed, illegally-shipped luxury products, as well as Roland's possible death and dismemberment. She hadn't even noticed that Honey had finished her business at the counter and was standing next to her.

"Howdy-do Carol-Barbara!" Honey said it with a rare mix of what Carol-Barbara assumed was Honey's attempt at Southern twang mixed with a screech of Jersey.

"Oh, Honey. You startled me." Carol-Barbara jumped. Thank God Honey couldn't read her mind.

"Got something to mail there?" Honey glanced at the stack of invitations in Carol-Barbara's hand.

Almost forgetting why she'd come to the post office in the first place, Carol-Barbara looked down at her hand. "Oh, right. Yes, I have to buy some stamps to mail these."

"You know, you can get stamps out of that machine right over there. You wouldn't have to stand in line." Honey pointed behind Carol-Barbara.

Of course Carol-Barbara knew she could get stamps out of that machine over there. Hadn't she lived in Dogwood County all her life and been coming to this post office since stamps were three cents apiece? She also knew that machine only sold the plain-looking "Forever" stamps; the ones that would never go up in price even when the post office decided to raise the price of stamps to the point that she could hop in the car and drive a letter somewhere and it would be cheaper. However, she wanted the special stamps sold only behind the counter. The pretty ones with the flowers, or maybe she'd go a little different this time and get the recently issued Ronald Reagan stamps. She did love him so, for his acting *and* his politics.

Yes, she knew she could get those boring stamps out of that machine and be out of the post office lickety- split, and she didn't need somebody who just moved to the area to tell her how she could get those tired old stamps out of the machine.

As was typical of Carol-Barbara, she thought all of these things in her mind, but what came out of her mouth was a little more tactful. "Oh, right. Thanks for reminding me, but I wanted to get something a little different for these invitations. They're kind of special."

Suddenly, Carol-Barbara remembered she had an invitation in her hand for Honey. After all, she couldn't very well invite her to the inaugural meeting of The National Association of Kindred Elderly Dames and then exclude her from the next meeting, could she? She fished through the pile of envelopes and found the one addressed to Honey. At least this would save her the cost of one stamp, and wasn't hand-delivering so much nicer, really?

"I guess I could give this to you now." She held the envelope out towards Honey.

"For me?" Honey looked truly surprised.

"Yes, it's the invite for the next meeting of the uh, NAKED Ladies." She forced herself to say it. "We're going on a field trip to Richmond."

Carol-Barbara continued to hold the envelope out, waiting for Honey to take it, which never occurred.

Instead Honey asked her, "Would you mind mailing it to me? I get so few invitations to anything, and I'd love to be surprised by what stamp you choose."

Once again, Carol-Barbara's heart sank for the woman, and she suddenly felt like a jerk for trying to save a stamp. She carefully placed the invitation back on top of the stack. "Of course. I'd be happy to do that."

An awkward moment passed between the two ladies.

"Guess I'd better go," Honey offered. "That box was heavy as a dead body!" She rubbed her arms as though they were sore, and didn't notice the look of shock on Carol-Barbara's face. "See ya around!" Honey turned to go.

"Honey, wait!" Several people in line turned around to look as Carol-Barbara called after her and Honey turned around. "Honey, I'm going to be shamelessly curious. What was in that giant box, anyway?" She had to know.

"Shoes." Honey replied.

"Shoes?" Carol-Barbara questioned.

"Yes, I have so many shoes I don't wear, and there's a program that sends shoes to people that can use them. You know, like in third world countries and all."

"Oh," Carol-Barbara felt even worse about herself as a human now, not only for asking, but for all the bad things she'd been thinking were in the box. "That's really nice."

"Well, bye!" Honey left the post office in a whirlwind of fake boobs and leopard print that had even two men in their twenties making comments. Carol-Barbara couldn't help staring after her as well. Honey was a constant surprise.

Carol-Barbara thought about what a nice gesture it was for Honey to send her un-needed shoes to people in depressed areas of the world. Still, knowing Honey's sense of style, she couldn't help picturing a bunch of women in some war-torn country wearing Honey's old four- inch stilettos. It didn't seem right, but she guessed it was the thought that counted.

When Carol-Barbara got to the post office counter she perused the postage offerings, and decided to go with a sheet of stamps that was a little more expensive than the others, for good reason. Each stamp had a different Norman Rockwell-style drawing of a child on it. For each one of these sheets of stamps purchased, the post office would give a dollar to the Children's Society, a group that helped find loving homes for abandoned children. If Honey Van Honk could be philanthropic, then, darn it, so could she.

Part 11

Gainfully Employed

Carl had given forty years of his life to the Dogwood County telephone company. As a lineman, he had received the company's distinguished Golden Telephone award three times for his hard work and perseverance under pressure. When he started at the company, he had been a strong, young man of twenty-three, and the company had dealt strictly in traditional phone lines. However, since the advent of the computer, the company had changed its name to Dogwood County Communications, DCC for short, and it cornered the market on internet service in the Dogwood County area. There was simply no other option. If a person wanted internet service and lived in Dogwood County, he had to use DCC.

Carl and the internet did not get along, mainly because he didn't understand it, and that had been a huge factor in his decision to leave the company. His job had changed drastically when internet connection was added to the list of services that DCC provided. Young men and women, still reeking of their college graduation keg parties, and who knew more about computers than he could ever hope to know, sauntered in to DCC and took over. Carl had been ordered to decommission phone lines he had dutifully installed decades before, and doing so had crushed his soul. He hated every minute of it, but he stuck it out as long as he could, until the company took sympathy and offered him early retirement.

Retirement had been hard in its own right. Carl's feelings of unproductiveness had been overwhelming at times, and he knew his wife's patience had been pushed to the limit by having him under foot for the last couple of years. Carol-Barbara had her own schedule to keep, her friends at the Y, and now the support group she'd started. She needed him to have a life again, and so did he.

Carl hated being unemployed almost as much as he hated the internet, which was why he had to thank God that he'd finally be able to work as a greeter at the local All-Mart. He thought about his new job as he sat outside the All-Mart manager's office waiting to hand-deliver his application.

Now that he had been given a clean bill of health from Dr. Bowman, Carl wanted to get his application turned in so that he could start working as soon as possible. His job entailed much more than smiling and saying, "Welcome to All-Mart!" whenever someone graced its doors. Carl would also have to make sure the carts were brought in from their corrals in the parking lot. He wouldn't actually have to bring the carts in- some teenager they had hired would do that- but he'd have to make sure it got done, and sometimes those teenagers were not the hardest workers, what with their brains being all saturated with hormones and sugar from the endless sodas they poured down their throats. It was a scientific fact, he'd heard, that the frontal lobe in the brains of those teenage boys was simply non-functioning. Not until most of them reached the ripe old age of twenty-five.

For an All-Mart greeter, there was also the matter of giving stickers to the young kids that came shopping with their parents. Handing out the little green happy face stickers to the children had become an All-Mart signature. Sometimes, the store mascot, who was actually an All-Mart employee dressed as a giant green happy face, showed up to advertise special savings. He danced around, bringing attention to whatever the deal of the day was, and giving out hugs to the kids.

Sometimes, Carl thought the All-Mart mascot looked a little too much like Mr. Yuck, the green face that appeared on product labels to mark them as poisonous if ingested. He wondered why All-Mart hadn't chosen a different color for its mascot, but the little children didn't seem to mind. They looked forward to seeing that round green guy and getting that sticker just as much as their parents enjoyed saving money at the All-Mart.

It hadn't always been this way, though. When the first rumblings of conversation started about an All-Mart coming to town there had been an uproar. There were concerns about what would happen to the local mom and pop shops. The ramifications of moving All-Mart into town had been discussed at county meetings and special forums until no one wanted to discuss it any more. In the end, people just wanted their cheap groceries and green happy face stickers like the rest of the country had, and so All-Mart had been built. The retirees were certainly happy. Not only did the prices at All-Mart fit their fixed incomes, but it also provided the best place for a part-time job.

In addition to his other job duties, Carl would be responsible for putting the little red stickers on shoppers' return items when they came through the front door. Yes, there was a sticker for everything.

All-Mart couldn't have anyone trying to sneak past the door without getting the proper authorization. Carl stopped short of thinking anyone in Dogwood County might do something criminal, but he did know those few Dogwood County residents who were less than honest, and might even try to return something they hadn't actually bought at the All-Mart; maybe even something they'd received as a gift and knew darn well had come from the J-Mart three counties away. It had happened before. People tried to break all sorts of rules, and what kind of heck would break loose if the rules weren't followed?

Perhaps even another incident such as the one that befell his friend Lewis Albright, who had been a greeter since the All-Mart opened. Lewis had been working alone one busy Saturday morning when there was a sudden store-wide shortage of carts. The teenager who was supposed to be working the cart corrals that morning had called in sick, and so Lewis had been trying to keep things under control when a line of people formed, each waiting for a cart.

Try as he might, things were getting out of hand for Lewis, and the morning was becoming an organizational nightmare. Somehow, during the course of trying to get someone to bring in carts while making sure all the kids got their green happy-faces, a woman made it past Lewis without getting her red return sticker.

Instead, thinking she could save time by swapping out the under-sized shirt she had in her bag for an identical one in the proper size, she had gone to the ladies' clothing section, taken the unwanted shirt out of her bag, and replaced it with a new one. The security guard watching the closed circuit televisions in the back of the store looked up from his coffee cup just in time to see the woman taking a shirt off the rack and stuffing it into a bag. To him, it looked like certain shop-lifting.

Gathering two managers for backup, the three met the woman at the front door as she tried to exit the store. Naturally, she was flabbergasted. As it turned out, not only did she have a receipt for the purchase, but as she was being held by the security guard, the managers went in the back of the store to view the security tape and clearly saw what had actually happened. It was all a big misunderstanding.

This type of thing, Carl considered, would never happen on his watch. Yes, a job at the All-Mart was not to be taken lightly, but only with the utmost seriousness.

As Carl shuddered to himself at the ramifications of not doing a stellar job as All-Mart's newest greeter, a familiar voice called his name. Carl stood, straightening his tie as he did. Looking up, he caught the eyes of who would soon become his new boss. It was none other than his quirky new neighbor, Roland Van Honk.

Part 12

The Truth Comes Out

Finally, the day of The National Association of Kindred Elderly Dames' big field trip to Richmond; but first the group's founder had to do the same thing she did every morning of her life. Carol-Barbara Hoofnagle sat at the kitchen table with her first cup of coffee and opened the Dogwood County News Dispatch to the Obituary section.

For as long as she could remember, Carol-Barbara made a daily ritual of checking the obituaries in the newspaper. This had been going on since she was a teenager. She had picked up the habit from her maternal grandfather, who had lived with her family the last few years he was alive.

Gramps used to say he checked the Obituaries to make sure he wasn't in them. Then, he joked, he would know how to plan his day. Carol-Barbara knew that he really wanted to see who he'd outlived; it gave him strength somehow. At first, Carol-Barbara thought the habit mean-spirited, assuming he was gloating over who he had outlasted, until she realized it was just one of the ways he managed to stay alive so long.

Gramps wasn't a supremely religious person, but he did worry about what side he'd be playing for in the afterlife. When he spoke about the dead, which he often did, he sounded as though he was keeping baseball stats. He had even dubbed the teams the Devils and the Angels. When he came across an obit of someone he knew in the paper he would assign them to either team, depending on his opinion of the person. He even kept a running tab on a piece of paper stuck in his old tattered Bible. For example, when his old school chum Buck Ramsey passed away, Gramps had decided he would definitely be playing for the Angels, and had scribbled Buck's name and date of death on the side of the paper marked "Angels." But when a guy Gramps was sure had screwed him over on a car repair died, he'd been placed under the heading marked "Devils." Of course, he knew he didn't have the final say, but it made him feel better to do it like this.

Gramps had been doing it this way since his beloved Barbara passed away. Barbara was listed in his Bible as Angels' team captain.

Carol-Barbara hadn't known the grandmother who had given her the second part of her name. She died before Carol-Barbara was born, but by all accounts, she was exactly as her Gramps described her- an angel.

The first part of Carol-Barbara's name had been given to her in honor of her other grandmother, her father's mother, who she knew, physically, but in actuality not very well because the woman was as stern and severe as a girls' school marm. Carol Holloway always had a wall up, and Carol-Barbara hated going to visit her in Charleston, South Carolina. Every day she spent there was like a finishing school. Every social faux pas was pointed out and corrected, every dress code infringement punished. It was impossible for her to be herself while visiting Grandmother Holloway, as she insisted on being called.

Even though she never met her grandmother Barbara Simmons, Carol-Barbara had preferred to grow up thinking she was more like the woman that Gramps had fallen in love with. She had been, by all accounts, a caring, loving, patient woman. She had also been a tomboy in her youth, as well as a real daredevil in her adult life.

Grandma Barbara had learned to fly a plane at age 50, and was well on her way to receiving her pilot's license when she started feeling poorly and was given the diagnosis of Stage 4 breast cancer. Gramps said that she had known for some time that something wasn't quite right, but didn't want to go to the doctor. She was of the belief that every time a person got an official diagnosis, it was all downhill from there. Instant sickness was assured, even if the very day before the person had been out flying a plane and gardening.

For this reason, when Grandma Barbara got the news she had breast cancer, she refused to be the kind of person who gave up life to start treatment. She lived every moment after her diagnosis to its fullest, including getting her pilot's license. On a beautiful October day she took her inaugural flight as a bona fide pilot from the Dogwood County airport to Charlotte, North Carolina, and back. She said it was the best day of her life, aside from the day she married Gramps, of course. The next day she fell into a coma and never woke up again. The cancer had gone to her brain. Gramps buried her three months later, along with the piece of paper stating she was an "Official Pilot."

Carol-Barbara's sense of adventure and her need to live life to the fullest wasn't the only thing that her Grandma Barbara had given her. Sadly, she had also passed along the gene for breast cancer. Unlike her grandmother, though, Carol-Barbara approached the disease with a warrior's attitude. When Carol-Barbara received the phone call confirming her diagnosis, she had immediately signed up for the hard-hitting treatment she could get at Dogwood County Memorial Hospital. She had even arranged to go stay with a cousin who lived near Duke University for even more aggressive treatment, if the need arose. Thankfully, it hadn't. Now, Carol-Barbara had been cancer-free for nearly two years.

For a while after her diagnosis, Carol-Barbara had given up reading her obituaries for fear that, like her grandfather, she might open it up and see her own name staring back at her from the black and white pages. She even went through a bleak period where she wrote her own obituary as if her death were a result of her breast cancer and the three rounds of chemo she had to endure. She would go through a ritual of writing it, then burning it up in the fireplace in an attempt to erase that fate from existence. Carol-Barbara so desperately didn't want that obituary to appear in the Dogwood County News Dispatch that she swore that was what had gotten her back on her feet, but the day after her doctor pronounced her officially in remission, she went right back to reading the obits.

Carol-Barbara was on her second cup of coffee, and reading a particularly poignant obituary about a local man who had survived being taken prisoner in World War II, amassed a fortune in a crop-dusting business, and outlived three wives, only to die in his sleep, alone and in a nursing home at age ninety-eight. His fortune had gone to his favorite charity because, as the lengthy obituary pointed out, there had been no known survivors.

Carol-Barbara was considering how sad it was that a man could live nearly a century, suffer in a war, amass a fortune, find love three times, and yet still die alone, without anyone to carry on his family name, when her husband sauntered into the kitchen, their dog, Bubba, close at his heels.

Carl seemed deep in thought, so much so that he didn't even notice that he was wearing his shirt inside out.

"Having a rough morning?" She asked him, point blank.

"What's that supposed to mean?" Carl didn't have a clue what she was referring to. As far as he was concerned, he was up and ready in plenty of time, and looking good, for his first day of work as a greeter at the All-Mart.

"Your shirt is on inside out." Carol-Barbara stood from her chair and motioned for him to put his arms up. Though he felt a bit like an idiot when she told him, he did so without question, like a child waiting for his mother to help him get dressed.

Carol-Barbara slipped Carl's official orange All-Mart greeter's shirt over his head, turned it right side out, and put it back on him, smoothing his hair after she did so. How many times had she done the same thing with their kids before they slipped out the door to school?

One thing was for sure, Carl wouldn't die alone. Penniless, probably, but certainly not alone. Even though they didn't see their son and daughter as much as they would like, she knew they would be here at any sign of trouble.

Carl still looked amiss. "What's wrong?" Carol-Barbara knew he'd been waiting for this day for so long. She wondered why he didn't look happier.

"I'm worried," Carl confessed.

"You're not still fretting about Roland Van Honk being your boss, are you?" Carol-Barbara questioned.

Carl looked out the window and whispered, as if he might be over heard. "There is something wrong with those people over there." Carl pointed to the house next door.

"They're a little bit odd, but nothing to worry about, I'm sure. Weren't you the one who convinced me of that a few weeks ago?" Carol-Barbara wondered where Carl's sudden change of heart had come from.

"There's something I didn't tell you," Carl confessed.

It wasn't like Carl to keep things from her. She worried about what could be in store.

"Well, what is it, for the love of Nixon?" Carol-Barbara used one of Carl's own expressions.

"Remember how I told you Roland said that Honey gave him that limp?"

"Yes, I remember," Carol-Barbara feared the worst, and she got it.

"The truth is, Roland said Honey shot him."

"I'm sure that was an exaggeration," she assured him. "Surely he was kidding."

Part 13

Dear Carl

Carl was devastated. His wife had left for her day trip to Richmond with nary a thought about what he would eat for lunch; and on this, his first day of work as a greeter at the Dogwood County All-Mart. She'd fixed his wardrobe, but hadn't even waited until he got out of the bathroom having his morning constitutional to say goodbye.

Carl looked through the refrigerator for the fourth time, sliding last night's leftover casserole dish out of the way. He was still hoping there was a slight chance it might be blocking his view of the bright red, soft-sided lunch cooler Carol-Barbara always used to pack his food in on occasions such as this. No such luck.

Not only was there no red lunch cooler, there was also nothing in the refrigerator that looked safe for him to easily pack. He was still unsure of what was okay to eat since his pre-diabetic diagnosis. Sure, he was capable of throwing some of the leftover turkey and vegetable casserole into a Tupperware dish, but then, how much was too much? He didn't want to risk blowing his diet or even, God forbid, cause himself to have some kind of gastroenterological attack. That had happened once after a trip to an all-you-can-eat buffet with his friends from the Moose Lodge. After that incident, Carol-Barbara had taken a bigger part in keeping Carl's diet in check.

She was the one who reminded him to check his blood sugar every day, as well as the one who kept track of his diet every day. She always got him back on the straight and narrow, which was why he was now filled with confusion, disbelief, and just a touch of heartache that his wife had forgotten to make his lunch.

Carl assumed that she had been so busy getting herself ready for her big field trip with her ladies' group, that his needs had taken a back seat. He felt guilty for being so needy, even as he now stood in the center of the kitchen, looking dazed and confused, wondering how he would get through his day. After all, wasn't he a grown man of sixty-four who should be able to take care of himself? And didn't Carol-Barbara deserve to go on a nice day trip with her friends? Though he told himself these things, and for the most part believed them, he continued to sulk around the kitchen trying to decide what to do.

He found himself making a last ditch effort to find the red cooler, looking for it in the least likely places, as if she may have hidden it just out of his sight. Perhaps it would be in the bread drawer, or maybe in the pantry next to the dog food. The more he looked, the more he realized it was not like Carol-Barbara to play hide and seek with his lunch. He finally gave up looking for the cooler he imagined would be filled with good things to get him through his day.

He had resigned himself to the fact that he might have to take one of those diabetic replacement meal drinks Carol-Barbara had bought him. The thought of it made him queasy. The last one he'd tried had been horrible-tasting. The label had led him to believe it was chocolate-flavored, but the taste had been more like the chalky Barium drink he'd once been force-fed before an abdominal scan.

Just as Carl decided that he might rather starve than drink another one of those, there was a knock at his back door. The hand knocking on the door belonged to none other than his peculiar new neighbor, who also happened to be his new boss at the All-Mart. As Carl reached for the doorknob to let one Roland Van Honk inside, he wondered how his morning could get any more stressful. After all, most people didn't have their bosses living next door.

"Hi there, Roland. What can I do you for?" Carl tried to sound light-hearted, lest Roland sense his anxiety.

"Think I could get a ride into the store this morning?" Roland got right to the point.

"Uh, sure." Carl leaned out the door trying to get a glimpse of his neighbor's Cadillac in the driveway next door. It wasn't there. "Got car trouble, do ya?"

"You could say that," Roland teased. "Honey drove the car to Richmond."

Carl had forgotten for a moment that Roland's wife, Honey, would be on the art museum trip with Carol-Barbara and the rest of the NAKED ladies.

The reference to this acronym occurred on a regular basis, despite Carl's desperate plea to Carol-Barbara that every time she referred to her friends as NAKED, he was bombarded by mental images of those women that he might never get out of his head. They hadn't all aged as gracefully as his Carol-Barbara had.

"So Honey drove to Richmond to join the rest of the girls, did she?" Carl used the word "girls" jokingly, as the youngest member of the group was sixty, if she was a day.

"Yeah," Roland paused. "Even though she wasn't supposed to," he added.

From the tone in Roland's voice, Carl knew there must be an interesting story there. He pried a bit. "So she left you without any wheels?"

"You could say that." Roland was clearly irked by the fact that Honey had taken the car.

"Didn't she know you had to get to work?" Carl pressed a little more.

"That's the least of it," Roland offered. "Honey's not supposed to drive, on account of the terms of her probation.

"Oh," Carl lingered. "I see." Suddenly, the fact that Carol-Barbara had forgotten to make his lunch seemed inconsequential compared to whatever it was that Roland's wife had done. Good Lord, what *had* she done? Probation? Carl tried to imagine anything that his own wife might do that would put her name and the word "probation" in the same sentence. He was at a loss. The fact was, Carol-Barbara would never do anything to break the law. Not knowingly, anyway. He decided not to pry further.

"So, can I?" Roland asked.

Lost in his thoughts, Carl had forgotten for a moment what it was that had brought Roland to his back door. "Can you what?"

"Have a ride into the store," Roland reminded him.

"Oh, sure." Carl got his wits about him. "Let me just grab my keys." He reached over and grabbed his keys off the counter. That's when he noticed his wife's keys were still lying right beside his own. How, he wondered, had she gone anywhere without her keys?

Roland noticed the confusion on Carl's face as he stood holding two sets of keys in his hand. "What in the world?" Carl said aloud.

"Didn't you know?" Roland announced. "Carol-Barbara rode with Honey."

The blood ran out of Carl's face as he mulled over the possibilities. It wasn't like Carol-Barbara to get into a car with someone she didn't know like a sister. And she certainly hadn't mentioned that she was riding with someone else all the way to Richmond. This was Honey Van Honk they were talking about—heavy drinking, stiletto-wearing, silicone-breasted Honey!

Hadn't he just told Carol-Barbara that very morning that Roland walked with a limp because Honey shot him? At least that was what Roland had told him. At the time, Carol-Barbara had convinced Carl that Roland had been kidding, but now Carl wasn't so sure.

Honey was on probation! For what? And what more was she capable of doing? Kidnapping? Ransom? Had Carol-Barbara been taken against her will? Carl tried to stay calm. Roland was his boss. He couldn't let him see that he was panicking about the fact that his wife had gone off with his potentially criminal spouse somewhere.

He took a deep breath. Maybe, Carl thought, this was all a misunderstanding. He would have to believe that was so, or he definitely wouldn't make it through his day. Maybe it was simply that Carol-Barbara didn't know Honey wasn't supposed to drive, and was just giving Honey the benefit of the doubt about everything else. Wasn't that just like Carol-Barbara to give a new friend the benefit of the doubt? Of course, that had to be the answer. Carol-Barbara would never have done something like that had she known what she was doing. He had almost convinced himself of such when he imagined poor Carol-Barbara sitting in the front passenger seat of that souped-up Cadillac, wearing her blue pea coat, and blissfully clueless to the fact that she was in grave danger. Why, oh why hadn't he bought her that cell phone before he retired from the phone company? There was no easy way to get in touch with her.

"We'd better go or we're going to be late," Roland's voice made Carl jump. "Don't want to be late on your first day, do you?" Roland snickered.

"No, even if I am giving the boss a ride," Carl countered, trying hard to crack a smile.

He took one final look around the kitchen and decided to grab one of those diabetic drinks after all. At least it would keep his blood sugar level. The two men made their way to Carl's car, which was parked in the garage right next to Carol-Barbara's car. The sight of it only served to remind him how much he had to worry about today.

As he unlocked the door to get in, something bright red in the seat of his car caught his eye. His red lunch cooler! A small feeling of relief washed over him. Carol-Barbara hadn't forgotten about him after all! He carefully opened the top and took a peek inside. Carol-Barbara had carefully packed a nice ham and cheese sandwich, an apple, a small bag of pretzels, and two sugar-free cookies. Along with the lunch was a note written in Carol-Barbara's neat and tidy handwriting. It read:

Dear Carl,

I knocked on the door while you were in the bathroom, but I guess you couldn't hear me with the fan on and the water running. I think you need to get your hearing checked. I decided to ride into Richmond with Honey. She's letting me drive her Cadillac! Isn't that exciting? You will do fine at your new job today. Enjoy your lunch, and we'll talk when I get home from Richmond.

P.S. You don't need me there to hold your hand.

Love, Carol-Barbara

"Boy, I wish Honey would pack me lunch and a love note" Roland submitted, as he looked over Carl's shoulder.

Carl was reminded that he always had, and always would, need Carol-Barbara to hold his hand.

He only hoped she got home safely so he could tell her that in person.

Part 14

Bad to the Bone

Carol-Barbara had **never** driven a car the likes of
the one she now piloted through town and onto
highway 64 East towards Richmond. She was sure
the car must be causing quite a ruckus among those
she sped past.

The paint on the exterior of the 1964 Cadillac
could best be described as eggplant; a deep color
that looked almost black until it caught the sun in
just the right way, when it would shine a beautiful
purple. The tires had rims on them that shone silver
like the most highly polished piece in her tea
service.

Honey had only moments earlier described the
vehicle as "Jersey-luscious." There was, after all,
that sticker on the bumper which added to that vibe,
and certainly made it stand out in Dogwood County,
Virginia. Carol-Barbara didn't know exactly what
Jersey-lucious meant, but she thought it must refer
to the feeling of power that she got from driving the
car. It had been a very generous and trusting gesture
for Honey to let her take the wheel.

The inside of the car was no disappointment,
either. Of course, there were the obligatory dice
hanging from the rear view mirror. The seats were
covered in inch-high plush gray material. It felt like
real fur to her, but Honey had assured her it was
faux. Carol-Barbara's hands gripped a steering

wheel that was covered in a suede-like fabric that closely matched the exterior color of the car.

There was no doubt that this car was extraordinary. Had Carol-Barbara been a cursing woman, she would have called it "one bad-ass Cadillac," but since she wasn't the type to let foul words fly out of her mouth, she would think it to herself, and keep a silly grin on her face for the next ninety miles or so until they pulled into Richmond.

The subject of music had never come up in the few conversations she and Honey had, so Carol-Barbara hadn't considered what kind they might listen to, if any, during their trip. Normally, when she and Carl travelled, they listened to a little AM talk radio, or perhaps a book on tape, since the 2000 Toyota Camry she usually drove still sported a cassette tape player instead of a CD player like most newer models. However, they rarely listened to music.

Knowing what she did about Honey (that she dressed like a loose teenage girl and had an affinity for cheap alcohol), Carol-Barbara expected her taste in music to be second-rate as well. So, when Honey reached for the knob on the stereo, Carol-Barbara was surprised to hear one of her favorites wafting out of the high-quality Bose speakers. It was a song she remembered dancing to at her own wedding to Carl, "It's Not for Me to Say" by Johnny Mathis. The thought of Carl made her wonder for a moment if he had found the lunch she left for him on the seat of his car before she'd gone, but that contemplation was quickly interrupted by Honey's voice.

"It's not for me to say you'll al-ways c-a-re!" Honey sang out loud and turned the music up a notch. She explained that it had been one of her mother's favorites, and that every time she heard it, she thought of her. She stretched out her long skinny-jean covered legs, tapped her stiletto-clad heels to the music, and continued to sing.

Honey didn't seem to have any concern over the fact that Carol-Barbara had never been responsible for getting a car like this to and fro in one piece. In fact, she seemed downright relaxed, even urging Carol-Barbara to kick it up a notch, especially since the speed limit had recently been upped to seventy miles per hour on this particular stretch of road.

Carol-Barbara hesitated at first, but wasn't the whole point of this ladies' group she'd founded to do that which they had never done before? So without further ado, she made her right foot like lead, and pushed the pedal to the metal. The engine went from purring to growling, and they were on their way.

Today's plans were the first on a list of activities Carol-Barbara was in the process of organizing for her club. She'd started a sort of "bucket list," much like people who know they don't have much time left, and have a list of things they want to accomplish before they "kick the bucket." The group's list was more like a "drop in the bucket" list at the moment, but she intended to add more to it as ideas came to her.

In Richmond, they would be visiting a world-class art museum that was hosting a Pablo Picasso collection. Picasso had always been one of Carol-

Barbara's favorites, and she hoped her friends would feel the same way. It wasn't just his artwork she liked, but the stories that went along with the paintings that got her so involved. His work always seemed to reflect what was going on in his life at the time he did the painting, and, since he led a sinfully exciting life, the stories made the artwork all the more interesting.

Carol-Barbara had done all the planning for the trip, including purchasing the ladies tickets to the art exhibit, and making sure they had reservations at The Slippery Squid, which didn't sound appetizing, but www.JourneyCounselor.com had given it the best evaluation of all the sushi restaurants in the area. "Sashimi to die for!" The critic had written in the online review. "Don't leave without trying the Yellowfin Tuna!"

There were two other cars in a caravan behind them. Each contained the remaining NAKED Ladies.

One car contained Naomi Martin and Anne Townsend, with Charlene Updike driving, while the other one transported Susie Perkins and Diane Suffolk and had Martha Fitzgerald behind the wheel. The cars had been divvyed up in that manner by random draw because Carol-Barbara knew that too often the ladies got clique-y, and she wanted to shake things up a bit. She wondered how things were going with the others so far, but it was becoming harder to locate them in the rear-view mirror the faster she went, and anyway, she was having too much fun to really care.

Besides Carol-Barbara and Honey, there were two other people in the purple car. Directly behind Honey sat Debbie St. James, and behind the driver's seat was Debbie's sister, Elsa. The sisters had insisted on driving with Carol-Barbara and Honey. Carol-Barbara wasn't sure why, but she wasn't going to let it spoil her fun, and she truly did enjoy Elsa's company.

What Carol-Barbara didn't know as she sped down the highway, nor Elsa either, was that the car she was driving wasn't the only "bad-ass" in the bunch. Debbie St. James had her own agenda for being with the group that day, and it didn't include making lifelong friends with the rest of the ladies, especially a low-life like Honey.

Debbie had always been one who wanted to rise through the social ranks. When she was a little girl growing up in Fairlakes, Alabama, she told her parents, at age four, that she wanted to be the Queen of Fairlakes. She was referring to the beauty pageant in which the recipient of the crown was named Queen. She got what she wanted at age 17 by being the youngest woman ever to be crowned Queen of Fairlakes.

After that she got whatever else she wanted along the way. The very next year she was named the first female Valedictorian at Fairlakes High. She went on to the University of Alabama on a full scholarship and became a member of the Kappa Kappa Gamma sorority, where she quickly rose through the ranks to become the youngest ever President of the University of Alabama chapter of Kappa Kappa Gamma, and initiator of the chant "Kappa Kappa Gamma ! We love Alabama," that still rings through the halls of the Kappa Kappa Gamma sorority house today.

Nothing Debbie desired ever eluded her, including Dixon St. James, whom she met when she came to Dogwood County, Virginia on a visit to her cousin's house. Though he was engaged to her cousin at the time, Debbie sank her claws in and stole him away. Dixon was good-looking and successful in business, and, more importantly to Debbie, from the right breed of family.

However, the whole of Dogwood County knew what was really going on; Dixon had a proclivity for women to whom he wasn't married. Debbie knew about her husband's "issue" but had convinced herself that if others fulfilled his needs in that area it would free up her time for things she was more interested in than sex. In short, she believed those women were doing her a favor.

Elsa was Debbie's younger sister. It is often said that in many families one child will get the looks while the other gets the brains. Not so in this case. Debbie seemed to have gotten everything, while Elsa got nothing.

Elsa, never married, moved from Alabama to Dogwood County to be close to her sister after their parents died, and lived on a small farm where she grew mushrooms and rutabaga and sold them to the local farmers' markets. Elsa did whatever her sister told her to do, which was why she was now sitting in the back of Honey's car. Elsa had no idea what Debbie was really up to, and in Debbie's mind was probably too stupid to figure it out. Elsa had only been invited by Debbie as cover, to make it seem like they really gave a hoot about the ladies' group, and to give Debbie someone to boss around.

Debbie rode along in the purple Cadillac, hoping no one of substance had seen her in it as they rode through town. She gripped her fingers into the backseat and listened to the banter going on in the front of the car. She could tolerate Carol-Barbara, and actually had some degree of respect for the woman, but she considered Honey to be an embarrassment to Dogwood County.

The screech of Honey's voice got on her very last nerve, and it took everything in her not to strangle the woman with her purse strings from the back seat. She would have to calm herself, though, for her scheme relied on her poise and politeness. How else could you get people to bend to your whim? And besides, this wasn't just for her benefit, it was for Dixon, who had been working so hard, and who deserved to get what he wanted.

Part 15

Greedy Little Monsters

So far, Carl's day had not gone as anticipated.

He had emerged from his morning constitutional in the bathroom expecting his bride of four decades to be ready and waiting for him with a peck on the cheek and a winning motivational speech to get him through his first day at his new job as a greeter at the All-Mart. This was, after all, the first job he'd had since retiring from his forty year career as a lineman with the phone company two years prior, and he was very nervous about taking this first step back into the working world.

Instead of a warm send-off, he'd received not even a "Goodbye," from his wife, as upon his exit from the bathroom he'd found Carol-Barbara had already left for her day-trip to Richmond with her ladies' group. She had, at least, been thoughtful enough to leave him a letter of encouragement on the seat of his car, along with a hearty lunch to get him through his day, but he still felt as though he had been somewhat neglected.

In addition to that unexpected turn of events, Carl's new next-door neighbor, Roland, who was also, coincidentally, his new boss, had showed up at his door asking for a ride into work. His own car had been hijacked by his wife, Honey, who was on the very same trip to Richmond with Carol-Barbara. Carl had learned through the letter Carol-Barbara left on his seat that she would be the one actually driving the Van-Honk's car, as for some reason as yet unknown to Carl, Honey was not legally allowed to drive. Carl wasn't sure he wanted to know why Honey's license had been revoked. Whatever the cause, it would only be a matter of time before he found out, and it would be one more thing he could add to an ever-expanding catalog of reasons he had to worry about living next to his unconventional neighbors.

So far, the list included the fact that the Van Honks owned a cat that had been dyed the color of a pink Easter egg, and which had escaped once already, leading Carl's poor dog Bubba into a briar patch when he gave chase to the puffy pink fur ball.

The record of offenses also included the fact that Honey smoked Marlboro reds, the butts of which she flicked across the hedges separating the two houses, and into Carl's vegetable garden. His pumpkins, nearly ripe for picking, had been assaulted by the ends of Honey's cigarettes on more than one occasion. He had also seen with his own eyes her preference for the drink. She had tied one on in his very own living room the night she had joined his wife's ladies' group.

There was also the matter of Honey's choice of daily attire. Though Carl had originally given Honey the benefit of the doubt, trying hard not to judge a book by its cover, her actions said something about the class of lady she must be; certainly not up to par with his Carol-Barbara. So, he convinced himself, it wasn't just the fact that she had fake boobs, wore stilettos, drank heavily, flicked her cigarette butts into his garden, or the fact that she had committed a violation bad enough to be on probation. Rather, it was everything combined that was beginning to make him nervous. And now his wife had driven off in the Van Honk's Pimpmobile.

Yes, the list of un-Dogwood-County-like behavior coming out of the Van Honk household was growing faster than he cared to acknowledge. Granted, Roland hadn't personally done anything to paint himself in a bad light, but wasn't being married to Honey enough? If the saying was that behind every good man was a better woman, what did it say for the man when the woman presumably wasn't so good? And yet, Carl couldn't very well say no when his boss asked him for a ride into work, could he? And so it was that Roland now tagged along in the passenger seat of Carl's Honda Civic.

The two men had spent the 15 minute drive into town having a conversation about how different Dogwood County was from the very busy town of Newark, New Jersey, where Roland and Honey had lived before Roland's job as a manager with the All-Mart had transferred him to Virginia. First of all, Roland pointed out, people in Virginia were way too nice and accommodating. (No, really? Carl sarcastically thought to himself.) Second, there wasn't a decent Italian restaurant in the whole of Dogwood County. Personally, Carl had never been a fan of Italian food. After all, wasn't pasta really just funny shaped bread with sauce on it?

For Carl it was all about fried chicken and mashed potatoes with butter, and butter beans on the side, and more butter, and coconut pie for dessert. He told Roland as much. Those foods were the ones that had gotten him into his high blood pressure mess in the first place, and the reason the red lunch bag Carol-Barbara had packed him today contained a much healthier option than what she'd packed every day he worked at the phone company.

When the two men pulled into the parking lot of the All-Mart, Carl took a deep breath and walked into the store, exchanging pleasantries with a few people he recognized. With a wave of his hand, Roland requested that Carl wait near the front door for a few minutes. Roland headed back to his office and returned with the customary orange All-Mart apron which all the store employees wore. Carl slipped it on and decided he must look like he was anticipating a hunting expedition in his blaze orange get-up.

The job was easy, Roland explained; if a customer entered with a return item, slap a red sticker on it and direct the person to the customer service desk. If someone entered with a young child, offer the kid a green sticker. And always, always, greet every customer with a smile and the words, "Welcome to All-Mart!" Roland asked Carl to give it a try once out loud.

"Welcome to All-Mart," Carl uttered, in his most dignified voice.

"Louder, and say it like you mean it," Roland requested.

"Welcome to All-Mart!" Carl had shouted.

Roland was pleased with Carl's enthusiasm, giving him a pat on the back and assuring him that anything else he might need to know he would learn on the job.

Carl's first customer of the day was a woman who had purchased a cake from the bakery the day before. She had taken it home and served it to her family. Apparently they didn't like it because she was now back with half a cake proclaiming it didn't taste like she thought it would and now she wanted a refund. Due to All-mart's satisfaction guarantee, she felt the store ought to credit her for her dissatisfaction. Carl disagreed, but he couldn't say it out loud, and besides, his job was not to decide what should be returned and what should not, so he placed the obligatory red sticker on her half-eaten cake, and directed her towards the customer service desk.

A few more people trickled in past him. A little boy complaining about shopping with his mother came through the automatic doors. Carl gave him a green smiley-face sticker, and the boy grinned, ceasing his complaining as he fixed the sticker on his shirt and admired it.

"Thank you," whispered the grateful mother.

For the next couple of hours, this was how it went; people with returns, kids needing stickers. It was all very easy.

It was announced on the store's speaker that there was to be a treat for both customers and employees alike. The store mascot, in all his big green, smiley-faced glory would be coming in around lunchtime. Carl made sure he took an early lunch so he wouldn't miss the big entrance.

At around one o'clock everyone in the vicinity of the front doors got what they had been waiting for. An employee, unidentifiable due to the big green smiley face costume he was wearing, sauntered in through the automatic front doors and began greeting the patrons.

As was customary for the mascot, another employee, dressed in plain clothes, escorted the costumed character into the store. This was for the costumed employee's safety, as well as to provide an air of importance regarding the mascot, whose name was Smiley.

"Please don't crowd Smiley," the escorting employee would say. "Let's give Smiley some room."

At first, everything was going smoothly. Smiley met and greeted patrons, posed for pictures, all while his handler doled out stickers to the kids and coupons to the parents. Then something happened that Carl never could have foreseen. Smiley's attendant announced that free packages of All-Mart brand sausage would be handed out to the first ten people who could get to aisle twenty-seven.

Like animals they were, trying to get to their free sausage. In the chaos, someone knocked Smiley flat on his round, green ass.

One day as a greeter had spoken volumes to Carl about the human condition.

Part 16

True Colors

The drive to Richmond went off without a hitch, and the caravan of ladies from Dogwood County arrived at the Fine Arts Museum within five minutes of one another, despite the fact that Carol-Barbara had driven faster than she'd ever driven in her life.

For a while she'd lost sight of her friends in the other car in her rear view mirror. Driving fast had been at Honey insistence, of course, and since it was Honey who owned the purple Cadillac they were cruising in, she'd gone along with it.

It had been fun, Carol-Barbara had to admit, to pilot that beautiful vehicle down the highway, but it was still a wonder to her that she hadn't gotten a ticket. She guessed it was due to the fact that the speed limit on highway 64 had been increased so much in the past decade that it was nearly impossible for that to happen. Seventy miles an hour! Carol-Barbara still felt like fifty-five had been too much.

She thought of a song her son had listened to full-blast in his room over and over again when he was a teenager in the eighties. "I Can't Drive Fifty-Five!" The rock singer would scream.The words had taken on a whole new meaning for Carol-Barbara. Driving fifty-five now would mean getting run over by all the other cars racing seventy-plus down the highway!

Unbeknownst to Carol-Barbara, Debbie had left nearly permanent claw marks in the back seat upholstery of the Cadillac. This was not from the fast-driving, which she was used to since she had dated a NASCAR driver during her youth in Alabama. Rather, it had been from Honey's constant singing, which Debbie likened to someone scraping long, garishly-painted New Jersey manicured fingernails down a chalkboard. The noise had nearly driven her to jump out the Cadillac window.

The only thing that had stopped her was the thought that her husband was counting on her to obtain information from these women. He needed it for his next big business venture. For Dixon, and the money the venture was sure to bring, she would take a deep breath and try to make it through the day, despite the fact that she already hated Honey with every fiber of her being.

The ladies convened in the parking lot of the museum, stretching their backs after the long car ride, and teasing Carol-Barbara about her lead foot. The second carload of ladies had a less entertaining ride, in which the most exciting occurrence was that half-way through the trip Charlene realized she'd forgotten her heartburn medicine, and wondered if she was going to survive the day without it.

The ladies were right on time for the Picasso showing, which was exactly as Carol-Barbara had wanted it. She hated being late for anything.

"It's nearly 10:00," Carol-Barbara spoke up, and herded the ladies towards the front of the museum.

The docent stopped the group just inside the door and checked the time on their tickets. Then she led them through another set of doors and into a waiting room. She explained that there was a strict rule about how many people could be in the exhibition room at one time.

"Fire code," the docent explained.

Ten minutes went by and still they hadn't been let in. Honey was getting bored waiting, and so she started to sing one of the Patsy Cline songs she'd been crooning in the car, only this time there was no music to back her up. The quality of her singing, which had been less than stellar to begin with, was even further diminished. The vast empty waiting room further echoed the fact that she was truly off-key.

Debbie tried hard to control herself, but found it difficult, even with her Southern manners, to hold in her true feelings.

"Must you do that in here?" Debbie asked Honey.

Still, the singing went on, as if Honey hadn't heard a thing Debbie said.

Debbie asked again, louder this time. "I said must you do that in here?"

The other ladies recognized the tension, but tried not to stare, except Martha, who liked a good fight, and felt the possibility of one coming on.

Honey stopped singing for a moment. "Are you tawlkin' to me?" she asked in her heaviest New Jersey accent.

"Yes, I am talking to you!" Debbie put the emphasis on the word "talking" as though she were trying to teach Honey how to properly say it.

"Well, sorry," Honey said, then tried to make light of the situation, "I guess somebody doesn't like Patsy Cline!" She giggled and looked around at the other ladies for support. Only Naomi Martin, who was trying to pass the time by having a snack directly under the sign that said "No food or drinks allowed," had the spirit to speak up.

"Oh, I love Patsy Cline!" Naomi offered as she shoved a sugar-free cookie into her mouth. She hadn't been in the car with Honey on the drive to Richmond, and so it was new to her. Besides, being the easiest-going of the bunch, Naomi had a hard time being annoyed by anyone or anything.

"Patsy Cline isn't the problem, "Debbie said out loud, then mumbled under her breath quietly, "It's you I can't stand."

Just then the docent entered the room and opened the door to the exhibit which diverted the ladies' attention from the scene between Debbie and Honey, and alerted them to the task at hand.

"Ladies," the docent announced, "Welcome to the world of Pablo Picasso!" She led them through the doors and into the exhibit.

Debbie and Elsa pulled up the rear. Elsa was the only one who had heard Debbie say she couldn't stand Honey, and that was only because she'd been sitting on a bench right next to Debbie.

"What was that all about?" Elsa asked.

"Don't worry about it." Debbie leaned in close, "Trust me. That woman is not worth it."

"I sort of like her," Elsa announced to Debbie. "She's funny."

"Yeah, funny like a heart attack," Debbie dismissed Elsa's comment, like she dismissed almost everything Elsa ever said.

"Please don't start a scene," Elsa begged Debbie."

"Don't tell me what to do, you nincompoop," Debbie purposely walked faster, leaving Elsa ten paces behind.

Carol-Barbara was over the moon to be walking through an actual exhibit of Picasso artwork. She had to admit, some of it looked like a first grader had painted it, but it was more than just the skill, or lack thereof, as seemed the case in some pieces, that got her excited. Truth be told, she like reading about the crazy escapades Picasso had pulled throughout his life, and then seeing the artwork that came out of those wild, sinful times in which he lived.

Her favorite story was the one about him meeting Marie-Therese, the young lover he took when he tired of his first wife, Olga. Marie-Therese had been just seventeen when she met the 45 year-old Picasso and became his lover. Only seventeen, and he was a grown, married man! Why, Carol-

Barbara thought, when she had been seventeen she was so shy that if Picasso had even looked at her, she probably would have passed out, but this woman, this *girl*, had been Picasso's lover. If Picasso were around now he'd have been arrested for even thinking about Marie Therese. And rightly so, she concluded. Yet, out of their time together had come the painting of Marie-Therese titled Le Reve that was now in front of her. She stared until her eyes practically burned a hole through the canvas.

"Like that one, do ya?" Martha whispered to Carol-Barbara.

"Oh, I do. I do very much," Carol-Barbara sighed.

"Come on, there's more to see," Martha dragged Carol-Barbara away to peruse the rest of the exhibit.

Painting after painting captured Carol-Barbara's interest. The vibrant colors spoke to her as they never had from a magazine or even a print, of which she had two framed and hanging in her own home. It was as though all copies paled in comparison to the real thing; but in what she saw now the colors hadn't faded a single bit, not in all the decades since Picasso had put paintbrush to canvas. She was in heaven ogling each and every piece.

After what seemed like a short time, the docent came back and told the group their time was up. Carol-Barbara didn't want to leave, but the fact was other people were waiting their turn. With a sigh, she reluctantly left with her friends.

If she had to go back to Dogwood County right now, she thought, she'd be a happy woman, but the trip wasn't over yet, and she was grateful that she still had lunch at The Giant Squid to look forward to.

Part 17

Shrimp- It's what's for Dinner

Days before the ladies made the trek to Richmond, Carol-Barbara called ahead and made reservations for eight at the restaurant. Now they were actually there, and as they were being seated by the Kimono–clad waitress, Carol-Barbara realized it was everything the online review said it would be.

The menus were printed in Japanese, with an English description. Carol-Barbara thought it was very authentic, but Martha was less impressed.

"Why can't they print the damn menu in English," Martha spoke up. "We're in America, aren't we?" Culture was not Martha's forte.

As each lady began to peruse the menu, there was much conversation about what would be ordered. The menu was so extensive that it seemed as though every kind of sushi that existed must be available, which made choosing even harder.

There was Namako, which was the Japanese name for a slimy sea slug that, much like lobster at a seafood restaurant, was to be hand-picked from a tank before being sliced alive in front of the customer and served with a yellowish pottage made from soy sauce and citrus juice. It was definitely not for the faint of heart. There was also more traditional fare on the menu, and most of the ladies stuck to that, either going vegetarian to avoid having to eat anything raw, or making sure that cooked fake crab, the likes of which made Louis

Kemp famous, was substituted for anything that might cause an undesired digestive response later. Charlene was particularly worried about this.

"I'm going to hate myself later," she said quietly, but loud enough for Martha to hear.

"I told you I'd buy you some Tums, now just enjoy yourself," Martha encouraged.

Carol-Barbara, for one, promised herself she wasn't going to take the easy route. The whole point was that she branch out and order something that wouldn't be on a menu in the whole of Dogwood County. While she wasn't willing to eat a sea slug, she did want to order something interesting. After much deliberation she set her mind on the Iku-Tama; Salmon roe with Quail eggs. She was pretty sure that had never been on the menu at The Sizzler in good old Dogwood County.

Honey was seated next to Carol-Barbara, and had expressed her love of shrimp while looking over the menu. Carol-Barbara directed her towards ordering a shrimp roll, never knowing that by doing so, she was becoming party to what would soon be known in Dogwood County as "the shrimp scandal."

The ladies drank hot tea from tiny cups and chatted as they waited for their food, except for Honey, who had ordered a Coke and now sipped it through the straw she had requested. Carol-Barbara was positively starving, despite the hearty oatmeal she'd had for breakfast. She needed to take her mind off her hunger pangs while she waited, so she took a deep breath and decided to strike up a conversation with Debbie, who sat opposite her at the table. Debbie looked more than a little annoyed at the moment, so why not try to be nice, she thought.

"How are things, Debbie?" Carol-Barbara tried to seem genuinely interested.

"With what?" Debbie shot back.

"I don't know, like with Dixon's new shindig," she referred to Debbie's husband and his new job as Dogwood County manager.

"Fine." Debbie was less than forthcoming.

"I see," Carol-Barbara didn't know how much she should pry.

"Does he have any plans for fixing those potholes on Route 58?" piped in. "I'm tired of having to get new tires every six months." Martha was referring to the road that led to the subdivision where many of the ladies lived.

"Oh, he's got plans, alright." Debbie replied. "Let's just say that if he has his way that road will not be a pothole trap anymore," she snickered.

"Oh, then he must have the transportation board on his side already?" Carol-Barbara tried to sound excited. More than once she'd hit one of those potholes, and doing so had nearly caused her teeth to vibrate out of her head.

"Let's just say that with Dixon's plans, Route 58 will no longer be a bother for you to drive on." Debbie's reply was vague, and Carol-Barbara didn't like the way it sounded. She wanted to pry, but just then their lunch was served by the waitress in the beautiful purple Kimono.

The sight of the food quickly put a close to the conversation at hand. Dishes were laid out on the table. Some of them couldn't identify what they were being served as being what they had actually ordered, but everyone was so hungry it didn't seem to matter. They all dug in.

Honey began devouring her shrimp, and Debbie couldn't help but watch how uncouth she was when she ate.

"Try chewing with your mouth closed," Debbie shot a look at Honey.

"You know, you need to lighten up, Miss--- *Saint*, is it? Far from it, I think." Honey shoved another shrimp roll into her mouth, deliberately chewed it with her mouth open, and followed it with a swig of her Coke. "You've been out to get me all day."

"*Saint James*," Debbie corrected her, "And how dare you talk to me like that!" Debbie was indignant that she was being talked to in such a manner.

"Listen, you've treated me awfully since you first laid eyes on me. Looking down at the car I drive, how I talk, sing and eat. All these ladies have welcomed me into the community, but you—you seem to have a problem with the fact that I'm even in your near vicinity!" Honey was hurt, but she was also mad.

"I guess I just don't like it when someone who doesn't fit in moves into Dogwood County.

103

You don't belong here." Then she looked down her nose at Honey and continued. "And I'm surprised you would even order shrimp."

"What's that supposed to mean?" Honey asked, upset now.

"Well, shrimp are nothing but the cockroach of the sea, and I wouldn't think you would eat your own kind." Even though it was a silly comparison, Debbie looked pleased with herself.

Honey looked for a moment like she might cry, and Carol-Barbara stood by with an extra napkin in case the tears started to flow. Debbie could really be a nasty person. She had made all of them feel less than worthy once or twice over the years.

Instead of crying, though, Honey picked up another of her shrimp as if she were going to continue eating and let the whole conversation go in one ear and out the other. However, just before the shrimp reached her mouth, she paused, then hurled the crustacean like a dart towards Debbie. "Here's what you can do with these shrimp!"

It hit Debbie right on her recently-botoxed forehead, and, thanks to the cocktail sauce Honey had dipped it in, it stuck.

The entire table was silent, with mouths open and aghast at what had just transpired.

Part 18

Truth and Consequences

Needless to say, the lunch Carol-Barbara had so carefully planned for her ladies' group hadn't quite gone off as she imagined it would. Honey had just hurled a sticky shrimp, tail and all, at Debbie's forehead. It had stuck briefly before sliding down Debbie's face like one of the sea slugs in the restaurant aquarium, leaving a stream of cocktail sauce down her nose before finally falling to the table in an unappetizing pink lump.

Debbie was oddly controlled about the whole thing. Too controlled. She picked up her napkin and wiped her face, which did little to remove the sauce from her face.

Honey looked as surprised as the rest of them at what had happened. "Oh, dear-what have I done?" She reached for a napkin and dipped it into her water glass. "I'm so—sorry." She stood up and reached across the table towards Debbie's face, hoping she could clean up the mess she had just made.

"No!" Debbie put her hand up in a defensive motion. "You've done enough already." She stood up. "Elsa, get up. We're leaving." Debbie announced to her sister, who sat beside her.

"But I haven't finished my food," Elsa protested.

"Get up!" Debbie demanded of Elsa, who finally complied, but with her head slung low. Before turning to leave, Elsa pulled a twenty dollar bill from her pocket and placed it on the table. "For our share." She declared to the others, looking humiliated. The table was silent. A few of the women looked at Elsa with pity.

Elsa gathered her belongings, including the bag with the Picasso poster she'd purchased at the museum gift store. "Sorry." she said sheepishly.

"Stop apologizing!" Debbie spat at her to Carol-Barbara.

Carol Barbara reached out her hand and touched Elsa's. "It's okay. We'll talk later."

Elsa turned back towards her sister. "But how will we get home?" She had tears in her eyes.

"Certainly not in that trash-mobile that we arrived in. I don't care if I have to take an Uber cab all the way back to Dogwood County." Debbie meant it.

"But, Debbie, that will cost a fortune! And I don't have-" Elsa was cut off abruptly.

"Elsa!" Debbie shushed her as she had done since the two were children. "Get up, or else take your chances with these low-lifes."

"Low-lifes? I will thank you to keep your insults to yourself," Martha spewed. She'd had enough of Debbie's uppity attitude. "Let me tell you, I've wanted to throw something at your ugly face for years. I can't blame Honey. You're an evil person, Debbie St. James."

"You people are all going to be sorry. I can't believe I decided to join you today!" Debbie was fuming.

"Why *did* you insist on joining us today?" Carol-Barbara finally asked the question that had consumed her for weeks.

"Well, I supposed there's no reason to put on airs now, so I may as well tell you." Debbie straightened herself to her full height. "Dixon is unveiling his new plan for Dogwood County. It's going to be fabulous. A mall, with all the stores that matter, Nordstrom's, Saks, Crate and Barrel."

"What exactly does that have to do with us, Debbie?" Carol-Barbara questioned.

"Because the new Dogwood County mall is going to be situated in your subdivision," Debbie was full of herself.

"You mean, *near* our subdivision." Charlene said, correcting Debbie.

"I mean *in place of* your subdivision!" Debbie snapped. "Dixon was going to give you top dollar for your land, more than it's rightly worth. My mission today was to tell you about what a wonderful financial opportunity it would be for your golden years, but now- well-- now you can rot for all I care!"

"But our homes aren't even for sale." Naomi was confused.

"Doesn't matter if your homes are for sale or not," Debbie explained. "Dogwood County is in economic trouble, and it needs something to keep it going. This mall, in that location, will do just that. It's more important than your middle class dwellings. And that's how the Dogwood County planning commission will see it after Dixon is finished with them."

"You can't just buy our land if we're not selling," said Anne. Her words were loud and clear, despite the fact that she was still in speech therapy after her stroke.

"Au contraire," Debbie haughtily replied, "Ever heard of eminent domain?"

"Eminent domain?" Questioned Charlene, who had lived in her home alone since her husband died several years before. "Isn't that when the government seizes someone's property to build a road?"

"Sometimes a road, sometimes other things," stated Debbie, "And my Dixon has found a loophole that will allow him to build right where your homes are currently located."

"He wouldn't!" Diane jumped up from her seat. "I've lived in that house since I was a little girl! My brothers helped our Daddy dig that basement with their bare hands!"

"Too bad," Debbie responded unapologetically, "If you would play your cards right you'll get enough to keep you in Hillside Manor." Debbie referred to the retirement home in the county. "Play your cards wrong, and you'll end up living on the streets."

"You wouldn't!" Diane was shaking as she spoke.

"Oh, I would. And you can thank your friend here for that!" She glared at Honey. "She has made me feel less than generous." Debbie finally paused for a breath. "Now come on, Elsa, we're leaving!"

"I'm not going with you." Elsa stood her ground for once.

"Excuse me?" Debbie was incredulous.

Elsa took a step away from her and back towards the table. She took her seat. "You're a mean, spiteful person, Debbie, and I'm not going anywhere with you."

"Suit yourself, then. I see you've chosen your side. Don't expect anything else from me ever again." With that, Debbie stormed from the restaurant. By this time, the other patrons were all staring.

Carol-Barbara patted Elsa's hand. "I'm proud of you, Elsa. Real proud."

Elsa nervously smiled. "That's been a long time coming.

"What have I done?" Honey suddenly cried.

"There, there, Honey," Carol-Barbara consoled. "You didn't do this. Debbie has clearly been planning this for longer than you've even been a resident of Dogwood County.

Still, Honey continued to cry. "I guess I really am nothing but a trouble-making six-legged cockroach!

"You are not." Martha silenced her. "Besides, you clearly have just two legs. Can you imagine what it would cost to deck out six legs in those stilettos you wear?"

This brought unexpected laughs from the whole table, but the smile on Carol-Barbara's face only served to hide the fact that she was scared to death they were all about to fall prey to Debbie and Dixon's dreadful plan. Could the county really take their homes?

Part 19

Dirt Bag

"And then Honey threw the shrimp in Debbie's face!" Carol-Barbara raised her arms in the air and dropped them to her side, still disbelieving what had happened, though she had witnessed the unpleasant incident with her own eyes.

Carol-Barbara had been recounting the story to Carl, who listened with all the rapt attention he could muster, considering he was only half-listening.

He was scraping mud off his shoes into a trash can sitting in the garage floor. He had taken Bubba for a walk in the woods at the end of their street, and the ground had been much wetter than he had anticipated; so much so that he'd been forced to give Bubba a bath when they returned home. This was a process both parties disliked.

Bubba hated baths mainly because he considered them a punishment. As a hound dog, there was nothing Bubba enjoyed more than carrying around the stench of whatever he'd rolled in. A little mud added to it was just icing on the cake, as far as he was concerned. Baths made him feel as though he'd lost his identity.

Carl hated giving Bubba a bath almost as much as Bubba loathed receiving one, but for different reasons. For Carl, Bubba's bath time was nothing short of torture, with Carl ending up soaked from head to toe; the victim of a sort of canine water-boarding. He considered for a moment that the next time Bubba was due for a bath he might just pay the fee at The Dapper Doggie pet shop and have Bubba groomed properly.

"Are you even listening to me, Carl?" Carol-Barbara's voice interrupted Carl's thoughts.

"Of course I'm listening. Honey threw a squid in Debbie's face at The Giant Shrimp."

"No, Carl, it was a shrimp she threw, and the name of the restaurant was The Giant Squid. It's like talking to a wall sometimes, I swear..." Carol-Barbara trailed off.

Just then a knock at the garage door startled them both. Carl knocked over the trash can containing the dirt he'd been scraping from his shoes.

They both looked towards the door, wondering who would be knocking at this hour. After all, it was past eight o'clock.

In walked Martha without waiting for invite, and in true fashion, she got right to the point.

"What are we going to do?" These were the first words out of her mouth.

"Good evening to you, too, Martha," Carl derided.

"No time for sarcasm, Hoofnagle," Martha addressed him by his last name, as she so often did. "We've got bigger fish to fry."

"I prefer mine with tartar sauce on the side," he replied.. When it came to Martha, Carl found it hard to curb his sarcasm.

"This is serious." Martha then turned her attention to Carol-Barbara. "Have you told him yet?"

"Is this about what happened at lunch with the flying lobster?" He joked again

"For the last time, Carl, it was shrimp!" Carol-Barbara corrected him sternly.

"I'm talking about what happened after the flying shrimp," Martha explained.

"I haven't gotten that far," Carol-Barbara took a big breath. She had intended to ease Carl into the other issue that had come to light at lunch. Besides, she wasn't even sure if Debbie had been serious about her threats, and she didn't want Carl to worry. She considered his blood pressure would shoot through the roof when he found out.

"Tell me what?" Carl asked for the second time as he stood and brushed the last of the dirt from his shoes and picked up the overturned trash can. A pile of dirt remained on the floor.

Martha stared at Carol-Barbara in an attempt to give her one last chance to come clean before she would take over and start talking. Carol-Barbara took the hint.

"It's nothing. Probably just Debbie making idle threats." Carol-Barbara tried to be nonchalant.

"Such as?" Carl could feel his cheeks getting hot. He hated when Debbie caused stress to those he cared about.

Martha could no longer hold her tongue "Such as the fact that Debbie and her husband, Dixon, are going to bulldoze our homes down and build a mall!"

"They're going to do what?" Of all the things he had expected to hear, this hadn't been one of them.

Carol-Barbara took over. "Debbie claims that Dixon has a plan to build a shopping mall right where we are standing. She says he can get the plans passed due to something called eminent domain. She claims they are going to bulldoze our subdivision down."

Carl had a vision of Dixon in his bowtie and sockless loafers, sitting alongside his wife in her designer clothes; the two of them piloting a bulldozer through their subdivision. The vision was almost laughable. Carl's mouth broke into a grin.

"Do you think this is funny or something, Hoofnagle?" Martha piped in.

"Nope, not at all. I just can't picture the two of them bulldozing anything. And I'm sure whatever Debbie said was just an angry reply to having shrimp thrown in her face." Carl tried to talk the situation down.

Carol-Barbara wasn't sure she agreed with him, but she took note that he'd at least gotten the flying crustacean right this time.

Carl continued. "When are you two going to learn to take everything that woman says with a grain of salt?"

"I'm afraid she might mean it this time, Hoofnagle. She and Dixon might just have a case."

"What in the world makes you say that?" Carl questioned.

"I made a phone call on the way over here, to a contact I have in Washington. It's someone who knows a lot about this sort of thing," Martha explained.

Carl and Carol-Barbara knew better than to ask her who her contact was in D.C., for she was fiercely loyal and private about the people she knew.

They had always been aware that there was more to Martha than met the eye. They had known her since high school, and she'd always danced to the beat of her own drum.

After college, Martha had spent some time overseas under the guise of back-packing across Europe. This had been back in the day when women didn't generally do this sort of thing.

No one who knew Martha in high school believed her backpacking story, but they all respected her too much to ask what she was really doing. When Martha returned from Europe she seemed to know people in power, much like the St. James family did. Unlike the St. James family, though, Martha's contacts weren't tuxedo-wearing, benefit-schmoozing kind of people. They were more like sitting-in-the-dark-in-an-undisclosed-location-getting-things-done-under-the-radar kind of people. For decades Martha's contacts had remained nothing but nameless, faceless entities that popped up every so often to give her advice.

"So what did your contact say?" Carl pressed Martha for an answer.

"Unfortunately, he said that the St. James's may actually have a very real case. This sort of thing has happened before, and it didn't turn out pretty." Martha was straightforward. "He said he would check into a few things and get back to me."

"How soon?" Carol Barbara asked.

"Not sure, but I'll keep you in the loop. Look, you two, I have to run, but I will be in touch." She stepped over Carl's pile of dirt on her way out. "You gonna clean that up, Hoofnagle?"

"Yeah, Martha, I'm going to clean it up." Carl assured her.

With that, Martha was out the door, as quickly as she'd arrived.

Suddenly, Carol-Barbara remembered something. "I didn't even ask you about your first day of work at the All-Mart."

"Let's just say the angry mob on aisle five doesn't compare to this."

"That good, huh?" Carol-Barbara queried.

"Yeah. That good." Carl stared at the pile of dirt on the garage floor, and it looked to him oddly like Dixon St. James.

Part 20

The Center of Everywhere

Five days a week Dixon awoke at 4:00 in the morning and ran 7 miles on his treadmill before the sun ever peeked over the horizon. This morning he was feeling so good he decided he would do 10 miles, just for the fun of it. Dixon settled into his running pace, and began the controlled breathing that had allowed him to easily finish twelve marathons during his life, with a thirteenth coming up next spring in Atlanta.

After his run he would also lift weights for a half hour before finally going downstairs to his breakfast of half a grapefruit, exactly two pieces of toast spread with exactly two tablespoons of peanut butter and one cup of black coffee. It was the same breakfast he'd had every morning for thirty years. His regimented exercise and unwavering breakfast had kept him in shape. He looked fitter than most men half his age. This made him feel good about himself, and it didn't hurt that the ladies noticed, either. At least he knew they weren't just after his money and prestige, but they also found him physically desirable.

Recently, at his wife Debbie's request, he'd added swimming laps to his exercise routine on the two mornings he didn't run. Debbie participated in her water aerobics class on the same two mornings, and she suggested to Dixon that going to the YMCA would be a good way for them to spend quality time together. He knew it was really more of a way for her to keep up appearances. If they were seen by her friends and acquaintances exercising at the "Y" together, it was all the proof she needed to convince them that things were just fine on the home front. Dixon knew it was also her way of keeping an eye on him.

He had argued with her at first about going, claiming he didn't have the time to add yet another workout to his routine. After all he had his building development business to run; but he had gone along with it after he got a look at the cute female lifeguards who worked at the lap pool. Dixon had vowed that one day he would fake a heart attack just so he could have one of them give him mouth-to-mouth.

Dixon knew his wife would be very aware that scantily clad women at the pool would be in full view of him. Yet, knowing her as he did, he also understood her thought process would be that of "better a devil she knew than one she didn't." She was right. If it hadn't been women at the pool, it would be women somewhere else he would be reaching out to for the physical love she denied him.

Dixon knew Debbie wasn't oblivious to his extracurricular activities. While she loved the life he'd given her, it had been a long time since she actually loved him. He hated to say she had made him this way, but it was true. Withholding of love can make someone seek it elsewhere, he told himself.

Dixon loved Debbie in his own way, mainly because she let him get away with things, but also because marrying her had allowed him to get ahead in life. They'd had what could best be described as an arranged marriage by their families, who wanted to grow stronger by breeding their offspring with other families that had equally good names and genes. Debbie and Dixon were like horses in that respect.

Rather than his latest love conquest, it was his business success that made him feel so virile this particular morning. Today's good vibrations had everything to do with his latest business venture; one which he would be announcing to the Dogwood County commissioner later today.

Dogwood County had always been a quiet little place, with Mom and Pop stores that lined the main thoroughfare through Waynesville. These tiny shops had been okay in their prime, but the rest of the world had moved on, leaving Dogwood County looking like something out of a 1950's issue of *Look* magazine. It was no way to do business in the modern world, and Dogwood County revenues were suffering for it.

For decades, the motto of the place seemed to be "Let sleeping dogs lie." Dixon had decided there would be no more of that. It was time to wake this puppy up. Just as in a greyhound race when the rabbit is dangled in front of the canine's nose to get him moving, Dixon planned on enticing the residents of Dogwood County and surrounding areas with something that would get them moving into the future; and would make him a whole lot of money in the process. He called it his ten million dollar idea.

Dogwood County was located smack dab in the middle of the state of Virginia, and therefore a half-day drive or less from anywhere in the state, as well as Maryland, D.C. and much of North Carolina and West Virginia. Dixon envisioned his little shopping Utopia as a kind of center of everywhere, where people would come for a day or a weekend of restful relaxation and shopping.

Dixon's dream involved cobblestone streets, a sprawling maze of shops and restaurants, upscale department stores the likes of which could be found in big cities like Atlanta and Dallas, and maybe even one they could lure over from Europe. His dream also included a fancy hotel with a day spa. He did so enjoy a good spa day.

The shopping center would include services such as Wi-Fi, and a "green" outlook on the world, meaning each store would focus on making the smallest carbon footprint it possibly could. People who spent too much money loved that sort of thing. It made them feel less guilty for having money in the first place and spending it on things like five dollar cups of coffee.

He even imagined adding penthouse-only living spaces for only the most discriminating tenants, of course. He envisioned Debbie and himself living in the nicest one during their old age, surrounded by other equally as beautiful and worthy senior anchors of the community. Forget about that retirement home on the hill.

To the people of Dogwood County, it would be a hard sell at first. They didn't like change. But, later, after it was bringing much needed money and recognition to the area, they would probably name a street after him or something. They were always naming streets after people who gave back to the community, and he considered himself to be giving back in a big way. Hell, maybe they would even decide to name the actual development after him. - *St. James Place*. It had a nice ring to it, and he really didn't care that Parker Brothers had used the name first in the Monopoly game.

Dixon had the perfect spot for his Utopia- right smack in the middle of Forest Glen subdivision, which was located just off the highway; and which, he had discovered, was ripe for the picking due to a tiny, centuries-old glitch in record-keeping. Now all that was left was to convince the powers that be that Dogwood County's empty pocketbook would benefit more from this than it would a bunch of aging old cronies squeezing out their last few years in their outdated houses. Dixon ran his last two miles with a spring in his step just thinking about it.

Part 21

Murder, She Wrote

A week after their trip to Richmond, Carol-Barbara called an emergency meeting of The NAKED ladies. It seemed only appropriate considering the circumstances surrounding their last outing.

Despite the fact that Honey had pushed Debbie over her proverbial edge, it wouldn't have changed the fact that Dixon was determined to go through with his selfish plan. Had it not been for Honey *shrimping* the information out of Debbie, as Carol-Barbara's husband Carl had taken to calling it, the ladies might not have known about Dixon's plan until it was too late. At least now they knew what Dixon was up to, and would have time to find a way to prevent him from succeeding. Carol-Barbara considered they should all be thanking Honey for forcing Debbie into giving them a heads up.

Needless to say, Debbie was no longer welcome at the NAKED meetings, and during the past week, Martha had gone into action and contacted one of the government associates from her earlier days working in Washington, D.C. She'd discovered that Dixon might have an actual case against the Forest Glen subdivision. This is what they were here to discuss, and how to prevent it.

Betty Horton, who had lived for decades in the house Honey and Roland now occupied, had joined the group tonight via Skype, and she didn't seem too surprised to learn what Dixon was up to, and had pointed out that she had never trusted him as far as she could throw him. At 90 years old and 85 pounds soaking wet, that wouldn't have been very far. Were she able, Betty assured Carol-Barbara, she would have thrown him all the way into the next county and let them deal with him for a while.

But since she couldn't do that, and since she couldn't even attend the ladies' gatherings in person, she had asked Carol-Barbara to conference her in tonight from North Carolina She put the "National" in The National Association of Kindred Elderly Dames.

She neglected to tell everyone she would be Skyping while she was having her evening bath at the nursing home. Suddenly, she was yelling at the top of her lungs. "Damn it, Naomi! I told you I can't stand it when you hover over me while I'm washing. It makes me nervous. Now get the hell out of here!"

"Who was that??" asked Martha.

"Her nurse," Carol-Barbara explained.

"Mrs. Horton, it's almost time for your medication. You have to finish up your bath now." The ladies heard the voice of Betty's nurse in the background and all tried to stifle their laughs.

"I'll be out when I'm good and ready!" Betty squawked. "And make sure I have milk tonight. You know I can't take my medication without my milk."

"Alright, Betty, knock it off, we've got work to do." Martha commanded.

"Is that you, Martha, you old coot," Betty teased. "Which one of your mysterious friends is going to fix this mess for us?"

'"Don't you worry about it, Betty. You just listen up. All of you listen up. We have a real problem here with Dixon St. James, and I need to know what you all think about it. Do we give in and move into that sorry excuse for a retirement home in town, or do we fight for our homes and live out life on our terms?"

"I say we sue him!" Diane suggested.

"That costs money, and according to my contacts in Washington, he's got a pretty good case against us. If we sue him, we might just be throwing our money away. Then we won't even be able to afford Happy Acres Retirement Home, or whatever it is they call that place."

"Sarah Jennings lives there and says it's kind of nice," added Susie.

"Sarah Jennings doesn't know nice from a hole in her—"

"Martha!" Carol-Barbara stopped her.

"What? I was going to say head," assured Martha. "Anyway, it doesn't matter if it's nice if it's on Dixon's terms. I don't know about you all, but I want to go out of here on my terms."

They all agreed that it would be best to have the freedom to decide. Betty agreed, too, and then signed off, saying they had her support, but that she had to get out of the tub before her nurse went off duty and left her to fend for herself. She wouldn't have minded except for the fact that she was shriveling like a prune in the tub and really did need her nightly glass of milk. "Whatever you ladies decide to do, I'm behind you," and she hung up.

At that, Charlene spoke up, "Can we get this wrapped up?" she complained. "I have to go home and research where I'm going to live. I can't afford a retirement home."

"Now listen, there's going to be none of that talk," Martha declared. "We're going to figure out a way to stop Dixon.

At that moment Honey, arriving late to the meeting, came busting through the front door without knocking, and she was clearly under the influence of alcohol. "I think I have an idea," She pulled a gun from her handbag and waved it in the air. "We'll just shoot him."

All mouths dropped open, and Naomi ducked and covered as best she could in her wingback chair.

"What? I was kidding," Honey settled in to the last empty chair in the living room. It's just a water gun. She squirted it in the air.

Oh, thank goodness," Naomi said with a sigh of relief. "I thought you were serious."

"Too bad, because I think that's the best idea I've heard yet," Martha stated.

Part 22

Aw, Shoot!

"Try not to shoot anyone while I'm gone," Carl joked as he sat in a chair at the kitchen table, struggling to pull his boots on. He was preparing for his shift at the All-Mart, and today the impending rain necessitated wearing the duck boots he received as a gift from Carol-Barbara on Christmas Day, 1983.

The boots were from LL Bean, and even though they showed their age they still kept the rain out. He considered their longevity a testament to American-made products, and categorically refused to get a new pair. His socks stayed dry, his feet warm, and that was all that mattered. Until his feet got wet, he was resigned to keeping them. Even then, he considered, LL Bean offered a lifetime, 100% guarantee on all their products. He still had the shoebox from that Christmas, and the piece of paper inside it that stated that fact. He could probably send them back and get a new pair. Unless, of course, the company had been sold to the Chinese since then. He sure hoped not.

Carol-Barbara sat at the table across from him and sipped coffee. Carl's remark about shooting someone was precipitated by the fact that Carol-Barbara had just finished recounting the goings-on at her meeting of the NAKED ladies the night before, during which a very tipsy Honey had suggested they shoot Dixon to stop him from going through with his plan of razing their neighborhood and building a mall. The strangest part, Carol-Barbara had just explained to Carl, was that their friend, Martha, had agreed with Honey's suggestion that it might be the easiest, quickest way to get rid of him.

"Honestly, I'd like to shoot him myself right about now," Carl confessed. "But I'd also like to see our granddaughter every so often, and without a glass window and a guard between us, you know?" Carl joked. "And besides, you know Martha didn't mean it. She'd never do anything like that. He paused. "Now Honey, on the other hand," Carl's voice trailed off.

"Oh, stop it, Carl. There will be no shooting of anyone by anybody, okay? I can't believe you would even say such a thing. Or that Martha, in all her wisdom, would even entertain such a thought."

Carol-Barbara had always known Martha to have a good head on her shoulders, so she just could not understand why their meeting last night had ended with Martha and Honey in the same corner.

"I see those wheels turning, CB. What's going on in there? Are you thinking I might be right?" Carl knew when Carol-Barbara had that far-away look she was thinking hard on something.

"You don't really think Honey would resort to violence, do you?" Carol-Barbara asked.

"I don't know. You remember that comment Roland made to me about Honey supposedly shooting him, don't you?" Carl reminded her.

127

"Of course I remember, but I don't know if I believe it," Carol-Barbara thought on it for a moment. "If Honey had actually shot her husband, wouldn't *she* be the one behind a glass window with a guard watching her every move?"

"I guess so," Carl admitted, "But what about the incident at the restaurant with Debbie?" Carl questioned.

"That was a shrimp she threw, Carl!" Carol-Barbara rose her voice in frustration. "That's hardly the same as shooting a gun at someone. Besides, a girl can lose her temper, can't she? Especially when Debbie is involved."

"Well, you're right about that," Carl agreed.

"Oh, Carl, what are we going to do?" She struggled with the reality of the situation. Tears hadn't shown in Carol-Barbara's eyes since she'd learned her cancer was in remission, and those had been happy tears. Now tears of frustration flooded her eyes. She lowered her head and pressed the backs of her hands into her eyelids to try and stop the flow.

Carl rose from his chair and went to stand beside her. He placed a loving arm on her shoulder.

"Look at me, CB." Carl's voice was soft, but serious. Carol-Barbara raised her head and looked into the eyes of the man who had cared for her physical and emotional well-being every day for more than forty years, just as she'd done for him.

Carl's eyes were as bright and clear as the day she met him, though now they held nearly a lifetime of memories. The skin around them was as weathered as leather from all his years working for the phone company, climbing telephone poles out in the elements. This only served to make the blue in his eyes stand out more. The wrinkles around his eyes were like frames surrounding two nearly identical paintings. Each one could tell tales of love and happiness, as well as sadness and loss. Together the pair told the whole story.

When she looked into those eyes she found it impossible to choke back her emotion anymore. The tears flowed down her cheeks. "We could lose our home, Carl."

Carl leaned in close and kissed Carol-Barbara on the forehead, the way he had done so many times during their life together; in the hospital when the twins were born, when she learned of her mother passing, and again with her father, when she was diagnosed with cancer, and again when she was given word that it was in remission. She loved those kisses. Of course, she loved the passionate ones they had shared in the past as well, and still did sometimes, despite the fact that their grown children thought people over sixty didn't get "those feelings" anymore.

However, it was the kisses on the forehead that meant the most to her. Kisses on the forehead meant business. They meant he understood, and that he would do whatever was in his power to keep his loved ones safe.

Carl continued. "We are not going to lose our home, CB. I feel confident of that, but just remember, even if we were forced to leave this place, for me it's not these four walls that makes this a home, it's you."

Now Carol-Barbara was really choking up, but still Carl continued. "But I promise you I will do whatever I can to make sure you don't lose your home. "Well, short of shooting him, that is."

He paused and turned towards the counter to get his red cooler with the lunch she'd made him. "I'll leave that to you girls," Carl smiled, trying to lighten the mood. He started for the door then turned back towards her. "Hey, I have an idea."

"What's that?" Carol-Barbara rose to take her coffee cup to the sink, wiping away the last of the tears with her napkin.

"Why don't you give Elsa a call? See what she knows about the situation." He suggested.

"Elsa?" Carol-Barbara was surprised by Carl's suggestion.

"Sure. You haven't talked to her since you dropped her off after Richmond, right? She's always been a decent person. Maybe she'll know more about what Dixon is up to. It's just an idea. Love you." With that, he walked through the door, waving his goodbyes as he went.

Carol-Barbara considered that Elsa might be willing to tell her what she knows, if she wasn't too scared of Debbie's wrath. It had seemed like she turned a corner at the restaurant, though, standing up to her and all.

Years ago, and for only a short time, Elsa had been a much-beloved babysitter to Carl and Carol-Barbara's children during a financially difficult time in their lives. The phone company had gone on strike. Carl, wanting to work, but being unable to, had lost two months wages. In a desperate attempt to help their situation Carol-Barbara had filled in as a receptionist for someone on maternity leave, while Carl helped a friend put roofs on new houses. Elsa had agreed to pick the children up from school and keep them until they both got home at night, and she was willing to do it for free. She had received quite an inheritance from her father, who must have known Elsa wouldn't marry rich like Debbie, and she'd been able to live on it quite comfortably without having to work. She'd focused her life, instead, on volunteer work.

Elsa's job with the children not include helping the children with their homework, as academics had never been her strong suit. Her sister, Debbie, had gotten not only the looks in the family, but also the brains. However, it turned out Elsa had other gifts. First, she was wonderfully patient with children, as well as great fun; and second, during their time together, she taught them both to bake. They spent afternoons in the kitchen making the most delicious sweets that Carol-Barbara had ever tasted. She felt Elsa had surely missed her true calling.

Life had been so hectic at that time that there had been nights that Carol-Barbara had simply made cheese sandwiches and opened cans of soup for dinner. Then, after the kids went to bed, and being so tempted by the treats Elsa left behind, she would gorge herself on chocolate-banana muffins and orange scones with homemade clotted cream. She

131

gained ten pounds during that two month period. Pounds that didn't come off until years later when she went through chemo and was so sick she couldn't eat a thing.

The kids' special time with Elsa was put to a stop by her sister when Debbie convinced Elsa she shouldn't be working for free, and threatened to cut off their father's money, which Dixon controlled for Elsa.

Both Elsa and the children had been devastated when Debbie stepped in and stopped all their fun, but Elsa always seemed to listen to everything Debbie said, and that was just the way it was. By then the telephone company strike was over, and the woman Carol-Barbara had been filling in for also came back from maternity leave. Everything returned to normal.

Thinking about what Carl had said about calling Elsa made her reach for the phone. She could still remember Elsa's phone number. She picked up the receiver and started to dial. Then, having second thoughts, she hung the phone up and reached for her rain jacket hanging on a peg in the laundry room. Forget calling, she would pay the woman a much-needed visit instead. Maybe, if she was lucky, she would even get a chocolate-banana muffin out of it.

Part 23

Hoecakes and Honey Wine

Carol-Barbara was behind the wheel of her Toyota Camry and heading farther out into the countryside where Elsa lived. She turned onto the dirt road that led to Elsa's house. She hadn't been down this road in years.

Elsa was so different from her sister, and Carol-Barbara had to wonder how the two were even related. Elsa preferred to live in a rural setting, keeping to herself most of the time, caring for her plants and baking; while Debbie had to live in town, in the heart of the action, meddling in affairs that sometimes weren't even hers to meddle in, and with a social calendar that rivaled that of the first lady.

Elsa was so quiet and sweet. She would do just about anything to make another person's life easier, even to her own detriment, Carol-Barbara considered. Elsa had been Debbie's lackey for so many years that it seemed she'd lost her own identity in the process.

She pulled her car into the driveway of the little house with the white picket fence. The bareness of autumn was currently masking the fact that, come spring, the little yard would be bursting to its brim with flora of every kind, as the only thing Elsa enjoyed more than baking was gardening.

Fall leaves covered raised beds where in a few months lavender, rosemary and basil would fill the herb garden, releasing their intoxicating aromas as the sun heated them. Other areas of the front yard would hold massive bouquets of Virginia flowers such as Bluebells, Tulips, and Daffodils. Not a single space in the front yard went to waste. If Elsa thought something could grow there, she planted it.

Carol-Barbara hadn't been in the back yard of Elsa's little abode for many years, not since Elsa used to baby-sit her children, but she imagined that underneath the chilly, hard ground were volunteers of every kind waiting to burst forth into the sunshine as soon as Mother Nature gave them the okay to do so.

Elsa's back yard would be a cornucopia, spilling its treasure of tomatoes, bell peppers, spinach and squash of all varieties. Vegetation of all kinds seemed to spring into life of their own volition around Elsa. To say she had a green thumb would be putting it mildly. There would also be the new seedlings that Elsa would grow in a small greenhouse during the winter, to be planted when the ground warmed up. She tended to them as if they were her children, and in a way they were, since Elsa had never married, and didn't have any children of her own. She lived alone in the little home.

The perimeter of the front yard was bordered by Forsythia planted so closely together it appeared as one giant bush snaking its way around the yard. In the spring it would be hard to tell there was a fence behind all that foliage at all, except for the fact that there was a gate at the only location where there was a break in the Forsythia growth.

Now though, Carol-Barbara could see the fence, and she could also see that it was in dire need of repair. Several of the fence posts were falling down, and the whole of it needed to be painted. Perhaps, she thought, she would send Carl out to do the repairs and slap a coat of paint on it.

Though it housed only one person, the home was more alive than many of the big houses Carol-Barbara had seen, with their chemically induced green lawns and meticulously landscaped gardens. Those places seemed alive at first glance, but a second look found most of them to be fake, even dead inside- like Debbie.

Carol-Barbara imagined that Debbie's house must look like one of those House Beautiful magazine covers, where everything seemed lovely and perfect on the outside, but on the inside was something dirty and false. Carol-Barbara had never made in into the gated community where Debbie and Dixon lived. She'd driven by many times, though, and jokingly wondered if the gate and guardhouse was really meant to protect the residents from the rest of the world, or the rest of the world from them. Gated communities were so unwelcoming.

Not Elsa's house, though. It had always been the definition of hospitality, so Carol-Barbara wondered why she felt just the slightest bit nervous about knocking on Elsa's door unannounced. After all, it wouldn't have been like Elsa to treat Carol-Barbara any way but polite. It simply wasn't her way. She imagined her anxiety stemmed from the fact that the two hadn't had a real conversation in years, and that Elsa was probably still feeling horribly about

Debbie's behavior in Richmond. She had cried the whole of the way home that night.

Carol-Barbara hoped that in the comfort of her own home Elsa would feel free to speak her mind. She took a deep breath and readied herself, but before she could get out of the car, the front door to the house burst open.

"Carol-Barbara?" A voice hollered from the porch. "Is that you?" The voice was friendly, excited. It was pure Elsa.

Carol-Barbara slipped out of the car and waved towards the plump woman at the door. "Yes, it's me, Elsa!"

"Well, don't just stand there! Get on in here!" Carol-Barbara's anxiety immediately melted away. She could see that Elsa was wiping her hands on a dishtowel, and she was hopeful those hands were dirty because Elsa had just finished crafting something delicious to eat.

Carol-Barbara made her way through the squeaky gate and up the steps to the porch. The mouth-watering smells wafting from the house confirmed her hopes. Elsa grabbed Carol-Barbara in a giant bear hug, nearly knocking her off her feet. Then, she grabbed her hand and dragged her into the kitchen.

"Try one of these. Hot and ready." Elsa shoved a crispy yellow Hoe-cake into Carol-Barbara's hand. "Have some honey wine with it. Nothing like honey wine with hoe-cakes." Elsa poured golden liquid from a stoneware pitcher into a matching mug and handed it to Carol-Barbara. She took it willingly, although for a moment she wondered about the ramifications of drinking something called honey wine at 10:00 in the morning.

Elsa sat her mind at ease. "It barely has any alcohol. I made it from the honey in my bee hives out back."

Carol-Barbara held the mug of golden liquid to her lips and took a swallow. It was delicious; more like sweet tea than wine, but there was a little kick to it.

Elsa insisted they sit at the kitchen table and chat. She brought the plate of hoe-cakes and the jug of honey wine with her. For about thirty minutes they chatted about Carol-Barbara's kids, what they were up to, how the grandbabies were doing, making no mention of what had happened in Richmond.

Elsa made Carol-Barbara promise to tell her daughter she wanted her to teach her little ones how to bake. "Never too early to learn how to get your hands dirty and a little flour in your hair. Little ones love that. I know yours did back when I was watching them."

Carol-Barbara assured Elsa she would pass that along. Then, she started to feel guilty. Here she was enjoying this woman's generous hospitality, when the real reason she was here was to talk about the issue with Debbie. She gently turned the conversation in that direction.

"I need to ask you a question, Elsa."

"Anything, Carol-Barbara. You know that." Elsa advised.

"How much do you know about what your sister and her husband have planned for Dogwood County?" Carol-Barbara came right out with it.

"Ugg" Elsa stood up from the table. "I should have said ask me anything, but that." She paused. "Though I kind of figured after what happened in Richmond you hadn't just come out here for idle chit-chat and hoe-cakes." She admitted.

Carol-Barbara tried to lighten the mood. "A big part of my coming here was the food, actually. I mean, I could have just phoned you, right?" She laughed.

Elsa tried to smile. She knew Carol-Barbara was not just using her for information, and that they shared a long and trusting history together. Still, though, she couldn't address Carol-Barbara's question.

"Please, Elsa. I need to know if I am going to lose my home." Carol-Barbara implored her.

Elsa sighed. "Debbie has my hands tied," Elsa tried to explain. "You know how she is."

"Oh, yes. I know how she treats people, especially you, Elsa, but what I don't understand is why? What is this hold she has over you?"

"Oh, CB." Elsa resorted to calling her the nickname by which she'd heard Carol-Barbara's husband refer to her years ago. "It would take a lifetime to explain how Debbie has sunk her claws into me, and why I can't remove them."

"I don't get it. You are such a different person when she isn't around." Carol-Barbara pointed out the obvious. "So strong and independent."

"I know," Elsa paused. "Let's just says something happened a long time ago, and Debbie has held it over my head ever since."

"I'm sorry, Elsa. I won't pry into your past, but if there is anything I can do to help set you free from her, I hope you know all you have to do is ask. And if you know anything that might help our situation, I do hope you will speak up. I promise I won't tell a soul I heard it from you." Carol-Barbara meant what she said.

Elsa was quiet for a moment, even pensive. Then she spoke up. "I'll make a deal with you, Carol-Barbara. If I ever decide I can safely divulge any information, you'll be the first to know."

Just then the back door flew open and Debbie pitched herself through like she owned the place. Elsa and Carol-Barbara were both surprised.

Elsa quickly got her wits about her. "Hello, Debbie," she replied meekly.

"Hello yourself." Debbie stated, with suspicion in her voice. "And hello to you, too, Carol-Barbara," she added. "Fancy meeting you here."

Carol-Barbara wondered how much Debbie had overheard, and what kind of price Elsa might pay for it.

Elsa's Hoecakes

Ingredients:

Dry:

1 cup all-purpose flour

1 cup yellow cornmeal

3 ½ teaspoons baking powder

1 tablespoon sugar

½ teaspoon salt

Wet:

2 eggs

1/3 cup water

¾ cup buttermilk

¼ cup vegetable oil

Plus more vegetable oil for frying

Mix dry ingredients together in one bowl. Mix wet ingredients in another. Then mix the two together.

In a heavy skillet heat a couple spoonsful of oil. When hot, pour about ¼ cup of the batter onto the skillet and fry one side, then flip cake to other side and fry until cooked through. Add more oil as necessary while cooking additional cakes. Enjoy with honey or syrup of your choice.

Part 24

Angels and Devils

Under normal circumstances, Carol-Barbara would not have dreamed of interrupting Carl at work, but this was not a normal circumstance. She found herself navigating her Camry to the All-Mart on her way back from Elsa's. She just had to talk to her husband about what had occurred earlier that morning.

At first, the two ladies thought their conversation had been uncovered, but then Debbie acted as if she hadn't heard a thing, claiming she was only surprised to see Carol-Barbara at her sister's house so early on a Saturday morning. After that, things got so weird between Debbie and Elsa, that Carol-Barbara stayed just long enough to make sure Debbie knew she hadn't intimidated her. Then she left the two sisters alone. Now, she hoped Elsa was okay and not facing the wrath of Debbie.

As she sped through town, Carol-Barbara saw the big orange sign for the All-Mart looming up ahead. Carl would still be working, so why not stop and see him on the way home and let him know of this recent development? She had to go right past the All-Mart on her way home, and she did need to pick up some asparagus to go with the rosemary chicken she planned to make tonight. Elsa had given her the Rosemary on her way out.

...

The morning rush at All-Mart was finally over. Carl had spent the past few hours validating returns and giving out stickers, as well as utilizing a giant helium tank to blow up balloons for the many kids that joined their parents for Saturday shopping. He'd spent a considerable amount of time blowing up second, and even third, balloons for kids who'd let go of theirs, and watched them float high up into the rafters inside the building. Those balloons joined many others in various stages of deflation, and even some that had become permanently lodged in the ceilings; their ribbons dangling from the ceiling long after all helium had escaped from them. When the kids would come crying, Carl would blow up another balloon, consoling the child as he did so.

Carl also had to reprimand a group of teenagers for inhaling helium from the tank while he was assisting another customer with a return. Kids these days- they would try anything to get high. As he scolded them, the boy who had sucked the helium from the tank replied in a squeaky voice, "Screw you, old man!" His friends laughed like hyenas. They left the store in a pack, and Carl would have gone after them, but who knew what those hoodlums would have done to him? He could only hope that somehow, someday, someone younger, and healthier, would teach them a lesson.

He sat down and wished he were just home with Carol-Barbara right now.

Just then, he saw Carol-Barbara push past the pack of teenage boys and through the double doors into the store. She saw Carl sitting on the bench, looking forlorn. He turned his head towards her, and his face lit up just as it had the first time they met.

"Well, think of an angel and she shall arrive." Carl stood and walked towards her, kissing her on the cheek. His heart still skipped a beat at the sight of his bride.

"Were you thinking of me?" She questioned.

"I was. What are you doing here? Come to take advantage of the Saturday rump roast special?" Carl knew Carol-Barbara could not pass up a good price on a rump roast.

"You could say that," she playfully smacked him on his rear.

"Hey, that's bound to be grounds for harassment," he joked.

"Actually, I'm here because of a more serious matter," she informed him.

"What's wrong? Is it one of the kids?" Carl was concerned that something serious had happened.

"No, no. Just more news involving Debbie and Dixon." She paused. "I just came from Elsa's, and Debbie showed up."

"I thought you were going to call Elsa? You mean to tell me you actually went over there?" Carl was surprised.

"I did, and let me tell you, Debbie is holding something over Elsa's head, threatening her with some sort of blackmail. I just know it. You should have seen the fear on Elsa's face when Debbie walked in and Elsa thought she had overheard us talking," she explained.

"Did she know why you were there?" Carl was concerned now.

"No, it doesn't appear she did. But if she had I can tell you Elsa would be paying for it dearly." She paused. "I don't want to involve Elsa anymore. This fiasco is not her fault. She just happens to have the bad luck of being Debbie and Dixon's family. You know what they say. You can't choose who you are related to."

"Speak of the devil," Carl nodded towards the double doors as they opened automatically. In walked Dixon.. He looked out of place, dressed in his designer duds, and sauntering into All-Mart.

"He must be slumming it," Carol- Barbara whispered. Normally, she assumed, Dixon would shop at one of the full-price stores in the area, or better yet, leave the shopping up to the housekeeper they employed.

"Hello there, fellow Dogwoodians!" Dixon, always the politician, sang. It was hard to believe this was the same man who had plans to raze their neighborhood. Never one to be sheepish, Dixon looked them straight in the eye as he walked past.

Carl and Carol-Barbara, taken aback by his over-confidence, simply stared at him, unsure of what to say. If Dixon noticed their stunned silence, he didn't react to it, but instead continued to make his way past them, greeting everyone he encountered in the same rehearsed manner. He made his way down the aisles to the jewelry counter, where he stopped.

"That cocky son-of-a-bitch," Carol-Barbara whispered.

144

They saw him amble up to the counter, where an attractive brunette, at least 30 years Dixon's junior, arranged gold-plated necklaces on a stand. The young woman seemed to know him, and also seemed happy to see him; perhaps too happy. Carl and Carol-Barbara could see them clearly, but they were too far away to make out what they were saying to one another.

As they watched, Carol-Barbara spoke up. "Surely he doesn't buy Debbie jewelry at All-Mart," she stated matter-of-factly. "Seems like he could do better than that. And he seems overly familiar with the jewelry counter girl. Do you think that woman is one of his conquests?"

"I don't know, but let's not jump to conclusions," Carl paused. "He could just be comparison shopping."

Carol-Barbara looked at Carl as if he had just suggested the Earth was square, or that E didn't equal MC squared. Before Carl could respond to her, a man about Dixon's age came racing through the double doors and into the All-Mart. He headed straight for the jewelry counter. In one smooth motion, he grabbed Dixon by the back of the collar and swung him around.

"I thought I told you to stay away from her!" Carl and Carol-Barbara heard the man yell. "My wife doesn't want anything from you!"

Dixon said something back to the man, which they couldn't hear, but they could see that the girl had begun crying. She slipped from behind the counter and ran out of the store, right past Carl and Carol-Barbara.

"Now do you see what you've done?" The other man shouted and ran after the girl. He glanced back at Dixon with one final warning before running after the jewelry counter girl. "I swear, Dixon, don't make me do something I'm going to regret! Stay away from her!"

Carl and Carol-Barbara looked at one another. "Looks like the devil finally messed with the wrong man's wife," Carl stated.

"Yes," Carol-Barbara agreed. "Yes, indeed."

Part 25

Suffragette

Very early Sunday morning found Carol-Barbara already seated at her kitchen table, frustrated about her lack of quality sleep. Rather than remaining in a state of exhausted stupor, she went about making the first pot of coffee, carefully measuring out the amount of ground beans and water so that the life-giving liquid would taste exactly the way she wanted--not too weak, not too strong.

She knew that if Carl had been the first one up, which happened only on rare occasion, she could count on her coffee being so strong that even after she added her powdered creamer, the concoction would still look brown as mud. Carl's ratio of coffee to water was way off in her opinion. The end result was bitter, and made her shaky. Her method left her pleasantly awake, without the jitters of a caffeine overdose.

As she waited for the coffee to brew she peeked outside. The sun was just rising over the mountains. Though she was naturally an early riser, this time of day was early even for her. With the unusual stress going on in her life, she found it harder and harder to go to bed at night, and she had been spending far too much time lying in bed wide-awake, and worrying. She especially worried about what was going to happen to their close-knit community if Dixon's giant mall moved in. Damn that man. He was ruining what should have been a golden time in her life, free from stress.

147

Carl had always been a sleeper, and the impending doom seemed to have zero effect on his ability to get eight hours, or more, of shut eye. It angered her on some level, thinking of Carl peacefully snoring in their bedroom, while she sat up wondering how to fix things. Maybe Martha and Honey were right, someone needed to just shoot Dixon and put them all out of misery. Problem was, she'd never been the violent type. Besides, there had to be a better way to take the wind out of Dixon's sails.

As she fretted over the current situation, she realized it was so early that she had not yet heard the familiar clunk of the newspaper hitting the driveway, or the engine of the car that delivered it roaring away. Gone were the days when a dimple-cheeked boy delivered the newspaper on his bicycle. Apparently, someone had decided that being a newspaper delivery boy was too dangerous. One amendment or another meant to protect children from some perceived danger had taken away yet another thing that could teach them the satisfaction of a job well done, and the value of money. This recent change made it impossible for children to experience the joy of personal responsibility by running their own newspaper delivery service. Carol-Barbara sighed at the thought of the loss.

One thing was sure, when one of those boys delivered the paper so many years ago, he certainly had delivered it earlier than this. She had never waited even a moment for its arrival. There it had been every morning, reliable as the milk delivery— and there was another thing that had gone the way of the dinosaurs.

Since there was no newspaper for her to read yet, Carol-Barbara flipped on the small television she kept in the kitchen. The local news would not be on for another fifteen minutes, so she watched the tail-end of a beauty product infomercial. The sole goal of the "Booty Pop" as it was called was to make a woman's hind parts appear larger and more rounded under her clothing. It promised to make the wearer have a rear end that "attracted attention."

Funny how times had changed, she considered. As a younger woman she had done everything in her power to make her curvy parts not stick out, including wearing girdles that were so tight she could hardly breathe. Now the thing to do was to make your rear end look like something akin to a baboon butt. The infomercial ended with an offer to buy one "Booty Pop" and get a second one free. "Just pay separate shipping and handling," the announcer boasted. Why anyone would need two, Carol-Barbara could not understand. After all, a girl only had a single rear-end to "pop" at any given time.

By the end of the infomercial, Carol-Barbara was halfway through her second cup of coffee and feeling more like she could take on the day. She heard the familiar sound of the newspaper delivery car coming up the road, then the distinct clunk of the newspaper hitting the driveway. Carol-Barbara hadn't gotten dressed for the day yet, but she knew the possibility of someone seeing her in her nightdress at this hour was remote, so she opened the front door and dashed out to the end of the driveway to grab the paper. As she headed outside, she remembered the days she had tried to teach their dog, Bubba, to retrieve the paper. Bubba had showed little interest in learning, though he did enjoy the treat she gave him as an incentive. After a while she had just given up and continued retrieving the paper herself. Besides, lately Bubba was known to sleep in later than Carl some days; poor old dog.

Carol-Barbara grabbed the paper and headed back into the house, the door slamming behind her as she did so. When, she wondered, was Carl going to get around to fixing that spring so it wouldn't slam every time someone entered or exited the house?

She returned to the kitchen, and sat down at the table to begin reading the paper. Rather than switching the television off, she muted the volume with the remote and let the screen continue bathing the kitchen in flickering light. She opened the paper to the local news just as the weather report for the week caught her eye on the television screen. Alternately, she looked from the television to the newspaper, comparing reports. On the television report, it showed rain starting Monday and continuing for the next three days. She compared it to the local newspaper weather report, which called for partly sunny skies over the same period. Who was she supposed to believe? Why couldn't these weather guys get their acts together?

Next on the television was a story about a local girl who had won an art contest. Fluff story, she considered, not real news, and looked back towards the newspaper. There, she saw a review of last weekend's cotillion ball, announcing the couples who had been chosen king and queen of the dance; more filler, although the pictures of the young couples were nice. Wasn't there any real news in

Dogwood County? Hadn't any of those investigative journalists caught wind of what Dixon was up to?

Then, something caught her eye. It was almost hidden among the announcements of engagements, weddings and meetings of the local chapter of the Dogwood County Chamber of Commerce. The small article urged people to remember to get involved in the local special elections for seats which were coming up, including the seat Dixon held as Dogwood County Manager.

It had honestly slipped her mind that Dixon's job was up for grabs, as two years had gone by since he had been elected to the post. Something caught her eye on the television. As she looked up, there was Dixon's face, taking up nearly the entire screen on her tiny television set. "Local position up for grabs. Current county manager as yet unopposed."

Unopposed? Carol-Barbara was surprised. Surely, in the whole of Dogwood County there was someone who was qualified to run against Dixon for the position of county manager. If not, what did that say about Dogwood County? What did it take to run for that office, anyway, if Dixon qualified? He had no more political experience before his election than anyone else.

She took another giant gulp of coffee and thought for a moment. Who could she think of that cared about Dogwood County? Who knew what Dogwood County needed? Who would serve Dogwood County in the manner it deserved?

She would, that's who.

The answer came to her just as Carl sauntered into the kitchen, having been awakened by the sound of the front door slamming.

"What's going on?" He questioned, rubbing his eyes and immediately pouring a cup of coffee.

"I'm running for office," Carol-Barbara announced.

"Really?" Carl questioned. "I didn't realize you were interested in being President." He took a sip from the mug that announced he was "World's Greatest Grandpa."

"Not for President, you nincompoop," Carol-Barbara snapped. "For the office of Dogwood County Manager, against Dixon St. James."

"By golly, CB, that's infinitely more serious than the office of the President," Carl teased.

"Stop. It's much too early to joke around, and I haven't had enough sleep to think of a good comeback." She paused, "Besides, I'm as serious as I can be."

"I'm serious, too," Carl submitted.

"You don't seem surprised," she noticed.

"I'm really not. I don't know why we didn't think of this before." He then added, "I think you'd be great, and you've always wanted to give back to this community. You finally have time in your life to do that now. It makes perfect sense to me." He paused. "Besides I know once you've decided to do something, there's no talking you out of it."

Short of shooting him, running for office seemed the best way she knew to outsmart Dixon at his own game. She stood from the table to face Carl.

"That's it then. I'm doing it," she stated matter-of-factly. "And I think I have as good a chance of winning as anyone else."

Carl held up his coffee mug as if to make a toast. "Well then, to the new nominee for Dogwood County Manager," He took a sip of his coffee." Why not?"

Carol-Barbara met his mug with her half-filled one. "Why not, indeed."

Part 26

Hit Me with Your Best Shot

It was Friday afternoon, and Carol-Barbara was preparing for her meeting of The NAKED Ladies by making two recipes she had torn out of Simple Southerner magazine in her dentist's office. She had been waiting for an excuse to make the Chili Cheese Cornbread Casserole, and a chilly rainy day like today was all the excuse she needed.

At the kitchen counter, she carefully layered the meat and beans, sauce, cheese and cornbread batter into her largest stoneware casserole dish and slipped it into the top part of her double oven. It would be hot, bubbly and scrumptious just in time for the meeting. Into the bottom oven she slipped a tray of seasonal vegetables including acorn squash, sweet potatoes and parsnips tossed with olive oil and rosemary. She set the timer so they would roast to a golden color, and then turned her attention to decorating for the occasion.

She had planned a special red, white and blue affair in honor of her decision to run for county manager. Though it was nowhere near Independence Day, Memorial Day, or even Flag Day, she felt the color scheme would be appropriate for the situation. She draped her living room in festive red, white and blue crepe paper. On the dining room table she placed a patriotic striped table runner that she had left over from a July 4th celebration at church. She also blew up balloons, some of each color, and taped them to the backs of the chairs. The night before, she had also taken the time to make an old standby for dessert- a Jell-O salad in which she had used strawberries, blueberries and cream cheese, in keeping with the color palette she had chosen for the evening. It was now chilling in the spare refrigerator in the garage. She would place it as the centerpiece. No matter what time of year, the colors red, white and blue screamed democracy and independence! And in this case, it would mean independence from the clutches of Dixon St. James and his dastardly plans for Dogwood County.

Carol-Barbara planned to tell the NAKED ladies all about her political aspirations at the beginning of the meeting, so the rest of their time could be spent gathering ideas from each of them as to how she should proceed with her campaign. She had already slipped quietly into the county government office earlier in the day and filled out the paperwork necessary to start her process as a candidate.

While she was there, she had recognized the administrative assistant at the county office as an acquaintance from her breast cancer treatment days; a woman who had gone through chemo at the same time and with the same doctor. Her name was Sherri Armstrong.

Sherri told Carol-Barbara that even though she technically worked for Dixon, she so disliked the man that she promised she would keep the details of Carol-Barbara's candidacy a confidential affair until the official announcement came out at the next county planning meeting, which would be held on Monday. Sherri told Carol-Barbara that no one else had expressed any interest in running for the job, and as far as she knew, Dixon, in all his arrogance, assumed he would be un-challenged.

Carol-Barbara planned to be at that meeting, and to hold her head high and lock eyes with Dixon as he was shocked by the news that she would be his rival. Carol-Barbara thanked Sherri for her confidentiality, and had even invited her to come by the house this evening to gather with the other ladies, and Sherri had promised to try and stop by. Carol-Barbara left the county office happy that she had, hopefully, recruited another NAKED lady, and exhilarated by the fact that she would officially be giving Dixon a run for his money.

Aside from Carol-Barbara's election years ago as PTA president, this would be her first foray into the world of politics, so she wanted a capable person as her campaign manager. She could think of only one person for the job, and that was Martha. She was a good person to involve in matters such as these, as she tended to know more than the average person about all things political since she had worked in that capacity in Washington, DC for much of her life. Carol-Barbara trusted her opinion. She had already taken the liberty of calling to let Martha know about her plans, and asked her on the phone to represent her.

At first, Martha had balked at the idea, advising Carol-Barbara she had no idea what she would be getting herself into, or the level of mud Dixon was capable of slinging at an opponent. Carol-Barbara assured her she could handle anything Dixon threw at her. Let him hit her with his best shot, she told Martha. She also reminded Martha that he would be hard-pressed to find any mud to sling, since Carol-

Barbara had led an honest and ethical life. Though far from a saint, she'd never done anything that could be remotely construed as controversial.

Unless someone wanted to make a big deal about her ripping recipes from her dentist's magazine, there would be no one from her past coming out of the woodwork to reveal anything negative about her. She had never smoked pot in college, or had an illicit affair, or swindled funds from her employer. That was one good thing about having lived a fairly simple life in a small town—there would be no dirt to dig up. After the initial worry, Martha had finally agreed to play the part of campaign manager, and Carol-Barbara could see through Martha's rough exterior that she was actually honored and excited to be asked.

By six o'clock most of the ladies had arrived at the house. Even Sherri Armstrong had showed up. She knew Carol-Barbara had not revealed her plans to the rest of the ladies yet, so upon her arrival she secretly mentioned to Carol-Barbara that she had been scared to death all day that Dixon would come into the office and go through her files or want updated information about the county meeting on Monday. Luckily, he had stayed away, choosing instead to leave the office early to pack for his weekend Rock-fishing excursion to the coast. He was so sure of his re-election that he hadn't even asked if anyone else had decided to join the race. The overconfidence of the man infuriated Carol-Barbara, but it would also work to her advantage, as her announcement on Monday would have the element of surprise.

By 6:15, the only person who hadn't graced the rest of the ladies with her appearance yet was Honey, and that was nothing new. Honey was usually late, so Carol-Barbara called the meeting to order and began reciting the NAKED ladies pledge.

She began, "I am a woman, smart and strong." The ladies repeated after her. She continued, "To the union of womanhood, I belong," They repeated after her again. "Though I may know some times of strife-"

And this is where things got crazy, as she was interrupted halfway through the pledge by Honey, drunk as a skunk, stumbling through the front door.

"I've shot him!" she yelled. All eyes were on Honey as she fell to the floor in a heap.

Carol-Barbara's mind started racing. All she could think was that Honey must have made good on her idea that she shoot Dixon to get rid of him. Thoughts reeled in her head. On the one hand, if he was dead, this would basically make her a shoo-in for election. On the other hand, she absolutely did not want to be associated with something as controversial as the shooting of her political rival on the very day she put her name in the hat.

If Honey had shot him, there would be no end to the speculation that Carol-Barbara had something to do with it. No longer would her reputation be unsullied. Something like that would be horrible for her campaign. Then there was also the fact that she never really wanted the man to be dead anyway. She would never wish that on anyone.

Carol-Barbara shook herself from her thoughts and lunged towards Honey, grabbing her arm and trying to pull her up from the ground where she lay sobbing and wailing.

"Who? Who did you shoot?" Carol-Barbara pleaded with her.

Honey sat up. "I was cleaning my gun, and I accidentally shot him! I shot Roland!"

Carol-Barbara pulled away from Honey. "Carl! Come quick!"

Within moments Carl had gone next door to assess the damage. He was initially irritated that he was missing the conclusion of Matlock, but soon realized this was a serious matter. As luck would have it, Roland was snoring peacefully in his recliner, having no knowledge that he had nearly been Honey's target. The television set, however, was blown to smithereens. Carl could tell that the bullet had ricocheted off the arm of his recliner while he slept. Roland hadn't heard a thing because Honey had placed a silencer on the gun. Why Honey had a silencer for a gun, Carl could not even imagine. Carl roused Roland from sleep to let him know what had happened.

"Honey almost shot you," he told him matter-of-factly.

Carl's response? "Not again."

Part 27

Second Chances

Honey had not shot Roland after all. The bullet had come close, but as Carl pointed out, close only counted in horseshoes and hand grenades. This fact did not make anyone feel better about the events of the evening. The NAKED ladies could not wrap their heads around what had just happened.

At some point during the evening, Martha had made a comment about Honey being from New Jersey, and didn't that "say it all," to which Diane replied by reminding Martha that her own truck had a gun rack in the back window.

"That's for hunting, and an entirely different situation, my dear. The only reason a person has a handgun with a silencer is for murdering someone," Martha countered.

Though they probably should have called the police about the shooting, no one did. For that, Honey had been supremely grateful, since she was already on parole, and, as she pointed out to the group, even handling a gun right now could get her thrown in jail. Since no one asked, and Honey didn't offer, it was still a mystery as to why she was on the bad side of the law.

Later that evening, Honey was escorted back to her house by Carl, and saw for herself what she had done. By that point Roland was up from his nap, and angry that he couldn't watch television in the den. Other than that, things seemed normal between

Honey and Roland, so Carl had left the house feeling secure there would be no more violence in the neighborhood that night.

Carol-Barbara was another person who was glad the police were not notified, as being even indirectly involved in an accidental firearm incident could have ruined her chances for election. The unanticipated events of the evening had caused her a delay in sharing her campaign news with the rest of the ladies. When she finally did, she was disappointed that, though they were proud of her, their reaction was largely subdued. Her announcement had clearly taken a backseat to Honey's antics.

Saturday morning after the "TV assassination," as he would find himself referring to it, Carl drove out of the garage to work his shift at All-Mart. The remains of the victim lay by the curb, waiting to be picked up by the trash truck. Its screen was blown up and its insides were hanging out like a dead robot. As he drove away, Carl wondered if the garbage man would notice that the television had been the victim of a shooting. Probably wouldn't be the first time, he laughed to himself.

Martha spent Saturday morning at Carol-Barbara's going over her strategy for the election. She was especially worried because Sherri had told her that early on in the race there would be a debate, which would be broadcast on the local public television station. Martha wanted Carol-Barbara ready for any question the panel of judges might throw at her, or any accusation Dixon may sling. They sat in the living room, with red, white and blue crepe paper from the night before still hanging from the ceiling, and partially deflated balloons rolling around on the floor. Carol-Barbara had been too tired to clean up from the mess after Honey's stunt. Martha sat in one of the wingback chairs in the living room, and Carol-Barbara sat in the matching one across from her.

"Carol-Barbara Hoofnagle, what makes you qualified to be Dogwood County Manager?" Martha asked, in her best impression of Barbara Walters.

"Well, I was born here. Well, I was raised here, too---""

"Weren't we all," Martha cut her off. "Give them something important, something Dixon doesn't have."

Carol-Barbara thought about it. What did she have that Dixon didn't have? Honesty and integrity to name two.

"Well," Carol-Barbara tried to continue.

"And stop saying 'well.' It makes you sound insecure." Martha was never one to beat around the bush.

Maybe, Carol-Barbara's inner voice considered, asking Martha to be her campaign manager hadn't been the best choice. In fact, perhaps she had jumped the gun deciding to nominate herself for office at all. She had been pretty hopped up on coffee the morning she made the decision to run. Could it have been the caffeine talking? Her outer voice said as much, prompting Martha to put in her two cents.

"You're not acting like half the woman you are today, CB. Are you going to let one pushy little A-hole make you doubt yourself?" Martha didn't mince words.

"Are you referring to you or Dixon?" Carol-Barbara teased.

Martha ignored her comment, took a deep breath, and let out a sigh. She asked her original question again. "Carol-Barbara Hoofnagle, what makes you qualified to be Dogwood County Manager?"

Carol-Barbara straightened herself, took a deep breath and thought about the matter-of-fact way she used to run the PTA when she was President all those years ago. She could be straight-forward and confident when she needed to be. She dug deep to find that confidence again, and began answering Martha's question.

"As a lifelong resident of Dogwood County I have been involved in many aspects of our residents' lives; from heading up the school PTA to serving on church councils, to sitting on the board of the YMCA. I know people all over the county. I know what residents out in the rural areas need, like better roads and access to faster internet. Just because someone lives on a farm these days doesn't mean they don't want to be able to order something off Amazon or email their kids once in a while.

I also know what the people living in town want, such as buses so that people living in the East end of town can get to the West end to work in the businesses there. And better sidewalks so they can walk to work if they want the exercise. I also know

*what they don't want or need. They don't need to
lose their homes or businesses so that some mall
can move in with overpriced stores hardly anyone
in the county can afford. Building this mall will
make someone rich for sure, but not the residents of
Dogwood County. Maybe some executive living in
some other part of the country, and certainly my
opponent, Dixon St. James, who I have on good
authority will be making a tidy sum off the deal.*

*And in a few years, when it's too late, when
neighborhoods have been destroyed and families
displaced to make way for this so-called super mall,
and everyone realizes it was a mistake in the first
place, the stores will sit there, like giant empty
boxes. A big eyesore is what they will be. Vagrants
will make their homes in vacant storefronts.
Druggies will lure people there to make deals.
Gangs of skateboarders will turn the vast, empty
parking lots into their playgrounds, and weeds will
propagate where flowers once grew!"*

She was out of breath from her tirade, and
Martha was staring at her.

"That was certainly better. You kind of lost me
with the skateboarders and the weeds, but you
definitely got your point across." Martha applauded
her. "You keep practicing and I'm going to the
kitchen to get some more coffee."

While Martha was in the kitchen, Carol-Barbara
perused the catalog Martha brought with her. It
contained pictures of products that could be
personalized; bumper stickers, hats, and yard signs
could all be emblazoned with Carol-Barbara's name
and passed out during the next few weeks before the

election. The problem was, all these items cost money; money that Carol-Barbara didn't have. It was yet another thing she should have considered before signing up for this endeavor.

Dixon and his campaign manager wife had plenty of money. They would be able to fill the county with Dixon's name and face. People might vote for him simply because he would be all they could see. Carol-Barbara worried they might not even know she existed. She understood now why politicians went to such lengths to obtain money through fundraising. Only a wealthy person, like Dixon, would be able to advertise himself otherwise. And what kind of world would it be if only the extremely wealthy had a chance to make a difference? As she pondered this thought, the doorbell rang, and when she opened it, there stood Honey.

"Oh. Hi." Carol-Barbara wasn't sure how friendly she should be to Honey after what happened the night before.

Honey held her pink cat in her arms. The beast looked as though it had recently been dyed, as the color was even brighter than the last time she had seen the feline. Honey wore a pink sweatshirt that nearly matched the color of the cat's fur.

"How can I help you?" Carol-Barbara managed to ask.

"I just came to apologize about last night. I'm really sorry if I ruined your evening. I understand if you don't want me in the group anymore, and I want to thank you for not calling the police." Honey seemed genuinely apologetic.

Carol-Barbara didn't know how to reply. It was too much, too soon. Of course, she accepted Honey's apology, and she guessed she would give her another chance. That was her way, and wasn't the group all about supporting each other?

But Carol-Barbara did have questions. Why did Honey have a revolver if she was on parole? Didn't that disqualify her from owning one? How could she be so careless as to clean it while it was loaded? And the biggest question of all, why was she on parole in the first place?

Carol-Barbara wasn't able to ask Honey any of these questions because Martha had returned from the kitchen, and was approaching them.

"Well, well if it isn't New Jersey's version of Annie Oakley!" Martha chided.

Carol-Barbara piped in, worried things might escalate between the two of them. "Honey has come to apologize for last night," she informed Martha.

"Have you frisked her? She's not armed, is she?" Martha joked.

"No. no. I don't normally carry loaded guns around." Honey was surprisingly understanding of Martha's sarcasm. She continued. "Well, I just wanted to apologize. I've done that now, so I'll just be taking Poopsie home now." She kissed her cat on the top of its pink head, and turned to leave.

Carol-Barbara felt bad. She didn't know what to say, and it turned out she didn't have to. Martha did it for her.

"Hey, I was only kidding. Nothing wrong with owning a firearm. Myself, I prefer shotguns. Though I can't say I've ever shot a television set with one. There's just no chase in it, you know? I like the chase." Martha joked. "Hey, why don't you come in and help us with the campaign?"

Oh, Martha, what are you doing? Carol-Barbara thought.

"Campaign?" Honey questioned.

Of course, Carol-Barbara realized, Honey had gone home before she made her big announcement the night before.

"I'm running for the position of County Manager, against Dixon St. James," Carol-Barbara told Honey.

"Really? That's so brave of you! Oh, I hope you win and put that SOB in his place!" Honey was truly excited, and her lack of filter when it came to word-choice rivaled that of Martha.

"That's right, Honey. She will be putting that SOB in his place, and she could sure use some tips on what to wear. You know all about that stuff, right?" Martha asked.

Honey was flattered, but unsure about whether Martha was teasing or not. "Are you seriously asking me to help?"

Carol-Barbara, too, was flabbergasted. Though she had to admit Honey's enthusiasm almost made up for her friends' lack of it the night before. And so, in a flash of pink, Honey Van Honk became Carol-Barbara Hoofnagle's official campaign stylist.

Part 28

Now is the Time for All Good Women

The day of Carol-Barbara's big political announcement had arrived. She dressed herself in the outfit that Honey picked out for her. She had to admit she looked pretty good. With Honey in charge, her first thought had been that she might end up looking like a two-bit hooker, or at best a mid-rate one.

Instead, she looked perfectly appropriate. The outfit was surprisingly conservative, considering that Honey usually draped her own body in skimpy outfits and sky-high heels. Carol-Barbara really had to give it to Honey. She knew how to style a girl to fit her personality.

She admired herself again in her bedroom mirror. She and Honey had gone into town that morning for a visit to Maxine's dress shop. They had tried on dress after dress, as well as pant suits, and even a multi-colored muumuu that Honey insisted Carol-Barbara try on just for laughs. In the end they had gone with a smart-looking navy blue skirt, an elegant cream-colored silk top and a matching form-fitting jacket on top. It had been more expensive than Carol-Barbara thought necessary, but she justified the purchase by convincing herself she could wear it to church, and, of course it would come in handy should she actually be elected to the position of County Manager.

She carefully applied a little makeup, and adorned herself with the pearl earrings and matching necklace her mother bequeathed to her. Nude heels graced her feet because, as Honey explained, nude-colored shoes visually elongated the legs. Though Carol-Barbara wasn't sure why her legs needed to look longer, since that had little, if anything, to do with effectively managing a county, she gave in and bought the shoes. Then, while in the dressing room trying the whole ensemble on, Honey had noticed the state of Carol-Barbara's undergarments and, in true Honey fashion, made her views known.

"You have a decent figure, CB." Honey had taken to calling her that almost all the time now. "Must be all that water aerobics you do. So why do you do it a disservice by slapping on those two-dollar granny-panties and sad-sack bras. It's like chucking an All-Mart throw pillow on a Hepplewhite Settee."

"A Hepple what?" Carol-Barbara questioned

"A Hepple*white*. You know, the famous 18th century English furniture designer? Well, originally he was a cabinet-maker, but he was extremely talented and had a lot of ideas on furniture design, so he ended up apprenticing for a furniture manufacturer in Lancaster. Then he eventually opened his own shop in London. He's credited with introducing the style of furniture we now refer to simply as Hepplewhite, but the truth is Hepplewhite's work is so rare and unique there isn't a single piece thought to have been made by his hand in existence anymore. We mainly know about his work through a posthumous book published about his furniture design entitled The Cabinet-Maker and Upholsterer's Guide. It's a classic." Honey seemed pleased with herself.

Carol-Barbara was dumb-founded, and stared in Honey's general direction. She'd never heard Honey sound this way. She knew exactly what she was talking about, and never slipped on a single syllable. Her heavy New Jersey accent even seemed to dissipate with every word she spoke, and took on a more neutral tone. The only word that she could use to describe what she'd just heard out of Honey's mouth was "smart," and that was previously not a word she might have chosen to describe Honey.

"How is it you know all this?" Carol-Barbara finally asked when she could speak again.

Honey explained. "In college I majored in interior design in school, with an emphasis on 18th century furniture,"

Carol-Barbara was floored, and the look on her face must have showed it. Honey called her on it, and the Jersey accent was back in full force.

"What? You think just because I look the way I do, talk the way I do, act the way I do, that I can't have a brain?" Honey seemed upset.

Carol-Barbara wasn't sure what to say to fix this. Clearly she had insulted Honey.

"I'm sorry it's just that you surprise me every time I'm with you, Honey," Carol-Barbara told her. "I had no idea."

Honey softened a bit. "No, it's okay. You didn't know." She hesitated before continuing. "I had a full scholarship to NYU," she offered, looking regretful. "Then I screwed it all up."

"How?" Carol-Barbara was intrigued.

"No, really. I've said too much already," Honey shook her head.

"Are you sure you don't want to talk about it?" Carol-Barbara prodded.

"Let's just say I got involved with the wrong people," she wavered, unsure of whether to go on. "You ever hear of Sal "The Sandman" Pierogi?"

Carol-Barbara shook her head.

"Let's just say if he puts you to sleep you don't wake up." Honey looked serious.

"Sal The Sandman Pierogi?" Carol-Barbara repeated. "Sounds like something out of an old mob movie," she joked.

"Uh, yeah. It sure does." Honey quickly changed the subject. "So, back to my original point. You are as rare and unique as a Hepplewhite, and you deserve to be dressed that way. Besides, Carl would like it if you bought some sassy new lingerie, wouldn't he?"

Carol-Barbara didn't push for any more information, and suddenly she felt a little down when Honey mentioned Carl. Like most men, Carl had been a "boob-man," and when she had opted for a double mastectomy she felt guilty for taking that part away from him. Naturally, Carl had told her

172

she was silly for thinking such a thing, and had showered her with love ever since.

"You know I had breast cancer, right? Things aren't really great up top anymore, even with the reconstruction I went through," she admitted to Honey.

"Sweetie, you think these things look this great before I get my foundation on? Even with a boob job, we all need some help. Believe me, you won't be disappointed."

Carol-Barbara blushed. "I guess I have always wondered what Victoria's secret really is, and why she looks so smug about it. Okay, I'll do it." Carol-Barbara caved. "Where do I start?"

Now, at home and standing in front of her bedroom mirror, Carol-Barbara had her own little secret underneath her pristine navy blue suit, and she had to admit it did make her feel powerful.

The meeting would be starting at 7:00pm. Carol-Barbara had eaten before she got dressed so she wouldn't spill anything on her ensemble. She hadn't eaten much, though, as her nerves were on edge, and she had just over an hour before she had to be there. Martha had quizzed her again over the phone so she would be prepared for any questions Dixon or the other members of the board might throw at her. Honey had given her tips on how she should walk to exude an air of confidence; chin just a little higher than normal, shoulders back, a distinctive spring in her step.

She had practiced these moves earlier in the living room in front of Carl and it hadn't gone well.

He'd told her she looked unnatural, uptight, and that her gait looked a little like Neil Armstrong when he first walked on the moon, bouncing in the anti-gravity of space. Carl also suggested that the look on her face was one of severe constipation. He meant to be helpful, but this whole process just wasn't his thing, so she took another look in the mirror. The confidence she had felt when she first got dressed and saw herself in the mirror dropped. She went back to square one.

She'd seen what he meant about the look and had rectified that first. With practice she now looked more like she was just mildly gassy. It was an improvement overall. Next she worked on her walk, backing up across the room and going towards the mirror. A little less bounce, a little more stride. Finally, she brought her chin down just a hair so she wouldn't appear to be looking down her nose at the good people of Dogwood County.

When she had practiced for another twenty minutes, she came out and showed Carl again.

"Much improved," he'd stated.

Then, feeling flirty, she opened up the top couple of buttons on her shirt and flashed her new purple bra at him. And what about this, Carl? Is this much improved, too?" What had gotten into her?

He diverted his eyes more than briefly from the evening news. "Well, yes. That is quite nice. Where did you get that?"

"Honey helped me pick it out. She said it would make me feel powerful. From the look on your face just now I would say she's right," she joked.

"I might have known she had something to do with that." Carl stated. "Well, I'll give it to Honey this time, she did a nice job of styling you, so maybe she is good for something."

"Oh she's good for something alright. Did you know that she apparently has great taste in interior design and is a wealth of information on antique furniture?"

"I could have told you that. You should see the inside of their house. It's like a museum."

Carol-Barbara was about to ask Carl when he had seen the inside of the Van Honk house when she remembered he had walked Honey home the night of the shooting.

"Well, did you also know that I think Honey might have gotten in trouble with the mob when she was younger?"

"Now why doesn't that surprise me." He told her.

"You know what should surprise you?"

"What?" He asked.

"It's almost time to go and you're not even dressed." She told him.

"Don't try to use your newly acquired style tactics on me, CB. I'll be ready." She had lost his attention and he turned back to the television.

Carol-Barbara never understood why men had it so easy with everything. Just throw on a shirt and pants and they're done. Had that apple Eve bit into caused all this?

Part 29

Hear Ye, Hear Ye

Carol-Barbara's big moment had arrived. The night of the Dogwood County planning meeting was upon her. Soon everyone would know she would be running for the position of Dogwood County Manager.

Ten minutes before she and Carl were to leave for the meeting, Carl had finally changed his clothes. He now wore a smart-looking navy blue jacket, light blue button down shirt and paisley tie, along with khaki pants. The whole ensemble complimented Carol-Barbara's navy skirt suit perfectly, and she pointed this fact out when he sauntered into the kitchen, walking stiffly and looking a little like an uncomfortable teenager dressed for the prom.

Carl had never enjoyed dressing up, but he obliged her by taking an extra measure of care with the night's attire. He'd intended to all along, but just liked to see her stew a bit. They'd been married so long that he knew he could push her buttons, and she would respond accordingly. They took part in the game all couples who have been together for any long period of time tend to play; and they both played their positions well. Carol-Barbara knew in her heart that Carl generally ended up doing the right thing, but she still gave him the satisfaction of letting him think he had an edge. She knew that he never would have arrived at the meeting looking anything less than debonair, even though he hated it.

Carl did, however, have to draw the line when Carol-Barbara suggested they take her car for the night, and he had his reasons. Carol-Barbara tried to convince him that they would be more comfortable in her car, not to mention the fact that she was never sure about the fuel status in Carl's automobile. His gas gauge had long since been broken, so that the arrow was always stuck at the halfway point. How he kept track of what was really in the gas tank she didn't know, and tonight she really didn't feel like taking chances. She didn't need this evening to end up with them hitching a ride to the meeting with her in her new suit and pumps! However, Carl was insistent they take his car. He assured her that he had gassed up the car earlier that day. Since she had won the battle with his clothing, she decided to let him have this one.

"Fine, we'll take your car," she conceded. "Let's just go. I'm a nervous wreck. If I stay here and wait any longer I'm going to explode." She grabbed her purse off the kitchen table and took two steps to reach for the doorknob to the garage. Carl jumped in front of her to open the door.

"After you Madame future county manager," he said as she passed through the door.

"Well, well, aren't we full of ourselves tonight?" she teased.

Carl did the same thing when they got to the car. He raced to her side and opened the door for her.

"My, I haven't been treated this royally in a very long time," she noted, and slid into the passenger seat. When she did, she saw why Carl was adamant about driving his car tonight. She immediately began crying happy tears when she saw what he had done. The entire inside of the car was plastered with sticky notes bearing words of encouragement about her big night. There must have been at least 50 of them stuck to every part of the inside of the car.

"Carl, when did you do all this?" Carol-Barbara looked around, reading the motivational phrases. *You can do this!* And *Dogwood County is lucky to have you!* One even predicted that she would eventually be the next President of the United States.

"I was working on it while you were primping yourself in the bedroom for all those hours." He confessed.

"And here I thought you had just been lying on the couch watching Matlock in your dirty shirt." She wiped the tears from her face, trying not to muss the makeup Honey had so carefully applied.

"Well, honestly, I did a little of that, too, while I was writing the notes." Carl reached over and hugged his beautiful wife. "Now let's get you to your show."

Carol-Barbara calmed down during the drive, busying herself with reading all the notes Carl had put so much time and love into, but when they pulled into the county government complex and she saw the vast amount of cars parked in the lot she became overwhelmed again. Apparently, this election was more important to people than she'd previously thought.

"Maybe I can't do this. Really, Carl." She looked to him for guidance.

Carl could see she was visibly shaken. "Look around at all your notes. Take a few with you and stick them on your notebook where you can see them while you're giving your speech," he urged her.

Carol-Barbara looked around; trying to decide which ones would give her the most peace during this whole ordeal. And then it became obvious.

"I'll just take this one. It's all I need." She pulled it off the front of the glove box and stuck it to cover of the notebook in her lap. It simply read, "*I love you.*" She looked into the eyes of the man who had loved and supported her for so many years and began to cry again.

"Now, now stop it. You'll muss your make-up, and I know you and Honey worked hard on that." He pulled a tissue from the box next to him and dried her eyes.

"Carl, you're so wonderful to me. How come, after all these years, you're still so good to me?"

"Because you're so easy to be good to, CB, and you do the same for me every day." With that, Carl kissed her on the lips in a way he hadn't done in a very long time. When he pulled away, she felt invigorated, positive, even excited.

"You're right. I can do this." She gave him a peck on the cheek. "Let's go shake things up a bit, shall we?"

"Now look who's full of herself." Carl teased.

Inside the meeting room, Carl and Carol-Barbara sat next to Martha. She'd gotten there early to save the seats she thought would put Carol-Barbara in the best view. Behind Martha sat Honey and her husband, Roland, who looked as though he'd been unwittingly dragged along. They all greeted each other.

Roland leaned forward to talk to Carl. "Want you to know I'm missing the Knicks game for this, Hoofnagle," he only half- joked.

Roland was not into politics, nor did he care too much that Honey had been recruited onto Carol-Barbara's political team. He clearly wanted to go home. Carol-Barbara turned around in her seat to face him.

"Thanks for taking the time out of your evening to come to this, Roland. It means a lot," she said, and meant it.

Roland's face softened. "Hey, nuttin' personal, Carol-Barbara. I'm just a die-hard Knicks fan. Oh, and you're welcome." He leaned back in his seat and stopped talking, clearly embarrassed that Carol-Barbara had heard him complaining.

Carl leaned in close to Carol-Barbara so Roland wouldn't hear. "Hey, already buttering them up. You're pretty good at that, CB."

Dixon sat on the stage with the rest of the county team. He looked so self-righteous that Martha, for one, couldn't stand it. "Look, he has no clue does he?"

The meeting began with the pledge of allegiance, and then a young girl from one of the local schools sang The Star Spangled Banner, after which Honey hollered, "Play ball!"

Then, straightaway the town mayor got down to the business of asking for nominees. In accordance with county rules and regulations, Martha stood up and nominated Carol-Barbara.

"I nominate Mrs. Carol-Barbara Hoofnagle to run for the office of county manager," she stated.

Just like that it was done. As they had planned, Honey stood up right after Martha finished speaking. She wore a leopard print dress and sky-high black heels. With her hand on her hip, and in her thickest Jersey accent, she proudly made her announcement. "And I second the motion." She winked at Carol-Barbara.

They only required two motions, and so it should have stopped there, but it didn't. One after the other of Carol-Barbara's friends stood up. Diane Suffolk gave the motion a third, Susan Perkins a fourth, and so on and so forth, until seven people were scattered through the crowd, standing up for her. She tried hard to keep tears from springing to her eyes. After her friends' dulled reaction when she announced her plan to them at the meeting, she had no idea they had organized this.

Mayor Humphrey, the moderator of the meeting, stood up and told everyone to sit down, but before they did, one last person stood and said "I give it an eighth motion." It was Elsa.

The look on Debbie's face as she turned around from her usual perch in the front row was priceless. Dixon tried to look unaffected, but it wasn't working.

The mayor jokingly threatened to call security, but by then it was done, and it was the most beautiful show of support Carol-Barbara had ever seen.

When the excitement died down, and her friends had taken their seats, the mayor spoke again. "Well Mrs. Hoofnagle, you have quite a following."

Carol-Barbara was speechless for a moment. Then she stood. "I had no idea." She looked around at her dear friends, and her husband who reached up to squeeze her hand.

"Well, are you going to get up here and accept, or not?" The mayor asked her.

Part 30

I is for Ice Cream

As if there had ever been any doubt that she would go through with her run for Dogwood County Manager, Carol-Barbara got up on stage and publicly accepted her nomination in front of her friends and neighbors, the entire Dogwood County Council, and most importantly, Dixon and Debbie.

Dixon got up from his seat and gave Carol-Barbara an obligatory handshake. It was remarkably weak, and if there was one thing Carol-Barbara couldn't stand it was a man with a weak hand-shake. Worse than that, though, the look on his face said everything Carol-Barbara needed to know; he thought her attempt to take his position was nothing more than something annoying, possibly cute, but not something that need worry him.

Debbie was visibly fuming because Elsa stood up in support of Carol-Barbara. When the meeting was over Carol-Barbara saw Debbie cornering Elsa and visibly berating her. Nobody made a mockery of Debbie St. James and got away with it, least of all her sister, Elsa.

Carol-Barbara still didn't know what Debbie was holding over Elsa's head that made her so afraid, but one thing was for sure; Elsa's determination to go against her sister's wishes could mean only one thing, Debbie's stronghold over Elsa might be deteriorating.

After the meeting was over, people trickled out of the building, some of them shaking Carol-

Barbara's hand. Her friends all gave her hugs, and then it was time to go.

Carl said he felt like getting some ice cream. Carol-Barbara knew he shouldn't have ice cream due to his borderline diabetes, not to mention his cholesterol levels, but she decided to go along with it since it was a special occasion. They could have gone to Dairy Queen in town, but instead they headed to the dairy bar that was on the rural road not far from their home. Carl liked The Purple Cow's homemade ice cream. It had been around forever, and in fact had been one of the first places he had taken Carol-Barbara on a date all those years ago.

The ice cream shop was slow tonight, but upon entering, they learned they weren't the only ones from the meeting who had decided to finish the evening off with a little frozen concoction. In the farthest corner sat the only other people in the place. One of them was Dixon, and the other one was not his wife. Across from him was a young lady they did not recognize.

"Another conquest?" Carl considered out loud.

"Shhhh. He'll hear you," Carol-Barbara silenced him.

They placed their orders. Carl got a giant banana split, which was way more than Carol-Barbara thought he should have, but she let it slide. She ordered a single serving of raspberry sherbet. The teenage boy working at the counter served them, and they sat down on the opposite side of the room from Dixon and his companion. Carol-Barbara tried not to look at the pair, but she couldn't help herself.

The girl was in her mid-twenties, and was pretty, maybe even beautiful by some standards, and Dixon was staring at her while she ate her ice cream as if he were watching the most alluring, entertaining vision he'd ever seen. Dixon didn't have any ice cream in front of him. Carol-Barbara reasoned that Dixon probably thought ice cream was too fattening. Judging from how thin and obviously fit he was, sugar had probably never passed the man's lips. In her opinion it was strange for a man to be so into his looks.

Then she had a thought. What if, she considered, Carl was the type of man to worry about what he ate, obsess over his gut size, or waste hours at the gym trying to look twenty years younger than he was. She glanced over at her husband devouring his banana split as if he was afraid that at any moment she was going to change her mind and take it away from him, and felt a whole new appreciation for the man, belly and all.

Dixon had glanced at Carl and Carol-Barbara when they came in, and did not acknowledge their presence in any way; yet he also didn't seem to be bothered by the fact that he had been spotted. He allowed the girl to finish her ice cream, and they chatted, though what they said Carol-Barbara could not hear. It was a full ten minutes before he stood, placed his arm gently around her shoulders, and assisted her in standing. The ice cream shop wasn't very wide, and Carol-Barbara noticed that Dixon made a point of making sure the girl was on the far side of him as he guided her from the restaurant.

When the two got outside Carol-Barbara expected a big to-do of smooching and romantic goodbyes, but instead Dixon walked her to her own car and gave her a hug before making sure she was safely seated in the driver's seat. She even saw him go as far as to pull on her seatbelt once she was buckled in as if to make sure it was working properly. She was surprised to see that Dixon seemed to genuinely care about this young lady.

Carol-Barbara couldn't help but notice that the girl was driving a brand-new bright-green Jeep Wrangler, though. A present from her sugar daddy, probably. The license plate read SKTRUTH and it had Alabama license plates. She saw Dixon drive away in his white Lexus.

"All finished?" Carl asked her, patting his belly.

"Almost." Carol-Barbara replied.

"You probably would have been done by now if you hadn't been staring at them," he chided.

"Was it that obvious?" Carol-Barbara was embarrassed.

"Oh yeah. I think it was." He remarked.

"I can't help it. What do you think he was up to with a girl half his age, and all the way out here where no one can see him? Do you think this is their regular meeting spot?

"Well, why don't we ask?" Carl joked.

The teenage boy from the counter was now wiping down a table across from them.

"Excuse me," Carl said, "That couple that was just in here. Have you ever seen them before?"

Carol-Barbara couldn't believe what Carl was doing.

"Oh sure, he and his daughter come in here every Monday night," the teenager said.

"Oh, I think you are mistaken. The St. James' only have sons." Carol-Barbara piped in. "And they live out of town."

"Well," the teenager continued "I'm just telling you what he tells me every time he orders. She always orders the same thing, and he always says the same thing, 'My daughter will have a scoop of your homemade chocolate peanut butter ice cream with extra peanut butter sauce on top.' That's what he says, alright."

"Are you sure?" Carol-Barbara couldn't believe her ears.

"CB," Carl piped in, "He says he's sure. Now let's get out of here." Then he whispered. "I have got to use the bathroom and I'm not going to do it here."

"Fine, let's go," Carl-Barbara stood up. She decided not to say anything else about the Dixon situation until they got in the car.

As they drove the short distance home, Carol-Barbara couldn't help but pick Carl's brain.

"Do you think that teenager knows what he's talking about?" she asked

"Probably not." Carl stated. "Teenagers rarely do."

"Then why would he say that? He seemed very sure of himself."

"He may have been, because maybe that's just the story ol' Dixon tells people when he's out fooling around with some young thing." Carl suggested.

"The thing is, Carl, they didn't seem like they were fooling around," she pointed out.

"Well, not in front of us, anyway." Carl justified.

When they got home, Carl headed for the bathroom, and Carol-Barbara immediately called Martha. She wanted to run past her what she had seen and heard that night at The Purple Cow. She gave Martha the scoop, and told her about the Alabama license plate.

"So what do you think, Martha?" Carol-Barbara asked. "Know anybody who can get to the bottom of this?"

"Well, I might be able to pull some strings," Martha assured her. "With a personalized license plate it sure makes things a lot easier."

"I guess that's a start." Carol-Barbara conceded.

"Why the interest anyway? I mean aside from basic curiosity about what your opponent is up to?" Martha asked.

"Just a feeling, Martha. I know I probably don't have a right to pry into his business, but—"

Martha stopped her. "Hey, this is Dixon St. James we're talking about. You never know what that SOB is up to. We need to be proactive with him. You know I'm always happy to help. Shouldn't be hard to have a friend of mine do a little background check on the girl. Won't hurt a thing."

"I don't know how you do it, Martha." Carl-Barbara was always amazed by her friend's abilities.

"No, CB, you don't. I mean I could tell you, but,"

Carol-Barbara interrupted Martha this time. "Yeah, yeah, I know. You could tell me, but then you'd have to kill me. I've heard it all before."

"And you still don't believe me, do you?"

"Oh, I'm not saying that, but just in case, don't tell me. Then we can stay best friends, okay?"

"Always," Martha laughed.

Part 31

Truth in Pie

Carol-Barbara stood at the kitchen counter measuring out brown sugar and flour. This would be the last year that she would be hosting Thanksgiving, as next year her son and daughter-in-law would start hosting at their house. However, Carol-Barbara wasn't ready to entirely hand over the reins to them just yet. She planned on easing them into the recipes over a longer stretch of time.

There were certain dishes she had prepared for years that could not be replicated without careful teaching. So, she determined, she would let her daughter-in-law Brooke, prepare the turkey next year, especially since it hardly ever got eaten after everyone filled up on appetizers and sides. It usually ended up being reserved for sandwiches and soup the next week.

Brooke would also use her own china, the set that Carl and Carol-Barbara gave them for their wedding. The important things, though, Carol-Barbara would still prepare; the spoon bread, the corn soufflé, and the brown sugar pie Carl loved so much, which had most certainly played a part in his borderline diabetes over the years.

Carol-Barbara always had to make three pies; two to be served at room temperature for Thanksgiving evening and another for the weekend following, during which Carl would watch TV and snack on brown sugar pie straight out of the refrigerator. He liked it chilly because it made the filling gooey, which he loved. Carol-Barbara would also make appetizers for the feast, including her Virginia peanut soup, and chicken liver pate.

Attending Thanksgiving at Adam and Brooke's house next year would mean they would have to drive almost 100 miles to Roanoke to get there, which was a pain, but in some ways it would mean a load off her back. For years she started about three weeks before Thanksgiving shopping and preparing for the big day. After this year, there would be no worrying about cleaning the house or taking out all her fine silver and polishing it. This, and not having to prepare the house beforehand, was a big relief; or so she had convinced herself.

She had been hosting Thanksgiving since before her own kids were born as her own mother had no interest in doing it. As much as it was a relief to not have to worry about certain things, it also felt like she was being phased out, and that she didn't like at all; all the more reason to spend time slowly passing the torch to Brooke. At least by then her beloved granddaughter would be a little older and easier to manage while her mother did all that was necessary to prepare a feast fit for royalty.

Carol-Barbara also convinced herself that this year there was a valid reason to start giving up some of the responsibility of the holiday. She had started to fantasize that she would actually beat Dixon in the election. That would mean next year at this time she could actually be manager of Dogwood County. It was so exciting to think about, but also daunting, and she couldn't imagine doing that and having to prepare a Thanksgiving meal as well.

The way the election was being held this year was a little off from the usual way things were run. Due to some calendar changes, the election was actually being held the second Tuesday in January rather than November. This meant that during the holiday season she would be busy with her campaign. Martha was in the process of ordering bumper stickers and yard signs which read Hoofnagle for County Manager. They didn't have a lot of money to work with, and would have had even less if an anonymous donor hadn't slipped a money order for $1000 into the Hoofnagle mailbox while they were at church the previous Sunday morning. In the memo line of the money order it read "For your Campaign." She promptly turned it over to Martha since she was her campaign manager, but not before Carl got a look at it. He had nearly fallen over when he saw it.

"Lord, CB! I definitely went into the wrong line of work. I should have been a politician." He joked.

"It's not like it's really for me, Carl. It's for the campaign," she had argued.

"But you are the campaign, CB. Somebody really wants you to win." he countered.

She considered he was right. Someone out there wanted her to win so badly they had given $1000 of their hard-earned money to make sure she had a fighting chance. After that Martha made an announcement in the paper that all campaign donations should be sent to the county office to her attention and would be swiftly deposited into the campaign account. Within a week, checks started coming in the mail for $10 here and $50 there. It wasn't a lot compared to what Dixon could probably raise, but it was more than she ever expected.

While Martha worked tirelessly on the campaign, Carol-Barbara decided she would be selfish one last time and spend this week of Thanksgiving and focusing on the cooking since it could be the last year she had any control over the meal. She would make each recipe with utmost care.

She began by pouring her ingredients for the brown sugar pie filling into a saucepan over low heat. She stirred, and as the mixture came to a boil, the phone rang. It was Martha.

"Well hey there, Martha. I was just thinking about you and the campaign." Carol-Barbara turned the heat down on the stove so her sugar didn't burn.

"Got some news for you, CB. It's about your Jeep girl." She paused.

"Well, don't keep me hanging, Martha. Who is she?"

"The DMV brings up the name Ashleigh Winston," Martha revealed.

"Ashleigh Winston? That doesn't ring a bell. Maybe a married name?" Carol-Barbara questioned.

"Nope, never been married," Martha quickly spouted.

"Well, her last name isn't St. James, so if she's his she's not legitimate. I still think she's just some girl he's messing around with." Carol-Barbara glanced over to the stove. "Oh, no! My sugar is starting to crystallize. I have to go. It just won't be right if it crystallizes."

"Okay, you go un-crystallize your sugar and I'll be in touch if I find out more details." Martha hung up.

Carol-Barbara put the phone back on the receiver. She stirred her sugar mixture and wondered what Dixon could be hiding.

Carl's Favorite Brown Sugar Pie

Ingredients:

2 cups packed brown sugar

1 ½ cups evaporated milk

4 Tablespoons butter

½ teaspoon salt

1 teaspoon vanilla extract

6 tablespoons all-purpose flour

Turn oven on to preheat at 400 degrees.

Combine flour and sugar in a saucepan over low to medium heat

Add milk, butter, salt and vanilla.

Stir continuously until the whole mixture starts to boil.

Turn heat off and pour the mixture into an unbaked pie shell.

Bake for 5 minutes at 400 degrees and then turn the oven down to 350 and bake 25 more minutes until set. If your crust starts to brown too much, cover the edges with foil during cooking.

Part 32

Here We Go Again

It had been several weeks since the ladies gathered for an official meeting, though Carol-Barbara had seen several of them when they stopped by to help with this or that for the campaign. Susie helped her make campaign buttons with a kit they bought from the craft store. Carol-Barbara thought about using some of the donations that had come in to have them made, but Susie's motto had always been if you can do it yourself, why pay someone else to do it for you?

Martha had been at the house nearly daily to check on how things were going, and to also update Carol-Barbara that there was no more information about the girl.

Even Honey stopped by one morning with her cat, which was suddenly not dyed pink anymore, but a light blue.

"Poopsie needed a change," Honey explained. "She was tired of pink."

While she was there, Carol-Barbara asked Honey to go through her closet and cull any outfits she thought could be useful during the campaign because she just could not justify spending one more penny on new clothes. Honey had actually come up with several ensembles that Carol-Barbara had never even considered. She had to admit it yet again; Honey was a pretty good judge of fashion, despite what she put on her own body.

And so, after several weeks of little time for anything but campaign work, one early Friday afternoon Carol-Barbara had an idea. She had just spent the morning writing a piece the local newspaper requested about her background and why she would make the best candidate for the job of Dogwood County Manager, and she was spent, politically speaking. She decided to call the gals for an impromptu get-together; one that didn't include any talk of politics. She found herself craving a roomful of friends gathered for light conversation and food. The conversation, at least, she could try to keep light. The food, on the other hand, always seemed to end up a bit on the heavy side. They all loved the assortment of fat laden cheeses that seemed to end up on the table, and of course someone usually brought a rich, decadent dessert to share.

She began making her calls and, surprisingly, even on such short notice, almost all the ladies were available. Diane even said that a bird must have whispered in her ear of an impending get-together, because that morning she had awakened with an overwhelming urge to make a giant tureen of banana pudding layered with vanilla wafers and cool whip. She had sampled a little after her lunch, but other than that the vat of pudding was untouched, so she said she would bring it over.

When she got Martha on the phone, in true fashion she stated she would not be cooking anything on such late notice but that she would stop by the KFC for a bucket of popcorn chicken and if Carol-Barbara didn't like the way the red and white paper bucket looked on her fancy dining room table she could dump the chicken into something more suitable.

Carol-Barbara had even called Sherri, from the county office. Unfortunately, when Carol-Barbara got Sherri on the phone she learned she was down with the flu, but promised she would join them next time.

The last call she had to make was to Elsa, and she had to admit she was a little nervous about doing so. She hadn't talked to her since she saw Elsa's sister, Debbie, berating her after the campaign announcement. She knew she should have been a better friend and called to see how she was doing, but things had been so busy. Still, it was no excuse, and this nervous feeling was her punishment for not having checked in with her earlier.

Carol-Barbara knew Elsa didn't have an answering machine, so she let the phone ring seven times before she considered hanging up. Then, on the eighth ring she heard the click of the receiver.

"Hello," came a weak-sounding voice from the other end.

Carol-Barbara was immediately worried because Elsa usually sounded so chipper. "Elsa, it's Carol-Barbara. You okay?"

"Hi, Carol-Barbara. I'm sorry. I'm just tired," Elsa explained.

"Are you sure? You sound more than tired. Is something wrong?" Carol-Barbara was truly worried.

"It's just not a great day," she paused. "Did you need something?" Elsa was short, to the point, not like herself at all. It wasn't like Elsa to not chat.

"I just want you to join us tonight. I'm having the girls over, just a casual gathering. We can talk and eat. Please say you'll come." Carol-Barbara implored her.

There was a pause. "I can't. I'm sorry I have plans."

Plans? Now Carol-Barbara was really curious. Elsa hardly ever had plans. "Well, Elsa, if you change your mind, the invitation stands."

"Thanks, Carol-Barbara. Bye," and she hung up just like that.

"What in the world?" she said out loud.

Carl walked through the back door, having just finished his morning shift at All-Mart, and heard the tail-end of Carol-Barbara's call.

"Getting the ladies together for a wild night?" He asked her.

"Oh yeah," Carol-Barbara stood up and walked over to give him a peck on the cheek. "We are going to party hard tonight. You know us," she joked.

"Did I hear you talking to Elsa? How is she doing with that witch of a sister and evil brother-in-law?"

Carl didn't usually call names. It made Carol-Barbara wonder if he'd had a particularly stressful morning manning the door at All-Mart.

"Everything okay, dear?" She asked.

"I'm fine. Just a bratty little kid kicked me in the shin when I gave the last sticker to the kid in front of him. What's happening to kids today? Our kids never would have done that."

"Let me see," Carol-Barbara urged him to lift his pant leg up. The spot where the kid kicked him was black and blue. Carl tended to bruise easily because of the blood thinner he was on. "Good grief," she said.

"And you know the worst part? The mom didn't do a thing. Just told him to come on and she'd buy him a pack of stickers. The kid actually got rewarded! Can you believe that?" Carl adjusted the cuff of his pants. Then he changed the subject. "So what about Elsa? She doing okay?"

"I couldn't tell. She said she can't join us tonight. She sounded tired."

Carl was a little disappointed because he knew from past history that if Elsa was coming to the get-together she would be bringing some of her amazing home-baked goodies. They had always been one of his downfalls.

Certainly there would be other good food available though, with all those women in the house. He made a mental note to sneak a plate into the den while he watched the USA network pre-

Thanksgiving Matlock marathon. He retired to his den, mouth watering.

The ladies arrived, save Honey. The dishes were set out on the dining room table, KFC bucket and all. Since this was a little more of a casual night, she was going to forgo formalities and dispense with saying the NAKED pledge, thereby getting right to the eating and chatting.

However, Martha insisted they say it, and began, "I am a woman, smart and strong." The rest of the ladies joined in. Having all her friends there reciting the words she'd written brought tears to her eyes, and when it was over she raised her glass.

"You all are just the best. To my friends!" She raised her glass of cider in a toast and they all drank.

That was when Honey came tearing through the front door. Carol-Barbara nearly choked on her drink.

"Something has happened!" Honey was out of breath.

"My God, it's like déjà vu all over again," Martha joked. "Who'd ya shoot this time Van Honk?"

"It's Dixon. He's been shot!" Honey announced.

There was a hush in the room. Carol-Barbara finally spoke up. "You didn't, Honey did you?"

"Not me! And I don't know who did, but Roland said it happened outside the All-Mart. He called me and told me to come over here and let you all know."

Now there was anything but a hush in the room. Like hens in a hen house they all sounded, thought Carl, who entered the room under the guise of getting to the bottom of what all the panic was about, but couldn't help scooping up some of Anne's blueberry salad on the way in. "What's going on ladies? Why all the squawking?"

"Dixon's been shot," Carol-Barbara informed him. "Outside the All-Mart."

"Dang it, why does all the exciting stuff happen after my shift is over!" Carl half-joked.

"Oh, be serious, Carl!" Carol-Barbara jumped at him.

"Well, we all knew it was just a matter of time. So who did it?" Carl asked.

Honey piped in, "Roland doesn't know. He just called me and said the ambulance had just taken him to the hospital."

Unlike the last time Honey had blown through the front door with a life and death emergency, this was real. Dixon had actually been shot. A bullet had actually made contact with Dixon, and he had been taken to Dogwood County Memorial for emergency surgery. Carol-Barbara wondered how dire the situation was, and she also couldn't help but wonder who had finally had enough of Dixon. There must have been a list a mile long of people who didn't like him, but not liking a man, and actually shooting him, were two very different things.

Part 33

Suspicious Minds

Dixon had finally gotten what he deserved, or so most of the NAKED ladies thought. Of course, since most of them were church-going women, they did hate to think about anyone actually dying, but a little gunshot wound; well, most of them thought as long as it didn't put Dixon 6 feet under, it might be just what the man needed to help get it through his thick skull that he couldn't treat people the way he did.

Even after the ladies learned of Dixon's shooting, there was no real reason to break up the party and go home. What could any of them really do about it anyway? It was what it was. Someone had finally had enough of Dixon to put a bullet in him.

The group wasn't aware of Dixon's exact medical status yet. For all they knew he could be dead already, but knowing Dixon as they did, it was more likely that the bullet had missed all his vital organs and he was probably at the hospital giving all the pretty young nurses a pat on the butt and an intentional peek up his hospital gown. Dixon was the type of man who rarely had to own up to his wrong-doings. Yes, he was one lucky bastard, Perhaps, though, his luck had finally run out.

They all filled their plates and sat down to discuss possible motives and suspects. There was speculation of all kinds as to who could have done such a thing. In some of their minds, even though

Honey had been the one to deliver the news of the shooting, she was suspicious simply because of her past history. Martha couldn't help but bring that fact up.

Honey was busy defending herself to Martha, and Martha was giving her funny looks, as though she didn't buy anything Honey said. Shootings never happened in Dogwood County, and at the very least Martha wondered if Honey had brought some of her New Jersey bad luck down with her when she moved to Dogwood County.

"Van Honk, are you telling me you had nothing at all to do with this? You are the only one who arrived to the meeting late, and without an alibi. And we all know how much you hate Dixon." Martha half-teased. "Of course we all do, though."

Being accused of shooting Dixon was just enough to bring out Honey's sassy side.

"Listen Martha, I was soaking in a hot tub and enjoying a glass of Fine Swine liqueur when Roland called me with the news. He had been listening to his police scanner in the car on his way home from the All-Mart. Furthermore, I don't think I like what you are implying." She put her hand on her hip and stood her ground with Martha, which few people ever did.

Martha seemed to be enjoying herself. "Your track record precedes you, Honey. If there were anyone in this room who might have shot Dixon, I would bet on you."

Honey took a step forward, "Oh, yeah, Martha Fitzgerald? Didn't I see you buying ammunition at the All-Mart the other day?" Honey questioned.

"That was for target practice!" Martha countered.

Honey had had enough. "Like the target on Dixon's overly-taut butt maybe?"

"You know something, Honey?" Martha started, then gave up. "Oh, never mind. Whatever I say is just going to rile you up, and I am tired of hearing your voice."

"Alz I'm sayin' is, don't shoot the messenger," Honey put an end to their conversation.

Carol-Barbara really didn't think Honey had a thing to do with the shooting. Personally, Carol-Barbara's immediate thought was that it all had something to do with the woman she'd seen Dixon hanging around with; the one the ice cream shop employee had said he introduced as his daughter.

It was too much of a coincidence that this girl had come into the picture recently, and now Dixon was in emergency surgery for a bullet wound.

Carol-Barbara tried to remember more about that day a few weeks ago when she and Carl witnessed the jewelry counter girl's husband storm into the All-Mart and tell Dixon to stay away from her. Maybe he was the one who shot Dixon? Carol-Barbara wondered if she should inform the police about the incident. What if it had been him and she didn't say anything? Then she would have to live with the consequences. But if it was just a coincidence, then she might be getting an innocent man into trouble.

Susie had already decided the whole thing had something to do with a sex crime, but she watched too many episodes of Law and Order SVU and thought everything could eventually be tied to a sex crime. In this case, though, she might be right.

Diane sarcastically suggested that Carol-Barbara might have shot Dixon to ensure the election would go in her favor. Carol-Barbara didn't think that was one bit funny and let Diane know as much.

They were all dying to know Dixon's status when Carl hollered from his den that the shooting had made the early edition of the evening news. The ladies crowded into Carl's den to watch the television. The announcer stated that a local man had been shot and was being treated at the hospital and was in critical, but stable, condition. The media wasn't releasing who the victim was, though they all knew, until the next of kin had been notified.

Good Lord, could it be possible that Debbie didn't know yet?

According to the newscast Dixon was still alive, but in critical condition. As much as they all disliked him that really was the important part. If he was alive, he might be able to confirm who shot him, and that would be very interesting; very interesting indeed.

Blueberry Salad

Two- 3 oz packages raspberry JELL-O

One 16oz can blueberry pie filling (or pint of fresh blueberries)

One 16oz can crushed pineapple (with juice)

One 8 oz package cream cheese

One cup sour cream

½ Cup sugar

Nuts for topping

Dissolve JELL-O in 1 cup boiling water. Add blueberry pie filling and pineapple. Pour mixture into 9x13 pan. Refrigerate to congeal. Mix cream cheese with sour cream until smooth. Add sugar. When salad is congealed, spread mixture on top and sprinkle with nuts. Refrigerate until ready to serve. Serves 6-8. Enjoy!

Part 34

That's Debatable

Within three days of the incident the news had traveled, and it was the talk of the town. Dixon had been shot, and the bullet had wounded him in one of the most sensitive of all places. He had been shot squarely in the left buttock. He would survive, and the wound would heal, but no amount of squats, lunges or running at the gym would ever fix the dent in his pride.

There were still no suspects, and the culprit either had very bad aim, or purposely went for an area that would not kill him, but would make a real statement. That it did, since Dixon's perfectly sculpted body was among his most prized possessions. Even though the damage would heal, it would keep him off his feet and out of the gym for several weeks.

As it turned out, Dixon's wife, Debbie, had not been notified of her husband's situation until the morning after the occurrence. She had been in Richmond on a shopping excursion and had been staying overnight in The Jefferson. She made the trip to the posh hotel a few times a year whenever the monotony of shopping in little old Dogwood County started to get the best of her.

The story went that after a long day of shopping, and a delicious steak, topped off with a bottle of fine champagne, she had fallen into a deep sleep. She'd turned her cell phone off at some point. When she awoke the next morning and found out about

Dixon's shooting, via the concierge, she got back to Dogwood as quickly as she could. She made her way straight to the hospital.

Sharon Halsey, one of Carol-Barbara's church friends, worked as a nurse at the hospital on the floor where Dixon was being cared for. Several days after the shooting Carol-Barbara ran into her at the hair salon, where Sharon recounted the story of Debbie's arrival at the hospital to Carol-Barbara. Sharon sat next to Carol-Barbara, her hair in rollers, waiting for her perm to take, while Carol-Barbara, hair-do already complete, listened eagerly.

"You should have seen her, Carol-Barbara," Sharon laughed as she told the story. "She came flying down the hall with her Coach handbag in one hand and her Nordstrom bag in the other. *Where is he? Where's my Dixon? I got here as soon as I could!*" Sharon imitated Debbie's extreme Southern drawl. "She had new silk pajamas for him and made a big deal about how he couldn't be expected to wear that scratchy hospital gown. I swear the performance was worthy of an Oscar."

"I believe it," Carol-Barbara responded. "Debbie's always had a touch of the drama in her."

Sharon changed the subject slightly. "So are you getting your hair done for the big televised debate against Dixon?" She asked.

"I needed a little touch up, you know? I have to be down at the local television station at 5:00 tomorrow evening." Carol-Barbara looked in the mirror. "Not bad, huh?" She touched her newly coiffed hair. She'd had it cut and colored in an attempt to look fresh and young for the debate, which she had been assured would still happen, despite Dixon's condition.

"Can you believe Dixon is going to do the debate from his hospital bed? Do you think he's trying to get the pity vote?" Sharon asked. She was referring to the fact that Dixon had arranged for the local television station to have a camera crew show up and do a remote debate with him at the hospital, while Carol-Barbara would be filmed at the station.

"I wouldn't put it past him," Carol-Barbara stated.

"I'll be there you know. At the hospital, I mean," Sharon told her. "It's taking place during my shift. I switched tomorrow with one of the other nurses so I can be with Henry during the day when he goes for his doctor's appointment." Henry was Sharon's husband.

"How is Henry doing?" Carol-Barbara asked her. Sharon's husband, Henry, had been diagnosed with pancreatic cancer. The doctors had caught it early, thanks to Sharon's diligence in getting the right tests done. It helped that she had connections at the hospital. The last Carol-Barbara had heard, Henry had a good shot of beating it, which wasn't always the case, but Sharon had nearly run herself ragged with working and taking care of him.

"Oh, he's coming along," Sharon told her. He's able to eat better now and finally gaining a little weight. The whole ordeal's been so stressful for both of us.

Carol-Barbara thought for a moment. Why hadn't she asked Sharon to join the NAKED ladies? She knew her well enough, and certainly, with a life like Sharon's, she could use all the support she could get.

"Sharon, are you interested in coming to my meeting next time we get together?" Carol-Barbara carefully posed the question, not wanting Sharon to feel pressured.

"Meeting?" Sharon questioned. "Is it like a Bible study or something?"

"Not exactly," Carol-Barbara replied. "Although I do enjoy a good Bible study," she noted. "This is something different. I started this club because I thought my friends and I needed an outlet. You know, for whatever we might each be going through."

"So what do you do at the meetings?" Sharon questioned.

Carol-Barbara thought about it. Lately it seemed like all they had done was dodge bullets of various kinds, and eat. She told Sharon as much, and added that when the election was over she intended to plan more outings. The weather would be better by then.

"Sounds good to me. I like food. And I can dodge bullets just as quick as the next gal," she joked.

Later that day, Carl drove Carol-Barbara to the tiny Dogwood County television station a little before five o'clock. She was nervous about the debate, and as they walked into the building she told him as much.

"How should I act? I've never been on TV before," she questioned him.

"You will be fine, CB," he assured her. "Just be you. That's who everybody wants to see. Don't try to be someone you're not."

When they walked in the building Carol-Barbara was immediately whisked away to the make-up room for a touch-up, so Carl parked himself in a chair in the corner of the lobby to read a magazine.

The debate was to start promptly at five. A moderator was to be there asking random questions that had been emailed to the television station earlier that week from Dogwood County residents.

Normally, the debate participants would be standing right beside each other at podiums, but since Dixon was still at the hospital, there would be a separate cameraman at the hospital. The viewers would see a split screen with Carol-Barbara standing at a podium at the station and Dixon presumably lying in his hospital bed. *Awkward* was the first thought Carol-Barbara had about the whole situation, but the show must go one. With the holidays there would only be time for one more debate after this one, and that would be right before the election.

As she sat in a chair, the makeup girl at the station was applying what looked like way too much blush on Carol-Barbara's cheeks. The expression on Carol-Barbara's face as she looked in the mirror must have said it all about what she was thinking because the girl was quick to respond.

"I know it looks extreme, but the camera really has a way of washing a person out. We have to put on extra makeup to fix that. Don't worry. You won't look overly made-up on screen," she assured Carol-Barbara.

"Are you sure?" Carol-Barbara was already worried about the way she looked, even though she wore the new outfit Honey had helped her pick out, and which she knew she looked great in.

"Positive." She paused. "I'm quite skilled at what I do," she continued. "My other job is doing makeup on cadavers at the Ettrick funeral home down the street. Talk about a body looking washed out."

It was an off color joke, but it served its purpose. Carol-Barbara suddenly felt a lot less anxious. She recanted with a joke of her own. "I'm nervous, but definitely not scared *to death* anymore. Thanks."

"You're welcome," the girl stated.

Just then a man wearing a headset came through the door. He introduced himself as the producer.

"Ms. Hoofnagle, it's time. Come with me please." He held the door open for her.

She followed him down the hall and when they got to the newsroom she could already see Dixon on a screen. It was a live shot, though they weren't on the air yet. Dixon lay in his hospital bed, and Carol-Barbara could see her friend Sharon, the nurse, tending to his last minute needs. He looked well, except for the fact that he was in the bed. She suddenly wondered if they could see her, too. As if the producer could read her mind, he spoke up.

"Pretty cool, huh?" He pointed to the screen showing Dixon. "We can see them because we need to be able to set the camera up right and make sure we are logged in remotely, but they won't be able to see us until the debate starts."

For Carol-Barbara, that was welcome news. She didn't like the idea of Dixon seeing her in her final moments of debate preparation. The producer asked her to stand behind the podium so he could set up the camera. He made a few adjustments and then told her it was time. He then got a on a speaker and called for the moderator.

"Doris, can you come in here please? We're ready." He told her.

A middle-aged woman entered the room and Carol-Barbara recognized her as one of the local newscasters.

"Hi, Ms. Hoofnagle. I'm Doris Blair," she introduced herself. She explained that she would be randomly scrolling through the emails that had been sent in and would read some of them aloud to them. They would each have one minute to respond to each question. The whole debate would last about thirty minutes. A coin had been flipped and Carol-Barbara learned she would be going first. She settled herself behind the podium and took a deep breath.

"Here we go. Three, two, one," the producer counted down. "And we're live."

Part 35

Mr. Shady

Carl watched the debate between Carol-Barbara and Dixon from the green room of the television station. There was a nice big flat panel television screen attached to the wall, and a comfy couch on which he perched himself. He was the only one in the room, and could have made himself quite comfortable had he wanted to, but he stopped short of removing his shoes and stretching out. Never mind the fact it would have likely been frowned upon by the production crew, he was too nervous for Carol-Barbara to do anything but sit on the edge of the couch and sip decaf coffee.

His coffee had been freshly brewed for him by the nice new Keurig machine in the corner. The production assistant had showed him how to use it, and it really was one of the neatest pieces of technology Carl had ever seen. There was no filling of paper filters with coffee grounds or waiting for the pot to brew. Rather, there was a wide variety of pre-filled pods, and with just one push of a button, in about 20 seconds he had the hot beverage of his choice. He decided then that he and Carol-Barbara must own one of these fine pieces of machinery. Among the pods he'd found a decaf one, and chose that since he was already hyped up over the fact that his lovely wife had to face-off against her nemesis. The last thing he needed was caffeine.

The debate set up at the local television station was actually quite high-tech, he considered, especially for little old Dogwood County, but what did he know? Never mind Keurig machines, he still thought remote controls were high-tech.

When the debate started, it showed Dixon laid up in his hospital bed milking his injury for all it was worth. He would be using the fact that he had recently been shot to his advantage. Of course the fact that someone had shot him didn't speak highly of his likeability around Dogwood County, but it also made him seem somehow vulnerable, and some people might be easily swayed into voting for someone who had been targeted during an election.

Then again, when he considered the possibilities, for all he really knew Dixon may have shot himself in the butt cheek in order to gain the sympathy vote. Maybe he knew his chances of getting reelected were as slim as the gluteus maximus that had taken the bullet. Carl wondered, as he sat waiting for the debate to begin, if it was even physically possible for someone to shoot himself in his own backside, but he didn't put anything past Dixon. He was a shyster, no two ways about it.

Carol-Barbara was ready, and it was a good thing, as the debate moderator, one Doris Blair, was live now, and she began explaining to the audience how the debate would work. She would click a button on her computer and the questions that had been submitted via email by local residents the week before would randomly come up on the screen. Neither the moderator, nor the candidates, knew exactly what would be presented. Carol-Barbara began to worry. What if she didn't know how to respond? What if she came out looking like an idiot in front of everyone watching? She wondered how many viewers there actually were.

The first question was from a man who signed his name Mr. Know-it-All. He wanted to know which of the candidates could do something about lowering the price of gasoline. Clearly he didn't know everything; since it was obvious Dogwood County had zero impact on the going rate of a barrel of crude oil. Carol-Barbara froze. She didn't know the first thing about crude oil, or what it had to do with Dogwood County politics, and even though she had been chosen to answer the first question, Dixon used her hesitation to his advantage. He quickly joked that if he could do anything about the price of crude oil he would probably be president of the United States. He then suggested he might get in touch with his buddy who was a retired Wall Street commodities trader to see what he could do about it.

This only served to demonstrate that Dixon was clearly educated on topics that belonged in higher levels of politics, and that he had friends in high places; whereas Carol-Barbara wasn't even sure how gas was made, or how the price of gas was determined, much less what a commodities trader did. Was she really supposed to respond to that? Thankfully, the moderator made a funny look, asked Dixon to please wait until he was given the go-ahead to speak when a question was asked, and quickly moved on by stating that the question didn't have any relevance to this particular election. She threw the question out.

Another question popped up on the screen. "This one is for Ms. Hoofnagle," the moderator sternly announced. "Our local park hasn't been redone in years. Benches are broken, the playground equipment is lacking, and what does remain is ugly at best and certainly dangerous by today's standards. What can be done about this?" It was signed Susan P.

Carol-Barbara knew that must be from Susie. She also knew her friend had done her a huge favor by asking it. From her years serving on the church beautification committee, along with Susie, Carol-Barbara knew everything there was to know about designing and landscaping a place both children and adults would want to spend time in. She answered like a pro, and this gave her the confidence to continue.

The next question was Dixon's. It asked what he would do about the panhandlers who sometimes stopped in Dogwood County hitchhiking their way across the state. He answered that he would make sure every panhandler was prosecuted according to the full extent of the law.

More questions came and went. The two went back and forth with their answers. Some questions were silly and off-topic. One person wanted to know how any of this would affect the price of tea in China. Someone else asked what would be screened at the local movie theatre during the upcoming weekend. The moderator made a joke that perhaps someone should have screened the questions first.

Some of the questions were valid, though. Could something be done about all the potholes on Main Street? What were the candidates' thoughts on installing a stoplight at the corner of Garland and

Grapevine where so many accidents occurred each year?

Then the big question popped up on the screen, the one Carol-Barbara had been waiting for someone to address. It read, "I've heard rumors that there are plans to build a giant shopping mall just on the edge of town. What impact would this have on residents?" It was signed Carl H.

Carol-Barbara didn't know Carl had sent in a question, much less that he knew how to send an email, but how many Carl H's would have sent in that particular question? She knew it hadn't been sent from their joint email address because she probably would have seen it while poking around in her account during the past week.

The construction of a mall wasn't public knowledge yet. Dixon was visually surprised. However, it was not his turn to answer. He took a long gulp of water to try to hide his shock, though Carol-Barbara couldn't imagine that he didn't expect it on some level. After all, at one point he had sent his wife Debbie to do his dirty work with the people who would be most affected by the existence of a super-mall.

This was the question for which Carol-Barbara was really prepared. She had practiced over and over again just exactly what she would say if this question arose, and once again it was her turn to go first. She began, "I am against the construction of a mall on the outskirts of town-"

Dixon interrupted her. "Is this really something that needs to be addressed right now?"

"Mr. St. James, I asked you before to please wait your turn." Doris Blair reminded him.

"I just don't see how rumors should have any place in this debate," he added.

"Mr. St. James!" Doris Blair had no patience for his interruptions. "Ms. Hoofnagle, please answer the question."

Carol-Barbara started again. "I am against the construction of a mall. It would only serve to line Mr. St. James's pockets, as he is the main investor in this mall. It would also put long-time residents out of their homes." There, she had said it. How would Dixon respond?

In the only way he knew how, of course—by appearing to have a heart attack. Suddenly Dixon was clutching his chest. Bells and whistles were going off all around him, and his nurse was running to his aid.

Now everybody knew about Dixon's plans to displace residents, and if Dixon made it through this second crisis, he'd have to answer to all of Dogwood County.

Part 36

King of Hearts

The day after the televised debate, Carol-Barbara received a phone call from Sharon, the nurse who worked in the unit where Dixon was hospitalized.

"I shouldn't even be disclosing this to you, what with patient confidentiality and all, but I have some good news and some bad news," Sharon told her. "I'll start with the good news."

She said that while no heart issue should ever be taken lightly, in Dixon's case it had been very mild. He was very physically fit, and because he was already hospitalized, the medical response had been so quick that he was expected to have very little lasting damage from the event. It couldn't even be classified as a real heart attack.

She pointed out that Dixon's attack probably seemed more dramatic than it was because of the bells and whistles that went off when it occurred. He was already plugged up to machines to monitor his condition, so when his heart began beating erratically it was very evident something was happening. Alarms began sounding and the doctor came running, all before the television people could get the cameras shut down. It was broadcast to everyone watching.

"It was more dramatic than an episode of ER! The only thing missing was George Clooney!" Sharon joked.

Carol-Barbara tried to laugh. She was glad Dixon was going to be okay, and now that she knew he would be, yet again, that same worry crept back in. For one, she was upset that her chance to really "wow" the residents of Dogwood County during the debate had been cut short by the incident, and she also worried that all this drama would gain him the sympathy vote. Or, could it be that the universe was simply working against her? Maybe she wasn't meant to serve Dogwood County. Maybe Dixon was meant to go through with his development plans. The thought was sobering.

Logic told her that as sheisty as Dixon was, he likely hadn't had anything to do with his shooting, and he certainly hadn't given himself a semi-heart attack. She also wondered, though, how this could have happened to such a physically fit man. Dixon worked out every day and was the picture of health. She asked Sharon as much.

Sharon explained that the heart problem may have been due to the stress of the gunshot wound. "Or" she stated, "He may have been induced into having a heart attack."

"Induced?" Carol-Barbara questioned.

Sharon continued," Remember I said I had some bad news, too? Well, depending on how you look at it, since I know Dixon isn't the most beloved citizen of Dogwood County. Some people might find some sick pleasure in what I am about to say."

"Sharon, what in the world? What are you talking about?" She could only imagine what other drama could possibly be woven into this already twisted scenario.

"I probably shouldn't be telling you this, but there is speculation among the nurses that someone may have tried to kill him," Sharon told her.

"You mean the gunshot, right? We already know that. He obviously didn't shoot himself," Carol-Barbara reminded her.

"I'm not talking about the gun shot. I'm talking about the heart attack. It may not have been a natural event, especially if someone tampered with his IV," Sharon presented the possibility.

"Someone tampered with his IV?" Carol-Barbara was shocked.

"Let's just say the nurse on duty in his room later that night noticed after all the excitement was over that some settings had been changed. She was really concerned, so she told the doctor on call. More so to placate her than anything else I think, he sent what was left off to the lab to see exactly what was in the IV bag. You know, to determine if anything had been added that wasn't supposed to be there."

"You mean someone may have poisoned him?" Carol-Barbara was flabbergasted that this was even a concern. Didn't hospitals have safety precautions in place to prevent this sort of thing from happening? "How could someone do that without anyone noticing?" she asked.

"Well, it's probably just all conjecture, but there was a lot of activity in that room in the hour prior to his heart attack," Sharon explained. "He had people in and out of there, a business partner, his wife, even people from the television station were setting up their equipment. It's probably just that someone inadvertently jostled something around,"

Carol-Barbara sighed a breath of relief. "Of course. That's probably what happened then. Someone just accidentally hit something."

"You have to understand, though, we do have to rule out any criminal activity, especially since someone already tried to shoot him," Sharon told her. "But you're right. It's probably just a fluke."

Sharon changed the subject. "So when are you getting the girls together again for one of your meetings?"

Carol-Barbara remembered that she had promised Sharon an invite. "So you want to be part of the NAKED ladies, huh? You sure about that? We seem to be drumming up drama wherever we go," Carol-Barbara joked.

"Sounds like fun to me," Sharon told her.

Carol-Barbara was suddenly motivated to plan something; anything to get her mind off of the current negativity surrounding the election. "Let's do it, then. How is Friday?"

"Perfect," Sharon paused. "Hey, do you like Salsa?" She asked.

"You mean like with chips?" Carol-Barbara figured Sharon was asking what she could bring.

Sharon laughed. "No, like dancing. There's a restaurant Henry and I used to go to before he got sick. It's in Charlottesville, so it's a little bit of a drive, but on Friday nights after dinner they have free Salsa lessons followed by a DJ and dancing."

Salsa dancing? Carol-Barbara had never considered such an idea.

Sharon continued. "In fact, if you don't mind, we could all go. I know it's supposed to be ladies' night, but Henry is feeling so much better now. I would love to take him out. It would do him a world of good to see some old friends."

Carl and the others guys Salsa dancing? Carol-Barbara couldn't imagine it. While the ladies had taken a vow to be open-minded and experience new things, their significant others never had. Sharon sounded so excited, though. How could she say no? Somehow the guys would be volunteered, and a NAKED ladies date night it would be.

"That sounds exciting," she told Sharon. "Plan on it. I'll call all the girls."

Sharon hung up giddy. Carol-Barbara hung up confused as to how she would pull this off. Carl had a big heart, and would do almost anything to help a friend, but Salsa dancing? She wasn't sure she could count on that.

Carl walked into the kitchen for a snack just as Carol-Barbara hung up with Sharon.

"Hey, you wanna hear a joke?" Carl was infamous for his bad jokes.

"I have a feeling I don't have a choice," she told him.

Carl began, "Two trees are growing side-by-side. One tree says to the other, 'Do you come here often?' The other one replies, 'I never leave.'" Carl paused for effect. "You're not laughing. Get it? Leave?"

"Oh I get it. Hey, you wanna hear something even funnier?" It was her turn to pause for effect. "You're going Salsa dancing Friday."

Part 37

Chips and Salsa

To say Carl was distressed about learning to Salsa dance was an understatement. He did, however, like to see Carol-Barbara happy. So, if putting on his dancing shoes and making a fool of himself did that, then, darn it, he would be the biggest fool in Dogwood County. And, he wouldn't be alone in his foolishness, since several of the other husbands had agreed to go.

According to Carol-Barbara, the plan was that the group would caravan to Charlottesville. Once there, they would enjoy a Spanish-style meal at a restaurant called Calientè. Upon completion of the meal, they would convene on the upper level of the restaurant where a group of professional Salsa dancers would give them a 45 minute dance lesson.

She had tried many times to get in touch with Elsa, but to no avail. She felt a little guilty, as she was sure Elsa would have enjoyed this evening.

The caravan went off almost without a hitch, but for the fact that Diane backed out, saying she had to take care of a sick cat and didn't like dancing anyway. It was typical Diane, so Carol-Barbara wasn't insulted. Diane said she'd stop by to visit sometime next week instead.

All the other suspects were there, plus Sharon and her husband, Henry, who Carl hadn't seen in months. He was glad to see him out and about.

The caravan finally departed. Their estimated travel time was only 30 minutes, but with Martha in the backseat of their car, Carl mused, it would seem twice that. Martha spoke incessantly about the situation surrounding Dixon, and the speculation regarding who had shot him; perhaps even a gang member.

Thankfully, just before Martha launched into a lecture about the gangs that had infiltrated Virginia and how a person could tell the difference between a gang hit and something else, Carol-Barbara reminded her that tonight was supposed to be about letting go, getting away from it all for a while, and certainly not talking about Dixon, so the conversation changed to something more light-hearted. Soon they were pulling into the restaurant.

Inside Calientè, the hostess got them seated. It turned out that Martha was good for something, and she had had the forethought to call ahead and reserve them a giant table. Calientè, it turned out, was hot in more ways than its name. Apparently it was the hottest place to be on a Friday night, and was packed full of people. Had Martha not made reservations, they would be waiting with all the other people who had forgotten to make reservations. Instead, they waltzed, or rather salsa-ed right to their table.

Drinks were ordered, and everyone settled in. Honey ordered a margarita the size of her head, and some of the other ladies, including Carol-Barbara, joined in. The men mainly ordered cervezas, except for Roland who amped it up a notch, and ordered a tequila shot along with his beer.

"How do you drink that stuff?" Carl asked him.

"What, this? It's mother's milk," Roland explained.

Yeah, if your mother is a car battery, Carl thought. He'd never been much on hard liquor.

As is par for the course in a Spanish restaurant, baskets of chips were placed on the table. Carol-Barbara had to remind Carl not to fill up on them before dinner arrived, and it was a good thing, as dinner was beyond delicious. A family style dinner of burritos and tamales, chile relenos and mounds of rice and beans was brought out. How were they supposed to dance after all this food? Carl wondered. He would need a wheelbarrow to carry him away from the table.

And what Spanish restaurant would be complete without a mariachi band, Carl considered, as one made its way to the table to sing a sweet, slow song, about which the subject matter Carl didn't know, since it was in Spanish, but it sounded romantic, and it seemed to make the ladies happy. When it was over, tips were expected, and Carl pulled out his wallet.

"I should have learned to play the guitar," he whispered to Roland, as he slipped the musician a ten spot.

Just after the empty dishes were taken away, Carl noticed a familiar sight in the corner of the restaurant; something he hadn't noticed before. It was Debbie's sister, Elsa.

"What in the world is she doing here?" He whispered to Carol-Barbara.

231

"Who?" Carol-Barbara strained to see in the dim light.

"Isn't that Elsa?" Carl nodded his head in the general direction.

"Good Lord, Carl, I think you're right. Who is that she's with?" Carol-Barbara tried not to stare at Elsa, who sat at a corner table with a gentleman neither recognized.

"I've never seen him before." Carl confirmed.

Just then, Elsa caught Carol-Barbara's eye, and the look on her face was that of pure horror. Elsa whispered something to her companion. She excused herself from her table and came towards them.

"Hi, Carol-Barbara." Elsa looked meek. "Please don't tell Debbie you saw me here."

"No, no of course not." Carol-Barbara hesitated, trying to change the subject. "You look beautiful, by the way."

Carol-Barbara could not recall ever seeing Elsa wearing her hair in any way but her trademark bun, and now it was down, her long gray hair flowing down her shoulders. She even had a flower in her hair, and wore a beautiful turquoise blue dress. Her glasses were gone, too, so Carol-Barbara could see that the blue in her eyes nearly matched that in her dress. Carol-Barbara had never realized how attractive Elsa was, and not in the same made-up way as her sister, but in a natural, almost farm girl way.

"What are you all doing here?" Elsa asked, trying to seem normal, looking around to the group.

"We're being forced to learn to Salsa dance," Carl piped in, trying to lighten the mood.

"I tried to call and invite you, but you never answered your phone," Carol-Barbara added.

"I've been otherwise engaged," Elsa glanced back at her companion and smiled.

Carol-Barbara thought how incredibly happy Elsa looked.

"I guess Robert and I will see you upstairs then," Elsa told them. We're staying for the dancing, too.

So his name was Robert. Carol-Barbara stowed it away in her memory. "I had no idea you liked this kind of thing," Carol-Barbara got right to the point.

"I've been taking dance lessons for years. Robert and I met a couple of years ago, but we started coming here on a regular basis last year. "Please don't tell Debbie," she begged again. "She would ruin it for me."

"Of course not, Elsa. I would never do that, and I'll tell the others not to mention it either," she assured her.

With that, Elsa relaxed a little. "I'd better get back to Robert. I'll see you upstairs in a bit."

"Well that was weird," Carl whispered after Elsa left.

"You can say that again," Carol-Barbara agreed. Elsa was sure surprising her lately.

The bill was paid, and a man came to their table to tell them their Salsa instructor was ready and waiting for them. The group was taken, along with the other couples in the restaurant, to the upstairs level.

Several professional dancers were lined up waiting for them. The head dancer introduced himself as Rico. From what Carl could tell, Rico was in his forties, but with the svelte dancer's body of a man half his age. Rico wore pants so tight Carl wondered how the man could walk.

Honey noticed, and in a way only Honey could express, she said so.

"Not hard to tell which way he hangs is it?" She leaned over and whispered to Carol-Barbara, yet loud enough for Carl to hear.

Carol-Barbara stifled a laugh, and Carl couldn't help noticing she was blushing.

"You like that, huh?" He teased her.

"Carl! You know I'm not like that!" She defended herself. "Although I think it's to the left," she giggled.

"It was just the one margarita you had, right?" He questioned her.

"Well I'm not drunk if that's what you're asking," she told him matter-of-factly. "Can't a girl have a little fun?" She paused and looked around. "Where is Elsa anyway?"

"Maybe she doesn't need the lesson," Carl pointed out. "After all she said she comes here all the time."

Rico introduced himself as a former Brazilian national champion of the Salsa dance. He spoke with a heavy accent, which Carl was sure must make all the women swoon.

Rico spent the first 40 minutes showing them the basics of the Salsa dance, using the female participants randomly as partners. Carl and the rest of the guys kept up the best they could.

"Now for the finale!" Rico announced. "You will learn to do the hip roll. This move is so seductive I must insist it only be done by those over the age of eighteen!"

With this statement he came close to Carol-Barbara and flirtatiously made an announcement.

"So, lovely lady, you will have to refrain from this move," he joked.

Carl saw Carol-Barbara blush yet again, and she giggled like a schoolgirl.

"This guy really has you on a leash, doesn't he?" Carl whispered.

Carol-Barbara rolled her eyes at him. "Let me enjoy myself, Carl."

Rico began the hip roll. The class tried along.

"No, no, no!" Rico stopped them. "You have to put your sex into it!" He practically yelled at them. "Your sex! Your sex!"

Carl wondered how the hell he was supposed to 'put his sex into it' without doing something practically illegal looking.

Rico came up behind Carol-Barbara to demonstrate. He put his hands on her hips. "Like this!" Rico dug his hands into her hips. "Now move them in a circle, like the sex!" Rico demanded.

Carol-Barbara realized she had definitely been missing out on something, as she'd never circled her hips like that in her life, and certainly not during 'the sex.' She couldn't help but laugh, and after what seemed an interminably long time, Rico removed his hands.

Everyone began trying the hip roll, some of them more productively than others, and Carl was sure he was going to throw his back out.

After the lesson, the DJ began spinning tunes, and the real fun began. Couples of various levels began to tear up the dance floor. Carl and Carol-Barbara prepared to give it their all. As they made their way across the dance floor, they noticed a couple join the crowd and begin dancing. It was Elsa and Robert, and boy, could they move. Carol-Barbara wondered what other secrets Elsa had.

Part 38

Josefina Estanga Torres Ruiz

The DJ cranked out song after song for the crowd of amateur salsa dancers. Carl barely had time to catch his breath in between each round. His heart was pounding and his back was killing him, but there was no way he was coming off the dance floor, not while Carol-Barbara was having so much fun. This was all for her, and he had already decided he would sway his hips and move his feet until he fell in the floor, or somebody told him to stop, whichever came first.

The Salsa instructor, Rico, walked the room, mingling and showing people new dance moves to incorporate into their ever-expanding repertoire. He danced his way across the room and made a deliberate effort to get to Carl and Carol-Barbara.

In an attempt to keep Rico from showing him up in front of his wife, Carl shook his hips more vigorously, which only served to make the pain in his lower back intensify. By the time Rico got to them, Carl was clutching his lower back as he tried to keep up.

"Hola, my friends!" Rico greeted them. "Are you having a good time?"

"Of course we are," Carol-Barbara blushed. "This is so much fun. I don't know why we didn't do this years ago."

Because I would be a cripple by now, that's why, Carl thought to himself as his lower back twinged in pain.

"You are really getting the hang of this, beautiful lady," Rico complimented Carol-Barbara and playfully hip-bumped her.

"Oh thank you, Rico!" She gushed. "But a student is only as good as her teacher!" She gushed.

Carl thought he would puke if he saw his wife fall all over Rico one more time.

Rico turned his attention to Carl. "And how about you old man? You doing okay there?" Rico playfully smacked Carl on his backside. Apparently, in Venezuela smacking another man on the rump was commonplace.

"Fine, Rico, just fine. Thanks for asking." Carl mustered.

"A little more hip action, eh my friend?" Rico shook his hips and danced right up on Carol-Barbara to demonstrate. It was nothing short of vulgar, in Carl's opinion.

Carl was not amused. He wondered if Rico was going to hang out here molesting his wife all night.

Luckily, that didn't happen. In a blessed reprieve the DJ announced he would be taking a short break, and suggested that everyone should enjoy a refreshment from the bar.

"Keep that beautiful young lady happy, old man," were Rico's parting words as he sauntered away.

"Sex maniac," Carl muttered under his breath.

"I think he's perfectly lovely," Carol-Barbara gushed.

"Of course you do. He's falling all over you," Carl pointed out.

Carol-Barbara looked Carl in the eyes and took his hand. "Do you think I don't see through his act? I know he's only after one thing from me, and he is absolutely going to get it."

Carl looked at Carol-Barbara like she had really lost her mind.

"A really good tip. Now come on, let's get a Pellegrino." She took his hand and led him towards the bar.

Damn it, Carl thought as Carol-Barbara pulled him by the hand towards the bar, someone else I'm going to have to tip.

When Carl and Carol-Barbara came off the dance floor, they joined Martha, who was already seated at the bar next to Elsa and her friend, Robert. Martha liked to socialize with her friends, and she had tolerated the Salsa lesson, but dancing all night was not her cup of tea, so she had been drinking bourbon and water all night at the bar.

Honey and Roland were there also, acting like two teenagers, dancing, drinking and talking. They stood at the opposite end of the bar. Sharon and her husband Henry seemed to be enjoying Roland and Honey's company, as well. They all sat together laughing at some inside joke. Carol-Barbara thought it was good to see them all enjoying each other.

Carl and Carol-Barbara sat down and ordered a large bottle of Pellegrino to share. They drank deeply, and waited for the cold bubbly liquid to replace the fluids they had lost while dancing. They made small talk with their friends, but just as they started to feel refreshed, their attention was drawn to a woman who had just walked through the door.

She was the kind of woman who, by her very looks alone, garnered the attention of every man and woman in the room. She was dressed in a traditional Spanish dress, red, of course, with a flower tucked behind her ear. Her long, dark hair framed a face that could only be described as one of timeless beauty.

"Who is that?" Carol-Barbara asked.

"That is Josefina Estanga Torres Ruiz," Robert answered. "She is half the reason I'm here."

"I thought the reason you were here was Elsa," Martha teased.

Elsa piped in. "Don't worry about me. I know where I stand against her," she joked.

Robert lovingly reached for Elsa's hand, and she smiled. "Elsa is the other half, but I have to be here to watch Miss Ruiz, as well."

Elsa piped in. "Robert is a retired FBI agent, but he still sometimes does consultant work. He's been following Josefina for some time."

"Why?" Carol-Barbara asked.

"She is bad news," Robert explained.

"How so?" Carl asked.

"They call her the Caracas carcass-maker," Robert offered. "On account of the fact that she's from Caracas, Venezuela, and apparently she has been responsible for the demise of more men than can be counted on all our fingers combined," Robert tried to explain.

"What do you mean?" Carol-Barbara questioned.

"Josefina is purportedly the leader of a particularly violent South American drug cartel," Robert explained.

"That lovely woman is the head of a drug cartel?" Carol-Barbara was shocked.

"Don't let her good looks fool you," Robert pleaded. "She is a monster. And she has taken a liking to our Salsa instructor."

"Rico?" Carol-Barbara was genuinely worried.

"It's why Elsa and I started coming here last year," he explained. "We used to go bowling every Friday night, until I got assigned to this case."

They watched Josefina make her way to Rico. The two embraced in what could only be described as a made-for-Hollywood moment. He swept her up in his arms and kissed her on both cheeks, then passionately on the mouth

"And Rico? He is involved as well, then?" Carol-Barbara questioned.

"I'm still trying to figure him out," Robert explained. "He is either the most naïve man who ever existed, or the best actor I've ever met. He would appear to have no knowledge of who he is involved with."

Martha was, for once, suspiciously quiet.

"So what happens now?" Carl asked.

"I've got people on the outside. They will follow them, and report back to me in the morning." Robert told them.

"And to think, I thought you led a quiet existence," Carol-Barbara told Elsa.

Elsa just smiled. "I do," she stated. "Except when I don't."

Part 39
Turkey Talk

Their night of Salsa dancing and socializing over, Carol-Barbara had driven the route home between Charlottesville and Dogwood County. Her margarita buzz had long since expired. Carl had snored loudly all the way home in the passenger seat beside her. While he did, she pondered the strange events of the evening. She had learned that Elsa was romantically involved with an FBI agent, and was now his side-kick in the hunt for a South American drug Queen.

So, Elsa did have a life of her own, separate from the controlling clutches of her sister, Debbie. Good for her, Carol-Barbara thought. Yet, how was it that Elsa could have this secret life, full of adventures, and no one know a thing about it? It was always the quiet ones, wasn't it, who ended up having the most to hide.

Of course, Martha had her secrets. Carol-Barbara always knew that, but that was just Martha, and had everything to do with her former career in Washington, D.C. Then there was Honey, who had moved to the area as one big secret she was trying to unravel. What about her other friends, she wondered. Did they have secrets, too?

If demure Elsa had been living a life worthy of a movie plot, what might some of her other kindred spirits be doing behind everyone's backs. Obviously there were things happening behind the scenes in Dogwood County.

Now, there was likely a connection to a South American drug cartel nearby. Was it possible all of these things had been going on right under Carol-Barbara's nose all these years and she had just been too involved in her plain Jane life to see it? Not anymore, though. She was part of what was going on, and as candidate for county manager, she had better get to the bottom of things before all hell completely broke loose, if it hadn't already.

The election was coming up fast. Soon the voters would be going to the polls to decide who the best candidate would be. First, though, Carol-Barbara had to make it through the holidays. Thanksgiving was coming up in less than a week, and Christmas would be here before she knew it.

Maybe, she thought, she would do things a little differently this year for Thanksgiving. With everything going on she'd scarcely prepared and frozen half the food she needed. Why, oh why had she been so stubborn? She should have passed on the Thanksgiving preparations to Brook already. What had she been thinking?

Maybe she would just pare down the meal so that she didn't have to work quite so hard. She had not anticipated how busy she would be. Certainly the kids would understand if she made that decision this year. Maybe she could even convince them to go out for Thanksgiving. They'd never done that before, and that would mean no cooking, as well as no cleaning up afterwards. What a treat that would be.

Home now after the long drive, and with Carl tucked into bed next to her, snoring gently, she picked up her cell phone and dialed her daughter's number. Lauren was a night owl, and would likely be up writing or watching television. The phone rang.

"Hi, mom. What are you doing up so late?" The voice on the other end was lively. She definitely hadn't been asleep.

"Hey, sweetie. I had a thought to run by you," Carol-Barbara got right to it.

"Shoot," said Lauren.

"I'm thinking this year we should pare down Thanksgiving. You know, cut back a bit, what with your Dad being on a strict diet, and everything else that's going on with my election. Maybe we could even go out this year, let somebody else worry about the cooking and cleaning," Carol-Barbara tried to sell it.

"Mom, are you joking?" Lauren didn't sound on board with the idea.

Carol-Barbara hesitated before answering. "Well, sure, it might be fun, a little more relaxed than years past. We might be able to talk more rather than work so much." The words coming out of her mouth sounded convincing to her, but didn't do the trick.

"No, Mom! Stop it. You cannot be serious. Everyone looks forward to your cooking. And we all chip in with the cleaning. Why would you do that to us?" Lauren was upset.

"I just thought…" She trailed off. "Never mind. Obviously it means a lot to you, and if it means a lot to you, then it means a lot to me, too. Forget I even mentioned it." She paused. "Will Tim be coming with you this year?" She was referring to Lauren's longtime boyfriend.

"Well, of course. That's okay, right? Or are you paring down the guest list as well?" Lauren questioned.

"Of course I'm not paring down the guest list! Don't get smart with me. Please, bring him! I'll be insulted if you don't." Carol-Barbara meant what she said.

"OK, if you're sure. Look, I have some writing to do before I hit the hay tonight. Did you have any more hair-brained ideas you wanted to run by me before I go?" Lauren joked.

"No, no. No more ideas. And do me a favor. Don't ever mention this to your brother. I have a feeling he will lay into me, too," she joked.

"My lips are sealed, Mom. I love you. Bye."

"Thanks, love you, too," Carol-Barbara hung up and let out a loud sigh.

"Not going for it, is she," said a sleepy voice next to her. Carl had awakened to hear the whole thing.

"Heck, no! I don't know how I'm going to get it all done," Carol-Barbara shook her head.

"I'll help you," Carl offered.

"Yeah, right. Your idea of helping is sampling everything as I cook," she smiled at him.

"I mean it. I'll help cook this year. Anything you need me to do." Carl was genuine. "Hey I have an idea. Invite Elsa and her man over for Thanksgiving. I'm sure Elsa would love to help you prepare, and I'm sure she would accept any offer that would get her away from her sister."

"You think she'd come? Even though she wants to keep things on the lowdown with him?" Carol-Barbara questioned.

"I think we can keep it quiet. Sure. I think she'll come," he urged her. "And you can find out more about Senorita Ruiz, as well!"

Carol-Barbara had to admit, it sounded like a great idea. She would call Elsa tomorrow and ask.

"You know, I can always count on you," she snuggled into Carl's arm to go to sleep.

"That's why you married me," he assured her.

The next day Carol-Barbara called Elsa bright and early. Elsa answered after one ring and sounded chipper. Apparently she was still happy after the night with her guy.

"Hi there, CB," she greeted her. "What's up?"

"Got any plans for Thanksgiving yet?" Carol-Barbara got right to the point.

"I suppose I'm expected at my sister's," Elsa sighed, suddenly not sounding very happy anymore.

"How would you like an excuse to get out of it? Bring Robert and come have Thanksgiving with us."

"Really?" Elsa sounded surprised. "Oh, I don't know. I'm afraid Debbie will find out, and I really don't want her to ruin things for me and Robert."

"I promise, you can count on us to keep it quiet. We'll pull the blinds if we have to, unplug the phones, and park Bubba outside to bark in case anyone shows up. Come on, you can do this. It will be so much more enjoyable than spending the evening with Debbie." Carol-Barbara urged."

"I can't argue that," Elsa laughed.

"Would it help if I told you I could really use your help? With the cooking I mean."

"You, CB? You're an excellent cook. You don't need me," Elsa reminded her.

"No," Carol-Barbara admitted, "I can manage, but it would be a heck of a lot more fun to have you there. And you can tell me all about how you met Robert, and more about Senorita Ruiz, too!"

"Oh, I can't tell you any more than Robert told you last night. I've been sworn to secrecy. You'll have to ask him," Elsa informed her.

"So does that mean you'll come? And to help the morning of, too? The guys can watch football while we cook," Carol-Barbara tried to sound so excited that Elsa couldn't say no.

"OK, we'll come. I'll make up some excuse to Debbie, but remember, not a word to her, right?" Elsa reminded her.

"I, too, am sworn to secrecy, my friend!" Carol-Barbara set her mind at ease.

Part 40

Stuff It

Thanksgiving morning arrived like any other morning, with Carol-Barbara Hoofnagle hitting the ground running.

She had so much to do on this Thanksgiving morn. The pies she had managed to bake and freeze a few weeks ago had been defrosted and were on the counter. Carl had purchased a turkey a few days ago after his shift at the All-Mart. The bird now sat fully defrosted in the refrigerator, ready to be roasted.

Carol-Barbara checked the clock. It was 5 a.m. Elsa was due to arrive at about eight to help with preparations. Elsa's friend Robert would be coming later, as he would be mainly there to keep Carl company and to watch football, and the games were still hours away. The rest of the Hoofnagle family wouldn't be showing up until around noon. Their son, Adam, and his wife Brook, would be driving from Roanoke with their brood. Their daughter Lauren and her beau, Tim, would show up from northern Virginia around that time as well.

Carol-Barbara put the coffee on to percolate, and didn't even go outside to retrieve the newspaper. She did glance outside to see if it would be waiting for her when she could take a break, but she didn't see it. Probably late due to the Black Friday advertisements that had to be stuffed into each bag., but there was something else at the end of the driveway she couldn't ignore. It was her neighbor, Honey, walking up and down the street looking as though she had been crying. Their eyes met, and Carol-Barbara gave a hesitant wave.

"Everything ok?" She asked Honey.

"Not really. " Honey replied.

Carol-Barbara knew she would probably regret it, with everything she had to do this morning, but she walked out to the street in her robe and slippers to talk to Honey.

"What's wrong?" Would she really want to hear the answer to this question, she wondered?

"It's just that it's Thanksgiving, and Roland and I have nothing planned. We don't have any family we can share this special day with, and we didn't even make a reservation at one of the restaurants in town. Now everything is booked up. I'll be lucky if I can find anything left at the grocery store to cook." Honey wiped tears from her eyes.

Instantly, Carol-Barbara felt as if someone else were in control of her thoughts and actions. She had a feeling she would hate herself for what she was about to do, but she couldn't help it. She could hear the words being said, but it was as if someone else was saying them. She had been possessed by the Thanksgiving spirit.

"Come join us for Thanksgiving." Oh, dear Lord, please let that have been my inner voice, she thought, but she could tell by Honey's reaction that the words had actually gone from her lips to Honey's ears.

"Yes! We would love to! Oh, thank you, Carol-Barbara!" Honey hugged her affectionately. "Is there anything I can do to help you get ready? I'm really good with stuffing!"

And that is how it was that Honey was enjoying a cup of coffee at Carol-Barbara's kitchen table when Elsa arrived.

The three women quickly got to chopping, mixing and baking side by side. Carol-Barbara was actually surprised by how well they all worked together. Things were getting done faster than she ever could have imagined.

By the time the guys gathered in the den for pre-gaming and beer, she actually felt pretty confident that things were going to go off just fine today. She even allowed herself to relax for a moment and get excited about the arrival of her children and granddaughter.

She considered that with the extra guests it wouldn't be one of her traditional Thanksgiving dinners. But, as the Indians and Pilgrims came together and shared a meal, thankful for their union, so would Carol-Barbara be thankful for all she had been given; her family, friends, and yes, even Honey, who could stuff a turkey like nobody's business.

Part 41

Giving Thanks

Honey had superbly stuffed the turkey and it was now basking in the 350 degree heat of Carol-Barbara's Kenmore oven, which had been installed when the house was built fifty years before. Carl was of the "if it ain't broke, don't fix it," mindset, and so the appliance, which seemed to be indestructible, remained.

Carol-Barbara joked with Honey and Elsa that the stainless steel double oven would still be standing when, and if, Dixon got his wish and knocked the houses in the area down to build his super mall.

"Hey, hey. No talk of Dixon today, please," Honey begged her, as she washed the raw turkey juice and stuffing from her hands.

Carol-Barbara promised she wouldn't mention his name any more, and instead questioned Honey about the way she was cooking the turkey. Honey had instructed Carol-Barbara not to open the oven for any reason for the next three and a half hours, but Carol-Barbara did not understand this method. Shouldn't a turkey be waited on hand and foot? Watched like a hawk? Or rather, like a turkey? Shouldn't it at least be checked on every now and again?

"Just trust me, CB," Honey assured her. "Three and a half hours. You'll have a perfect turkey. People say don't stuff a turkey for germ reasons, I say BS. Just wait."

Honey's method had not been unlike Carol-Barbara's up until she stuck it in the oven. She had stuffed the winged wonder with a homemade dressing of breadcrumbs, celery and spices, not unlike any other homemade dressing. Then she had slathered it with butter and salt and placed it on the roasting rack; again, not different from Carol-Barbara's own way. What was different was that Carol-Barbara had always religiously basted the turkey every fifteen minutes as though it was her full-time job. Honey, on the other hand, said a turkey should be left alone once it was dressed. Less being more was her theory. Plus, she had placed the turkey in a paper bag before sticking it in the oven. Another thing Carol-Barbara had never seen anyone do.

Carol-Barbara had a hard time leaving the turkey alone. As the three women cooked and cleaned and got about the business of the Thanksgiving preparation, Honey had to keep reprimanding her for opening the oven to check on the bird. Honey swore that the more the turkey was basted the soggier it would get.

Could Honey be trusted? Carol-Barbara wondered. After all, the woman had been drinking wine since 10 o'clock that morning, and her turkey roasting techniques went against everything Carol-Barbara had ever learned about cooking fowl; but she wanted to enjoy her day, and, rather than argue with Honey she decided that if a not-cooked-to-perfection turkey was all that went wrong today, she would be a happy woman.

For her part, Elsa had made two pies already and was working on a third. Though it was not her favorite, for tradition's sake, and because Carl had insisted, she made a pumpkin pie first. There were so many more interesting flavors than pumpkin for a pie. She didn't have anything against pumpkin mind you (she used it in soups and bread) but for pie she considered it just plain bland. So she also made a maple squash pie, and a coconut praline pie.

"Don't knock it 'til you've tried it," she told Carl when he snuck a peek into the kitchen in between football games. He and Elsa's friend Robert, as well as Honey's husband, Roland, had been watching football on TV in the den.

Carl, Roland and Robert had become fast friends. Before Robert arrived, Carl had told Roland he was going to ask Robert about his work as an FBI agent, perhaps try to garner some more information about what, and who, he was investigating, like Josefina Estanga Torres Ruiz. Roland shrugged when Carl told him of his plans. He could have cared less, as he had enough drama in his life living with Honey.

The truth was, Carl didn't want to talk about such serious subjects on Thanksgiving, either, and he quickly realized that neither he nor Robert cared too much for idle chit chat. Instead, the three men enjoyed staring at the TV and audibly showed their joy or disappointment in the outcome of the football plays with almost primitive noises.

From the kitchen the ladies could hear an "Ahh!" when the men were happy with a play, and an "Ugg" when they didn't approve of whatever had just happened. The men "Ahhed" and "Ugged" and sipped beer and laughed out loud at the commercials in between football plays. They seemed to genuinely feel comfortable with one another.

At about 3:00, the kids showed up, one right after the other. It was wonderful to see them. With Elsa there it had been even more special for the kids because they recalled when she had been their much-loved babysitter.

First to arrive had been their daughter, Lauren, with her longtime boyfriend, Tim. They brought with them gifts they had gotten her parents on their recent trip to Peru; a handmade wool sweater for Carl and a beautiful multi-colored scarf for Carol-Barbara.

"Handmade by real Inca women," Lauren informed her.

Then, their son, Adam, arrived with his wife, Brooke, and their daughter. It was beyond wonderful for Carol-Barbara to see her only grandchild. Even though it had only been a couple of months since she'd seen her. She seemed to have grown by leaps and bounds. The baby, Carly, named after her paternal grandparents, was now smiling and laughing at everyone from the comfort of her carrier. The last time Carol-Barbara had seen her she was much less aware of her surroundings.

"She's crawling now, too," Brooke told them. "Wait until you see." Brooke took the baby from her carrier and placed her on the ground. She promptly started to scoot around the room.

"Amazing!" Carl exclaimed. "Look how fast she is! She'll be a track star yet! Come to Poppy!" He scooped her up in his arms.

"Hey, Nana wants some of that, too," Carol-Barbara tickled Carly's chin.

"Can I tell them?" Brooke turned to her husband, Adam.

"Go ahead," Adam encouraged her.

"We're pregnant again," she told them.

"So soon?" Carol-Barbara exclaimed, as she hugged her daughter-in-law. "Is that okay?"

"The doctor says it's fine," she assured them. "If it's a boy we'll name him, Oliver Jackson, after my dad," she divulged.

"Oliver Jackson Hoofnagle, huh?" Carl stated. "It's got a certain ring to it." Brooke's dad had died years earlier, and he thought it was nice they would pay homage.

The group talked and laughed, watched football, took turns watching Carly run and crawl and play. Finally the turkey was ready. It was time to sit down to the meal.

As she sampled it in the kitchen before serving, Carol-Barbara had to admit it was the best turkey she had ever had, moist on the inside and with the crispiest, most delicious skin.

"I hate to say I told you so," Honey joked.

They sat down to dinner and toasted each other. They went round the table stating what they were each thankful for. Carol-Barbara went last.

"It may sound cliché," she started, "But I am thankful for my family, for my friends, and for the best turkey I think I've ever laid eyes on."

Carl began carving the turkey, and as he did there was an unexpected knock at the front door.

"Who would be showing up on Thanksgiving afternoon?" Carol-Barbara questioned.

"I'll get it," Honey stood up. "You all sit tight." She took her wine glass with her.

Honey went to the door, not knowing what to expect when she opened it.

There stood a young woman, just a few years younger than Carl and Carol-Barbara's children.

"Happy Thanksgiving!" Honey announced to the girl. She'd already had too much wine while cooking, and, to her, it seemed like a very happy Thanksgiving indeed.

"Hello. I'm sorry to bother you, but is Elsa here?" The girl asked.

"Yes, can I tell her who is asking?" Honey wasn't slurring her words, by any means, but she' had enough wine that she swayed a bit. She grabbed the door to steady herself as she stood and waited for an answer.

"Maybe I've made a mistake coming here," the girl said. She backed away from the door a bit.

Just then Carol-Barbara came to the door to see who it was that had been knocking. At first she didn't recognize the girl, but she quickly realized it was the young woman who had been with Dixon weeks before at the ice cream shop. She was shocked.

"Can I help you?" Carol-Barbara asked.

"I need to see Elsa, please," the girl pleaded.

"Ok, can I tell her who-," Carol-Barbara nearly finished repeating the same question Honey had asked, but was interrupted by Elsa stepping into the foyer.

The girl saw Elsa, and broke into tears.

"Ashleigh, what are you doing here?" It was clear Elsa knew the girl, but was beyond surprised to see her.

"I couldn't stay away any longer. I'm sorry. I need you!" The girl ran to Elsa, who embraced her.

After what seemed an eternity with Honey and Carol-Barbara staring at the two women, Elsa pulled back and held the girl at arms' length, taking her by the hands.

"You know you shouldn't be here," Elsa advised her. "What if Debbie finds out?"

"What does it matter? I'm a grown woman now." The girl cried.

"Elsa, is everything ok? Should we leave?" Carol-Barbara felt awkward, as if she and Honey shouldn't be there.

Elsa turned to them, never letting go of the girl's hands. "No, no. Don't leave. I want you all to meet someone." She turned back to the girl. "Carol-Barbara, Honey," she paused. "This is my daughter, Ashleigh."

Part 42

Truth Be Told

The women sat together in the formal living room of Carol-Barbara's house. Elsa and Ashleigh huddled on the couch together, while Carol-Barbara sat bolt upright in a chair. It was just the three of them now since Honey had tactfully made her way out of the room.

It wasn't that Honey didn't care. However, she didn't really know Elsa's history, save for what she had seen with her own eyes over the past couple of months. Even with the little she had seen, she could confirm a couple of things for sure. One, Elsa and her sister, Debbie, didn't seem to get along, and two, Elsa was hiding some pretty deep emotions. She didn't think she belonged.

Judging from the looks of it, Elsa's deep, dark secret had just showed up at the Hoofnagle's front door. Lucky girl, Honey thought. It was hard keeping secrets, and she oughta know. So, seeing the very private and liberating moment that was about to occur in the living room, Honey had decided her presence would be better appreciated if she hung out in the den with the guys watching football. Besides, the guys had beer, and she loved beer.

Now that Honey was gone and it was just the three of them ready to talk, Carol-Barbara tried to wrap her head around what she had just learned. Elsa had a daughter, and it was the very same girl that she had seen with Dixon at the ice cream shop.

How could it be that Elsa had a grown daughter and she didn't know about her? Furthermore, Dogwood County was small; how was it the entire area was in the dark about Ashleigh? Carol-Barbara had so many questions. Where was Ashleigh when her own kids were little? Who raised Ashleigh? What was she doing here now? How long had Elsa known she was in town? And most importantly, how did Dixon play into this?

Finally, Carol-Barbara decided to break the silence and just ask. "Elsa, forgive me for looking so shocked, but how is it I didn't know about Ashleigh?

"I know I have a lot of explaining to do." Elsa seemed sheepish, yet also proud, and she held her daughter's hand tightly, as if she had waited so long to get this secret out, and to be able to freely show her affection.

"I don't mean to pry, but it's just-," Carol-Barbara desperately wanted an explanation.

Elsa interrupted her. "No, you aren't prying. You deserve an explanation. First of all, it's your house we're sitting in; your Thanksgiving we are completely ruining."

Now Carol-Barbara stopped Elsa. "Let's get something straight. You're not ruining anything. This is important."

Elsa continued. "Thanks, CB. You have been there for me more than anyone in my own family over the years. You've never asked me to be anyone but who I am, unlike my sister," she paused. "I want to tell you everything, but please could I bother you for a glass of water first? I suddenly feel parched."

"Of course. Can I get you anything, Ashleigh?" Carol-Barbara stood from the wingback chair she was seated in.

"I'll have some water, too. Thanks." Ashleigh spoke softly, just like her mother.

"Back in a jiffy." Carol-Barbara left the room and headed towards the kitchen. Carl was standing in the kitchen peeking under the lid into a dish of deviled eggs. He had every intention of snagging one when Carol-Barbara walked in. He looked like a kid caught with his hand in the cookie jar.

Carl immediately jumped to his own defense. "I-I was just going to taste one, make sure it's alright before we feed them to the guests," he joked with her. The celebration had been put on hold for the time being.

"Not now, Carl. We have bigger fish to fry," Carol-Barbara snapped.

"What's wrong?" He asked her.

"You are not going to believe this," Carol-Barbara began as she retrieved three glasses from the cupboard.

"Is everything ok?" He was worried now. It wasn't like her to not want to immediately monitor what he was putting in his mouth, what with his blood-sugar and all.

"Remember the girl we saw with Dixon in the ice-cream shop?" She reminded him.

"Of course I do," he answered.

"Well, she just showed up at the front door," she told him.

"Here? Why?" Carl couldn't imagine what could have brought that particular young woman to their house.

"She's Elsa's daughter," Carol-Barbara stated matter-of-factly.

"What? Elsa doesn't have a daughter," Carl pointed out.

"Carl, she does. Elsa just confirmed it." She tried to make him understand.

Carl was full of questions. "How? When? Why?"

"And who? What? And where?" Carol-Barbara added. "I don't know the answers to any of those questions yet, but I'm going back in there to find out."

"This just couldn't be," Carl said. "There has to be a mistake. And anyway, the kid working at the ice cream shop said the girl was Dixon's daughter, so how could she be Elsa's daughter, too?" He naively questioned.

"If we have to have that talk about how that happens at this stage in our lives, then I'm not sure how we got those kids we have of our own in there, or our grandkids, for that matter" she teased him. "It takes two to make a child." She paused for effect, but the obvious was so far from anything that Carl could have ever imagined that he still didn't get what she was saying.

"I don't get it," he admitted, eyeing the deviled eggs again.

"Do I have to spell it out for you? I believe Dixon may be the girl's father and Elsa her mother." She finally told him.

"But that would mean," he paused. "No, they couldn't have. Dixon is married to Debbie!"

"And lots of people are married to lots of other people and have children by still different people. Remember, Carl, you don't get pregnant by putting a ring on!" she advised him as she filled the three glasses with water. She took a giant swig out of one of the glasses and turned to head back towards the living room.

"Let me know how it turns out," he called after her. "I'll hold the fort down!"

Back in the living room, Elsa and Ashleigh had clearly been deep in conversation when Carol-Barbara re-entered with the water. They stopped talking as she came in. She handed them each a glass and returned to her seat. They sipped their water in silence and then finally Elsa spoke up.

"Where to start?" She paused again. "I guess it's best to just say it, get it out." She looked at Ashleigh for approval.

"It's ok. Go ahead," Ashleigh encouraged her. "Aunt Debbie can't hurt us anymore, or keep us apart."

Elsa nodded and began, "So you know my sister and Dixon don't have any children together, right?"

Carol-Barbara nodded.

"Do you know why?" Elsa prodded.

Carol-Barbara was anything but tactful when she spoke, telling it the way she had always seen it. "I guess they have always struck me as rather self-centered people that just didn't have time for little ones."

"Well, it wasn't exactly that way at the beginning," Elsa informed her. "But it does seem to have turned out that way." She explained. "See, Debbie found out a few years into their marriage that she couldn't have children, and even though Dixon really wanted children, he accepted the situation. He did suggest adopting to Debbie, but that was out of the question. Lord knows, Debbie is just too self-involved and narcissistic to raise someone else's child. She decided that if she couldn't have one of her own, then she didn't want any. But the thing was, Dixon still wanted a child so bad. Well, one night he and Debbie had a huge fight about it. He came to me to talk. He used to do that from time to time. He always told me I was a good listener, and that he wished he could talk to Debbie like he talked to me. That particular night he had brought a bottle of bourbon with him. We sat at my kitchen table and drank it, chased it with sweet tea I'd made earlier. We were both rather tipsy when he told me he thought maybe he had married the wrong sister. As you can imagine, I was taken aback. I almost slapped him, but then, well, I don't know if it was the bourbon or the full moon or what, but I suddenly wanted this man so bad. I threw myself at him. We ended up making love, and Ashleigh is the result of that night."

She paused and looked at Ashleigh. "Sounds like she was a mistake when I tell it, but she's the best mistake I ever made," she smiled. Ashleigh smiled back, clearly at peace with the circumstances of her conception.

Carol-Barbara spoke. "Does Debbie know?"

Elsa shook her head no and continued. "How could I tell her I had slept with her husband? She would have killed me. When I found out I was pregnant, I told Debbie I had a one night stand and got pregnant. She hated me anyway for it; for the fact that I could get pregnant so easily and she couldn't. She's treated me badly ever since, told me I was a shame to the family, that if anyone ever found out I had an illegitimate child it would ruin all of us. That I was weak, and that I was." She paused trying to hold back tears. "And that I was a whore. She convinced me of that. So I went to stay with our cousin, Betsy, in Alabama. Her kids were teenagers by then. After Ashleigh was born, Betsy agreed to raise her. I knew Debbie would never go there because she hated Betsy, thought she was too country and way beneath her, so I knew Ashleigh could grow up without feeling Debbie's hatred. Betsy and I agreed that Ashleigh would grow up knowing she was adopted, and I went to visit often when she was little, but it nearly killed me to leave her, so I stopped going. I was so worried I was going to do something to ruin Ashleigh's chance at a normal life." She stopped talking.

"That must have been hard," Carol-Barbara couldn't imagine the pain Elsa must have felt. "How is it that Dixon knows about Ashleigh then?"

Elsa continued. "One night Dixon came over to "talk" again, and I knew how much it would mean to him to know he had fathered a child. So I told him about her. I made him promise he wouldn't try to meet her until she was at least out of college. He kept his word, probably because by then he knew what having a child out of wedlock would mean for his political aspirations, but suddenly Ashleigh was going to the best private school in Alabama. He was sending money to Betsy to help, and he even paid for college for Ashleigh, too, and graduate school. Then, a few months ago he decided he wanted to meet her, and she him. So he rented her a little house on the outskirts of town and she came up here. The rest is history."

"So Debbie still has no idea that Ashleigh is Dixon's child?" Carol-Barbara questioned.

Elsa and Ashleigh both shook their heads. "I don't think so," Elsa said.

Ashleigh spoke up. "I have so enjoyed seeing my mother. And seeing why it never would have worked out with my biological father. He's glad I exist, don't get me wrong, but he's a hot mess."

What a perfect description of Dixon St. James, Carol-Barbara thought to herself.

So, she thought, now she knew why Debbie treated Elsa so badly. Elsa had been given a gift Debbie never had, and she had convinced Elsa to hide that gift away, that she would only bring shame to her and the family. Poor Elsa! All those years without her daughter! Carol-Barbara couldn't imagine not knowing her own children like the back of her hand when they were growing up.

She suddenly remembered her own children and granddaughter were in the other room waiting for Thanksgiving to begin. They must be wondering what had happened to her, and Carl was probably running out of ways to keep them at bay.

Carol-Barbara made a split-second decision. "Ashleigh, do you want to join us for Thanksgiving?"

Ashleigh looked to Elsa for guidance. "Of course she does," Elsa patted her cheek. "I'll have a little explaining to do to Robert, so would you mind giving us a moment before we have dinner?"

"Of course not," Carol-Barbara said. "I'll go ask him to come in. Take as long as you need. We'll be in the dining room waiting for you."

Part 43

General Hoofnagle

It turned out to be one of the most meaningful Thanksgivings Carol-Barbara had ever had the pleasure of hosting. She was proud that she had been able to provide the venue for Elsa and her daughter, Ashleigh, to spend their first Thanksgiving together after so many years of separation.

Before dinner Elsa, with Ashleigh by her side, had cleared the air with her friend Robert in the living room, so as not to make a scene in front of the other guests.

Robert had been very understanding when Elsa told him of her big secret; how she and Dixon had ended up in a love tryst, her subsequent pregnancy, and how she had spent so many years in self-banishment from her beautiful daughter because she didn't want to ruin her chance at a normal life.

Robert held no grudges against Elsa, and as it turned out, he had fathered a child very young in life while unmarried. He had financially supported the child, and it hadn't been any secret that he was the boy's father, which made his situation very different from Elsa's. However, Robert told them he still had bad feelings about never having gotten to know his son very well. The boy was a man now, and lived clear across the country in California working as a computer software programmer. He was married and had children of his own. Once a year Robert got pictures of his grandchildren, but he had never met them in person.

"You know," Robert said to Elsa and Ashleigh, "You two have inspired me. I might just take a trip out to California soon, whether they like it or not."

"Oh, you should, Robert. You really should," Ashleigh replied. "I'm sure it would mean the world to them." Coming from Ashleigh, that meant a lot, and it made Robert really commit to the idea.

"Maybe Elsa will come along with me," he said, looking at her lovingly, and she smiled and nodded in approval. Afterwards, they had all joined the rest of the group for a delightful Thanksgiving meal.

During dinner, Elsa thought that even though Robert could identify somewhat with her situation of having a child out of wedlock, her circumstances were quite different from his. For one thing, the father of her child was her sister's husband, and that sister, the child's biological aunt, still didn't know the truth.

She also considered the fact that she was Ashleigh's mother, biologically, but technically she was her aunt, too, since Ashleigh's father was her sister's husband. And furthermore, if she considered the fact that her own cousin had raised Ashleigh, then that kind of made her a second cousin twice removed to her own daughter as well. The whole thing made her head spin, and the saying 'I am my own Grandpa' came to mind. Ah, well. Nothing to do but have another slice of brown sugar pie and a get over it.

After dinner, Honey and Roland excused themselves and went home; thanking the Hoofnagles for making them feel part of their family. Honey had, as usual, had a bit too much to drink, and could be heard singing Christmas carols across the front lawn as she headed back to her own house, while Roland walked behind her trying to keep her in a straight line.

Shortly after that, Carl and Carol-Barbara's son and his family headed for the basement where Carl had earlier set up several blow up mattresses on which they could all sleep. It had been a long day for them, and the baby was crying. Nothing but sleep would cure the poor girl.

Next, their daughter and her boyfriend retired to the guest room. Carol-Barbara never thought she would be okay with sending her daughter to bed with a man who was not yet her husband, but my how times had changed. It seemed to be what everyone was doing now, living out of wedlock. Besides, they were grown people, so who was she to say what they could or couldn't do.

That left Carl and Carol-Barbara sitting with Elsa, Robert and Ashleigh in the dining room. Carl suggested they retire to the living room where it was more comfortable. He offered everyone an after-dinner brandy, which he was only known to partake in once a year after the Thanksgiving meal. Robert was the only taker. The two men sat across from one another in the wing-back chairs, while the ladies all sat on the couch with mugs of coffee.

It became clear that Robert had something on his mind, and had stuck around for a reason.

He took a swig of his brandy. "I'd like to talk about Dixon St. James for a moment, if I could." It

272

was as though he were asking permission, knowing it was a touchy subject. He continued. "Under the circumstances, I feel there is something I should tell you all." Robert was serious.

Assuming he was referring to the fact that Dixon had fathered her child, Elsa encouraged him. "Of course," she said. "I know my news has been quite a shock."

"I appreciate that, Elsa," he reached over and patted her hand. "And while the ramifications of your past relationship with Dixon is of utmost concern to me, there is actually something else I need you all to be aware of. " He paused. "See, I am in a very difficult predicament here. In fact, the saying 'I could tell you, but then I'd have to kill you' comes to mind."

The room was silent for a moment while the others tried to figure out if this was an actual threat. Not knowing Robert very well yet, they weren't sure what to make of his comment.

"I'm kidding." Robert quickly tried to set their minds at ease. "Sorry, dry sense of humor."

There was a collective sigh of relief in the room.

"However, I am in a sticky situation," he admitted. "Elsa, you know how I continue to do work for the FBI."

"Yes, of course." she stated.

"The thing is, I have had Dixon under surveillance for some time. In fact do you all recall the woman I pointed out when we were at the Salsa club? Josefina Estanga Torres Ruiz? "

"How could I forget?" Carol-Barbara assured him.

"The thing is Dixon St. James' name has come up too many times for comfort in connection with her. As a matter of fact, I think she may be funding some of his ventures."

Carl piped in. "Don't get me wrong. Dixon is a real jerk. He's the kind of guy who would buy a vote, or pay a lawyer to find a way out of an air-tight contract; and he certainly is trying to screw the people in our neighborhood with that whole mega mall idea," He paused, "But in cahoots with a drug cartel? I just can't imagine it."

"I'm telling you Carl, I have my reasons to believe he got involved with her, and is now in over his head." Robert added.

"Do you think that's who shot him?" Carol-Barbara asked.

"That's a possibility I am exploring," he explained. "Listen, I could get in real trouble for talking about this, and I wouldn't even tell you about it except for the fact that I really care for you all, and with Carol-Barbara running against him in this election, well I'd just like you all to know who you might be getting involved with."

He paused and turned to Elsa. "And, it goes without saying that I think very highly of Miss Elsa here." He reached for her hand and she smiled. "I don't want her, or her lovely daughter, to suffer because of what this man might be involved in. And I need to let you all know it could get ugly."

"I can't believe he would knowingly be involved in something like that, but who am I to say," Ashleigh told him. "Whatever you have to do, I understand."

"Thank you," Robert told her.

Much as Carol-Barbara cared about Elsa and Ashleigh's plight with Dixon, she had her own battle to wage with him; and it was coming up faster than she cared to believe. Right after the holidays the special election would be held, and she now realized she had given far too little consideration to her bid for county manager.

Unfortunately, some of her Christmas traditions would have to take a back seat this year; no volunteering to get the church Christmas pageant up to speed, no ringing the bell for donations to the Salvation Army. She would be gathering her own army, composed of the NAKED ladies, and she would serve as their fearless leader. Her spirit had been rekindled, and as far as she was concerned, this meant war. If she could pull off winning the election, she would be giving Dogwood County the biggest present it could receive. Yes, Virginia, there is a Santa clause, and her name is Carol-Barbara Hoofnagle.

Part 44

Puzzle Pieces

Getting shot had turned Dixon's life upside down. He had been released from the hospital several days before Thanksgiving. The bullet was still lodged in his rear-side, and would be for the rest of his life. To remove it would have been too risky, as it was located right near some organs he desperately wanted to keep, namely right behind his testicles near the base of his spine. He had been warned by the medical staff that any extraction might cause him decreased sensation in that area, or paralysis. His doctor, whom he trusted, had told him that lots of people walk around with bullets lodged in their bodies. He had explained that scar tissue would just build up around it.

"Just come see me for a doctor's note before you travel on a plane so they'll know why you're setting off the metal detector," the doctor had said with a laugh. Dixon didn't think that was so funny.

So now he was home, his bullet wound healing nicely, but still there was no word on who may have shot him. This fact made him feel jumpy. He hadn't left the house since Debbie and one of the deputy sheriffs, there for security reasons, had escorted him from the car and settled him into his den, where he had been watching TV almost non-stop. He was bored, and becoming more depressed with every passing day.

He had been doing a lot of thinking. He thought about how one of the worst things about all of this getting shot mess was that he couldn't even exercise his stress away, as he was accustomed to doing. Going outside for a run right now seemed akin to putting a sign on his back that read "Close only counts in horseshoes and hand grenades! Here I am! Free second chance!"

Besides, even if he had the nerve to go running, his backside hurt too much to actually follow through with it. His doctor told him it would be weeks before he was back to normal. His only exercise had become lifting his hand from the cookie box to his mouth. At this rate, his muscles would have turned to mush by then. He could feel his six pack was more of a four already.

He also wondered for a split second if all this would affect his chances at re-election, but he was still Dixon St. James after all, and as far as he was concerned his job was not in jeopardy. Bullet or no bullet, in his mind Carol-Barbara Hoofnagle didn't have a chance at taking the title.

Mainly, though, he thought about his daughter, Ashleigh. Was she still in town? Had she gone to see her mother, Elsa? He thought about how Debbie still didn't know that he was Ashleigh's father. For so many years he and Elsa had kept the secret. He had to admit it was wearing him down.

Though Debbie knew nothing of Ashleigh's paternity, only that her sister Elsa had her out of wedlock, Dixon dreamed that someday they would be able to tell her the whole story; that perhaps so much time might have passed that how Ashleigh came to be wouldn't matter anymore. Ashleigh was such a lovely person. If only Debbie would listen to their story with reason and an open mind, perhaps she might be able to forgive her sister and him for sleeping together. Maybe then, Debbie could accept Ashleigh into her life.

Thanksgiving came and went. For the big day he and Debbie normally went out to a nice dinner at the Dogwood County Country Club with a group of friends. They usually stuffed themselves silly and then finished the night in the club bar laughing, drinking fine port wine.

This year, though, Dixon had asked Debbie to call their group of friends and cancel. He asked her to tell them he still wasn't feeling up to par. She did as he asked, but the truth was he probably could have made it to dinner. The real reason he didn't want to go was that he was still afraid to put himself out there as a potential target until the police knew more about who might have shot him.

Debbie wasn't much on baking, and had never hosted a Thanksgiving dinner of her own. Plus, most of her time recently had been spent either at the hospital or fielding calls from the media, who wanted more information about the shooting. So instead of the country club, at about three o'clock on Thanksgiving Day Debbie went to pick up Chinese food and bring it home for them. Dixon got cashew chicken and she got pork fried rice. For dessert they ate Marie Callendar's brand pecan pie with vanilla ice cream. Afterwards they opened their fortune cookies and read them aloud.

"You first," Debbie suggested.

Dixon reluctantly opened his cookie and held the slip of paper up to read. "You will live a long and healthy life." Yeah, right. He thought. Not with some potential killer out there after me.

"Now mine," Debbie began, clearing her throat. "There are big changes ahead for you," she read. "What the heck does that mean?"

"You know you can't trust these things," Dixon pointed out. "Look at me, I've got a bullet lodged in my ass and mine said I would live a long healthy life."

Debbie shrugged and cleaned up the dinner mess. Later they watched television highlights of the day's football games until Debbie got tired and went to bed. Dixon slept in his recliner that night, with one eye opened.

Several days later, he didn't know which day, as they were all running together now, Debbie had come home with several boxes of puzzles to help occupy his time. Did she really not know, after all these years, how much he detested putting puzzles together? The desire to not feel bored won out, though, and so he began working on one of them. He had been looking for the same piece for about thirty straight minutes. This is what he was doing when the noon television news came on. He was surprised to hear the newscaster say the following words:

"Much like millions of Dallas fans asked decades ago, *Who shot J.R?* The question around Dogwood County is *Who shot Dixon St. James*"

Dixon couldn't believe his ears. According to the news report, some people in the community were worried, and wondered if there was a killer on the loose. The newscaster did his best to get the people he interviewed all riled up and worried, but the general consensus seemed to be that the shooting was personal. One guy being interviewed even went so far as to tell the news man that he thought for sure that Dixon deserved it because he was "one of those damned politicians." Thanks guy, thanks a lot, Dixon thought.

What the newscaster and the others didn't know was that the police weren't worried at all for the rest of the community. They knew something that no one else in the county knew. Something they hadn't divulged yet because they didn't want to ruin the ongoing investigation.

The police had not even told Dixon this fact yet, but that was about to change. Deputy Sheriff Ron Johnson was about to make a visit to the St. James home to ask some questions. He rang the doorbell and Debbie answered.

"Mrs. St. James." He removed his hat and tipped it to her.

"Hello, deputy." Debbie recognized him as the man who had escorted Dixon home from the hospital, but she couldn't remember his name.

"Deputy Johnson," he reminded her. "Mind if I come in and talk to your husband?"

"No, not at all," Debbie led him in the house and down the hall. Before opening the door to the den and announcing him to Dixon, she asked the deputy a question. "Have there been any new leads since we last spoke?"

"Yes, ma'am, there have. That's what I am here to talk to your husband about," he told her.

"I see," she said, then paused, hand on the doorknob, but not turning it at all. It was an awkward pause, as though she were thinking about something. Then, she spoke again, "He's very delicate right now, you know."

"Yes, ma'am. I understand, but if you don't mind I really do need to speak with him," he urged her.

"Of course. Forgive me. I'm just so worried about him," she offered.

"Understandable ma'am, very understandable under the circumstances." Deputy Johnson waited for her to turn the doorknob.

"Well, in you go then," Debbie said as she opened the door. "Dixon, Deputy Johnson is here to talk to you."

Dixon looked up from the puzzle he was reluctantly working on. He started to stand up to shake hands, but his injury hurt, and the deputy urged him to sit back down. "Hey there, Ron," he said. The two men had known each other for years on a work level, and they were casual with one another.

"I'll just leave you two alone, then," Debbie closed the door behind them, but she didn't leave. Instead, she put her ear up to the door, trying to hear every word that was said.

Deputy Johnson sat down on the sofa. "I see you're working on a puzzle. Wish I had more free time. I love those things."

"Yeah? Well, I'll trade you places. I hate 'em. Debbie thinks I need to keep my mind active, though." Dixon pushed the puzzle away from him.

"I'll get right to the point, Dixon," the deputy said. "When you were in the hospital we had your car towed down to the station to give it a going-over, since the shooting happened so close to your vehicle. And well, we found something."

"Oh yeah, what?" Dixon asked.

"A tracking device was located on the underside of your car. Would you know anything about that?"

"A tracking device? No. I don't know anything about it. What does that mean?" Dixon was worried.

"It means that whoever shot you may have been following you for some time, and knew exactly where you would be that night," Deputy Johnson explained. "And there's something else," he paused. "We also located bullet holes."

Dixon had a concerned look on his face. "Bullet *holes?*" He questioned. "As in more than one? I thought the only bullet hole was in my rear end." He shifted in his seat uncomfortably.

Deputy Johnson continued. "We found two more in the car. Let me ask you a question, Dixon. Did you hear anything hit the car that night? Before or after you got shot?"

"Well," Dixon started, after I got shot I was pretty much focused on the pain, and before, no, I don't think I heard anything," he hesitated. "What does this mean, Ron?"

"I'm not sure yet, but a detective I know is working on putting the pieces together, to try and figure out exactly what happened that night, and where the tracking device may have come from. We're hoping the information might lead us to your shooter. Anything else you might remember from that night would be very helpful."

Well, well, Dixon thought. He was sure behind doing anything that might help catch his attempted murderer, and give him some peace back.

Dixon glanced at the puzzle on the table and suddenly noticed something that he hadn't before. It was the piece of the puzzle he had been desperately looking for before the deputy had arrived. It had been right in front of him the whole time; he just hadn't seen it. He picked it up and gently put it in place. All of a sudden he felt motivated about his life again. "Ron," he said, pushing through the pain and standing up from his chair with a sense of strength and determination. "I'll help in any way I can."

Part 45

The Old and the Relatively Tranquil

The best part about running for office, Carol-Barbara thought, was that she got to be someone she usually wasn't for a while. Commanding, confident, and downright annoying, according to her friend, Martha, who was busy putting campaign buttons together while Carol-Barbara barked orders at the rest of the NAKED ladies who had aligned themselves in the Hoofnagle living room to help their friend with her campaign.

Carol-Barbara inspected one of the buttons. "We should have made them bigger, bigger I tell you!"

"Pipe down, Castro!" Martha teased her, likening her to the much maligned dictator.

Honey was busy at work on Carol-Barbara's laptop designing a poster to be used for the campaign. Much to Carol-Barbara's surprise she discovered that Honey was quite skilled on the computer, and very creative to boot.

Honey showed Carol-Barbara a feature on the All-Mart website that allowed users to upload photos and original artwork to design posters and other fliers. The best part about it was the one-day turnaround for orders. This was important, since they only had a couple of days until they planned on getting out into the county to hand out the materials and drum up support for the election.

Honey had helped Carol-Barbara come up with a slogan she hoped would be easy for people to remember.

Carol-Barbara Hoofnagle- I don't have to be a saint to keep Dogwood County Heavenly.

She thought it summed up what Carol-Barbara was trying to do for the county if elected to office, but also added some humor to the whole event. It also served to make a slight political dig at Dixon St. James; yet not so obviously that she would be accused of slandering him by his fan base, if he still had one.

Since it would be a special election held in January instead of the usual November hodgepodge of political mess, Christmas would be falling right in the middle of things. Even though Carol-Barbara had told Carl that she thought it would be a good idea to dumb things down this year as far as decorations, Carl had other ideas.

When Carol-Barbara mentioned to him that they would be minimalists this year, he had put his foot down. Why should a damper be put on the holidays just because she was running in the special election? So, while the women were in the living room preparing for the election, he was busy hauling the decorations out of their storage area above the garage.

Theirs was one of the houses that people counted on to be decorated to the max for the holidays. He didn't want to disappoint the local kids, and it seemed to him that during the campaign would be the best time to show people they were all about family and community, and not to give up their spot on the county's tacky lights tour. So, with that goal in mind, he decided, they would go even bigger this year.

Plastic Santas, light up reindeer, the entire cast of Charlie Brown's Christmas in blow up form, and everything else he had spent years collecting was dragged out of storage. Also more lovingly unpacked was the pièce de resistance, the life-size, created- to-scale nativity scene. He had obtained it in the most interesting of ways. Years before it had been incorrectly delivered to the only Jewish synagogue in Dogwood County. The synagogue had ordered a giant electric light up menorah, but someone had made a mistake in taking the order, and they were delivered the nativity scene instead. By the time the mistake was discovered, the company they ordered from had gone out of business.

Carl bought the nativity, for next to nothing, with the intention of donating it to their church. However, their church was famous for their live nativity, so they decided they didn't need it. Instead, it became the annual centerpiece of his display. With that as the cornerstone of their Christmas centerpiece, at least no one could ever say the Hoofnagles didn't know "the reason for the season."

Even though it was barely the first of December, and he still had plenty of time to set up, weather-wise it was a perfect day to get outside and get to work. After all, people would be out shopping already, driving around, visiting family for the holidays, and he wanted to brighten their days as they moved through all of the holiday rush.

He even thought about giving Carol-Barbara's campaign a plug amongst the holiday decor. Maybe he would put up some red, white and blue themed lights around one of her campaign yard signs. A little patriotism in the middle of the holy season never hurt anyone. He didn't think baby Jesus would mind sharing the stage. That got him thinking. He imagined that if baby Jesus had a campaign team like the one Carol-Barbara had inside, they may not have needed a guiding star. Instead people would have been wearing buttons that read "Vote for the son of God!" and holding signs that proclaimed "Baby Jesus- He'll save your eternal soul!" You couldn't get a much better campaign slogan than that. After all, who didn't want their eternal soul saved? And that wouldn't just be an empty election promise. Oh, how Carl's mind did wander sometimes.

"You've got my vote, baby Jesus," Carl said out loud as he walked out front to set up the manger scene.

While he was setting up the decorations, he saw Roland had come out of his house to put up a few of his own. His collection didn't appear to be anything like the one Carl was hauling out, nor were most people's for that matter, but since it was the Van Honk's first year in the neighborhood, he was glad to see there was some effort there to brighten up the yard.

Rather than brightening, though, at the moment it looked as though Roland were struggling with a string of lights that had tangled into a ball. Carl waved towards Roland, then decided to walk over to help the man.

"Looks like quite a mess, there, Roland. Can I lend you a hand?"

287

"I won't say no," Roland replied.

"Here," Carl crouched down on the ground. "Let's try to stretch it out a bit."

Just as he took one end of the lights from Roland, a car turned onto their street. It was a dark-colored car with all of the windows darkly tinted, way more heavily than was allowed by Virginia law, and it drove very slowly by. Too slowly, in Carl's opinion, as if the person inside were scoping things out in the neighborhood.

From Roland's perspective, the way he was crouched down next to the boxwood bush he was hoping to light up, he didn't notice the car, and the car wouldn't have been able to see him either. Carl, on the other hand, could see it perfectly.

"Somebody you know?" Carl asked Roland.

"What's that?" Roland stood up, stretched his back, and upon seeing the car driving away down the street, appeared dumbstruck. "No, no I don't think so." He dropped the strand of lights he was holding. Carl noticed a look of real concern in his eyes.

"I'm sorry. I've forgotten something I have to tend to. We'll have to work on this another time." Roland said, and walked briskly back towards the house. He quickly disappeared inside.

Well, that was odd, Carl thought. Something had definitely spooked Roland, but what? And what in the world was going on in Dogwood County lately anyway? Every day there was more drama than he knew what to do with. It was like an episode of the

Young and the Restless, not that he purposely watched the program, mind you. He couldn't help that Carol-Barbara had it playing on the small kitchen television while he ate his lunch every day. He didn't mean to know that Victor and Nickie were back together for the eleventh time, or that Kay and Jill were at each other's throats again.

Unlike the young and restless people of Genoa City, up until a few weeks ago Carl had considered the people of Dogwood County older and pretty darn satisfied with life.

Yes, Genoa City had the Abotts, the Newmans, and their latest antics, and apparently Dogwood County had the St. James family, the Van Honks, and a host of other characters that had yet to be fully revealed.

Part 46

Mr. Suspicious

By the time Carl got Roland's Christmas lights untangled, all by himself, he was frustrated. So frustrated that he quit his own light show assembly for the day, and looked to drown his sorrows in the one thing he knew would comfort him-Christmas cookies.

He entered his kitchen from the garage. That day, all the ladies had been in the living room working on Carol-Barbara's campaign, so the back door was a safer way to enter the house without being caught. He saw the plates of cookies they had brought, neatly sitting on the kitchen table. Like a frat boy who had just turned twenty-one and ordered one of everything at his birthday bar crawl, so began Carl with the cookies.

He was not discriminating; an equal opportunity cookie killer, was he, destroying several peanut butter cookies, a handful of snicker doodles, two sugar cookies shaped like trees, with green sugar sprinkles, and even a red hot accessorized gingerbread man, though they weren't his favorite. He'd also eaten a fair amount of buckeye balls and one piece of peppermint bark to freshen his breath after his cookie orgy.

The best part about his binge? He hadn't been caught. Though he would pay for it later, with stomach cramps and a sick feeling that would make him wonder if he had sugared himself into full-blown diabetes. Oh, how he would suffer later that night, but every single cramp he would endure for those delectable morsels.

After his bender, he'd quietly made his way to his den where he'd fallen asleep on the couch, his own little self-induced sugar coma. And what a nap it was. He awoke an hour later, stretching with his eyes still closed, reveling in his own self-destruction, and debating whether or not to get up or sleep it off a little more.

He slowly opened his eyes, squinting against the little bit of light that came through the window blinds. That's when he saw her. Carol-Barbara was standing over him, and she didn't look happy.

"Carl, wake up," she demanded.

He sat bolt upright. "Huh? What's the matter?"

"I saw the crumbs, Carl. Have you been eating cookies?" She questioned.

Damn that woman, he thought, she had such an eagle eye.

"I had a couple," he admitted.

That sent her into another lecture. After listening to her yell at him for ten minutes about how he was going to end up in a real diabetic coma someday if he didn't watch himself, he had hauled himself off the couch, returned to the outdoor Christmas lights, and neglected to tell her about what he had witnessed with Roland.

Since then, five days had gone by. Nothing had triggered his memory about the car with the Jersey plates- until now. He had just arrived home from working his shift at the All-Mart. He had parked his car in the driveway rather than putting it in the garage because he knew they would be heading out again in less than an hour to go to church.

Wednesday nights were reserved for adult Bible-study, followed by a light meal in the fellowship hall. He'd brought home sliced cheese for the sandwich platter Carol-Barbara always brought, along with a few other things they needed for the pantry; including cans of tuna fish, which he'd been relegated to having for lunch since the cookie incident. Punishment was hell, but his blood sugar had been so high afterwards, even he was worried.

It was getting dark outside, that time of dusk when it's hard to make out objects clearly. Just as Carl was reaching into his car for the second paper bag of groceries, while trying to balance the first bag on his hip and hold his keys, he fumbled. His keys fell to the ground. He set the bags down and stooped to look for them.

The dusk, combined with the interior light in his car, made it difficult to see where they had fallen. He found he had to close the door, making the interior light shut off, and therefore diminishing the glare and shadows, but he still couldn't find them. Had they gone under the car? His only choice was to lay flat on the ground and reach as far under the car as he could. He felt like an idiot. He fished all around with his hand, finally feeling them with the tips of his fingers. How had they gone so far under the car? He was just able to hook his finger into the keychain loop and pull them out when he was startled by the screeching sound of a car coming around the corner and turning onto his street.

He got to his knees, but before he could stand up, he noticed the car pulling to an abrupt halt in front of Roland and Honey's house. It was the very same car with the New Jersey plates that he had seen five days before; the one that had presumably driven Roland to run inside his house like he had seen a ghost. Coincidence? He thought not.

He considered standing up to get a good look at what was going on, but then thought better of it. If Roland had been that scared, maybe there was reason to be; so he stayed in a squatting position, hiding.

The car idled in front of the house, and at first Carl thought the driver was the only one in the car, but then he noticed a figure in the backseat.

Not long after the car came to a stop, out tumbled Honey Van Honk. And almost as soon as she was out, the car sped away, doing a U-turn and heading for the main road. Honey looked left and right. As if she were trying to make sure no one had seen her get out of the car. She carried a briefcase with her, and clutched it to her body like it was a child. She headed for the front door, at about the same clip Roland had demonstrated days before. It wasn't until she got inside and shut the front door that Carl stood up, rubbing his back and wondering what in the world he had just witnessed.

About that time, Carol-Barbara opened the front door.

"Hurry up, Carl!" She hollered. I need that cheese to finish off the sandwich platter. What in the world is taking so long? I saw you drive up ages ago."

Carl picked up the two grocery bags and walked towards the door.

"Hold your horses, CB, and there's something you need to hear!"

As he hauled the groceries inside, he began to tell her about the car from 5 days ago, then, as she packed up the items she needed to take to church, he finished by recounting what he had witnessed tonight.

"You might be reading too much into this, Carl." She told him. "It might just be a relative visiting from New Jersey."

"You've heard Roland and Honey say they don't have any relatives. No kids, no family at all to speak of," he reminded her.

"Well, then maybe a friend," she suggested.

"What kind of friend would make Roland run for the hills, or Honey look so suspicious as she got out of the car? And besides, she was carrying a briefcase. Have you ever known Honey to carry a briefcase?"

"I have known Honey to do many things, and I wouldn't put anything past her. It was probably an accessory to whatever look she was going for today. Besides, what do you really think was in that briefcase, Carl?"

"I don't know," he hesitated. "Money? Drugs? Maybe the cremated body of Jimmy Hoffa?"

"Probably more like makeup, hairspray, and a bottle of liquor." Carol-Barbara changed the subject. "Now look Carl, we need to get to the church. I've been asked to make a little political speech before Bible study."

"Is that appropriate?" Carl questioned. "Talking politics before Bible study? Aren't we supposed to be discussing how there would be no Christmas without Hanukkah?"

"Pastor wants me to do this. He says maybe it'll drum up interest in Bible study if we have a local celebrity there," she informed him.

"Celebrity? Is that what you are now?" Carl teased.

"Pastor's words, not mine. Now, please, Carl, get in the car," she begged.

"Fine," he grumbled, but couldn't help glancing over at the Van Honk house as he slid into the driver seat. There was something weird going on over there. He just knew it.

Part 47

Run for Cover

Dixon stood in his front yard, dressed in his red track suit. He was bound and determined to go for a run, even if it killed him. Due to the fact that not one, but two different people had tried to shoot him mere weeks ago, with one making contact; he figured that might be exactly what happened.

He'd been feeling much better in the last few days, physically at least. The wound to his backside was almost imperceptible. The wound to his psyche, though? That would take a little more time to get over, since his perpetrators had not yet been caught.

Even so, he was suited up, had stretched his calves and quads, his hip flexors and hamstrings. There was nothing left to do but start running; to just put one foot in front of the other and go. The first step was always the hardest.

As he went over the route he'd chosen for himself in his mind, his neighbor, Bob, stepped out of his front door, wearing his robe and slippers. He reached down and picked up the Saturday newspaper that was laying on his porch, and then stood there, breathing the cool December air.

Please don't let him see me, Dixon thought, but it was too late.

"Hey, Dixon! Beautiful morning, isn't it!" Bob asserted.

Damn it, Dixon cringed, but ever the politician, put on his best game face. "Yes, just gorgeous!"

"Going for a run, are you?" Bob pressed.

Why had he decided to wear the bright red track suit? It was so obvious. He may as well have been wearing a Santa suit.

"Yes!" He replied. "Can't keep a good man down, you know!" That kind of confidence was what would ensure Bob's vote when the election came up next month, Dixon thought.

Bob stood stagnant on his front porch, as though he were waiting for Dixon to take off. Dixon stretched his legs one final time in an aggressive manner, as if to appear that he was taking himself very seriously. Clearly Bob wasn't going anywhere. After a moment there was nothing left to do but start running. Bob waved from the front porch as Dixon broke into a jog. He went down his front path and onto the street, running right in front of Bob's house.

Dixon's breathing became natural as he reached the end of his street. He would be heading through the security checkpoint of his gated community. He waved to the guard as he passed by and saw him jot down something in his notebook. Probably noting what time he saw Dixon leave. Well, he thought, at least if he didn't return someone would notice.

He turned onto the main road and ran along the shoulder, feeling stronger with every stride. What had he been so afraid of? It all seemed so natural. These were the same streets he had run for years without any kind of trouble at all. It was, after all, bright daylight, and the chances were highly unlikely that someone would make a violent move at a time like this.

As he ran, Dixon noticed the tiny ache in his buttock where the bullet had entered. It was nothing he couldn't bear, so he picked up his stride a little bit, gauging his breathing. He knew he had lost some of his stamina, but that would come back quickly. He'd been in great shape before the shooting, and he was feeling stronger with every step.

As he approached the intersection closest to his subdivision, he broke into a real run. It was just as exhilarating as he remembered, and he really fell into a good pace. He continued this way for several minutes until, a half mile or so down the road, he began to focus less on his own body, and more on what was going on around him. He noticed the birds chirping, the sounds of leaf blowers, and he noticed how bare the tress were.

He also noticed that there was a black car approaching him from behind, and he knew he had the right of way, so he kept his pace and didn't change a thing. The car, however was too close for comfort. It was as if the driver might be trying to scare him; but that was ridiculous, he thought. He was just being paranoid.

However, the entrance to Dogwood Park was just ahead of him, and he decided he would cut across it just to be safe. It was a rambling park, with running and biking trails laid out amongst trees and bushes. Cars were not allowed.

In the center of the park there was a fountain, which wouldn't be on at this time of year. He knew this because he'd helped design the park, and he knew that the fountain they had put in couldn't withstand temperatures below freezing. Even though it was in the forties today, the county planning commission had decided to have the fountain cut off every November 1st, because one never knew when the temperature would drop and the thing would freeze and break.

Dixon ran past the gates into the park. He knew he was being overly cautious, and there was little chance the car was following him; but damn it, he'd been through too much over the last few weeks to take any unnecessary chances.

What with people questioning his every move as county manager, he'd become a little suspicious. It could literally be any of the disgruntled members of the county who had shot him; and all because he was trying to bring Dogwood County into the 21st century.

Why were they so darned against a mall anyway? Hell, every town had a mall now; indoor, outdoor, low class or high fashion. The one he had in mind would definitely bring class to Dogwood County, which was something it was severely lacking now.

Dixon continued running until he had almost reached the center of the park. He could see the lake, and as predicted, the fountain was not running. The bones of it sat, centered in the middle of the lake, dead looking. In fact, the whole park looked dead.

As he ran he thought about how the park would look a few months from now when the weather warmed back up and noises of children playing would be loud enough to be annoying to many people.

Not to Dixon, though. He loved kids, had wanted a gaggle of them, and grandchildren to follow; but his wife, Debbie, couldn't bear children, they had learned shortly after marriage.

However, he had still been in love with Debbie. She was so strong, confident and beautiful. He was willing to go without becoming a father, as long as he had Debbie. Then things had changed. Debbie had become bitter, and pushed him away physically. He could do without kids, but darn it, he couldn't do without sex. That, combined with her attitude towards him, had driven him right into the arms of other women.

At first, it was just random women who were more than willing to satisfy him. He played the part of poor, neglected husband well. Soon, though, he needed more than just sex. He needed someone to talk to about his sadness with Debbie. Never one to go to a therapist, he ended up going to Elsa. Who better to understand his problems with Debbie than her own sister?

Just like everything else with Dixon, though, it had soon turned sexual. When he learned he had fathered a child with Elsa, he could hardly contain his excitement, though he knew he had to; for Debbie, for his career, for lots of reasons.

All these years later, though? Now he didn't care as much. He and Elsa had wasted enough years not knowing their daughter. He told Elsa as much right before inviting Ashleigh to come to Dogwood County. She had enthusiastically accepted.

And Debbie? Though he still loved her in certain ways, he was not in love with her. Theirs was more like a business relationship. She told him what he needed to do to be successful, and he did it. She was his counselor, his critic, and even his financial backer, since she had inherited all that money when her parents died.

It had been her idea to build the mall, but they had needed more money. She was good at finding money, coming up with a way to make more, so he had taken her word for it. Why would she do anything to hurt their bottom line? It was Debbie the people of Dogwood should be angry with if they didn't like the mall idea.

Yes, being shot had forced Dixon to take a long, hard look at his life. As he thought about it, he made one loop around the lake, then headed up the path towards the other side of the park. When he came out the other side, there was the same black car. It was idling near the crosswalk. His heart slipped a beat.

Just to be safe, he purposely changed his course a bit to avoid having to run right in front of the car, but it slowly started to follow him. He ran a little faster down the street, thought about crossing the street, but didn't want to seem scared. He shot his eyes to the left and to the right. There was literally no one else around. Damn it! Why had he not brought his cell phone? One call and he could have had the entire Dogwood County police department at his beckon call.

He ran a little faster. The car sped up. What to do? He suddenly remembered what a very wise Kindergarten teacher had told him many years ago while he was being chased by a couple of little girls hell bent on kissing him.

"Dixon," she had said softly, getting down on one knee so she could look him in the eye, "If you don't run, they can't chase you." He had taken her word for it, bracing himself for a myriad of kisses from the girls when he finally decided stop running.

Instead, the girls had stopped in their tracks, perplexed by why he was no longer trying to escape them. Suddenly, just as his Kindergarten teacher foretold, the girls ran the other way. They had never considered they might actually catch him one day and be able to plant a big kiss on him.

He decided to try the same tactic here. He slowed to a stop, tried to catch his breath, then raised up to his full height and turned around. The car was coming to a stop beside him. The windows were heavily tinted, and there was no license plate on the front of the car. He stood, looking at the area that he imagined was exactly where the driver sat, and stared into a pair of eyes he couldn't actually see, but knew must be there.

Suddenly, the rear passenger side window rolled down, and he recognized a face he'd seen only once before. There sat Josefina Ruiz. What in the world,

Dixon wondered, was she doing in Dogwood County, and what did she want with him?

Part 48

Wheeling and Dealing

Dixon was surprised to see Josefina staring at him from the open window of the car. He had stopped running and was standing at the edge of the road. He had nowhere to go. If he ran, the car would likely just follow him. There would be no escaping a vehicle while he was on foot. He thought about running back into the woods, but that would make him look like an idiot, and besides, he had a feeling that the driver would just circle around and meet him at the other side of the park. What was he supposed to do, stay in the woods all night? Anyway, she apparently already knew where he lived, because she had followed him practically since he'd set out on his jog.

So he stood and stared at the woman in front of him. He had recognized her instantly, though he had only met her once before. That had been enough, though. Her first impression would stay with him forever. It had been about a year since he first laid eyes on her, and now, as he stood on the side of the road the entire night flashed before him again.

He and Debbie had gone to a local fundraiser; one of the many they attended for one charity or another. Debbie served on numerous boards. She was involved in so many he couldn't keep track, but that didn't really matter, because what Dixon remembered most about that night was meeting Josefina.

He had seen her from across the room, wearing a purple dress; long, dark hair flowing down her back as she sipped a martini. She was exotic looking, with legs that could have only come from a pure and distinguished pedigree. Women didn't just get lucky and end up with legs like those. They were passed down from generation to generation, evolving, with slight DNA changes making each pair even lovelier than the last. She was the most beautiful woman he had ever seen.

Josefina was drinking and laughing with a group of men. She didn't seem to mind that she was the only woman in the group. She seemed to relish in it, in fact, throwing her words and moving her body in the most delightfully confident way he had ever seen a woman do. He had been unable to stop staring.

The men she was with Dixon recognized as some of the most influential people in Virginia. Dixon considered himself a fairly big wig when it came to social position in Dogwood County, but these people made even him feel a bit small. Yet, Josefina seemed confident, even casual among these people.

He didn't know all of their names, but he did instantly recognize Tom Thurston, the owner of Thurston Aviation Company, with his big, roaring laugh, and even bigger belly. Dixon first met him when they were paired up for a charity golf tournament. That day, Tom had confided in him that his aviation company wasn't doing too well financially, and that he had met a woman, a financial backer from South America, who claimed she could help dig the company out of the mess it was in. Dixon had put two and two together and realized this must be the woman who stood with him now.

The other man he knew for sure was Congressman Paul Worthington; a shifty tool of a man who was known to have his hands in ventures both in and out of the country. He spent a lot of time in South America, which, Dixon surmised, was probably how he knew Josefina. As he watched Josefina and her dealings with the men, it became clear that she was a queen holding court among them, and he wondered if all the men in the group had ties to her. Once, Josefina caught Dixon looking at her. She kept her cool, and simply lifted her glass in a gesture of cheers towards him.

At some point that night, Debbie took the podium to give her worn-out speech about how important it was for those with money to help take care of those less fortunate. Dixon knew it was all just ass-kissing. Debbie didn't have a compassionate bone in her body. She only did it because it made her look good.

While Debbie was speaking, Dixon realized that Josefina had moved to stand next to him. He felt her more than saw her. It was as if there was heat coming off her body. After a few minutes she leaned in and whispered in his ear.

"She does drone on, doesn't she." She stated.

Dixon thought he would melt. Her voice matched her beauty. It was both sweet and spicy, with an accent one would expect to hear from a woman who had grown up in Venezuela. He thought briefly that he should explain that was his wife she was talking about up there at the podium, but he was unable to respond, as the heat coming off Josefina had somehow had the opposite effect on him. He felt quite literally frozen.

After Debbie finished her speech, she walked towards Dixon and Josefina. By then Dixon had found his voice and proper introductions were made all around. Josefina explained to them that she was a venture capitalist, with an interest in helping to put Dogwood County on the map.

"It's beautiful here. You shouldn't have to beg for money. People should be flocking from all over the world to see these mountains, breathe this air. It reminds me of my own dear Venezuela."

Debbie piped in. "What we need is something that will draw people here. I have some ideas, but it will take money."

"You have ideas. I have money. Let's talk," Josefina had told her.

Later, Tom Thurston would quietly tell Dixon to stay as far away from Josefina as possible. "She'll own you," Tom had muttered under his breath.

While Dixon could never, even in his own mind, be the epitome of moral character, he knew when to take a piece of advice, and he certainly didn't want to be "owned" by anyone. Debbie already made him feel like a piece of property.

Dixon relayed Tom's information to Debbie and urged her not to have any goings-on with the woman, and as far as he knew that had put an end to it. Until now, because now Josefina was right in front of him, and she did not appear happy.

The driver of the car got out and opened the door to the back where Josefina sat. Dixon saw those long legs stretched out in front of her and very nearly went weak in the knees.

"Dixon, my love, we need to talk." The words dripped from her mouth.

"We do?" He questioned.

"Get in the car," she commanded.

Dixon had no choice but to do what she asked. As he slipped in beside her, he wondered briefly where the authorities would find his body later.

Josefina spoke Spanish to the driver. Dixon couldn't understand what she was saying, but he quickly realized that she must have told him to close the partition between the front and back of the car so they could have privacy. The car didn't move, but the engine remained running.

"Your wife, she has greatly displeased me," Josefina stated.

"Debbie?" Dixon questioned. "What did she do?"

"Don't play dumb with me, Mr. St. James. I'm talking about the money. I have seen nothing in return for my part of all-- this." She moved her hand in a circle as if to encompass some situation she was summing up for him. Something he was clearly supposed to know about, but didn't.

"I honestly don't know what you are talking about." He must have looked genuinely confused because she backed off a little.

"I told your wife there would be consequences if I didn't see things moving along. So far I see no sign that there is anything being done with my money. You have one month. No more, no less. Now get out of my car," she ordered.

Suddenly his car door was being opened from the outside by the driver. He wondered, did Josefina have some signal, some button she pushed to let the driver know it was time to open the car door? Dixon got out. He was shaking.

"One more thing, Mr. St. James," she paused. "How is your wound healing?" She smiled, then pushed the button to close the window and disappeared behind the dark glass.

Dear God, he thought, as the car drove away, what has Debbie done?

Part 49

D' Nile Ain't Just a River in Egypt

Dixon couldn't run fast enough. Josefina Ruiz had put the fear of God in him; perhaps more than getting shot had. The two miles he had to run home from the park seemed more like ten. On the way he could think of only one thing; finding out from Debbie what sort of alliance she had formed with Josefina, and figuring a way out of it.

Up until today, the extent of his knowledge regarding their relationship, was that they had never spoken again after their first meeting, which had been more than a year ago at the fundraiser. Now, he had been rudely informed, the two women had made some sort of business deal; one that may have gotten him shot already, and, he knew for a fact, could get him killed in the very near future if he didn't fix the situation.

Naturally, he hoped that money was all Josefina wanted. Still, it sounded like it could take every bit of savings he had squirreled away for retirement to do it. He wondered if he could use the funds set aside for his campaign. Surely his supporters would understand that he needed the money for a good reason, especially if they wanted him to continue serving Dogwood County in the capacity to which they were accustomed- alive.

Damn his wife, he fumed. As Ricky Ricardo used to say, she "had some 'splainin' to do," and he planned on getting every detail from her, even if he had to drag every torrid word out of her big fat mouth. As he ran, he realized that his anger towards

Debbie was causing him to feel invigorated, and he used that feeling to run faster.

Soon he was rounding the corner into his subdivision. He was breathing hard, but was determined to keep up his pace until he reached his driveway. He passed the gatekeeper's house. The same guard who was working when he left for his run waved him on through.

As he ran the final two blocks to his house, he half-expected to see Josefina's black car with the tinted windows waiting for him, but certainly, she couldn't have made it past the gatehouse.

Finally, he could see his house in the block up ahead. There was no ominous black car sitting in the driveway. In fact, nothing looked out of place, save for the fact that the grass on his front lawn was getting too long. He'd really let things slide since his shooting, and was surprised the Home Owner's Association wasn't all over him.

Just a few more houses to run past before he reached home. His neighbor, Bob, who had been diligently cutting his grass when he started his run, was now using a weed whacker on the edge of the yard closest to the street. Damn it, he calculated, there was no running past him without being noticed, and he literally could not afford to stop and talk.

"Hey, Dixon!" Bob hollered.

"Not now, Bob!" Dixon ran right past him.

"I have to ask you a question!" Bob pleaded.

"Later, Bob!" Dixon yelled back, trying to use a light tone that might make his snub seem friendlier. Bob would just have to get over it, as Dixon had to focus on the task at hand.

As he approached his house, he didn't see Debbie's car in the driveway, but that wasn't unusual. She generally parked in the garage. God forbid her convertible Volkswagen get even a drop of bird crap on it. For a moment he worried. What if she had already left for her water class at the YMCA? Then he would be forced to wait for her to get home, and she often didn't come straight home. This needed to be dealt with now.

He stopped running at the end of the driveway, tried to catch his breath, as he wanted to have lots of it available to let loose on Debbie. As he tried to steady himself, the automatic door to the garage began to open. He watched as it reached full height, and he saw Debbie's car begin to back out.

Dixon couldn't help himself. He ran up behind the car and started waving his arms. At first Debbie didn't see him. She continued to back out, but Dixon wasn't budging. Thank God for the backup camera, because the car alerted her to the fact that there was an object behind her; that object being a flailing, angry Dixon.

Debbie rolled the window down. "Dixon, what exactly are you doing?"

"I'm trying to get you to stop, damn it!" He lunged towards her window, leaned in towards her. "I need to talk to you."

"Dixon, you know I do my water class on Saturday morning. Can this wait? I don't want to be late." She said impatiently.

"I think being late to your class is the least of your problems right now. This can't wait. Get out of the car." He demanded.

"Excuse me?" She replied angrily.

"I mean it, Debbie. Get out of the car," he commanded.

"Don't order me around like a servant. I will get out of the car when I return from my class," Debbie growled. "Now, get out of my way."

Dixon decided to break out the big guns already. "It's Josefina Ruiz. She followed me today," he told her. "She says you owe her money."

Debbie looked like she was the one who had almost been run over by a car. "What do you mean she followed you?"

"I mean she hunted me down like an animal and told me she had better get her money or else," he told her. He paused, took a deep breath. "Debbie, what have you done?"

"Don't worry about it," she replied.

"Don't worry about it? I was just threatened, life and limb, and you tell me not to worry about it?" Dixon was fuming.

"I simply made a little deal with her." Debbie responded calmly, as if his being threatened meant nothing to her.

"What kind of deal, Debbie? One that's going to get us both killed?" He questioned.

"We are not going to get killed. Believe me, once this is all done, we'll have more money than you could ever imagine." Her voice softened. "Dixie, have I ever steered us wrong before? Trust me. I know what I'm doing." She paused. "Can I go now?"

"This is not over, Debbie." Dixon stepped away from the car. Debbie began to back out quickly, then suddenly stopped. She stuck her head out the window.

"Hey! Since you're feeling so much better, why don't you go mow the damn grass!" And then she was gone.

He contemplated the details regarding what kind of agreement she'd made with Josefina; but, he considered, when it came to Debbie and money, never the two shall part. He decided for the time being to trust her. What other choice did he really have right now?

Besides, there was a shiny red Honda push mower in the garage calling his name.

Part 50

Don't Eat the Meatloaf

The second Saturday of every month the Moose Lodge held a dinner for its members and their guests. The busy month of December was no exception to the rule.

In twenty years, Carl and Carol-Barbara had missed only two of the dinners. That had been when she was first undergoing her chemotherapy, and the thought of eating, or of being around people, had turned her stomach.

Tonight they would be attending with their fellow Moose Lodge members. This included some people they enjoyed socializing with, as well as others they didn't care to see as much, such as Dixon and Debbie.

Carl graciously invited Roland and Honey to attend with them. At first the couple declined, but a little prodding convinced them it might be fun.

Honey dressed in her typical fashion, with a tight Cheetah print dress and black stiletto heels; cleavage exposed to the nines. She topped off her outfit with a shiny red sequin bag.

Thank God that it was chilly outside, Carol-Barbara thought, because this forced Honey to put a black cardigan sweater on over her dress. It, too, was tight, but it did cover her up a little, thereby playing down the swell that was pouring out of her dress top. Carol-Barbara hoped it would be chilly in the lodge. Maybe Honey would keep the sweater on all evening.

The foursome drove to the Moose Lodge in Carol-Barbara's car because after much discussion, it proved to be the most comfy, and Carol-Barbara sure as heck wasn't going to pull up in front of the Moose Lodge in the purple pimped out Cadillac that Honey drove. Though it had been exciting driving in it, once had been enough.

The Moose Lodge was roughly three miles from their house, so any discussion was brief, and the topic of conversation included mainly how Carol-Barbara's campaign was going. Roland asked her if there was anything he could do to help.

"I could hang signs or something," he had quietly offered.

"You know, Roland, I might just take you up on that," she had said, and thought again what a nice peaceful man Roland was. She couldn't help but to think once again how Roland had gotten together with Honey. They do say opposites attract, though, she considered.

They pulled up to the lodge and parked just as Martha was getting out of the back seat of the car beside them. She'd come along with Susie and her husband, John.

"Fancy meeting you here," Martha quipped.

They shared greetings amongst the group, and walked towards the lodge together. Carol-Barbara thought that it was good to see Susie and John out and about. They'd been dealing with so much grief since the death of their son, Eric, who had been a Marine stationed in Iraq. It had been hard on the whole family, especially John, who had been so very close to Eric.

Eric had grown up with the Hoofnagle's kids, and Carol-Barbara had a recollection of John coaching Eric and her own son, Adam, in football when they were kids. John had been so proud of Eric, who had gone on to be the star high school quarterback. It was clear Eric would do great things in life, and he had. Apparently he had died while diverting a woman and her two children away from a roadside bomb he and his battalion had just discovered.

Eric had been awarded a posthumous silver star for his heroic actions. The news of his death six months ago had been hard on the whole town, actually, as he was their hometown hero in many respects.

In fact, Susie had recently told her that the high school was putting together a 5k in his name to raise money for injured members of the military.

The group made their way into the lodge. It was to be a sit down meal, and the group of seven sat down at a large round table and waited to be served. Dinner tonight would be meatloaf, mashed potatoes and peas, along with all the rolls they could eat. The White House rolls were already in a basket on the table. Carol-Barbara gave Carl a look as he reached for one and began slathering it with butter. He shoved the first bite into his mouth before he realized she was watching him.

"What?" He said with his mouth full. "I'm just having one."

Carol-Barbara shook her head. She'd let him have his roll with butter, but after that he'd better watch it.

The group noticed that Dixon and Debbie had just walked through the front door.

"Oh boy, here comes trouble," Martha wisecracked to Carol-Barbara.

Carol-Barbara noticed that Dixon looked tired, and had he gained weight? It wasn't like him to put on even an ounce.

She watched as Dixon took Debbie's wrap from her shoulders and hung it on the coat rack. He hung his own beside it. The pair walked to a table where several of Dogwood County's finest residents sat, including the mayor. Dixon pulled Debbie's chair out for her. Carol-Barbara noticed that the entire time since they entered the lodge, neither had spoken a word to each other. More trouble in paradise? She wondered. Perhaps it had something to do with Elsa and her daughter, Ashleigh? At any rate, the pair looked decidedly unhappy with one another.

"Stop staring. Your eyes are going to bug out of your head," Carl whispered to her.

"I was not staring," Carol-Barbara was momentarily embarrassed. She quickly returned her attention to the people at her own table.

"Were to," Carl teased.

Just then the waitress brought out their meals. It was brought out family style on big platters, and passed around the table. It smelled wonderful. As far as meatloaf goes, the Moose Lodge had the best there was. The cook there had perfected a secret recipe that made it taste like steak, without breaking the bank. It was home style comfort food at its best. The potatoes were creamy and piping hot, and the peas were still bright green, not overcooked or mushy.

The group enjoyed their meal and made idle chit-chat. Carol-Barbara was glad Carl had invited Honey and Roland, as they turned out to be great conversationalists, and watching the two of them banter back and forth with one another was great fun. They teased one another about virtually everything. He told her that her dress was too young for her, and she told him he was a fuddy-duddy. They seemed on some level like a couple that had been together forever, and yet Carol-Barbara got the sense they really didn't know one another at all. For example, he had seemed surprised to learn that she didn't like peas. How could someone who had been married for so long not know his spouse didn't like peas? Had he not listened to her, or did he just not care?

They were in the middle of their meal when Martha decided she had to use the ladies' room.

"I'll be back momentarily," she announced, and left the table.

Shortly after she left there was a ruckus at the next table. A woman was standing behind her husband trying in vain to perform the Heimlich maneuver.

"He's choking on his meatloaf!" The woman was frantic, and rightly so.

Other people tried to help her. A big man got up from his table and pulled the woman from behind her husband so he could try using more force. The choking man was turning blue, and it appeared he lost consciousness. He became like dead weight and even the big man couldn't hold him up. He began to slide to the floor.

"Someone call the paramedics!" The big man hollered.

No one seemed to know what to do, but another woman at that table got out her cell phone and called 911.

At that point Honey stood up from the table. "That'll take too long. We have to do something."

Carol-Barbara almost didn't recognize the voice that came from Honey's mouth. It was calm, cool, and collected, and all business. For a moment her New Jersey accent had been replaced with something else; something Carol-Barbara couldn't place. She was astonished to see Honey run towards the man.

Honey stripped off her sweater in an effort to move with less constraint, and in doing so exposed her skimpy dress top, and her cleavage in all its glory. She threw herself down on top of the man and straddled him like a horse.

"Roland, my bag!" Honey shouted. Roland quickly brought her sequined bag to her. She opened it and pulled out a small pocket knife.

There, in front of everyone, she performed an emergency tracheotomy, finishing the process by grabbing a straw out of the nearest iced tea glass, and placing it into the hole she had cut in the man's throat. She began breathing into it, until after a minute or so, the man's chest began rising and falling.

That's when Martha emerged from the bathroom.

She took note of the situation. "Good God! What happened?" Martha questioned as she exited the ladies' room.

"He was choking," Carol-Barbara explained. "She saved his life."

Just then the paramedics arrived on the scene. They raced to the side of the man, who was breathing, thanks to the straw in his throat, but was still unconscious. Honey stayed by his side holding the straw in place and calmly waiting for them to take over.

There was definitely more to this woman than any of them knew, and Carol-Barbara planned to find out exactly what it was.

Part 51

Spies Like Us

After the rescue squad showed up at the Moose Lodge to transport the choking man to the hospital, the regularly scheduled Bingo game went by the wayside. Most people left right after the event, too shaken to even finish their dinners.

It turned out that the man, who had come close to dying, was the brother of a Moose Lodge member. He and his wife were visiting from Maryland. They had planned to stay only one night, and then head out Sunday morning to continue on to Florida for a vacation. Now their one-night stay would include a couple of extra nights in the hospital, and their vacation would be cut short, but at least he was alive.

A member of the rescue squad stuck around for a while to ask Honey some questions about what had happened; and, just to make it all legal, a police officer showed up to make sure there hadn't been anything sinister about the occurrence. After they questioned her, they took down her contact information. Ultimately, though, they thanked her profusely, and told her that the man would probably not be alive if it weren't for her courageous act.

Carl and Carol-Barbara heard most of the conversation between Honey and the authorities, as they had stuck around to help clean up, and because they were Roland and Honey's ride home.

In the car there wasn't much talking, as no one was sure what to say. Carl and Carol-Barbara did, of course, make a point of telling Honey how amazing she had been. Honey played coy, acting as if what she had done was something that happened every day.

"I just did what anybody else would do to help a fellow man," she replied.

Roland seemed nonchalant as well, as if he'd seen her perform in that way a hundred times before. Carol-Barbara couldn't help but wonder why he wasn't as impressed by her actions as everyone else was.

More than fifty people in the Moose Lodge had seen Honey Van Honk give a man an emergency tracheotomy. With good reason, most of them had been so caught up in the fact that a man was choking to death on the floor that they didn't even question who was doing the saving, just that he was being saved, thank God. Yet, Carol-Barbara knew better.

She had known Honey for a couple of months now, and had seen her do some crazy things; most of them not extremely impressive. However, last night she had saved a man's life, and not in any ordinary way. She had basically carried out surgery right there on the Moose Lodge floor.

It was now Sunday morning, and Carl and Carol-Barbara were up, getting ready to head out for the early service at church. They sat at their kitchen table sipping their coffee and discussing the events of the night before.

"Quite a night with Honey, huh?" Carl pointed out the obvious.

"I mean, she didn't even blink," Carol-Barbara retorted. "Where would she have learned to do something like that?"

"Maybe she worked in the healthcare field at one time?" Carl was reaching for an answer.

"She's never mentioned that," Carol-Barbara replied. "And besides, why wouldn't she have just said that's where she learned it when we questioned her about it in the car?" She paused. "No, there's definitely something we don't know about our Honey."

Carl nodded. "And did you notice how cool Roland was about the whole thing? Not just in the car, either. I was watching while we were at the Moose Lodge. He seemed almost bored or even annoyed by what she was doing. He even took a couple bites of his food while the whole thing was going on." He shook his head. "I just don't get it."

"Did you notice the change in her voice, even her mannerisms, as she worked on him?" She questioned.

"No, but I was too busy watching her slice into the guy's throat to hear anything she was saying. What did she sound like?" Carl wondered.

"Like someone else, not like Honey at all. I can't place it. I actually thought for a minute I heard something different in her voice, and that's the second time that has happened. Remember when she was telling me about her college days?" Carol-Barbara pondered.

"Maybe in the excitement of things she just forgets to sound so New Jersey?" Carl offered.

Carol-Barbara stood up from the table, coffee cup in hand. "People don't just lose and gain accents like that, and I, for one, want to know more." She headed towards the kitchen counter, slugged down the last of her coffee and placed the cup in the sink.

"How?" Carl posed.

Carol-Barbara thought for a moment, then walked towards Carl. "I'll tell you how," she said with determination in her voice. "After church I'm going to walk right over there and ask her." And with a glint in her eye she added, "And you are going to go with me."

After church, when they were sure it wasn't too early to make a house call, Carl and Carol-Barbara made their way to the Van Honk residence. Carol-Barbara had decided they would show up under the guise of delivering bagels and cream cheese as a kind of show of appreciation to Honey. On the way home from church, Carol-Barbara had asked Carl to make a detour to the bagel shop in town. While Carl waited in the car, she'd gone in and picked up a nice box of assorted bagels, some savory, some sweet, along with two kinds of cream cheese. She'd chosen plain, and one called honey almond, in honor of their local heroine.

Carl expressed concern that they were going to disturb the Van Honks, who may have been sleeping in after a night of excitement, but Carol-Barbara reminded him that Roland and Honey had seemed very unexcited by the events of the evening, and were probably going about their Sunday morning as usual. Still, this was not something that Carl was gung-ho on doing. As curious as he was about the whole situation, his position was that, at this point, things might be better left alone. With Carol-Barbara in charge, though, and on one of her missions, did he really have a choice?

They walked over to the Van Honk abode, box of bagels in Carol-Barbara's hand, and rang the doorbell. After a minute or so there was no answer, though both the pimped-out Cadillac, as well as Roland's less flashy Honda, were in the driveway.

"See? They're still asleep," Carl stated.

"They're not asleep, Carl. No one our age sleeps this late."

"They're a few years younger than us," he pointed out, to which Carol-Barbara's response was to give him a simmering glare, and to simply ring the doorbell again. There was still no answer.

"Maybe they're out back." Carol-Barbara made her way down the steps and started around the corner of the house. Carl reluctantly followed.

As they rounded the corner to the back yard, they could see no sign of the Van Honks, but the back door was slightly ajar. Carol-Barbara walked towards it.

"CB, no." Carl urged. He knew what she was thinking.

"I'm just going to holler in, make sure everything is alright."

"Hello!" She called through the open space. There was no answer.

"See, I told you. They are not here." He stated.

"No, you said they were asleep. Their cars are here, so they must be here," she said matter-of-factly.

"Maybe they went on a walk?" Carl offered.

"And left the back door wide open? I don't think so." She pushed the door open a little more, and called out to them again, but still got no answer. She made her way just inside the door.

"I can't believe you are doing this," Carl was visibly upset.

"I just want to make sure they are alright. Just stay here." She disappeared into the house.

Carl stood on the back patio, unsure of what to think about his wife's actions. Sure, it made sense as a good neighbor, to check on them, especially after what had happened the night before. Yet, Carl knew his wife had an ulterior motive. Little spy, he thought. What exactly was she doing in there?

After a minute or two, she peeked around the door.

"Carl, you have to come in here!" She said in a loud whisper, and then disappeared inside again.

Carl jumped. Something must really have happened to the Van Honks if she wanted him to come see something. Now he was worried. Not knowing what in the world he was walking into, but trusting his wife implicitly, he followed her, but when he got inside he didn't see her.

"Where are you?" He asked, in the same loud whisper she had used with him only a moment before.

"In here," came her voice from the next room.

Carl cautiously made his way into the room, unsure of what he was walking into. It turned out to be the dining room, where he found his wife standing over a table full of stacks of cash. He had no idea how much there was, but he knew that on an All-Mart manager's salary, there was no way Roland should have so much money lying around.

"Good Lord!" Was all he could muster.

Carl noticed also that there was a television set on in the next room. It was tuned to a station he didn't recognize, and it was loud enough that he could hear it. He could tell it was a newscast of some sort, but the people were not speaking English. He couldn't make out what language it was, but why would the Van Honks be listening to any foreign news channel?

Carol-Barbara saw him looking at the television.

"I noticed it, too. Weird, huh." She stated. "So why do you think they have so much cash lying around? And with the back door wide open!"

Carl glanced back at her. He noticed something else that caught his eye, more than the television, and just as much as the wads of cash. Behind her on the wall there were three large military-style guns propped up against the wall. He pointed and she turned around.

"Probably because they have plenty of protection," he pointed, and she turned to look at the guns that had eluded her before.

Suddenly, the Van Honk cat, Poopsie, freshly dyed pink again, hopped up on the table with the cash and scared the hell out of both of them.

"CB, I think we need to get out of here. Right now."

Just then they heard the front door open. They panicked, both of them practically tripping over their own feet, as they headed for the back door. They made it out and ran around the side of the house, racing through the front yard as best they could, finally arriving at their own back door, and into the safety of their home.

"Oh, God," Carol-Barbara said, when she finally caught her breath.

"What is it?" Carl asked.

"The bagels. I left them on the table next to the cash. They're going to know we were there."

Part 52

Vandals and Hoodlums

They both felt so awkward about running out of the Van Honk's house, and for going into it in the first place. Carol-Barbara admitted she should have left well-enough alone and that she had let her curiosity take over, but now they were home and the two unlikely criminals would spend the next several hours secreted away in the safety of their own den.

One of the local television stations was hosting a Sunday movie marathon and, since it was December, the whole day's line-up was based on movies with a Christmas theme; so they turned on their 15 year-old television set and settled in for the afternoon.

Carl and Carol-Barbara could never be defined as a couple that had to keep up with the Joneses, so to speak. They firmly believed in the saying "if it ain't broke, don't fix it," though admittedly Carol-Barbara could not bring herself to use the word "ain't" and, being a person who tried to be grammatically correct as much as possible in life, said "If it isn't broken, don't fix it." Carl never thought it had the same ring, but the important part was they were on the same page with their priorities in life.

This is why, when they tuned the television set to channel 5, they did so on a television set that was big and bulky and still utilized a tube to make it function. When new flat screens and even flat panels, (Carl didn't know what the difference was) had entered the scene, and many of their friends were upgrading, the Hoofnagles repeated their mantra and decided they would keep the set they had until it broke. That had been five years ago. Some of their friends had already had to replace their new sets with even newer ones because the technology just hadn't lasted, but the Hoofnagle's set was still going strong.

When channel 5 advertised that it was having a Christmas movie marathon, they really weren't kidding. It had started at midnight and was to run until the following midnight; twenty-four hours of Christmas. When they first started watching they caught the last thirty minutes of "Christmas Vacation " which was decidedly more risqué than any of the other movies channel 5 had on the lineup for the day, but which contained one of Carl's favorite lines ever. Chevy Chase could be heard saying "Hallelujah, holy shit, where's the Tylenol?" Of course, channel 5 bleeped out the foul language, which was fine with Carl because he still understood where Chevy Chase's character, Clark Griswold, was coming from. He'd spent many a Christmas feeling like he needed a Tylenol to get through, especially if a lot of family was visiting. Sure, he loved their families, both sides, but trying to keep everybody happy was an over the counter pain killer worthy task.

"Miracle on 34th Street" played next, which was one of Carol-Barbara's favorites. And after that "Holiday Affair" with Robert Mitchum and Janet Leigh, during which Carol-Barbara reached over from the couch to Carl's recliner and held his hand. At some point Carl dozed off. The movies were definitely taking their minds off what had transpired earlier next door. During a commercial break

331

several hours later, Carl woke up, and announced that he was hungry.

"Sure wish I had that bag of bagels," he said, as he turned down the volume on the commercials and stood up to stretch his legs.

"You want me to go over there and ask for them back?" Carol-Barbara joked, then paused. "So really, Carl, what do you think that was all about over there?"

Carl thought for a moment. "Maybe they don't trust banks?" He offered.

Carol-Barbara knew as well as Carl did that in all likelihood that wasn't the case. "And the guns?" She questioned.

"Maybe they don't trust their neighbors, either, and for good reason, too." Carl smirked.

Carol-Barbara simply shrugged off his comment. "I was only trying to check on them, especially after what happened last night. Put it all together, Carl. It doesn't add up. Average people don't know to do emergency tracheotomies, or have thousands of dollars of cash on their dining room table-"

Carl interrupted her. "It looked more like a million."

Just then something on the TV caught Carol-Barbara's eye, and since the volume was turned down, she pointed. Carl turned towards the television set. There, on the screen, in 24 inches of glory, was Dixon St. James' face.

""Quick, turn it up!" Carol-Barbara was insistent.

Carl used the remote to raise the volume, and they heard Dixon's voice speaking alongside the picture, while the words "Dixon St. James for County Manager" scrolled along the bottom.

"A commercial?" Carol-Barbara was incredulous.

"Well, it is a campaign. People running for office sometimes do that." Carl stated.

"But I can't afford something like that. That's not fair." She was dissuaded.

"Now, CB, just because he can afford a television commercial doesn't mean he's going to win." Carl tried to pacify her.

"But everyone will know who he is, and not me!" She was furious.

"Don't you think everyone already knows who he is? And not necessarily in a good way." Carl expressed his expert opinion.

Tears looked like they were going to spring from Carol-Barbara's eyes. "Maybe I've made a mistake. I mean, with everything going on in our lives, it just seems like a bad idea now. Maybe we should just move to that tropical paradise you're always talking about and forget about all of this."

"Are you kidding me, CB? You have put so much work into this. Your friends are ready to start handing out all the buttons and campaign fliers they've helped you make. You have as much chance as he does of winning. I want you to stop that negative talk right now. You're just having one bad day." Carl hardly ever raised his voice, and even now it wasn't in anger, but rather out of concern, and encouragement. "And I promise you, we will go to that tropical paradise one day, but just for a visit. You know you would miss Virginia too much, not to mention the kids and grandkids."

Just then the doorbell rang. It startled them both. Carl started towards the door with an intent to answer it, but Carol-Barbara jumped up from the couch. She grabbed the sleeve of his arm.

"No, Carl! What if it's the Van Honks?" Her eyes grew wide.

"What if it is?" Carl shrugged. "We've got to come clean sometime."

Carol-Barbara knew he was right. Better to get it over with now so they could get on with their lives and stop hiding in the den. She let go of his shirtsleeve and he went towards the front door.

A knock followed the doorbell. Whoever stood outside that door was insistent. He took a deep breath and reached for the doorknob, turned it, and opening the door slowly, he could see Honey, tears streaming down her face.

"Carl, I need your help," she pleaded.

Carl prepared himself for the worst. "What is it?"

"Somehow the back door was left open and Poopsie got out. We can't find her anywhere!" She cried.

Carol-Barbara, hiding around the corner listening, heard Honey's plea and had a sudden feeling of relief. They didn't know it was them; hadn't realized they had been inside the house! Then she had another thought. They had left the back door wide open when they ran out. It was their fault that Poopsie had escaped, and so she came out from her hiding place.

"Of course we'll help you find her," she said. "Carl, get Bubba on the leash. You know that dog can sniff out that cat anywhere."

"Will do," he said. "You two wait here."

After Carl got Bubba leashed up, Honey followed along behind them, calling Poopsie's name as they roamed the neighborhood. She wore her stiletto heels. Carol-Barbara wore her white Reebok tennis shoes, which gave her a speed advantage as they searched. She remained several yards in front of Honey the whole time, still afraid to put herself in a position where they may have to talk about how the back door got left open. Even though she agreed with Carl that they would need to tell the truth at some point, in her opinion, now was not the time.

After about fifteen minutes of searching around the neighborhood, Bubba's keen sense of smell led them to a drainpipe on the other side of the road, across from the Van Honk dwelling. He seemed intent on getting inside it, though his sheer girth would not have allowed for that.

"I think we've found our runaway," Carl announced.

Or a rabid opossum, Carol-Barbara thought.

"Oh Poopsie! Are you in there? Are you hurt?" Honey bent down and yelled towards the opening of the drain. "Come to mama, love!" She pulled out a piece of catnip from her jacket pocket and handed it to Carl. "Here, she loves this."

Carl took the catnip from her and bent down towards the opening, gently pushing Bubba out of the way. After a moment, Poopsie peeked her head through the opening. Honey let out a squeal of relief. "Just pull it back a little and get her to follow it. She'll come out."

Sure enough, as Carl pulled the catnip a foot or two away, the cat followed. Once she got out far enough, Carl let her take it from his hand. Then, Honey snatched Poopsie up in her arms.

"Bad girl!" she scolded lovingly. "Don't ever scare mama like that again!"

Carol-Barbara breathed a sigh of relief. Carl scratched Bubba behind his ears. "Good boy."

"Now I can go home and eat those nice bagels someone left us," Honey stated. "Sesame seed is my favorite."

Carol-Barbara felt like she was going to throw up.

Part 53

SOVA

Carol-Barbara had just about lost the contents of her stomach when Honey mentioned the bag of bagels being left on the dining room table, but she hadn't let it show. Well, not immediately anyway. After a few moments, though, she was sure that Honey could sense the fear emanating from her very pores. Surely Honey knew that they had been in the house; had put one and one together. What would happen now?

Carl and Carol-Barbara exchanged glances, and she knew she had to come clean. The words poured from her mouth and she couldn't stop them. What she said came out in one long run-on sentence; throwing all grammar rules to the wind.

"Honey it was me I brought the bagels because I was worried about you after what happened last night at the Moose Lodge and I went into your house when I saw the door cracked open and I put them on the dining room table and I saw everything guns money everything and I ran out when I heard you come through the front door and I'm probably the reason the cat got out because I left the back door wide open." Here she finally paused for a breath. "I'm really sorry."

Honey just stared at her. Carol-Barbara didn't know what was about to happen, but she got the sense it couldn't be good.

Piping in, Carl admitted, "I was there, too."

Honey looked at him, then back at Carol-Barbara. She took a deep breath, stroked the pink cat she held in her arms, and finally opened her mouth. "Come on, we need to have a talk."

She turned to go towards her house, took a few steps and turned back around. Carl and Carol-Barbara still hadn't moved.

"Well, come on," she beckoned.

"Wait!" Carl glanced down at the leash in his hand and suddenly realized he still had Bubba. "What about the dog?"

"He can come, too," Honey replied.

Carl glanced at Carol-Barbara, who seemed to be frozen, unable to move. He gently spoke to her. "Come on, let's go make this right."

Carol-Barbara nodded her head almost imperceptibly, and took a step forward, then another. Carl followed. Honey resumed walking towards her own house, her two shadows in tow.

Neither Carl nor Carol-Barbara said another word during the brief walk back to the house, but they were both thinking the same thing. *Dear God, what have we done? Do we go with this woman, who up until yesterday we thought we knew? If we walk into this house with the guns and the ammunition, will we ever walk out again? Or will someone find our lifeless bodies somewhere, no one the wiser as to what happened to us?*

When they got to the front door of Roland and Honey's house, the door seemed darker, more menacing than it had before; like the entrance to a house out of an old scary movie. The kind where the audience watches in terror, knowing the main character shouldn't be walking up those steps, shouldn't be clanging the big old wooden knocker or ringing the ominous bell, but are powerless to stop him from doing so.

Honey stood for a moment as if thinking about what she should do next. Then, she turned back to the pair. "Let me go in and tell Roland you are here first."

She opened the unlocked door, and went in closing it behind her, leaving the two standing on the front porch. After a moment, Carl spoke.

"What are we going to do with Bubba? We can't take him in there with that cat." Carol-Barbara pointed out.

"We could make a run for it," he said only half-joking.

Carol-Barbara shook her head. "No. I started this, I have to see it through."

"I'll just hook the leash around the top of the hand rail. Hopefully, we won't be in there too long." Carl wrapped the end of Bubba's leash around the top of the rail. Bubba looked at him, displeased with the whole situation. His eyes said, *Wait a minute, I just helped you find that stupid cat, and now as a reward you're going to tie me up?*

"There," Carl said. "Now if we don't make it out, at least someone will see him and know where to look." "Stop it, Carl. I think you may be making this worse than it is. It's not like they're going to kill us," she snapped. Though inside, she'd been thinking the very same thing.

After about two minutes, the door reopened. Honey had removed her stiletto heels and stood barefoot in the foyer. She beckoned them in.

"Roland has been warned that you are here," she stated.

Warned? Carl thought. This didn't sound good, not good at all. Why did Roland have to be warned?

The Hoofnagles stepped into the Van Honk's home reluctantly. Honey closed the door behind them. She led them down the hall and to the one room they had ever spent any time in; the dining room. As they approached, Carol-Barbara's heart beat faster. This could be it, she thought; this could be how it all ends for us.

The swinging door to the dining room was now closed. Honey pushed it open and held it so they could go through ahead of her, which they did, with great unease. In a protective manner, Carl went first. Carol-Barbara closed her eyes and took a deep cleansing breath before following him, and when she opened her eyes, she was slightly relieved by what she saw.

Gone were the guns that had been leaning against the wall. Absent, too, was the pile of money that had been on the table. Replacing it was a large vase filled with flowers. Roland sat at the head of the table.

In front of him were the bagels and cream cheese Carol-Barbara had left there. They had been laid out on a platter, and spreading knives were next to each tub of cream cheese. Carol-Barbara could smell coffee, too, and assumed that was what filled the large pot that sat next to the bagels. Four small serving plates had also been placed on the table, along with four matching coffee cups. It was as though the Van Honks had known they would be having guests.

"Welcome," said Roland calmly. "Please, have a seat." His voice was friendly, but not overly so. Carl sensed discomfort in his voice.

Without saying a word, Carl and Carol-Barbara each took a seat at the table next to one another. Carl was closest to Roland. Honey took the seat next to Carol-Barbara. It was as though Roland and Honey were intentionally book-ending them. Perhaps so they couldn't make a run for it, Carol-Barbara wondered.

Honey started. "I'm sorry this is so uncomfortable for you." She seemed to genuinely mean it. "We never wanted you to find out like this."

As Honey spoke, Carol-Barbara noticed the same accent she thought she'd heard at the Moose Lodge the night before. It wasn't Honey's usual New Jersey accent, but something more sultry, and smooth.

Roland piped in. "Yes, Honey filled me in on what happened. I must say we were worried about who had been in our house. We were actually quite relieved to find out it was the two of you, and not," he paused. "Well, let's just say not someone else."

Honey started again. "We're not usually so careless, leaving the back door open like that, but we've become so comfortable here. Sometimes I just don't think about it anymore."

Think about what? Carol-Barbara wondered.

"Yes," Roland added. "You two have become like friends to us, and we never thought," again he paused. "We just never thought we'd be sitting here having to have this conversation with you."

"And we feel the same way," Carl interjected, seizing an opportunity to remind them, just in case there were any doubts, or that they had any plans to do something crazy, that they were their friends. Maybe, he thought, these people could be talked down from whatever they were planning, even if whatever "it" was that they were trying to tell them, happened to be one of those *I'm going to tell you, but now I'm going to have to kill you* things.

Honey stood from the table and walked around behind Roland, placing her hand on his shoulder.

"I'll take it from here. It's probably my fault they are having to find out like this anyway. I mean, if I hadn't pulled that stunt last night at the lodge, Carol-Barbara wouldn't have felt the need to check on me, and to bring the bagels." She paused. "By the way, would either of you like one? They certainly look delicious."

Carol-Barbara shook her head. "No, thank you."

Carl actually thought for half a second about taking Honey up on the offer. He was starving, and felt like his blood sugar was probably low. He even wondered if this bagel spread on the table could be their last supper. In the end though he, too, declined.

"Then I'll just get straight to the point," Honey resumed. "We are not who you think we are. My name is Hana Resnick. I'm an agent with SOVA. You have heard of this organization, yes?" She paused, waiting for a response. Both Carl and Carol-Barbara shook their heads.

"Ah, let me explain then. SOVA is the Slovenian counterpart to the CIA here in the U.S. We are an intelligence agency."

Carol-Barbara couldn't believe her ears. "So you're not from New Jersey?"

"Hardly," Honey responded. "In fact I have only been there once, and that was to meet my contact in Newark to pick up my orders and get a briefing on my mission, but that's where I got my character details."

"So Honey Van Honk is nothing but a character?" Carol-Barbara asked.

"That's all," Hana explained.

"That's too bad. I really liked her," Carol-Barbara said sadly.

"She really liked you as well," Hana assured her.

Carl spoke up. "Can I assume, then, that you are not really Roland Van Honk?"

Roland, or rather he who had pretended to be Roland, smiled. "No."

"Are you with SOVA, too?" Carl asked.

"Hell, no. I've never even been there. Not even sure where it is to be perfectly honest. I'm an American, born and bred. Grew up in Georgia actually."

"So you're CIA then?" Carl questioned.

"Retired, actually, but I still take a case now and again. My real name is Matt Booker. I got paired up with Hana here to keep her out of trouble."

"So you're not married then?" Carol-Barbara interjected.

"Not to each other, no. I've got a wife and kids back in Georgia. Five grandkids, too," he who was formerly Roland said proudly.

"My job has never allowed for such things," Hana said with a hint of sadness.

"This is crazy." Carol- Barbara stated the obvious. "So, what are you doing here?"

Carl nudged Carol-Barbara. "They probably can't say. I mean, if they did they might have to kill us or something, right?" He said with a nervous laugh.

"No one is killing anyone," Hana said. "Let me just set that straight right now. We did not call you over here to hurt you."

Carl and Carol-Barbara breathed a collective sigh of relief.

Matt Booker added, "We have really come to like you. Though we're quite used to playing different roles, we've both admitted that for the first time we've felt really guilty about lying to you. We want to set the record straight."

At this point he rose up and went to the side table near where some of the guns had been propped earlier. He picked up a folder with some papers in it and took out a photo. It was Josefina.

"The woman from the salsa place!" Carol-Barbara exclaimed. "The one Robert was tracking!"

"Yes. Miss Josefina Estanga Torres Ruiz. She's got eyes watching her all over the place. FBI, CIA, and SOVA, of course." Matt said. "It was a complete fluke that she was there that night, but boy did it make our lives easier. See, we knew she was in this area of Virginia, but had no idea exactly where. I was able to make a few phone calls that night and we tracked her to a house about twenty miles from here, up in the mountains. She's at home in that kind of terrain, seeing as how she grew up in the mountains of Venezuela."

Hana added, "And that gives us something in common, you see. I grew up in the mountains of Slovenia. And Matt, he spent summers camping in the mountains of Georgia, so if she thinks she can hide up there, she's dead wrong."

"So what happens now?" Carl asked.

"As far as you two are concerned, nothing. You are innocent civilians in all of this, and we need to keep you safe. This should never have become your problem in any way." With this, his voice became stern, commanding. "You will treat us as your neighbors who moved here from Jersey and you will continue to call us Roland and Honey at all times, in public and private. Your very lives depend on it." He paused, looked from one to the other. "Now, go home and live as if none of this ever happened," he finished.

Yeah, that'll be easy to do, Carl thought, as he and Carol-Barbara stood up from the table to go. Honey stood, too, and led them to the front door. Before opening it she turned to Carol-Barbara and gave her an unexpected hug.

"I really do think of you as a friend, CB," Honey told her. "And in this line of work I've never had many."

Part 54

Bigger than Life

Several days had gone by since their conversation with "the Van Honks" and Carl and Carol-Barbara had heard nary a word from their ever more mysterious next door neighbors. Carl spent some time putting last minute touches on the Christmas decorations; while Carol-Barbara was in and out of the house grabbing ingredients for the recipes she always made this time of year, and purchasing last minute Christmas gifts for friends and family. As she came and went she couldn't help but to steal glances at Roland and Honey's house. Every time she did, she saw nothing different or out of place than the last time she'd ventured to look that way. It was as though they had simply disappeared.

Carl walked Bubba more than was necessary every day, hoping to figure out what was going on with them. Carl noted that Roland hadn't been at work in a few days, but with Christmas right around the corner, he wondered whether or not Roland was taking advantage of a few vacation days. Now that he knew what Roland really did for a living, and that the All-Mart manager gig was just a farce, there was no doubt in his mind that a man like Roland would need to decompress from time to time. Or maybe, he thought, just maybe Roland and Honey had gone off to report to their higher-ups about what, and who, they'd found in Dogwood County- one Miss Josefina Ruiz.

Carl imagined that in their profession they must have to show up from time to time and debrief whoever they reported to. Perhaps somewhere in Washington D.C. Roland and Honey, aka Matt and Hana, sat in an office wearing black suits and the obligatory sunglasses people in their professions always seemed to wear even when they were inside. He imagined their orders were delivered to them via a cell phone that shortly after self-destructed, just like in the Mission Impossible movies. Carl mentioned this possibility to Carol-Barbara as she came into the den to bring him his afternoon tea one day.

"How many cell phones do you think they go through every year? And do you think they carry concealed weapons, and have a license to kill like James Bond?" Carl was clearly enthused at the idea.

"I think it might be less glamorous than the movies make it, Carl. It's probably quite dull at times. I mean, they have been sent to live in boring Dogwood County, Virginia after all," she reminded him.

"I wouldn't say Dogwood County has been very boring lately. What with Dixon being shot, and a drug Lord-ess living nearby. And then there's the election. That's definitely added some excitement to the atmosphere," he pointed out.

"Speaking of the election, tomorrow the girls and I are going to be up in your neck of the woods handing out the buttons and fliers we made. Martha arranged it."

"At the All-Mart? Why didn't you tell me?"

"With all the Christmas chaos, I just remembered," she told him. "I feel a little funny drumming up votes during the holiday season. It doesn't seem quite right," she worried.

"You gotta do what you gotta do, babe. You can blame whoever had the bright idea of planning the special election right after Christmas."

"Oh, I'm pretty sure Dixon had something to do with that. He probably thought no one would have the time to pull something together against him over the holidays. And you're right, if I want to win, I've got to bring my voice, face and name to this community as much as I can between now and then, holiday season or not." she paused. "By the way, I wonder when the yard signs Martha ordered will arrive?"

"Now that you mention it, a rather large package was delivered while you were out shopping," he casually dumped on her. "Probably your signs?"

Carol-Barbara was anxious. "Carl, why didn't you say something right away?"

"With all the Christmas chaos, I just remembered," he teased.

"Where is it? Oh, I can't wait to see." She practically bounced up and down like a little kid who sees the number one item on her list sitting under the tree on Christmas morning.

"I put it in the garage. Come on, I'll go with you." He stood from his recliner to follow her. Carl didn't fully show it at the moment, but he was as eager as she was that they had come, and he couldn't wait to put them up all around town.

In the garage there was a large flat box the size of a coffee table leaning against the wall. Carl grabbed a box cutter off the shelf and raised his hand high, preparing to slice the package open.

"Careful!" Carol-Barbara told him. "You might cut the contents."

"Okay, okay, I was trying to show off my strength," Carl told her. "Jeez, can't a guy have a chance to impress his girl every once in a while?"

"Just where did that attitude come from, huh?" she questioned him. "Wouldn't have anything to do with you finding out your friend and neighbor gets to shoot guns and chase after people, would it?" she taunted.

"Maybe," Carl admitted. "Why should he get to have all the fun?"

"Carl, you know brute force doesn't interest me. I'm way more impressed by the fact that you are willing to put all these signs up for me." She kissed him sweetly on the cheek. "Now, let's see what's inside."

"Using a more gentle technique this time, Carl cut into the top of the box and peeked in. He slowly pulled one of the signs out so he could get a look, but from her angle Carol-Barbara couldn't see.

"Oh, this is good," Carl said, and slid the sign back into the box so she couldn't get a look at it.

"Well, take it out already," she prodded.

"Uh,uh," he said. "Not until I get another one of those nice kisses."

Carol-Barbara giggled. It wasn't often Carl got mushy like that, so it really meant something. The signs could wait another minute.

"Of course." She leaned in and kissed him softly on the lips, let it linger for a moment, like she used to do during their courting days. Then she pulled away and gave him a tight hug.

"That's what I'm talking about," he said, relishing the tender moment. Now invigorated, and with his manhood restored, he reached into the box again. "Okay, let's have a look at these things."

He pulled one of the signs all the way out of the box and held it up for her to see.

"Oh, gosh! Carl, is it too much?" she paused. "Is it too much of, well, me?"

The sign bore a giant picture of Carol-Barbara. It was one Martha had taken of her just for the occasion. Underneath the picture, in bold, read **Carol-Barbara Hoofnagle for County Manager.**

"It's perfect," he noted. "You look beautiful."

"Really? It's just so odd to see myself in such a bold way, but it was so nice of Martha to order these! She must have spent a fortune. How will I ever pay her back?"

"I think the only payback Martha is looking to get is for you to beat Dixon at his own game," Carl assured her.

Part 55

Feliz Navidad

Every year, Dixon dressed up as Santa Claus and rang the Salvation Army bell. He'd started doing it because Debbie thought it made him appear a more caring, compassionate person, especially towards those less fortunate.

Actually, now that he considered it, having a husband who was willing to humble himself dressed as Santa and ring a bell asking for money, probably made Debbie seem a more compassionate person. The way he saw things, it generally always came down to Debbie and how she came across to the world.

He'd actually come to enjoy his time dressed as the jolly old elf, and he usually did it in front of the Kroger, but this year, for some reason he wasn't privy to, Debbie had arranged for him to do it in front of the All-Mart. He didn't argue.

Though he was mad as hell at her for conspiring with Josefina Ruiz, he agreed that with the election coming up, and considering all the bad press he'd had lately, he couldn't afford not to make a positive appearance in the community right now. With Christmas just a week away, there would be a lot of traffic coming in and out of the All-Mart. Even though he would be wearing a red, padded suit, Debbie had a big mouth, and she would be sure to let everyone know just who was behind that fake white beard.

Debbie insisted on driving him to his Santa gig. With Dixon dressed as Santa and sitting in the front passenger side of the car, she drove him straight up to the front of the store.

"I've got some errands to run," she told him. "I'll be back for you."

As Dixon got out of the car, the children who were coming and going with their parents and grandparents, stopped to gawk. The big man of the season was arriving in a silver Mercedes, and at the All-Mart no less. That wasn't a sight a kid saw every day.

Dixon waved to the kids as he walked over to relieve the guy who'd been ringing the bell since early that morning.

"Take a break, buddy," Dixon told him.

"Gladly, Santa," the man handed his bell over. "Good luck. These people are brutal," he said as he walked away.

Dixon took a deep breath and began ringing the bell. He immediately went into character. "Ho! Ho! Ho!" He hollered with enthusiasm. Secretly, he'd always loved the ho-ho-ho-ing part of the act.

Several minutes went by, with shoppers depositing coins and sometimes bills into his Salvation Army kettle. The guy before him may have had trouble gleaning supporters, but no one could resist Santa.

Dixon noticed a gaggle of women headed his way. At first glance he didn't recognize them, but within seconds he realized it was Carol-Barbara Hoofnagle and her entourage. They seemed to be converging on the corner opposite from him. With his get-up on, he was sure they didn't recognize him.

They each had a stack of fliers in their hands and other paraphernalia which they were attempting, successfully he might add, to give to passersby. He quickly realized what they were doing had nothing to do with Christmas. These women were in full election mode, and trying to garner votes for Carol-Barbara by handing out political trinkets.

Damn her, he thought. There she was in full view, everybody getting a good look at her, while he stood in disguise dressed as Santa. But why was he even worried? It wasn't as if she could really beat him. She could hand out all the photo buttons she wanted. He still didn't think she had a chance. He went back to swinging his bell and ho-ho-ho-ing loudly; loud enough to drown them out.

About an hour and a half went by, with Dixon pan-handling for Salvation Army dollars, while Carol-Barbara and her ladies begged for votes. As far as he knew, they still hadn't realized who he was.

Knowing Debbie would be showing up soon, Dixon rang the bell with more deliberation. He wanted to get all the donations he possibly could before his time was up. He bent down to talk to a little boy who had a whole dollar bill to give him, and who seemed enamored of the fact that Santa was taking donations.

"Thanks, buddy." Dixon thanked the kid and sent him on his way. When he stood up he saw a face he'd never wanted to see again. In front of him stood Josefina Ruiz. In her hand was a piece of paper, which she dropped into the kettle.

"I have a message for you," she said, and walked away as quickly as she'd shown up. Then, as if to add insult to injury, Dixon watched her head towards Carol-Barbara's group of ladies. She took one of their fliers.

With great concern Dixon took the note Josefina had left for him in the kettle. He unfolded it and, with great hesitation read it.

Two weeks and counting. Feliz Navidad, it read.

Part 56

'Twas

'Twas the night before Christmas, inside Dogwood County,

By now kids were dreaming of tomorrow's big bounty;

Honey and Roland tried to keep out of sight:

Having arrived home late from an international flight,
And Carol-Barbara in her nightgown and Carl in his shorts;

Watched the tail-end of the news, which ended with sports,

When out in the street they heard such a racket,

Carol-Barbara moved quickly to throw on her jacket;

Carl jumped from the chair in a sprint-like motion,

And yanked up the blinds to see the commotion;

The glow from the street-light showed a peculiar event,

Giving the onlookers cause to lament,

For what to their dismayed eyes should they see,

But a Volkswagen convertible smashed into a tree,

They knew this car, had seen it before,

And recognized the license plate the car wore;

1SAINT it read in the boldest of letters,

While a sticker in the window read I Love Irish Setters;

Inside, a person with deep county ties,

Someone perhaps they had come to despise;

Debbie St. James was the driver in plight,

But what was she doing at this time of the night?

As quickly as possible, the ambulance came,

The Hoofnagles stayed to give out her name;

It's Debbie St. James, wife of Dixon, they said,

Is it possible she could actually be dead?;

To the county hospital, to the emergency room,

Now out of the way, and give us some room!

As fast as NASCAR drivers the EMT's flew,

And now Carol-Barbara knew not what to do;

Back to the warmth of his den Carl retired,

While Carol-Barbara considered what had just transpired;

Calling Dixon was what she should do,

And after that Debbie's sister, Elsa, too;

One hand held the phone, the other a coffee cup,

As she dialed his number, hoping he'd pick up;

And then, after five rings an answering sound,

Dixon, your Debbie, in a wreck, she's been found!

As she told him what happened, he seemed not to care,

In fact to hang up on her did he dare;

She redialed again and he answered in spite,

Recounting to her that with his wife he did fight,

I wish not to see her, nor care what she does,

Our marriage will never be again what it was,

Call her sister, she'll tell you what it was about,

Don't call me again for I just want to pout;

So she hung up the phone, dialed Elsa in a flurry,

Who answered the phone straight away in a hurry,

Debbie knows, she knows about the daughter I had,

With her husband some years ago, oh this is bad!

CB, I imagine she was coming there to confront you,

'Cause she knows that you know, oh what a coup;

She was drunk off port wine when she left the house,

I can't believe she drove in that condition, the louse!

Carol-Barbara hung up, with a lump in her throat,

Carl, come here, put down that remote;

I have something to say, and it's bad, Carl, real bad,

I'm afraid Christmas won't be what we'd hoped, Egad!

A terrible thing has happened, I'm afraid,

More drama here in the county has been made;

And she heard Carl say as he shuffled to bed,

Well, Merry Dang Christmas, where's a BC Powder for my head?

Part 57

Nooner

Debbie's car was smashed up pretty bad, and so was Debbie. However, she wasn't dead. For that, her husband, Dixon, didn't know if he was disappointed, or grateful. Of course, in his heart he didn't really wish her dead; that would just be wrong. However, the hell that she had put him through over the past few months made him less inclined to care about her fate.

The hospital had called him shortly after Carol-Barbara called to warn him about what had happened. Thus, when the nurse made her official call, he sounded neither surprised, nor concerned. This had caused the nurse to be very short with him, as she sensed he really didn't give a damn about the fact that his wife had a broken arm, several cracked ribs, and that her face apparently looked like she had gone a few rounds in the ring with Mike Tyson.

He told the nurse that he had no intention of coming down to the hospital until the next morning, and then he very emphatically hung up. Now, the next day, he felt only slightly bad about how he had acted. This was mainly due to the fact that she had made the very bad decision to get in the car and drive drunk.

Sure, he would go see her in the hospital today. He had to, if only just to keep up appearances before the special election, but he wasn't happy about it.

Even as he got ready to go, he took his time; taking a long shower, making a pot of coffee, sipping two cups of it slowly. It wasn't until he turned on the television that he realized what day it was.

"Well," he said out loud. "Happy freaking Christmas to me."

Across town at the Hoofnagle household, the atmosphere was only slightly more celebratory. Carol-Barbara had risen early to make her traditional sausage and egg breakfast casserole, which she had prepared the night before, but which needed to bake in the oven for an hour before serving.

She'd had to drag herself out of bed, since sleep had escaped her for most of the night after the previous nights' events. She'd stayed up late worried about Debbie's crash, and had called the hospital at about three o'clock in the morning to check on her. Since Carol-Barbara wasn't a direct family member, the hospital had been reticent about giving her too much information. However, the nurse that was stationed on Debbie's floor must have been feeling a bit of the Christmas spirit, because she made the decision to give Carol-Barbara Debbie's status report.

"You didn't hear it from me, " the nurse began, "But she is pretty beat up, and yet I hear her husband won't even get out of bed to come see her until tomorrow," she added. "What a jerk."

Carol-Barbara had thanked the nurse for being so forth-coming. Based on her own phone conversation with Dixon right after the accident occurred, she wasn't surprised to learn that Dixon was being an ass about the whole thing.

As he sat at the kitchen table eating a thick slice of Carol-Barbara's casserole, Carl seemed less interested in the goings-on from the night before, although he did ask if Carol-Barbara would be making a trip to the hospital to see Debbie.

"After what Elsa told me last night about Debbie coming here in a drunken state to confront me, I don't think so," she answered. Then she added, "I mean, what did I really have to do with any of this, anyway? Sure, Elsa confided in me her deepest, darkest secret about having a love child with Dixon, but I mean really, I only just found out about it a few weeks ago. It's not like I've known all these years and have been keeping a big secret. But even if I had it's not like I would have betrayed Elsa and told Debbie about it! Why confront me?"

"She was drunk. Who knows what she was thinking when she decided to head over here." Carl paused. "Maybe you should ask her someday. I mean after she gets out of the hospital and all."

"Maybe. I don't want to think about it anymore. It's Christmas." Carol-Barbara poured herself another cup of coffee. Then she changed the subject. "You know, this is the first year we haven't had plans with either of the kids on Christmas. It's kind of lonely."

"Yes, but also kind of nice," Carl added. "We can sit around all day in our pajamas, nap if we want to, and eat." He took another huge helping of the casserole and plopped it on his plate.

Carol-Barbara threw him her look that's said "Pace yourself, buddy" but decided not to say anything and let him enjoy his Christmas.

Carl recognized the look, but didn't acknowledge it. She was going to let him slide today. He knew it, and, more importantly, she knew it. Still, just to make sure she didn't bring it up, he decided to throw an idea her way.

"How about after breakfast we crawl back into bed and get busy."

"Excuse me?" Carol-Barbara nearly choked on her sip of coffee. That was the last thing she expected him to say.

"You heard me. Like we used to do. A nooner."

"A nooner?" Carol-Barbara smiled. "Is that what they call it?"

"I believe so," Carl stated. "Whoever *they* are."

"Oh, Carl, you never cease to amaze me with your romantic ideas," she joked. "I tell you what, you finish your casserole, let me clean up, and I'll meet you back in the bedroom."

Carl finished his casserole in two big bites, then through a mouthful of food said, "You got it."

He stood from the table, put his dish in the sink and headed back to the bedroom. Sure, he was older now, but he wasn't dead, and enjoying a tryst with his lovely bride of 40 years seemed like the best Christmas present he could ever get.

Carol-Barbara shook her head in disbelief as Carl left the kitchen.

"That man," she said aloud to herself, but inside she felt like a million bucks that after all these years that he still found her attractive enough to want to get physical with her.

After quickly doing the dishes, Carol-Barbara darted into the bathroom to make sure she looked presentable. She still wore her pajamas, and she had to admit there was nothing sexy about them. They were made of purple cotton, and had been around the block a few times. In fact, she'd had them so long she couldn't remember where she'd gotten them. They would have to do, though. Besides, she thought, they're going to be off me anyway. She giggled to herself, and went back to the bedroom.

Carl was laying on top of the covers in his boxers. "Come here, you," he held out his hand to her, and there was something in it.

"Rub this lotion on my back?" He handed her the tube. "My skin is so dry."

"I don't think this is what they had in mind when they named it a nooner, Carl." She took the tube from him as he rolled over on his stomach.

"First things first. I'm itchy."

Carol-Barbara squeezed some of the lotion on her hand and began rubbing it on Carl's back. He jokingly moaned with pleasure. "Is it as good for you as it is for me?"

Carol-Barbara tossed the tube on the bedside table. "Turn over, you tease," she ordered as she playfully hopped into the bed beside him.

He laughed and embraced her. "Ah, I love you, you sweet thing." He squeezed her tightly and kissed her on the neck.

"Me too, Carl. Me too." They lay in silence for a few minutes, relishing in the comfortable familiarity and closeness of each other.

And then the doorbell rang.

"Now who in the world could that be?" Carol-Barbara asked, pulling away from Carl and sitting up.

"Whoever it is can wait," Carl urged her.

"But it's Christmas, Carl. I should at least go see who it is."

"Christmas. All the more reason not to be bothered."

"Really, let me just go peek out the window." She stood up and pulled the drapes back a bit, allowing her a view of the front door.

"Oh my gosh. It's Elsa!" She announced.

"Oh, no. I'm not going to get my nooner, am I?" Carl sounded like a pouty kid.

"Carl, I was looking forward to it as much as you were, but Elsa's at the door, and after what happened last night, it could be pretty important."

"I'm pretty important, too," he whined.

"Carl, come on. We'll just have to have an *afternooner* instead."

Elsa came to the door bearing gifts from her own kitchen. In a giant red and green Christmas basket there were Christmas cookies of all kinds, a loaf of sourdough bread and one of Elsa's famous pineapple-coconut bread, as well as a container with her homemade soft cheese, made from a recipe that had been handed down to her from an old Russian woman she had befriended years ago.

The three friends sat down at the coffee table and sampled some of the goodies. Though he had recently consumed two giant helpings of sausage and egg casserole, Carl spread a generous helping of the soft cheese on a slab of sourdough bread.

"Elsa, you've outdone yourself. This is delicious," Carl took another bite.

"Thank you, Carl, but I guess you both know that's not the only reason I stopped by. We should talk about the elephant in the room."

"Hey, I haven't eaten that much today," Carl joked.

Carol-Barbara shook her head in disbelief at her husband's bad joke. "Yes, let's talk about what happened last night," she encouraged Elsa. "How did all this start?"

"Debbie came by my house about eight o'clock last night. She'd clearly been drinking. She told me she knew everything about my indiscretion with Dixon years ago, and about our daughter, Ashleigh. I don't know how she found out. When I called Dixon he said he had no idea how she knew either, and that he didn't care anymore. He said he was tired of keeping secrets, and was glad it was all out in the open."

"I'm confused, though. Why was she on her way to talk to me?" Carol-Barbara questioned.

"I'm not sure, but somehow she knows that you know about the situation. She told me that. All I can figure is that she heard about Ashleigh and I stopping by at Thanksgiving. Or maybe she saw Dixon with her and started asking questions. Perhaps she's been following me? As much as I love having Ashleigh here, I knew it wasn't safe for her to move to town. Anyway, Debbie was so mad. She said she was tired of me, Dixon, and even you ruining her life, but I get the feeling maybe her beef with you has more to do with the election."

"Of course," Carol-Barbara said, "That makes sense. I've contributed to her nice quiet life being disrupted," Carol-Barbara realized. "Are you going to go to the hospital to see her?"

"I don't think that would be a good idea at this point," Elsa admitted. "Anyway, I have to get to church. I just wanted to bring you by your gift and have a chat. I'm glad I got to see you."

Elsa said her goodbyes and Carl and Carol-Barbara saw her out the door.

"Well, that was informative," Carl stated.

"Not enough, though. It doesn't explain how she found out about Ashleigh."

"Someone was bound to let the cat out of the bag. Bedroom secrets have a way of getting out." He paused. "Hey, speaking of the bedroom." Carl cleared his throat dramatically and nodded his head in that direction.

"What, you need a little more lotion on your back?"

"No, I need a little more of my CB in my arms," he replied.

Carol-Barbara's heart melted a little. Now who could say no to that?

Elsa's Pineapple Coconut Bread

1 stick of butter

1 cup of sugar

3 eggs

1 tsp lemon extract

2 cups baking flour

1 tsp baking powder

1/4 cup almond milk

1 can (20 oz) crushed pineapple (Don't forget to reserve the juice!)

1 cup flaked coconut

Preheat oven to 350 degrees

Mix dry ingredients separately from wet ingredients (minus the coconut) then mix the two together. Fold in coconut. Turn in to a 9 x 5 loaf pan and bake for about an hour. Test for doneness with a toothpick. Let cool for 15 mins and turn out on to a serving platter. Enjoy!

Part 58

Where in the World is Josefina Ruiz?

Josefina sat and considered her temporary abode in the mountains; with temporary being the operative word. She hated Dogwood County with a passion, but it was where she needed to be right now, since it wasn't safe for her anywhere else in the world.

Her mountain retreat had all the amenities one could want in a house. It had been built by a very wealthy, eccentric philosopher and his artist wife, and it boasted 6 bedrooms and seven bathrooms, as well as a gourmet kitchen that would impress even Julia Child. The original couple had decked the mansion out with the finest of everything, including chandeliers from French provincial mansions, reclaimed ancient hardwood from German castles and ceramic tile from Italian villas. In the spring it had beautiful gardens through which to walk, though Josefina had never done that because she had moved in during the month of September. The giant home even had both outdoor and indoor heated salt water pools in which to swim.

The real estate agent, who had been desperately trying to sell the place for several years since the owners died, had agreed to rent it to Josefina; and, since Josefina didn't know how long she was going to need to stay there, the agent had agreed to do it on a month to month basis. Her thought was that she may as well make some sort of money back for the owners' heirs, since just the upkeep alone had cost a small fortune the past few years.

Josefina had offered the agent $25,000 a month, plus an extra $25,000 just for her if she would keep her mouth shut around Dogwood County about having rented it out at all. It really was the perfect hideaway, since there was little chance anyone was going to come snooping around the big house with the chain link fence and only one main gate to the entrance, which required a code to get in. Besides, it was winter, and people didn't generally come up there to wander around in the woods at that time of year.

So here she sat, bored out of her skull in a house that presumably had everything going for it, but in a place that lacked anything a girl like Josefina could want.

Josefina had been born in Venezuela, but she'd spent her young life travelling the world with her father, spending time in the finest hotels from New York to Dubai, and spending her father's money in the most expensive shops from Paris to Singapore.

Josefina's mother had died when she was very small, and so it had just been she and her father for as long as she could remember. They had been a team, the two of them, but eventually her father decided she needed structure, and an outlet other than shopping, for her over active mind. So she'd been sent to boarding school in London, then on to University in Amsterdam, where she had acquired a business degree. Later, she'd been awarded an MBA from Stanford. Josefina was no dummy, and her father had known it from the start. He had big plans for her from a young age, and spent the money and time to cultivate her talents so that she could serve the purpose he had for her later. Those plans included her taking over "the family business," which consisted mainly of laundering drug money through various businesses around the world.

At first, Josefina had other plans for her life. She wanted to live in the United States, perhaps get a job in a big corporation and settle down. While getting her MBA, she counted her time in California among the best in her life, as she had fallen in love with a blond haired American man who had aspirations of owning a vineyard in Napa, but her father had put a stop to that very quickly, and had demanded she return to Venezuela as soon as she graduated.

When Josefina fought with him over it, he'd offered the young man in her life enough money to open a thriving vineyard, one that eventually became a big name in the vino business, but only if he would walk away from his daughter and never see her again. The aspiring vintner had been all too accommodating, leaving Josefina's heart broken. She was angry that her father had meddled, but even angrier that her young man had been so easily swayed by him. She'd never forgiven either of them, but where she came from, allegiance to her father was of utmost importance, and so she had done as she was told and gone back to South America.

Her father spent the next ten years teaching her the ins and outs of the drug business. When he passed away, the entire empire had been left to her to run, which she had ruthlessly and successfully done for the past several years, until recently.

Now Josefina was a wanted woman, having botched a big drug deal when she let her fiery Latin temper get the best of her. One of the biggest drug dealers in the Ukraine was trying to get a large shipment of cocaine from South America, but he didn't like the price Josefina was giving him, or the manner in which she intended his money to be "invested" in order to get the deal done and get his shipments moving.

When he confronted her about it, she'd lost her cool, even ripping the blue and yellow Ukrainian flag he had hanging in his office from the wall. He'd vowed he would ruin her, put her name out on the streets to anyone and everyone who might care; the CIA, Interpol, the UK's M1-6, Russia's FSB, and especially SOVA, since that operated in the Ukraine. He even swore he would alert her rivals of where she could be found. He'd done all that he promised, and more.

So, here she sat, in Dogwood County, Virginia, where she would remain until she could get operations in order elsewhere without calling too much attention to herself. She'd chosen this place because she figured it would be the last place on earth anyone would look for her, but she just didn't know how much more she could take.

It was actually too much house for Josefina and her entourage, which at this point consisted only of her driver, Esteban, who also acted as her bodyguard and her younger male cousin, who had been with her when the activity that placed a bounty on her head went down.

She'd intended on laying low while in Virginia, and hadn't meant to do business of any kind. It was to be a respite, until things cooled off, but then she'd gotten bored, had ventured into town, then to Charlottesville, and then on to Richmond, and in extreme secret to Washington D.C.

She'd made herself acquainted with some of the pivotal figures around the area rather quickly. Money talked, and when she began writing large checks for whatever cause they were trying to drum up interest in, it had quickly gotten her invited to some of the get-togethers that passed for high society around the area. That's how she had met that little vole Debbie St. James.

Josefina thought Debbie was a joke, but since she didn't have much else to do at the moment, she had listened to Debbie's plight about needing money for an upscale shopping center to be built in the area. Since Josefina could identify with shopping, and knowing that Dogwood County needed a better shopping option than the All-Mart, she had only too happily obliged Debbie with a loan, provided she would retain 51% of the mall after it was built. After all, she might have an interest at some point in the future of having a need to launder money through this area, and it was nice to have somebody like Debbie be indebted to her. She would do anything Josefina asked of her in the future, she imagined.

But Debbie was small-town, an amateur, she clearly didn't realize who she was dealing with, and she'd gone and done something with the money. Josefina still wasn't sure what that something was, but she planned on finding out today. She had demanded Debbie to come to Tyrandoah at two o'clock for one more chance to explain herself.

After taking a leisurely swim in the indoor pool, Josefina got dressed in a stylish black jumpsuit and heels. She applied her makeup carefully, arranged her beautiful long dark hair in a tight top knot so as to look more professional, and sat on her white leather couch to await Debbie's appearance.

At exactly two o'clock on the nose Debbie's car pulled up the long driveway to Tyrandoah. Josefina's bodyguard, Esteban, buzzed her in and made Josefina aware of Debbie's arrival. He let her into the living room where Josefina was waiting.

Debbie looked awful from her stay in the hospital. Her arm was in a sling, and she had some bruises on her face. Even so, she had put on her best clothes, some that she had purchased on her last trip to Atlanta, but which were, by Josefina's standards, still five and dime attire.

Josefina didn't even want her sitting on her fine couch in that ensemble, so she asked her to sit in the uncomfortably straight wing back chair, while she remained lounging comfortably; a princess receiving her court.

"You look like mierda." Josefina pointed out using her Spanish vernacular.

"I was in an accident," Debbie explained.

Josefina seemed uninterested. "So," she continued, as Debbie took her place in the chair.

Debbie looked scared. "Ummm…"

"Ummm? What is this 'Ummm'? Are you getting ready to sing to me?" Josefina cruelly mocked.

Debbie was speechless.

"You don't know who you are dealing with you idiot, you imbecile, you American redneck!" She shot the words at her like a bullet. "Where is my money? You were supposed to prove to me you had invested it by now."

"I did. Sort of." Debbie told her, uneasily.

"Sort of?" Josefina asked. "What is that supposed to mean? Sort of."

"I put it towards something that was supposed to be a sure thing," Debbie revealed.

"And where is it, this sure thing?" Josefina prodded.

"It actually didn't turn out that way," Debbie admitted.

Josefina jumped from the couch. She stood in front of Debbie, towering over her, then leaned in, her finger in Debbie's face. "You tell me where my two million dollars is right now, or I swear I will have your husband killed tonight!" She paused, started pacing. "Why is it that you even care about him? I told you before, he cheats on you. He has even fathered a child with your sister. He is not a good husband."

Debbie teared up. Josefina had been throwing this in her face since the moment she had found out about Ashleigh while trailing Dixon.

Unfortunately, Ashleigh had been naïve, and tricked into telling the exotic woman who was supposedly just travelling through town about her parents. Josefina had struck up a conversation with her at a boutique store she had followed her to after Ashleigh had ice cream with Dixon one Monday night.

Josefina had asked her what was wrong, and Ashleigh had been all too willing to tell her problems to the woman she would likely never see again. Especially when Josefina started talking about the death of her own mother at such a young age. It had been like therapy for Ashleigh, yet it was all a ruse.

Debbie was visibly shaken. Josefina was ruining every aspect of her life. How could she tell Josefina what had happened to the money? If she didn't tell the truth, she was signing Dixon's death warrant, and if she told the truth, she was possibly committing suicide as well. She was out of time, though. There was nothing else she could do but to tell her what she'd done.

"I put it on a horse." Even as the words spilled from her mouth, she couldn't believe she was actually telling Josefina. That wasn't all. In telling Josefina she was actually revealing a lifetime of addiction; one to gambling, although this was certainly the most she'd ever played, or lost.

"Are you saying you bet my money on a horse? As in a horse race?" It was the last thing Josefina had considered. Offshore bank accounts? The purchase of a remote island somewhere? All of these she had contemplated, but a horse race? It never crossed her mind.

"I have a problem," Debbie confessed. "One of which I am deeply ashamed." Debbie began to weep uncontrollably.

Josefina couldn't stand a woman who cried. Her instincts kicked in, and she smacked Debbie in the face, not just once, but repeatedly as she screamed at her.

"Get yourself together woman!" With every word she delivered another slap.

Debbie fell to the floor, gravelling. "Please don't kill me! Please!"

Josefina backed away. Stared. "You think only of yourself. Do you even love this man you call your husband? I said I would kill him! Today! And still you beg only for your own life." She spat on Debbie's ugly updo-ed hair. "You don't deserve him."

Debbie hung her head and sobbed.

"Esteban!" Josefina bellowed for her bodyguard. He came around the corner quickly, as if he had been waiting for his next order. "Get her out of my sight."

"What should I do with her?" Esteban asked nervously, having never enjoyed the more gruesome of Josefina's orders.

Josefina took a deep breath. The only thing that was keeping her from doing away with Debbie right now was the fact that she didn't want to call any more attention to herself.

"Get her to her car. Send her away. I need to think." She sat down on her pristine leather couch, tucking a piece of hair that had come loose behind her ear.

Esteban took Debbie by the elbow, helped her stand, and walked her out the front door and to her car.

Josefina was outraged, perhaps more than she'd been at her boyfriend all those years ago, or her father, and almost as much as the Ukrainian who had out-ed her. She stood up and went to the bar, made from a solid piece of ancient Redwood that had been lovingly crafted for the house. Taking a bottle from behind it, she poured herself a whiskey, neat, and considered her next move.

Part 59

Brownies and Beehives

New Year's Eve had come and gone with absolutely no pomp and circumstance for the Hoofnagle household. Carl and Carol-Barbara had tried to stay up and watch the whole of Dick Clark's Rockin' New Year's Eve celebration on TV, but sadly, the Times Square ball had dropped while the pair snored softly together on the couch in the den.

Besides, even though the program was still telecast with Dick Clark's name, (he must have had a hundred years claim to it was all Carol-Barbara could figure) the event just wasn't the same without Dick, who had passed away several years before. Even though the show still bore his name, it was run now by a new generation of young, svelte, and half-naked would-be celebrities, some of whom she'd never heard of, nor could she figure out why they were even celebrities.

Take the Kardashians, for example. Who were they anyway, and why would she even want to "keep up with them" as the name of their reality show suggested she might? The only celebrity she could even remotely identify, when she saw the advertisements for the program, was Bruce Jenner, who had been married to a Kardashian for a number of years.

Although, he looked so different now that she hardly recognized him. She'd seen a magazine cover at the grocery store reporting that he had decided to become a woman. That was fine, she'd thought, to each his, or her own, whatever the case may be, but in her opinion, his new look did not suit him. He'd been so handsome back in the day! She'd had a huge crush on him, but what woman hadn't? She just didn't get it.

While New Year's Eve had been a bust in the entertainment arena, the first week of the New Year brought for Carol-Barbara a new outlook on life, and a stronger desire to win the election. Any doubts she had about running had been replaced by a motivation she hadn't felt in a long time about anything.

In less than a week's time there would be one final public debate between Carol-Barbara and Dixon before the residents of Dogwood County were given the chance to exercise their right to vote. It was to be held at the county courthouse.

Carol-Barbara was not as nervous this time. So much had happened between the televised debate it seemed pointless for her to be nervous. It seemed to her that anything that could happen had already happened, even events she could not have imagined in her wildest dreams.

After Dixon's shooting, Carol-Barbara had learned that he had a love child with her old friend, Elsa. An international drug runner had been found to be living nearby and fraternizing with the locals. She had discovered her neighbors weren't merely an odd couple transplanted here from New Jersey, but rather a couple of federal agents after said drug runner. Then, most recently, Dixon's wife, Debbie, had nearly killed herself in a drunk driving incident practically in the Hoofnagle front yard. What else could possibly happen? Besides, she clearly had zero control over anything, so why fret? She decided instead to focus on something she could control- her hair.

Carol-Barbara made an appointment to get her hair cut and colored for the big event. Carl came into the kitchen just as she hung up with Tammy at The Beauty Mark salon. Carl heard the tail end of the conversation, and was surprised.

"What? Carl's Barbershop not good enough for you anymore, Mrs. Pol-it-i-co?" He emphasized each syllable of the informal word one might call a politician. Until she'd started the campaign he had often trimmed her hair for her.

"I just thought I could use a little all over freshening again. Tammy had a last-minute cancellation today and can fit me in at one o'clock." Gosh, had she really hurt his feelings? She wondered, then added, "Don't worry. I'll be back for an appointment with you soon enough. Can't keep paying almost a hundred dollars for a cut and color every two months.

"Well, I'll be waiting for you." Carl responded. "And I know you'll be back to see Carl the Barber. Where else do you get a kiss at the end of a haircut?" He bent down and kissed her on the forehead. Besides, I couldn't have fit you into my schedule today anyway."

"Oh, really? Business that good?" She joked.

"No. I only have one customer, but she is very demanding, now that I think about it," he teased, then ruffled the hair on her head with his hand.

He laughed. "Actually, I'm going to go in to work for a while. Roland is missing a few people who are out with the flu. He said he could use an extra hand."

"Roland, huh?" She replied. Now that they both knew Roland was not their neighbor's real name, it seemed funny to continue to call him that. "He's back then?"

Carl knew exactly what she was referring to. "Yes, and remember," he reminded her, "we are not supposed to even allude to the fact that we know Roland and Honey are not who they are pretending to be. It's best we forget about the whole situation. As far as I'm concerned, he's Roland Van Honk from New Jersey, and he's my boss at the All Mart. That's how he's going to remain until further notice. Got it?"

"Got it." She paused. "But you have to admit it's weird," she pointed out.

"It may be weird, but it'll hopefully keep us out of trouble. Those two were pretty darn serious when they said we had to keep things hush-hush."

What was it with all these people having to pretend to be someone they weren't? Suddenly, Carol-Barbara got a glimpse of the clock on the kitchen wall. She jumped from the kitchen table.

"Good grief. It's already 12:30. I've got to get out of here if I'm going to make it to that appointment in time. Can you get yourself some lunch?" She asked.

"I'll scrounge up something," Carl told her.

"Make sure it's healthy," she told him. "No junk, okay?"

"Humph," Carl fake pouted and crossed his arms like an angry child.

Carol-Barbara kissed him on the cheek, grabbed her purse and headed out the door to the garage.

Carl stood for a minute thinking about what he wanted to eat, then headed straight for the brownies Carol-Barbara had made for the pot luck at church tomorrow.

"One little one won't hurt," he said aloud, as if to convince himself.

Carol-Barbara arrived at The Beauty Mark, and since it was a Saturday, the place was hopping. Tammy had just finished up with her twelve o'clock appointment, and was accepting her payment at the front desk when Carol-Barbara walked in. The rest of the beauticians still had women sitting at their stations. The ladies were having everything done from perms to keratin treatments and even manicures.

"Good to see you again, Carol-Barbara!" Tammy welcomed her as she came through the door. "I'm just wrapping up with Mrs. Teaman. Give me just a minute. Make yourself comfortable."

"Thanks, Tammy." Carol-Barbara had a seat on the couch to wait. She noticed Mrs. Teaman, a well-coiffed woman older than herself, who happened to be sporting a traditional beehive hairdo, kept turning around to eye her. She started to feel a little self-conscious, as she knew she didn't know the woman, and wondered what she was looking at. Probably her own disheveled hair, she thought. Gosh, some women were so judgmental.

When Mrs. Teaman was done paying, she came over to where Carol-Barbara was sitting and extended her arm towards her. Carol-Barbara immediately tensed up.

"I just want to shake your hand," Mrs. Teaman said, matter-of-factly.

Carol-Barbara was shocked. "Who, me?"

"You are Carol-Barbara Hoofnagle, correct?" Mrs. Teaman asked, still holding her hand out.

Carol-Barbara, not wanting to appear rude, took the woman's hand. "I am."

"My friends and I are so proud of you, taking on that awful man in the election. We talk about you all the time. Dame power!" Mrs. Teaman raised the hand that wasn't clutching Carol-Barbara's in a fist of solidarity in the air.

Carol-Barbara didn't know what to say. Proud of her? Dame power? Was she supposed to know this woman who was clearly paying her such a nice compliment? She had clearly misjudged the woman, and could now feel a familiar pre-tear lump building in her throat, so she simply said, "Thank you."

Mrs. Teaman could see confusion in Carol-Barbara's eyes. "In case you're wondering, I go to church with your friend, Susie Perkins, and she gave me one of your campaign buttons, the one with the nice picture. That's how I recognized you. I adore that pin! I put it in my jewelry box to keep it safe because I just know it's going to be worth something someday. When you beat that awful man."

Carol-Barbara noticed that Mrs. Teaman never referred to Dixon by name. It was always 'that awful man.' She thought about something she could say to the woman, but she needn't have worried because it was clear Mrs. Teaman wasn't going to let her get a word in edge-wise.

Mrs. Teaman continued. "Oh, and Susie's told me all about your ladies' group, too. The NAKED ladies. What a hoot! By the way, my friends and I would love to start our own group. That okay with you? We'll give you credit, of course. Maybe you could even make a special appearance!" Mrs. Teaman finally paused for a breath.

Carol-Barbara hadn't considered other people may want to start their own chapters. How did she feel about that? She guessed that imitation was the sincerest form of flattery, and finally found her voice.

"Of course! I would be flattered, and thank you for the vote of confidence regarding the election with Dixon."

"No, thank *you*, and it's not just a vote of confidence. You've got my real vote in two weeks. Now keep up the good work." With those final parting words, Mrs. Teaman was gone.

Carol-Barbara's head was spinning.

"Ready, CB?" Tammy called to her.

"Ready." Carol-Barbara stood up, a spring in her step, and headed for the salon chair.

She sat down and Tammy started pumping the hydraulic lift on the chair to situate Carol-Barbara at the proper height.

"Carl doing ok?" Tammy asked as she leaned Carol-Barbara back to begin the shampooing.

"He's fine. Hobbling along." Carol-Barbara laughed.

"Oh, good." Then she paused, looking for something. "Darn it. I'm out of the conditioner I wanted to use on your hair. You really could use a deep conditioning treatment. There's some more in the back. Sit tight." Tammy walked to the back of the store, disappearing through a door.

Carol-Barbara laid at an uncomfortable angle, waiting for Tammy to reappear. As she lay there, she realized someone had walked towards her chair and was standing, not moving. Another beautician, Carol-Barbara wondered? She soon learned it was not.

A heavily-accented voice spoke to her. "I want you to have this."

An envelope was shoved into Carol-Barbara's hand. Though she couldn't see who was doing it, she had an inkling. No one else in Dogwood County had a voice like that. It could only be Josefina Ruiz.

Carol-Barbara loosely held the envelope. What was she supposed to do, let it drop? She had no idea what it even was.

"I heard you talking to that woman. Use it to beat that 'awful man' in the election." Josefina laughed. It was a maniacal laugh, as far as Carol-Barbara was concerned.

And then she was gone, and Tammy was back.

"Found it!" Tammy announced. "This conditioner will do wonders for your hair."

Carol-Barbara sat up in the chair.

"What's wrong?" Tammy asked.

Carol-Barbara opened the envelope. The contents included what must have been thousands of dollars, all in hundred dollar bills.

"Holy gosh!" Tammy exclaimed. "You shouldn't be running around with all that cash. Someone might rob you!"

"I'm not." Carol-Barbara told her. "It was given to me."

"By who?" Tammy asked.

"One of the customers, I think. As a campaign contribution." Carol-Barbara told her.

"Wow! She must really want you to win!" Tammy encouraged her.

"Oh, she wants something," Carol-Barbara assured her. *I'm just not sure what it is yet.*

Part 60

Return to Sender

Her trip to the salon over, Carol-Barbara immediately went home. Post-hair coif, she hadn't known what to do with the envelope full of money Josefina had handed her while she lay in the hairdresser's chair, so she'd stuck it in her purse to deal with later.

Then, she'd felt like such a criminal the entire time she was driving home from the salon; like a drug dealer carrying all that cash around. Especially since she was fairly sure that was how the money had been obtained. She thought about what would happen if she'd been stopped by the police with all that cash. How would she have explained it?

She'd made it home safe and sound, though, so she'd called a meeting of sorts. Now, she found herself sitting at the kitchen table across from Martha and Carl, the two people she trusted most in the world. She had been counting the money out loud in front of them for what seemed like an eternity. She was finally coming to the end.

"Nine thousand eight hundred, nine thousand nine hundred, ten thousand dollars." She paused, a look of disbelief on her face. "Ten thousand dollars," she said aloud again. "Who carries around ten thousand dollars in one hundred dollar bills?"

"Someone who doesn't trust banks." Carl offered.

"And drug dealers," Martha pointed out.

"And what does she want from me that she would give ten thousand dollars to my campaign?" Carol-Barbara asked with dismay.

"I think that's obvious," Martha stated. "She wants you to beat Dixon."

"But how did she know she would run into me at the hair salon to give me the money? I didn't even know I would be at the salon until thirty minutes before I arrived there!" She was perplexed.

"Maybe she's just been hoping to run into you somewhere." Martha offered.

"Maybe she's been following you, or even tracing your calls! Maybe she knew you were going to be at the salon. Maybe our phone is tapped!" Carl jumped up from the table, picked up the receiver and stared at it suspiciously.

"Maybe you need to calm down," Martha ordered. "Hang the phone up, Carl."

Carl did as he was ordered and had a seat back at the table. Martha had always scared him a little.

"I mean, it's not as though we run in the same circles," Carol-Barbara pointed out. "How did she know I was going to be there? And she was having her nails done, too, which means she must have had an appointment. Do you know how long it takes to get an appointment there? The Beauty Mark is not the type of place you just walk in and have your nails done, or anything else. The only reason I got in is because there was a last minute cancellation."

"I think you are overreacting. It was a coincidence, that's all. A woman like that probably carries around ten times that much cash. That was chump change to her." Martha paused for a moment. "The question is, why does she want you to beat Dixon so bad? I mean, what interest does she have in him? Ask yourself that."

"As far as I know, nothing. What makes you think they have any connection?" Carol-Barbara asked.

"Just something to think about. That's all. A woman doesn't move into the area from another country and just decide she's going to get involved in local politics, and just happen to give one of the candidates money to beat the other one for no reason. Perhaps she's been scorned by him in some way, and you know what they say about a woman scorned, especially a hot-blooded woman like Josefina."

"Oh, gosh. Do you think they were lovers?" Carol-Barbara questioned.

"I would hope she'd have better taste than that, but you never know. He's bedded half of Dogwood County's elite, hasn't he?" Martha concluded.

"I guess so," Carol-Barbara thought for a moment. "So what am I going to do with all this money?"

"Use it to beat Dixon of course!" Carl was adamant.

"What do you think?" Carol-Barbara looked to Martha to be the voice of reason.

391

"Hmmm… It would be nice to be able to do some last minute campaigning, on the radio, or even a television commercial, but I think it would come with strings attached," Martha pointed out.

"You mean like we could get in trouble for taking an illegal fund contribution and get fined or something?" Carol-Barbara asked.

"There's that, yes. Or worse. You don't know what you would owe her by keeping the money. There are strings, and then there are nooses, and with someone like her I'm afraid you could be hanging yourself. As far as the legalities, though, let's focus on those. First of all, it's likely illicitly obtained money, as we have already discussed. In the United States of America, one cannot fund a campaign with drug money. Even if we could prove it had been earned legitimately, there is the fact that Ms. Ruiz isn't even a resident of Dogwood County, or the United States for that matter. She can't even vote here. For that reason alone, she can't financially contribute."

"How will I get it back to her?" Carol-Barbara fretted. It's not like I can just mosey on up to her place and give it back. I don't even know where she lives."

"I do," Martha told them.

"How do you know that?" Carl asked point blank.

"I have my ways. You know that. Remember the old mansion up on the mountain?"

"Tyrandoah?" Carol-Barbara asked.

"That's the one," Martha confirmed. "She's been up there for months."

"Well we can't just show up there," Carol-Barbara pointed out.

"Why not?" Carl asked.

"I'm sure she has people milling about watching for trespassers, and guns at the ready!" Carol-Barbara exclaimed.

Martha, after listening to their logic, spoke up. "I'll take it to her."

"No, Martha, I can't put you in that position," Carol-Barbara demanded.

"As your campaign manager, which I do believe you made me back at the start of this whole thing, it falls within my duties to let her know we can't accept it," Martha trumped.

"Oh, Martha, I don't know…" Carol-Barbara's voice trailed off.

"I insist. There, it's done. This evening I'll make a little drive up the mountain and make a delivery." Martha stood up from the kitchen table, her move to end this argument here and now.

"I'm scared for you, Marty," Carol-Barbara called her dear friend by the moniker she'd given her years before.

Martha put her hand on Carol-Barbara's shoulder. "Don't be."

At this point Carl piped in. "Do you want me to go with you for protection?" He offered, only half-heartedly.

"No, Carl," Martha stifled a giggle imagining Carl as her protector. "That won't be necessary. Besides," she raised her jacket a little on the side to reveal the revolver she carried on her hip. "You know I've always got my own protection."

Martha made the long drive up the mountain to Tyrandoah. She carried the envelope of money with her. Even though she'd told Carl and Carol-Barbara that she wasn't scared about going up to see Josefina, she kept her revolver on the seat next to her.

She'd always been one to carry a gun, even had a concealed carry permit. In her former work with the government years before in D.C. she'd always just felt safer, especially as a woman, to pack a little fire with her wherever she went.

As she drove up to the house, she could see another car pulling out of the long driveway. She didn't recognize it, but when the car passed by her she definitely recognized the driver. It was Debbie St. James. Must have been a rental after her accident, Martha assumed. Thankfully, Debbie seemed to be preoccupied, and hadn't seemed to notice Martha.

What the hell was Debbie doing up here anyway? Martha wondered, but couldn't let it bother her at this moment. She had other things to worry about right now.

As she approached the gate to the house, she knew she must have to be buzzed in, so she slowed to a stop and pressed the button to be let in. A heavily accented male voice from the other end asked her to identify herself and wanted to know the nature of her business there.

Martha didn't hesitate. "Please tell Ms. Ruiz that it's Martha Fitzgerald."

After thirty seconds or so of silence, the gate opened, as she knew it would, and she was allowed to drive in. She parked her car in the circular driveway in front of the house, grabbed the envelope of money from the front seat beside her, and got out of the car. She headed towards the front door of the house, never missing a beat, or seeming nervous in any way.

She rang the doorbell and waited, and was rewarded with an almost immediate answer. Within a few seconds the door opened. A tall Hispanic-looking man ushered her in.

"Ms. Ruiz will receive you in the parlor," he stated. "Follow me."

Martha followed him into the elaborately decorated front parlor. There, on the chaise lounge, sat Josefina. She looked at her visitor for a long moment, then she finally spoke.

"Marta," she said simply, the word rolling off her tongue with familiarity, and in typical Spanish fashion, without the 'h' sound.

"Josefina," Martha replied with ease. "I've been trying to put off this visit since I found out you were here, hoping you would come to your senses and leave, maybe even turn yourself in, but I can no longer ignore you."

"Ha. It's so good to see you as well," Josefina joked. "It's been a long time," Josefina continued.

"That it has," Martha agreed. "And I must say I never thought it would be here in Dogwood County that we would be talking face to face again." She paused, then added. "How did you find me?"

"Oh, Marta," Josefina stood up from the couch. "Do you really think I couldn't find you if I wanted to? We both know the same people." She went behind the bar to refill a glass that had obviously become empty too fast, considering the gusto with which she poured it, then continued. "People who know how to find someone, even if they seem to have disappeared off the face of the Earth."

Martha said nothing in response, leaving the door open for Josefina to continue.

Josefina carried her now full glass of whiskey back to the couch, resuming her position. "You must have known you would hear from me, eventually."

"But why now, Josefina? After all this time? I thought we were done with these silly games. You told me you were going to turn your life around. That your father's parting words before his death had made you see the error of your ways." Martha seemed genuinely perplexed, and concerned.

"I tried, Marta, I really did, but it's just in me, you know? I am what I am, sure as you are what you are. We can't change. Neither one of us, which is why I am still a criminal, and you are a sixty-something year old woman who still thinks she can save the world." Josefina was nonchalant.

"I was not trying to save the world, just you. And I was only doing it as a favor to your father." Martha quickly replied.

Josefina was angry. "My father went crazy before he died. He didn't know what he was asking of you. He made me into what I am today, and then had some kind of guilty Catholic moment at the end. He was only trying to save his immortal soul."

"Your father loved you very much," Martha steadfastly told her.

If he loved me so much why did he let you turn me in? I had to go escape to Eastern Europe for God's sake! Do you know how cold it gets there?"

"As a matter of fact, I do. I spent many months there undercover," Martha had to stifle a smile. "It's where I met your father, God rest his soul."

At this Josefina jumped from the couch. "Stop talking about my father like he was some kind of a saint!" She began pouring what was left of the bottle of whiskey into her glass.

Martha took a deep breath. "Not a saint, just a reformed man trying to set things right."

"Thanks to you!" At this Josefina lunged towards Martha. Clearly, the alcohol was having an effect on her. Josefina stopped short of touching Martha, perhaps realizing she was about to attack a woman twice her age, and that would be physically unfair.

She backed away from Martha slowly, then grabbed her glass and headed back for more whiskey from behind the bar. "You know," Josefina spoke as she opened the bottle. "When I was in the Ukraine, and that awful man decided to out me to the world, this was the first place I thought of coming. Who would look for me in a place like this? And besides, I'm having fun messing with the people who live here. Like that idiot Dixon St. James and his ridiculously stupid wife."

"How in the world did you get involved with the St. Jameses?" Martha asked.

"It was all too easy, Marta. They want something and they think I can give it to them." She began pouring what was left of the bottle of whiskey into her glass.

"Do you think you need any more of that?" Martha knew she was being bold, but knew things would only get uglier the more Josefina drank.

"You are not my mother! Stop telling me what to do!" Josefina sounded like a spoiled child. "And just because you loved my father does not mean you get to tell me what to do." Josefina took a huge slug of the drink.

With this, Martha knew there was no point in trying to talk to Josefina. It was obvious she would remember very little of their conversation tomorrow. She made a decision to get back to the root of the reason she had come to see Josefina; the envelope of money, which she still clutched in her hand.

"My friend can't accept your money," she told her, and laid the envelope on the antique table next to the chaise lounge. She stood up from her chair and walked towards the door. "Please, I beg of you, out of respect for your father, try to remember the love you once had for him, and don't ruin any more lives in Dogwood County."

With that, she opened the door and departed, leaving a very angry, and very drunk, Josefina behind her.

Part 61

Boca or Bust

While her friends would be enjoying the pool at the YMCA morning water aerobics class, Debbie was at home, still recovering from her little drunk-driving accident. She was still in way too much pain to exercise.

Aside from venturing out to see Josefina when she was beckoned to Tyrandoah, Debbie had spent most of the last few days on the couch watching television. She spent mornings with Hoda and Kathy Lee, and her afternoons with Judge Judy, Maury Povich and Ellen Degeneres.

This lifestyle had given her way too much time to eat- she'd gone through two half-gallons of ice cream already, two family size bags of Martin's potato chips, and too many cookies to count, not to mention a fifth of vodka and several bottles of wine.

Being at home by herself had also given her way too much time to think, and she knew she had a big, bad problem; one that could only be solved by a big, bad solution.

She'd toyed with the idea of killing Josefina, just being done with her once and for all, but that wouldn't get her the money back that she'd lost, and she desperately needed that money. She wouldn't be able to get away with it anyway because Josefina had people protecting her at all times. If Debbie even got too close to Josefina, uninvited, she'd probably be shot on site, and even if she got away with it for a short time, there was no hiding from those people. They would find her wherever she went. So she'd been formulating a new plan.

Debbie's first mistake had been taking a drug dealer's money in the first place. Now, she had to pay Josefina back, in the hefty sum of two million dollars, plus interest, which was accruing every day at a quick rate; although not as quick as the rate at which the lines on her face were increasing due to the stress of it all. The copious amounts of junk food and alcohol weren't helping with her looks either. For someone who prided herself on how things looked, this was tragic.

Her second mistake had been gambling away the money in one fell swoop. When she first placed the bet, her thought had been that if she could win, then she'd have the money she needed for the mall plan, plus enough to replace all the money she'd lost over the past few years since her little "problem" had gotten in the way.

Gambling had become a terrible habit for her, one that had gotten out of control as the years went on. Dixon always knew she liked to put a little money in the slots from time to time on trips to Atlantic City; and he certainly knew she liked to place a few bucks at the Sunday races on their trips to Charlestown, West Virginia. However, he had no idea exactly how much she'd gambled away over the course of the past few years. It had depleted her entire personal savings, everything her father had left her when he died; all that money he had socked away for her after she'd married Dixon.

"Just trust me," her father had told her in private. "You're going to need this someday, whether you can see that right now or not."

Her father had been right, and she'd pissed it all away thinking she could make a big win and fix everything.

Now she had nothing; no money, no children to help her, her marriage had gone down the tubes, her sister hated her, and now she knew Dixon had fathered a child with said sister. She may have never known if Josefina hadn't told her a few weeks before.

At first she didn't believe it. Over the years, Debbie had often wondered if Dixon had fathered children with any of those women he had bedded. She used to allow herself to fantasize about the son he might have who would take after him; smart, good-looking, athletic. Perhaps he'd even secretly put him through a fancy private school, maybe even showed up on special occasions to watch the kid play quarterback on the football team; the same position he'd played in high school, and later in college.

So it hadn't been a son with some random woman, but a daughter and the mother was none other than her little sister, Elsa. She had come to hate both of them with every fiber of her being. Especially Dixon.

So, since desperate times called for desperate measures, her plan included vindication. It was one that would take care of her money problems with Josefina, and gain her a nice sum of money to take care of her the rest of her life. Her plan would have to be carried out very carefully, though, as she was already being watched by the authorities due to her previous indiscretions. She would shoot Dixon and get his hefty life insurance policy, plus his retirement fund. It was worth millions.

The first time she'd tried to shoot Dixon had been a huge mistake. She was actually trying to protect him from Josefina at the time. The night Dixon was shot was the night that Josefina became wise to the fact that Debbie had done something with her money besides invest it in the mall venture. It was also the same night that Dixon thought Debbie was on one of her shopping excursions in Richmond.

The truth was, she had gone to Richmond earlier that day. She'd stopped by Nordstrom's to try on a dress she'd seen online. She'd even gone so far as to check into the Jefferson Hotel; but then she'd gotten an idea.

With the help of her therapist, she'd managed not to gamble for quite some time, instead dealing with impulses by repeating the Serenity Prayer, the same one used by Alcoholics Anonymous. It had been working, but that day, it hadn't done anything to quell her addiction. Besides, in her mind, the gambling she wanted to do now would have a purpose. Any money gained would help with her cause to raise enough money to bring Dogwood County into the 21st century with a world class shopping center. She justified it by telling herself it would provide jobs and income to the people of Dogwood; *if* she won, that is, but she hadn't even considered the possibility of not winning because her bookie had assured her it was a "sure thing."

So she'd ended up at an off track betting site in downtown Richmond, placing her bet on one horse named *All About That Bass*. One million dollars was the bet. Her bookie had arranged for her to be able to place a bet that large in advance. What she didn't know, and what no one else knew, was that the horse had been bitten on the leg by a brown recluse spider minutes before the race. Bottom line was that she had lost everything.

She knew she'd have to tell Josefina what had happened, because the very next day the woman would be expecting an update as to where her money was being put to use. So, without checking out of the hotel, she'd gathered her belongings and headed back to Dogwood County to confront her. Josefina had been furious, of course, and had threatened that very night to go shoot Dixon that night as payback.

So Debbie had followed her for hours, and spotted her stalking Dixon. Debbie hadn't shot a gun in years, but she had a 38 Ruger in her glove box, and she planned on using it that night to protect Dixon.

Though she was always angry with him for being a philanderer, she still wasn't aware that night of the fact that he and her sister had a love child. That came later, so she still wanted to protect him to some extent. She certainly wasn't going to let Josefina shoot him. No, if anyone was ever going to kill Dixon, it was going to be her, but not then.

So when she finally came across Josefina watching Dixon from her car parked on a hill, she'd parked across from her. They were both waiting for Dixon to come out of the hardware store. Dixon's car was parked between the two women, one who wanted to kill him, and one who was trying, although misguidedly, to save him.

When he emerged and headed for his car, Debbie saw Josefina raise her gun and take aim. So Debbie raised hers, hoping to take out Josefina, or at least to hit something close by and scare her. Because she hadn't shot a gun in years, and because she was using a gun intended for close range when she was aiming at least 50 yards, she had misaligned the shot terribly. Instead of shooting anything in Josefina's general vicinity, she'd shot Dixon in the ass. At least it had knocked Josefina off her aim; hence the second bullet the police had found in the side of Dixon's car.

How apropos, Debbie thought, that she had been the one to shoot Dixon in his nether region. She wondered later, if only subconsciously, if she'd meant to hit him there. Just a little nick where it would wound him the most.

Now, though, after everything that had happened over the past few weeks, she actually wanted him dead. Her grand plan was to shoot him and make it look like Josefina did it thereby eliminating all of her problems. Josefina would certainly be caught and spend years in jail for the crime, and for everything else she was certainly wanted for, while Debbie would collect the money from Dixon's massive insurance policy and live out her years in Boca Raton, the grieving widow.

Pretty soon the people of the piss ant county of Dogwood, and her grand plans for a world-class shopping center would be a distant memory. For all she cared those lowlifes could go to their graves dressed in clothing from the All-Mart, and wearing cheap perfume and makeup from CVS. She was done.

Part 62

Que sera, sera

The night of the debate had arrived. Carol-Barbara was not nervous in the least. At this point, like Doris Day sang, it was que sera, sera; whatever will be, will be.

She was dressed yet again in the only thing she thought appropriate to wear; the outfit Honey put together for her all those months ago. Those days seemed like another lifetime now, and she thought about how much had happened since then.

Carl, also dressed very handsomely, had driven her to the debate. He would be attending, too, of course, as would all of her friends and family. Her daughter and son had made a special drive into town just to witness their mom in action. Her daughter in law had stayed back with baby Carly. Carol-Barbara reminded herself again about how it really didn't matter what the outcome of the election was, as she'd already been bestowed with so many blessings in life!

This debate would not be televised, so it was expected to be heavily attended, especially with all the ruckus that had been going on with Dixon lately, and in Dogwood County in general. He still had his supporters, those who didn't care what he did in his personal life, or men who were politically stuck in the middle ages, and didn't want to see a woman in the position, much less an aged in the wood woman.

However, Carol-Barbara had her army of supporters; her church friends, and her YMCA workout buddies, as well as all of her NAKED ladies, and of course anyone who couldn't stand Dixon. What the outcome of this election would be was anybody's guess, or so that's what she was told by Martha, her best friend, confidant and loyal campaign manager.

Carl dropped her off at the front door to the courthouse and went to find a parking space. When she entered the courthouse she was immediately greeted by a deputy, who was assigned to get her where she needed to be.

As she followed the deputy through the courthouse, she was surprised to see how many people were already milling about. She recognized a couple of faces. One woman she knew from the Y, but whose name escaped her now, hollered out, "Good luck," as she passed by. A little further in she saw Martha standing in the hallway.

"Remember what we talked about," she told Carol-Barbara as she passed by.

Carol-Barbara knew exactly what she was referring to, "Stay calm. Stay focused. Stay yourself."

Carol-Barbara was led by the deputy around the back of the courthouse halls and to the rear of the auditorium so she could enter without having to pass through the crowds of people who were already seated to watch the debate. She followed the deputy through a door that led to the back of the stage. There were some comfortable seats arranged as a waiting area. The deputy asked her to make herself comfortable, and then left. She was all alone.

She chose a chair and had a seat, arranging the note cards she'd made for herself and settling in to study them one more time. Martha had made sure she was prepared for any question that was thrown at her, and had even come up with a blanket reply for anything she couldn't answer. It read, "I'm still gathering information on that one and formulating an opinion. Let me get back to you on that." The reply sounded like something she might have heard any politician throw at a journalist when he didn't know a hill of beans about the subject at hand. Strangely, this sort of BS seemed to work, even for the President of the United States.

She'd been reading over the note cards for several minutes when she heard the same door she had been led through open again, so she looked up. The same deputy led Dixon through the door and asked him to have a seat. The deputy departed again, leaving the two opponents alone. They made eye contact briefly and nodded at one another, then he took a seat across from her. He had nothing in his hands, no notes, no laptop or tablet. She guessed he'd done this so many times that he didn't need a crutch anymore. Or perhaps he was just so confident that he would win that he didn't think it was necessary to prepare anything. After a few minutes, Dixon spoke up.

"You know, I'm not a bad guy, Carol-Barbara," he started. "I know you're aware of some of the things I've done. Elsa told me she talked to you, and I hope that you can forgive me."

Carol-Barbara may have fallen out of the chair if it weren't for the side arms holding her in. She didn't know how to respond. Thankfully, she didn't have to yet. He continued.

"Things have been falling apart with Debbie and me for a long time, and honestly all I want now is to get to know my daughter, and figure out some way to live a happy, meaningful life, with, or more likely without, Debbie."

Dixon sounded oddly a little sad about the situation with Debbie, despite the things she'd done lately. Carol-Barbara supposed it was because when you've been with someone that long, even when things were bad it was tough to think of a life without him or her.

Finally, Carol-Barbara found some words. "I think that's all any of us want, Dixon; to be happy. By the way, Ashleigh seems like a wonderful girl."

"Oh, she is, amazing really. She's smarter and kinder than I ever could be." He clearly felt great love and pride for the young woman, though he had been denied any responsibility, save his financial responsibility over the years, for the things that helped make her that way.

"I'm sure you'll have lots of time to get to know her now. You and Elsa."

Dixon nodded, "I hope so."

Just then the same door opened and the same deputy told them that the stage curtains would be opening momentarily and that they would each be expected to head to the podium that had their respective name attached to it.

"Good luck to both of you," he announced with every bit of unbiased political correctness he could muster. After all, Dixon was currently in a position of authority in the county, but for all the deputy knew, Carol-Barbara could be the one with the title after next Tuesday's election.

Dixon stood up and walked the short distance to Carol-Barbara. "Good luck, Carol-Barbara. You are truly a worthy opponent." He held out his hand to shake hers.

She stood up and extended hers. For all the reasons she didn't like Dixon, she couldn't seem to think of one right now. "Good luck to you, too, Dixon."

As soon as their hands parted, they heard the moderator announce that they would be beginning, and then the stage curtains opened.

The auditorium was packed. The lights from the stage made it so Carol-Barbara could only make out the first few rows of people. In the first row she spotted Carl right away. Martha had reserved a seat for him next to her. She gave Carol-Barbara a quick thumbs up when they made eye contact. Carol-Barbara could also see many of her friends who had arrived early and gotten seats up close. Susie and Diane were in plain view. She could even see Elsa in an aisle seat with her beau seated beside her. Beyond that, unless she squinted with great difficulty, she couldn't see much more. This was for the best, she contended, as being able to see the whole crowd clearly might be overwhelming.

The first few questions the moderator asked required only that the two be living, breathing and of a right mind to answer; name, place of birth, occupation. For occupation, Martha had recommended that Carol-Barbara reach back to her teaching days, though they were long since behind her, and make sure that the audience knew she wasn't just a housewife, not that there was anything wrong with that.

She also wanted to make sure they knew about all the volunteer work she'd done over the years; with the church, the local schools and the like. Martha had even suggested that Carol-Barbara might want to mention that she had recently started a support group for her friends, but Carol-Barbara was afraid the acronym for their group might get out and give people the wrong idea. The National Association of Kindred Elderly Dames had no place here in this court house; at least, not yet. When and if she was elected she might talk about it freely and set people straight on what it really meant to be a NAKED lady.

The next set of questions had to do with what each representative wanted for Dogwood County. Dixon stated he wanted to see it change and grow, and keep up with the times; more new subdivisions, new shopping areas, and attractions to bring more new people and businesses to the area. All of these things, of course, would better Dixon's bottom line, since he had always been in the building and contracting business.

Carol-Barbara's answer was more about keeping the area a modern version of what it had always been; a safe, wholesome place to raise children and one where the main economy was based on the industries that had long employed people in the area. There were plants that made textiles and electronics already there. Why not work with them to keep Dogwood County thriving?

It wasn't that she was against new things, and to prove that she added, "Why not make new friends, but keep the old. One is silver and the other gold." For that she got an appreciative laugh from several people in the audience, and she was proud of herself for ad-libbing it. Martha gave her an approving nod from the front row. Then it was time to take questions from the audience. The moderator left the stage with a microphone and, looking a little like Jerry Springer, went out to mingle with the crowd.

There were several rounds of exactly the kind of questions you would expect when the floor is open to such a diverse audience. One person asked when somebody was going to replace that yield sign with a stop sign at the corner of Maple and Route 330 before someone had an accident. That question had been for Dixon and he'd told the person he'd get right on it.

Another person wanted to know why he couldn't fish from the bridge that goes through downtown Waynesville. For this one, Carol-Barbara used her catch-all and said she'd been researching that herself for her husband and would get back to him on that. Of course, she hadn't, but she sure would now. Yet another person wanted to know from either of them if they knew if she was allowed to water her lawn on Sundays. Yes, Debbie and Dixon were in agreement, they knew no reason why she couldn't water her lawn on any given Sunday unless they were in a time of drought.

"This next one is for Mr. St. James," the moderator told them.

Then, from the back of the crowd, where Carol-Barbara couldn't see, she heard a familiar voice on the microphone. It was a voice that didn't quite fit in with the rest of the crowd, one with a heavy accent. It could be none other than Josefina.

"Mr. St. James," she began, "I'd like to know about your plans to knock down that neighborhood, thereby displacing all of those families, to build a shopping mall."

Dixon suddenly turned pale, and looked as though he was going to pass out. He couldn't get a word out. Just like when he was asked the same question in the hospital. Only now he had to answer to it.

"I-I-I" he stammered.

There was a loud whispering among the crowd, people trying to turn around to see who had asked the question that had been hanging over them all since the televised debate.

The moderator jumped in, "Now, now, everyone calm down. Mr. St. James, can you answer the question or not? "

Dixon found a voice. Not the one he usually used, but one that sounded a little more scared than usual, definitely not as confident. "I- I'm not sure about that idea yet."

There was a gasp from some people in the crowd, more muttering amongst them. The moderator continued, "So, just to set the record straight then, this is, in fact, a possibility?"

Dixon continued, albeit apprehensively. "I had toyed with the idea, yes, but now I'm not so sure."

At that point, the moderator lost his microphone to Josefina, who had apparently grabbed it out of his hand and stood up. "Mr. St. James, I have had enough, either I get my money back or someone is going to pay with his life!"

As Josefina stood up, someone had the presence of mind to turn the lights on, and now Carol-Barbara could see that Josefina was wielding a gun. The people who sat near Josefina could see it, too, and some of them started screaming and hitting the ground, trying to take shelter under their seats.

At this point, Martha stood up from her seat next to Carl and turned around to face Josefina. To Carol-Barbara's surprise, Martha pulled out a gun from a holster under her shirt. She aimed it carefully towards the ceiling so as not to frighten the people around her, or appear to be taking aim at them.

"Put the gun down, Josefina. Do you honestly think you're going to get away with this in front of all of these people? You can't kill all of us."

"No, but I can kill him," Josefina replied, aiming the gun towards the stage, and right at Dixon. She stumbled forward, seemingly drunk.

Carol-Barbara ducked behind her podium and urged Dixon to do the same. Dixon stayed frozen.

"Dixon, get down!" She urged him again, but still he didn't move. Perhaps he was too scared, or maybe with everything he'd been through, he'd just given up.

What no one in the building knew at that point, was that Debbie had put her plan in place to shoot Dixon that night, and was currently hiding in the ceiling above the stage, gun in hand. She planned on escaping through the maintenance access panel above the stage, then racing to the front of the building, feigning arriving late before anyone was the wiser.

However, she hadn't anticipated Josefina doing the job for her. She knew Josefina would likely be at the meeting, as she followed Dixon everywhere now. This was the reason Debbie made her plans for tonight, but she never imagined in a million years she would have begun waving a gun around. Josefina must have been desperate, as she was putting herself right in the hands of law enforcement.

In addition, something was about to go horribly wrong. Perhaps it was the extra weight Debbie had put on eating chips and Ho-hos, or maybe it just wasn't up to code, but for whatever reason, the tiny walkway she lay on had started to give way, and before she could get off, the whole apparatus fell, with her on it, leaving her in a crumpled heap on the stage floor. Her gun went flying.

While everyone's attention had turned from Josefina to what had just happened onstage, Josefina attempted to make a run for it, realizing Martha had every intention of shooting her if she had to. She didn't get far, though, as her high heels caught and she tripped over a baby carrier that had been left in the aisle while the mother held the baby in her arms. Josefina's gun also went flying, giving Martha just enough time to get to Josefina, put her smart-shoed foot on her back and aim her gun at her.

"Just hold it right there," she told Josefina, and to the crowd, "Everyone be calm. The situation is under control.

Even more to Carol-Barbara's surprise, her formerly discreet neighbors, Roland and Honey, who she thought only she and Carl knew to actually be undercover federal agents, came rushing through the doors to the auditorium, guns drawn. It was as if they'd been ready and waiting for something like this to take place. They raced to Martha's aid.

"Thanks, Marty," Honey told Martha, "We'll take it from here." With that, they swiftly apprehended Josefina, who was kicking and screaming something about small towns and small-minded people getting the best of her.

Onstage, Dixon finally crumpled in a heap on the floor. The deputy that had helped them to the waiting area suddenly came through the back door to the stage and to his assistance. Though also carrying a gun, he'd missed the entire ordeal as he'd been assigned to keep an eye on the lobby of the courthouse, probably never thinking anything like this would happen.

Several other people rushed onstage to try to pull Debbie from the wreckage. This, Carol-Barbara was sure, was not what Doris Day was thinking when she crooned the words, Que sera, sera.

Part 63

All is Revealed

News spread quickly about the goings-on at the debate, and pretty soon everyone knew about Josefina wielding a gun and threatening to shoot Dixon, and Martha subduing her, and Debbie falling out of the ceiling onto the stage.

The cat was also out of the bag about who Roland and Honey really were. That part was a relief to Carol- Barbara, as she didn't know how much longer she could keep that secret without letting something slip.

Josefina had been captured and taken to Washington, D.C. to be held until someone could decide what to do with her. Officially, she was being held on charges of attempted murder, and making threats of bodily harm. That was just until she could be slapped with the bigger drug charges, and officials could make them stick this time.

Martha had been forced to fess up that she'd never quite retired from her government position in Washington, which had been in international drug enforcement. She'd been brought back when her past with Josefina and her father had come to light, and it was discovered that Josefina had come to live in Dogwood County. That's when she'd been paired back up with Matt Booker and Hana Resnick, aka, Roland and Honey.

Martha, Hana and Matt had done work together back in the day, Martha told Carol-Barbara over coffee the day after the debate.

"We were a good team, the three of us," Martha told her. "We were responsible for the capture and subsequent incarceration of many of the world's biggest drug traffickers, but we could never seem to bring in Josefina's father. He was so charismatic, talked himself out of everything, and had the best lawyers in the world. Eduardo Ruiz was his name, but I called him El Tipo."

Carol-Barbara hadn't used any Spanish on a regular basis since she'd taken it in high school, but she knew what tipo meant, and she wondered why Martha would use this word when talking about a ruthless drug lord. She also thought she sensed something in Martha's tone when she talked about Eduardo Ruiz. Was it admiration? Sadness?

"You knew him well, then?" Carol-Barbara asked. "I mean, if my high school Spanish serves me well, tipo means kind."

"Let's just say I saw something in him, something other than just a criminal, and that after so many years of trying to get him to turn over a new leaf, or at least turn himself in before he got killed, it was cancer that got the best of him. I've always thought he was just about to see the error of his ways before that happened. I also happened to be with him on his death bed, and the last thing he asked me to do was try and get Josefina out of the business. He was so sorry he ever brought her into it. She was much less considerate of people than he was. It's been my biggest failure that I couldn't do that for him."

"She's a grown-ass woman, Martha. You can't feel responsible for her; and at least she's been caught now and won't be able to do any more harm."

Martha nodded her head. "You're right. I have to let it go."

Part 64

Naked at Last

Over a week had gone by since Carol-Barbara's conversation with Martha. The election had come and gone, and Carol-Barbara was glad it was over. It had been a long time coming, and she didn't want to think about it anymore. It had turned out the way the fates wanted it to. She would move forward from here, not dwelling on the past.

The election results had been overwhelming. More voters had turned out than ever before in Dogwood County history. The shenanigans leading up to and including the last debate had definitely had a lot to do with that.

So here she sat, on a cold morning at the beginning of February, alone, since Carl was at his job at the All-Mart, when she thought she heard a slight knock at the front door. The first thing she considered was that the doorbell must be broken. Nobody knocked when there was a perfectly good doorbell to ring, but she got up to check anyway.

When she opened the door, she got a shock. It was Dixon, in running clothes, and out of breath.

"Dixon! What a surprise. Did you run all the way here?"

"I did," he panted, the cold showing his breath in the air. "I was on a run, and decided I just had to talk to you, but I was afraid I might be disturbing you. I'm sure you're busy."

"Don't be silly. Come in," she urged.

"No, it's ok. I won't be long. I just wanted to say congratulations," he extended his hand.

She responded by shaking his hand vigorously. "It really could have gone either way, you know, Dixon," Carol-Barbara tried to play it off, though she had beat him by 10 full percentage points.

"No, no, Carol-Barbara, the people have spoken," he told her. "You beat me fair and square."

Carol-Barbara couldn't help smiling. "Thanks, Dixon."

"You're very welcome," he had finally caught his breath.

"You know, I was never fully on board with building that mall. That was mostly Debbie," he admitted, though sheepishly.

"All water under the bridge now." Carol-Barbara told him. "What will you do now?" She asked, not that he needed to do anything. Even with Debbie's poor financial decisions, she knew he probably still had enough money socked away somewhere to live out a comfortable retirement.

"I've never quite gotten out of the construction game," he told her. "I've been thinking about taking a little trip. I hear there's tons of opportunity in Belize; a real building boom, what with all the people buying up cheap property down there."

"Sounds fantastic," Carol-Barbara told him. There was an awkward pause. "Well, I could always use another good man to help with county decisions, if that falls through," she tried to be conciliatory, though she secretly hoped he wouldn't take her up on the offer. She was ready to do things the no-Dixon way.

Dixon shook his head. "I think I'm done with that." He paused. "But I do know someone who could use a job. She's bright, she's got a great education. I oughta know since I paid for it."

Carol-Barbara breathed a sigh of relief. "Ashleigh?" she questioned.

Dixon nodded his head. "My daughter is quite the whiz when it comes to business, and so tech savvy. She's even got her own computer blog, *The Dollar Diva*. She teaches other young women about finances. Ashleigh has moved in with Elsa so they can get to know each other, make up for all those years missed. She could really use a job until she gets her own thing off the ground, and I have no doubt that she will."

"Consider it done," Carol-Barbara told him. "As much as I could use a good man on my side, a good woman is even better." She winked at him.

Carol- Barbara hesitated, then asked him. "How is Debbie?"

"I'm afraid Debbie will be spending quite a while in a mental institution. She admitted she was trying to shoot me, so it was kind of the deal our lawyer had to strike to keep her from going to jail."

"Oh, dear. That's unfortunate," though she knew it was probably for the best.

"No worries. She'll be in the best place money can buy, and in the meantime I'll be working on our divorce. No marriage can be expected to survive all this. Well, I'd better be running along, no pun intended," he laughed, and jogged down the front steps into the yard, then turned around. "I'll send you a postcard from Belize!"

"Please do! Maybe we'll even come down and visit!" Had she really just said that? Yes, she had. She'd read about Belize and it sounded fantastic, so maybe that would be the tropical destination she and Carl would finally make it to someday.

She began to go back inside, but not before glancing next door. Matt and Hana, aka Roland and Honey, had gone back from where they came, and the Van Honk house now stood empty. There was no purple Cadillac in the driveway, and no pink cat to torment Bubba.

Carol-Barbara would miss her crazy friend, Honey. What a character she had been! She had taught them all so much about letting go, and just learning to be yourself. She had been the epitome of what it meant to be a NAKED lady; no holds barred, wide open, and free with your emotions! Carol-Barbara would cherish every moment she'd had with her. She would focus on the good times they'd had, and not look back.

Carol-Barbara knew she would be off to her first official county council meeting as Dogwood County's new manager on Monday, and her first act as manager? To repeal the hundred year old glitch that had caused all this eminent domain trouble in the first place.

But for now it was Friday, and she had to prepare her house for tonight's big meeting of the National Association of Kindred Elderly Dames! Monday she would get down to business, but for tonight it would be about letting it all hang out. Naked at last!

The End (almost)

Epilogue:

Carol-Barbara served two years as the Dogwood County Manager, during which much was accomplished, including saving her neighborhood, but also building a mid-size shopping center everyone was happy with. It was built on some land Dixon unexpectedly bequeathed to the county.

While Carl and Carol-Barbara never moved to a tropical island, after her service to the county, they did spend a glorious month on a tropical getaway in Belize. Dixon was quite the generous host, and oh the adventures they had! But that's another story!

Made in the USA
Middletown, DE
23 September 2020